Corey learned three important things that day.

The first was that there was a vital difference between what she had previously called work and what she was expected to do now. The second was that whoever invented four-inch heels was a sadist and an idiot, and anyone foolish enough to wear them deserved whatever pain they got. The third was that, despite the pain, if you looked good, you got bigger tips. She supposed life was a series of little trade-offs.

She'd earned forty dollars in tips that afternoon, and she couldn't help delighting in how good it felt to put that money in her pocket. It was a feeling she would never forget. If she could do that in half a day, she calculated, she could do twice that tomorrow. Maybe more if she got faster. She wouldn't have enough to buy a building, but she'd have enough to get her own place, buy a new pair of shoes, a coat, maybe even a tube of mascara.

Before it was over, she'd show them all that Corey Dobias was a survivor.

It wasn't over by a long shot.

Also by Terri Herrington

Silena
Her Father's Daughter
One Good Man

Available from HarperPaperbacks

HER FATHER'S DAUGHTER

TERRI HERRINGTON

HarperPaperbacks
A Division of HarperCollinsPublishers

This is a work of fiction. The characters, incidents, and dialogues are products of the author's imagination and are not to be construed as real. Any resemblance to actual events or persons, living or dead, is entirely coincidental.

HarperPaperbacks   *A Division of* HarperCollins*Publishers*
10 East 53rd Street, New York, N.Y. 10022

Cover photo by Herman Estevez

First printing: April 1991

Printed in the United States of America

HarperPaperbacks and colophon are trademarks of HarperCollins*Publishers*

10   9   8   7   6   5   4   3   2

This book is lovingly dedicated
to Michelle and Marie, for
understanding that I live in two
worlds at once and constantly
reminding me which is
the real one.

But yet thou art my flesh, my blood,
    my daughter;
Or rather a disease that's in my flesh,
Which I must needs call mine.

   —*King Lear* by William Shakespeare
      Act II, Scene IV

chapter

1

THE DELICATE RING OF BELGIAN CRYSTAL PUNC-
tuated the orchestra's rendition of a Bach sonata as
dancers glided over the marble floor. Boston's rich and
powerful clashed and mingled, but in this room, on
this night, one man's power shone brighter than the
rest. Retirement was only a pretext for the affair, but
everyone, from the highest government official in attendance to the lowest of the tabloid reporters, knew that
tonight was the culmination of a forty-two-year climb.
Tonight, Boston's elite, who had once shunned their
host as a nobody from nowhere, had come to laud the
empire that Nikos Dobias had built with his bare hands.

Late guests flowed with restlessness into the ballroom,
shaking Dobias's hand and showering his daughters
and granddaughter with the kind of flattery that only
money can buy.

Then, when they entered the throng of whisperers,
their praise altered as they considered the gaudy cluster
of rubies on Dobias's oldest daughter, Giselle's, throat,
and the ornate gown that failed to disguise the extra few
pounds on Rena, his middle one. They wondered aloud
about the conspicuous absence of Corissa, his youngest,
the one touted as his favorite. Rumors slithered about
his impending retirement, and the division of a significant part of his empire among his three children. Tonight was their arrival as well as his. But Corissa had
yet to arrive.

Nik Dobias glanced at his Rolex for the hundredth

time in an hour, then once again his gaze gravitated traitorously toward the foyer and the travertine marble staircase that led to his daughters' quarters. Behind the pleasant facade he wore with dignity and carefully cultivated charm was a seething unrest.

Things weren't working out for him tonight, Giselle thought, sipping her champagne and watching her father over the rim. All because of Corey. And now the temper that all three women knew to be so volatile in their father was nearing an explosion.

"I'm telling you, she isn't coming," Giselle said, hooking onto her father's arm and pulling him toward the dance floor.

Dobias discreetly pulled away from Giselle and shook his head. "I'm not in the mood to dance."

"Then mingle, for God's sake," she whispered through her teeth. "Look at all the people who came. Ten years ago these same people didn't even have the courtesy to respond to your invitations."

Dobias made a quick sweep of the room, and the discontent in his eyes gave way to a grim satisfaction. "Ten years ago I didn't own their asses." He glanced back at the archway leading to the ballroom. There was still no sign of Corey.

"Forget about her," Giselle said, reading his thoughts in his eyes. "Just enjoy the party. Everybody's here. Did you notice that Jinx Hollister isn't with his wife? He must have robbed the junior high to find that one." She took a glass off a passing tray and handed it to her father. He declined it.

"I tell her I'm giving her a hundred million dollars, and she hasn't the decency to show up on time."

"It's a matter of priorities," Giselle said, motioning to a waiter to take the glass. "No one told her she had to be present to win."

"This is not a lottery!" Dobias whispered, then caught himself and realized he had allowed his expression to reveal too much. Schooling his features to look more relaxed, he muttered, "And the moment I think one of you is treating it as such, I'll pull the rug out from under you so fast that you'll be begging for alms in the street."

Giselle's face flushed with the heat of his reprimand, and she swallowed her retort, thinking it wouldn't be wise to provoke him further. "I'm the last person who would think of it that way, Dad. Besides you, I've worked harder for the corporation than anybody in the last ten years. I've *earned* my share."

"Oh, have you now?" Dobias asked sardonically, regarding his eldest daughter directly for the first time that evening. "Have you really?"

"You know I have." Giselle hid her burgeoning chagrin behind a faltering hostess-smile. "By the time I pass it onto Emily, it'll be worth twice what you're passing to me."

Dobias lifted a skeptical brow and shook his head, but let his distracted gaze drift to the door once again.

A subtle ripple of excitement drifted over the room like a wash of cool air, and Giselle lost her smile and followed her father's gaze. Corey Dobias stood beneath the gold-leafed arch to the ballroom, looking like the phantom vision of her mother, wrapped in a tight gown of gold and black that even brought smiles to the most cynical of faces in the room.

Very nice, Dobias thought as a grudging smile played upon his own lips. He'd have to congratulate the designer himself. He glanced at the man with her, the man she clung to with all the pride and possession of a mesmerized lover, though Dobias hadn't a clue who the man was. He made a mental note to get his people on it right away.

"Another of Corey's toys," Giselle murmured. "Wonder if he knows anything about real estate."

Nik Dobias watched his oldest daughter cut through the crowd as his youngest became a part of it, dragging her escort, behind her, flaunting the fact that he didn't belong. Corey, he thought, was too naive to realize that men like that one crawled out of the woodwork, feeding on the smell of her pocket change.

He watched several of the women swarm around her, saw her lift her left hand, saw the ring that sparkled there. His smile collapsed.

Engaged, he thought. Without a word . . . without an introduction. He ground his teeth together and regarded her escort, who was grinning like a man who'd just won a hundred-million-dollar lottery.

"Not while I'm alive," he whispered aloud. Then, quickly scanning the guests, he found his attorney and motioned for him to follow him into the study.

"What's up, old boy?" Robert Gloster asked as they slipped out of the ballroom, the attorney falling into step with Dobias, who seemed on a rushed, urgent mission.

"Have I been hasty, Robert?"

The attorney tossed him a cursory glance and frowned. "What do you mean?"

"Am I making this too easy? Giving them all this without making them earn it?"

Robert laughed. "Of course you are, old boy. Their lives have always been too easy. But that's what they've come to expect."

They reached the study, and Dobias paused pensively on the threshold, stroking his chin and staring back in the direction of the ballroom.

"I want to make a change in the papers," he said. "I've been considering a better way, and I've just made up my mind. Before I hand those girls what I worked forty-two years to build, I've got to make fighters out of each of them."

Robert adjusted the wire-rimmed glasses that lent him the appearance of a nineteenth-century banker rather than the renowned attorney that he was. "But the papers are all drawn up, and they've made plans. Won't they be disappointed if you change it?"

"Disappointment was my first lesson when I was wearing second-hand shoes and figuring out ways to make three meals out of one," Dobias said as a final decision planted itself in his mind. "It's time my daughters learned about the strength that comes with struggle. I'll pass down my assets, all right, but I'll do it my way. When I'm finished with them, those girls won't ever be the same."

Dobias closed the hand-carved oak doors at his back. When he turned back to Robert, he wore a smile that bordered on the edge of laughter. "Besides," he added, "our guests came to see a drama. Tonight, they're going to get one."

chapter

2

ERIC GRAY STRAIGHTENED THE RENTED TIE THAT
had come with his rented tuxedo, and raked a hand
through hair that was a bit too long for a sophisticate,
though it fit his starving-artist image nicely. He wished
his father could see his you'll-never-amount-to-a-damn-
thing bastard son now, standing with Corey Dobias on
his arm.

He looked above the guests adorned with flash and
dazzle, and considered a chandelier that probably cost
more than he could hope to make in a lifetime. "God,"
he whispered. "You *live* here?"

Corey smiled, her blue eyes—eyes she had inherited
from her mother, along with a sizable trust fund that
she couldn't claim until age thirty-five—sweeping over
him with pride. "So what do you think?"

"I think I'm out of my league," he said, slipping his
hand possessively around her waist to the tight drape-
pleated skirt of gold and black tiger-striped lamé, a special creation by one of those famous designers whose
name he could never pronounce.

"No, you're not." She flipped back a trailing mane of
auburn hair mixed with various shades of brown, a look
that Vidal himself could not have duplicated. "You're with
me, aren't you?"

Eric worked to hold his expression, for he'd sworn to
both himself and her that there'd be no smart-ass retorts
tonight. But Corey didn't miss the strain on his face.

"Oh, Eric, I thought you were leaving your attitude at

---

home. Don't take things so seriously."

You've got some attitude. His father's words, so much like the ones Corey had just uttered, railed back to him with the inflated intensity of festering memory. *That martyred bastard son routine won't amount to bird shit in the real world.*

He grabbed a glass of champagne from a passing tray, threw back a gulp as if it were draft beer, and wished he could see his father's face when he heard who his son was going to marry. It might be worth inviting him to the wedding.

Recovering his smile, Eric looked down at Corey. "I did leave my attitude at home. See me smiling?"

Corey laughed, a laugh that could seduce a wildcat at forty paces, but that didn't disguise the innocence she wore without knowing it. Her mirth quickly died as her oldest sister touched her arm and feigned a kiss.

"So, you finally decided to make it, did you?" Giselle asked cordially. "Just in time to take the money and run."

Undaunted by her sister's barb, Corey slipped her hand back through Eric's arm. "Eric, meet my sister Giselle."

Giselle took his hand, then quickly discarded it. "So where did you find him?"

"We met at Harvard," Eric said, answering for Corey and forcing Giselle to look at him directly. "She's been hiding me."

"I have not." Corey cut her laughing gaze back to his. "I just thought it was best not to give Dad the chance to have him investigated, intimidated, and bribed while we were getting to know each other."

Giselle flashed the charming smile that made her seem so affable—and so dangerously harmless—to those she dealt with every day. "Well, there's plenty of time for bribery and intimidation now, isn't there?"

Corey tightened her hold on Eric's arm. "And you thought you wouldn't feel welcome here."

Giselle's amusement sparkled in her eyes, and she turned her back on them to meet her daughter, Emily, heading toward them with Rena.

A glint of determined humor flitted through Eric's eyes as Corey gazed up at him. "On my best behavior," he whispered, raising his hands innocently. "I didn't once call her a rich bitch."

"Don't," Corey warned. "She'd take it as a compliment." Her sister and niece approached. She reached out to push a wisp of hair out of Emily's face and winked at the eleven-year-old who had recently developed an awkward shyness toward handsome men. She'd noticed it earlier when she introduced her to Eric.

"Emmy, does my dad know I'm here? I haven't found him yet."

Emily self-consciously stroked back her dark curls and giggled. "Everybody knows you're here, Aunt Corey."

"That's true," Rena said, her smile conspiratorially coy as she leaned closer to them. "There's a rumor circulating that Eric is a European prince, though no one's figured out which one."

Rena's comment breathed new life into Eric's grin, and he took another drink of champagne, noting the way Giselle bristled at the idea.

Giselle's glance strayed to Rena's husband, John Keller, flirting with a starlet in a corner of the room. "Go rescue your husband, darling," she told her sister. "That actress, Sarah, Sylvie, whatever her name is. She's got him cornered."

Rena gazed around the room and saw her husband pull the buxom woman against him and begin to dance. The fact that her hipbones were pressed unashamedly against his was obvious to anyone who chose to look. It was even harder to miss his hand moving over her bare lower back.

"Oh, for God's sake," Giselle muttered. "If you won't put a stop to that, I will. That little tramp is making a mouse out of you."

Giselle sliced across the dance floor and unceremoniously cut in on his partner. Downing her champagne, Rena focused her dull eyes on the empty glass in her hand.

"So, where is Dad?" Corey asked, trying to divert Rena's sobering mood.

"I don't know," she whispered.

Emily perked up, hoping to salvage the moment. "He's in the study with Mr. Gloster," the child said. "Just think, in a little while you'll each be worth over a hundred million dollars!"

"Emily!"

"Well," Corey's niece said without remorse, "Mother says it's common knowledge. Besides, it was in the *Wall Street Journal* this morning."

Corey tossed an awkward glance toward Eric, who seemed surprised at the dollar figure the two of them had never discussed. She hoped it didn't matter. Turning back to Emily, she said, "Don't believe everything you read. And for heaven's sake, Emmy, don't repeat everything you hear."

She had no more uttered the words, when Nik Dobias and his attorney came back into the room, gesturing for the orchestra to end the song before its time so that he might have the floor. Corey applauded with the rest of the crowd as she watched her father step onto the dais he'd had built for such occasions, for there was nothing Dobias loved better than a speech with hundreds of people as his captive audience. He was probably having the doors bolted at that very moment, she mused. She saw the intoxicating spark of power and excitement in his eyes, and realized that she hadn't seen that spark in a very long time. It was the sharp, shrewd look of a predator after its toughest foe, and she wondered why retirement would hold such an appeal for him after he'd centered his life around making impossible deals.

"Would my three lovely daughters join me on the stage?" As the three started toward him, he went on, "Tonight you have come to celebrate my retirement, if you could call it that, from a long and very interesting career. I dare say some of you have aided in my climb to the top. Some others of you I've had to knock down and walk on to get where I am. No hard feelings, eh?"

Soft chuckles rumbled over the crowd, but in the faces of some, Corey saw hatred and enmity, and the secret vows to get revenge as soon as her father let his guard down. Perhaps they would use her or her sisters to exact that revenge, she thought with a chill as she took her place behind him.

Her hand rose to clutch the locket at her throat, the tiny trinket that looked incongruous against her lavish gown. She was glad Carolyne Roehm wasn't here to see it herself. She would surely have suffered a coronary at the sight of an eighteen-dollar trinket tainting the effect of her eighteen-thousand-dollar creation. Corey's gaze drifted to Eric as her father went on, and he winked at her, making her smile.

"My wife didn't leave me sons to take over the family business," Dobias was saying as if it were their mother's greatest faux pas, and Corey glanced at Giselle, whose cheeks burned with the same resentment that had followed her all her life, that she was his daughter, and thereby unworthy of the same respect he would have afforded a firstborn son. She glanced at Rena, whose eyes revealed no shame, for she had long ago accepted the status she held in her father's heart. And she knew that her father would not award them so great a prize as he planned tonight without some price. It wasn't his style, she thought, to inaugurate queens without first making them servants.

"Each of them has held a position in my company for the last several years," he was saying. "Giselle has been running one of my subsidiaries, Massachusetts Management, for ten years now, managing all of the properties Dobias Enterprises acquires, and saving the company a bundle. Rena, for eight years, has run Resources, Incorporated, which handles all of the purchasing for our buildings. And Corey, for three years, has run Dobias Designs, which does all the decorating for our holdings. Having them in the company, in positions of authority, has given me the chance to mold them and teach them. But there's still so much that they don't know.

"Each of my girls has her strengths and weaknesses," he went on. "Giselle is ruthless in business, a woman after my own heart, but she's never learned the art of cunning, and her judgment is sometimes so bad that it's a wonder she's come as far as she has. She can't stay in a relationship for more than ten minutes, she makes decisions based on whim, and the way she spoils her daughter is a crime—I should know, I did it myself."

The crowd murmured a low, obligatory laugh, each guest aware that it was at Giselle's expense. But her smile never faltered.

"With a little cunning," Dobias went on, "she might not have failed with some of the deals I've entrusted to her in the years she's been working for me. With a little more judgment, she might have known better than to choose a loser for a husband who would divorce her six months after their daughter was born."

A gasp swept over the room, and Corey looked to her older sister, who held her head high, despite the fact that all eyes were upon her, waiting for her to break. Anger swirled up inside Corey in defense of the sister she had never been close to, and in defense of Emily who stood near the stage with her eyes cast down.

"And then there's Rena," Dobias said, turning to gesture toward his middle daughter, who looked as fragile as a porcelain doll. "Rena, who has never had a backbone. Rena, who would dive from a twenty-story building if someone asked her to. Even if she owned it."

The guests murmured once again, but this time there was no laughter, for Rena's face clearly revealed that she lacked the fortitude Giselle possessed. "Ever since she was in diapers," Dobias continued, "she's allowed herself to be pushed ruthlessly around by anyone and everyone. She needs to learn to push back for her very survival, because until she does, she'll be trapped in the mousy life she's in right now, lurking in the background of everyone else's glory. No Dobias belongs in the background."

Corey ached to look at her sister, but some voice inside warned her not to, for she knew that there were probably tears glistening in her eyes, tears on the verge of falling. Still, she slipped her hand around her sister's, squeezed, and felt the tight clinging of Rena's trembling fingers.

Corey didn't disguise her outrage as her father continued his tirade about Rena's weaknesses. So this was the game he was playing, she thought. This was the price.

She bit her lip and told herself not to make a scene as her father brandished a hand her way. It was her turn, she thought, sucking in a breath and holding it like a weapon. But there was nothing he could say that could make her any angrier.

With his first words, however, she knew she had underestimated him.

"And then there's my beloved daughter, Corissa, who wouldn't know a real fight if it walked up and punched her out. She thinks she's got it all figured out," he taunted, "because she lived in the woods for six weeks last year, and climbed a mountain. She thinks because she got cold, suffered a few cuts and bruises, and missed a few meals, that she suddenly knows something that no one else does. But I say that it's time she learned about the real wilderness—the one where there aren't ropes to cling to on your way up, the one where dollar figures are the only way to keep score, the one with people who will vow brotherhood with you one minute and organize a hostile takeover the next. It's time she learned to climb the mountains that matter."

Again, Corey's hand came up to clutch the locket at her throat, the locket that Eric had given her, reminding her that there really was more to her than a pampered shell with free access to her daddy's hefty bank book. She wet her lips and tried to look as smooth, as unruffled, as Giselle did, but instead she feared that she looked as broken and surprised as Rena. She caught Eric's eye again, but saw that he stared at the floor. No one in the room uttered a sound, but despite their embarrassment and discomfort, Corey doubted one person in attendance would have missed the moment for the world itself.

"My original plan," her father was saying, "was to divide a portion of my estate three ways, creating independent corporations for each of them to run as they see fit, while I concentrated on a dream I've had for years—to operate the biggest and most exciting casino in the country. But I've changed my mind about letting go just yet."

A low rumble grew over the crowd, and Corey, reeling from the surprise herself, saw Giselle visibly lose her calm facade and step forward, as if she could physically stop her father with a little of the cunning he seemed to think so lacking in her.

Her father turned to face his daughters, and the ecstatic gleam in his eyes at their faces told Corey that no amount of money could have bought her father more pleasure.

"Instead," he went on, "I've decided to let them learn their lessons the hard way, the way I did. I'm going to let them fight it out."

He paused a moment as the roar of whispers over the room crescendoed and died, the guests waiting for the bottom line. "I'm creating a corporation in each of their names, and each corporation will be given a ten-million-dollar budget with which to work. Their husbands, past, present, and future, will not be permitted to participate. I did it alone, and I damn well expect them to. At the end of one year, the one who has achieved the most financial success with her company will get everything—lock, stock, and barrel. The other two—" he gave one last look at the astonished women standing behind him, and grinned in sheer delight, "the other two will get nothing."

Something in Corey's throat constricted, and she stood dumbfounded, gaping at her father in absolute disbelief. Giselle wavered, but Corey saw her sister force her chin defiantly up again, proudly bearing the weight of the challenge thrust upon her. Indeed, Giselle even managed to carve out a smile in her expression, hard and disillusioned though it was. Rena, on the other hand, seemed to shrink, as if she knew without even trying that she could never compete with her sisters. Corey didn't let go of her hand.

Her father turned around and made a great spectacle of embracing his stiff daughters, as if they had reason to thank him. When Corey saw that thanks was not only what he expected but what he *demanded*, a scorching blade of disgust twisted within her.

Giselle tried to speak, cleared her throat, then swept her smile over the crowd. "You know I've always loved the spirit of competition, Dad," she said. "Especially when it comes to business. I'll do my best to make you proud."

He turned to the next-born, the weakest one, and set his hands on Rena's shoulders. With incipient tears glossing her eyes, she looked up at him. "I know . . . I know I have a lot to learn, Daddy." Her voice broke off, and she swallowed, viciously aware of the hundreds of eyes fixed upon her, and the photographers flashing out the pictures that would make the front page of the society section in tomorrow's papers. "I hope I won't let you down."

He turned to Corey, whose face was expressionless, unreadable, and set his hands on her shoulders. "And you, Corey? Are you going to give your sisters a run for their money?"

Corey looked down at Eric, whose nod silently warned her to do as her sisters had done. But she'd inherited her nature from the very man who had inflicted this upon her, and it wasn't in that nature to acquiesce. "No, Dad," she said, meeting her father's intrepid eyes. "I don't think so."

A soft gasp whispered over the room, and Dobias dropped his hands from her shoulders as his whiplash eyes cut into her. "What did you say?"

Corey drew in a deep breath and steadied her voice, though her lips trembled with the strain of her words. "I said no. I won't compete with my sisters for your money, because I don't want it that badly."

Then, without waiting for the eruption that was sure to come, Corey stepped off the dais and walked away from him.

"Corey!"

The fury in his voice shook the very foundation of the room and silenced the whispers around them.

Corey turned back from the floor and glared up at her father, defiance in its purest form dancing in her eyes, like the white-hot center of a flame, the part with the most capacity to cause pain.

"You don't have the option to walk out on this!"

Something in Corey's hard, angry eyes changed, and her voice softened to a dull note. "I have all the options I could ever want," she said.

"Not anymore you don't!" He followed her down the steps, his face red with the strain of a foiled performance in front of all he held important in his life. "You walk out of here now, and you'll never come back. Your life will change so fast you won't know what hit you!"

"Well, maybe it's time I learned to climb the mountains that matter," she said. And with that, she went out the front door, leaving her father standing impotent with rage, but unable to do a thing to change his youngest daughter's will.

chapter

3

OUTSIDE THE DOBIAS MANSION, LIMOS WERE
lined along the drive, a dormant procession of status and financial might. Between the cars, uniformed
chauffeurs sat huddled over a game of cards that they
dealt on the hood of a Jaguar, and farther away from
the house, the valets stood in a ragged circle, trying to
stay warm in the January frost, passing a joint around
as they reviewed the celebrities they'd parked cars for
tonight, whom they'd come with, and how much they'd
tipped.

"Come on, Jack," one was saying as he waited for the
reefer to make its way around the circle and back to him.
"You can keep half of what I make tonight. Just drop my
script on Silverman's seat."

"Yeah, sure, Gary," the head valet returned, squinting his eyes against the potent smoke he drew into his
lungs, then released too quickly on a laugh. "Like he's
gonna see it lying there and rush home to read it."

The other valets snickered. "Hey, man, you never
know," Gary said. "Things like that happen all the
time."

"Not to people like you, they don't."

The others laughed again, making it clear to Gary
that his destiny was up to him alone. He'd show those
assholes, when he was counting his money in Palm
Springs and hiring peons like them to park cars at *his*
parties.

The doors to the Dobias mansion flung open and a

woman bolted out. Quickly, Jack dropped the joint in the grass, ground it out.

"Shit, that's old man Dobias's daughter," he said. "Somebody go see what she wants."

"I'll go," Gary said quickly, starting toward the woman who was already down the steps and dashing along the line of cars, searching for one in particular.

"Think maybe you can get her to read your script?" Jack asked, and the valets collapsed in derisive laughter.

Before he had reached her, the mansion doors opened again, and a man dashed out, a man with hair a little too long and stubble a little too thick. "Corey!"

Corey Dobias turned around at the sound of her name and saw Eric coming down the steps toward her, breathing with the speed and depth of one who'd had the wind knocked out of him.

"Come on, Eric!" she cried, angry that tears were stinging her eyes. Chafing her bare arms with her hands, she watched him come toward her. "Let's go."

"Are you crazy?" Eric railed, coming face-to-face with her. "You can't walk out of there and give up a shot at everything!"

"I don't want *everything*!" she shouted, alarming the valet who had almost reached her, but who wilted and turned away when he realized he was walking into something volatile. "Where did they park your car?"

Eric planted his feet, refusing to budge another inch. "You're acting like a spoiled child!"

Corey spun around, her long hair slapping into her face as she faced the man who, just two hours ago, had put an engagement ring on her finger. "How can you say that? You saw what he did up there."

She paced up the line of cars, looking for Eric's battered Chevy as she railed on in a quivering voice. "All my life, he's pitted us against each other. When we were kids and he'd bring us home new toys, he'd bring two so we'd have to fight over them. It was good for us, he said. Taught us how to be tough!"

"You're not the only family who's had sibling rivalry, Corey. Maybe he just figured out a way to make that into something positive."

She flung around. "What's the matter with you? I can't believe this is you talking!" She stepped toward him again, staring into his face and trying, once more, to make him understand. "He wants us to hate each other, Eric! He wants us to chew each other up! We're *sisters*!" She turned back to the cars, throwing up her hands. "Where the hell is your car? Tell them to get it!"

"No," Eric said, his face reddening even in the darkness. "I won't let you ruin your life like this. You don't have any idea what it's like to scrape for every penny. You can't survive without money! You turned down ten million dollars, for God's sake! Didn't you see how mad you made him?"

"Don't *you* see how mad he made *me*?" she asked, her breath sending white clouds over the chilled air. "You're the one who accused me of being superficial and pampered. Maybe you were right a few months ago, but I'm taking a stand now, Eric. And if you refuse to accept that, then you go back in there and drink my father's champagne and swap insults with my sister. I'm getting the hell out of here!"

She lifted the skirt on her gown and dashed around the side of the house, to the massive garage where the family's cars were kept. Quickly, she went in to her own BMW, the car her father had given her for her twenty-fourth birthday a month ago. She found the keys tucked under the seat, started it, and pulled out of the driveway.

As she started down the winding drive, she glanced in her rearview mirror and saw Eric kicking the dented fender of his car. Somehow, she suspected that what had happened tonight had changed things between them. Tonight, a lot had changed.

She only hoped she was strong enough to bear the consequences of her father's wrath.

"Get these people out of my house," Dobias ordered Robert Gloster as he took the steps two at a time to the master suite. "This party's over."

"But Nik, she's your daughter. Go after her!"

"Someone will go after her, all right," he said, "but it won't be me. Get one of the valets in here immediately. Giselle, Rena, come with me. You, too, John!"

Moments later, they all stood in silence as Gary, the aspiring screenwriter/valet, stepped into the room, clutching and unclutching his hands behind him, as if he were the messenger about to be sacrificed for bringing the wrong news.

Damn, he thought. This job was supposed to be an opportunity, not a chance to bear the brunt of Dobias's fury.

"Who did she leave with?" Dobias asked from the chaise longue where he sat, staring at the flames popping in his fireplace.

"Who, sir?" Gary asked. "Miss Dobias?"

Dobias snapped around, dropping his feet to the floor. "Who the hell do you think?"

"Uh . . ." The young man cleared his throat and tried again. "She left alone. There was an argument, sir," he said, as if that information might appease the tycoon. "The man with the Chevy. He refused to drive her, so she took her own car."

"Good. John, call the police," Dobias said, switching gears as quickly as he switched deals on an average day.

"That car is mine. Tell them to consider it stolen, and haul her ungrateful ass to jail."

"Daddy!" Rena's gasp surprised the others in the room, but she brought her hand to her mouth and forced out her words. "That car was her birthday present. You gave it to her!"

"I withdraw it!" he said, coming to his feet and stalking across the room to his son-in-law. "Make the call now, John! I gave that car to my daughter. But when she chose to defy me, she gave up that status. The car is still in my name. Call Mitch Easterman and remind him of that yacht anchored in the harbor. The one that no one would ever believe he bought on a police commissioner's salary, if it ever came out that it belonged to him."

He turned back to the valet, his eyes bitter and laced with venomous rage. "What the hell are you standing here for?" he bellowed. "Don't you have work to do?"

"Y—yes sir," Gary stuttered, then nervously backed out of the room, as if turning his back on the man would represent some disrespect.

When he was gone, Giselle's feigned composure snapped. "We can't have her arrested!" she shouted, as if the very volume of her voice would shake her father back to his senses. "It'll be all over the papers by morning as it is. How do you think our family will look if we have her thrown in jail for driving her own car? Dad, that just isn't *done*!"

Dobias slumped back on the gold-gilded chair, his dinner jacket heaped in a puddle on the floor where he had slung it. His shirt remained buttoned, however, and his tie remained knotted with a controlled neatness that contradicted his almost-defeated posture. He rotated a half-empty champagne glass in his hand, and stared at it with the intensity of a soothsayer searching for the answers he needed. In the fireplace next to him, the flames climbed, and his face reddened with the heat it projected.

"Dad." Rena went to her father and set a timid hand on his shoulder. "I'm sure she's sorry for what she's done. She had no idea—"

"No idea what?"

The outburst made them all jump, and Dobias snapped his head around to glare at them. "That she would humiliate me in public, or that there would be a price?"

Sensing the unstable waiver in their father's voice, the two daughters kept silent. But his son-in-law, who'd been one of his closest advisers, as well as a trusted attorney, for years, wasn't as wise. "Nik, how long do you intend to leave her in jail?"

Dobias burst out of his chair, and the glass in his hand flew across the room, shattering with a crash on the ornate wallpaper that Shara Dobias had chosen long ago. Champagne dripped down between the velvet brocade stripes. "I'll leave her there until she rots!" he shouted. "She's not my daughter anymore. And so help me God, if one of you lifts a finger to help her, you'll be thrown out of this house, too, and lose all that comes with it."

He stepped intimidatingly closer to his oldest daughter, his eyes boring into hers. "Got that?"

"Yes, Dad," Giselle said.

Dobias turned to Rena, who stared at the carpet beneath her feet, blinking back the tears welling in her eyes. "Rena?"

"Yes . . . yes, I understand," she whispered.

He turned to John, the one he had groomed to wed his weakest daughter. Before he had to ask, John Keller was nodding in agreement.

"I'm with you, Nik. Anything I can do—"

Before the affirmation had been entirely delivered, Dobias turned his back to the three again. Miserably, he dropped onto the chair and stared, unseeing, at the wall where the glass had hit. "John, tell Robert to have the papers ready for Giselle and Rena to sign in the morning," he muttered in a metallic monotone. "Instead of the competition going three ways, it'll just be between the two of them. And as a bonus for acting with propriety when their sister chose not to, I'll give Rena the decorating contract for the casino, and Giselle the management contract after it's operational. The contracts will be part of each of their corporations, and their budgets will be drawn up accordingly."

Surprise and the slightest rush of satisfaction flashed through Giselle's eyes, as if she knew she had the Dobias fortune won already. She regarded her sister, defeated by the tears she'd struggled to hold back. As if those tears confirmed some ineptness that she didn't have time to deal with, Giselle brought her gaze to Rena's husband. His eyes, too, shone with repressed eagerness, acknowledging that a year was worth the wait for three hundred million, and that, despite Dobias's provision that he stay out of the competition, he hadn't given it all up just yet.

"Thank you, Dad," Giselle said. "I won't let you down."

Rena nodded at the husband's nudging and forced herself to speak. "Yes, thank you. I'll—I'll do my best."

"Leave me alone now," Dobias said so deeply under his breath that they almost didn't hear. "I'm tired."

The women went to their father and kissed his cheek, each with the sincere devotion of children who had been offered the world—if only they fought hard enough for it. But Dobias didn't respond. Still he stared with lackluster eyes at the broken fragments of glass on his floor.

"Send someone to clean up that mess," he mumbled

as they left his room. "And don't forget what I said. One word between you and that girl, and you'll be just as broken."

Headlights loomed behind Corey as she negotiated the late-night highway traffic from Brookline into Boston, not sure where she would go but knowing that she had to get there soon, before the nausea roiling in her stomach overtook her. It was unbelievable, she thought, that the night her father was supposed to have granted her her independence had turned out to be such a vicious joke.

The headlights behind her blinked, and she set her jaw and told herself it was probably Eric trying to stop her, to malign her again for being what *he* had encouraged her to be. None of it added up.

A blue light suddenly flashed on the car behind her, and drawing her brows together in confusion, she pulled over. Had her father called the police to bring her back? Was he going to humiliate her further in front of their guests, who'd seen enough tonight to keep their grapevines humming for the next year? Miserably, she pulled over, lowered her power windows, and waited for the two officers to approach her car.

Murphy Johnson, the fifty-five-year-old cop who reached the car first, found the job distasteful at best, when he beamed his flashlight inside and saw the young woman squinting up at him with tears smudged beneath her eyes, oblivious to the game he was being forced to play with her. He didn't like it a bit, but he wasn't about to put his pension on the line by bucking an order from the commissioner himself. Besides, he thought, anybody driving a BMW and dressed in a get-up worth more than the house he lived in probably deserved a night in the cage.

"Was I speeding?" she asked when he shone his flashlight inside.

"Can I see your license and registration, please, ma'am?" he asked, trying to keep the ordeal as cut and dried as he could.

Corey Dobias mumbled, "Sure," and reached into her glove box for the license she kept there, tucked into a small purse, along with her registration. Handing it to the officer, she asked, "So what did I do?"

"Get out of the car, please."

Something in Corey's stomach flipped again, warning her that the nightmare she'd lived tonight wasn't finished with her, yet. Slowly, she got out of the car, the striped lamé of her dress reflecting against the lights. The thick stream of traffic continued around her. She hugged her arms around herself, and tried not to shiver from the cold.

Before she knew what was happening, the other, younger officer took her hand and slapped a cuff on her wrist. "I'm really sorry," he said, his voice shaking, "but I'm afraid you're under arrest."

"What!" Corey jerked around, chafing her wrist as she did.

"You have the right to remain silent—"

"Wait a minute!" She tried to wrench her other wrist free of his grip before he could finish snapping the handcuff. "What's the charge? You have to tell me the charge!"

"This car was just reported stolen," Murphy Johnson said.

"It isn't stolen!" she said. "It's my car. Check the registration again."

"This car is registered under the name of Nikos Dobias. He's the one who reported it stolen."

The cuff snapped, and Corey wrenched free and spun around, her hair beginning to stick to her damp face as she glared at the officer. "How much did he pay you?" she asked through her teeth. "Or did he bribe your boss? If he did, they'll need a scapegoat to explain it. It'll be you!"

The younger cop glanced at Murphy, his troubled eyes questioning him.

"You have the right to an attorney," Murphy said, taking her elbow and directing her toward the squad car. "If you cannot afford an attorney, one will be appointed to you."

"You bet I can afford an attorney!" she bit out. "Can you? You'll need one, you know, when they blame you for this stupid stunt. It'll be in all the papers. Idiot Cop Arrests Woman for Stealing Her Own Car. Somebody'll pay, and you can bet it won't be anybody at the top!"

She shook out of his grasp. "What are you going to do with me?"

"Our orders are to book you," he said, his voice a little too tentative, revealing to Corey that what she'd said had hit a nerve, but that he was as helpless as she.

And if there was anything Corey Dobias hated, it was helplessness.

"Then book me," she said, throwing herself into the car. "Book me and get it over with. He thinks it'll break me, but oh, is he wrong."

The two cops exchanged eloquent looks as they closed Corey Dobias into the car, her cat-striped dress shimmering with defiant extravagance as she sat stiffly in the seat with her hands clasped on her lap.

"She's got class. I'll give her that," the younger officer said as Murphy went around the car.

"She ought to. Her daddy paid enough for it."

Hesitating to get in, the rookie officer peered at Murphy over the roof. "What she said about a scapegoat. Is she right, you think?"

"Probably," Murphy tossed back as if he didn't much care. "But I can't buck orders. I got my pension to think about."

"And I have a family," the rookie lamented. "I need this job."

"Then my advice to you is to keep your mouth shut and play the game."

"But if she's right, nobody can win."

"Sometimes the object isn't to win," Murphy said with a grand sigh that defined his sage wisdom. "Sometimes it's just not to lose so big."

But two hours later, Murphy wondered at his own philosophy. Corey Dobias might just be right. If the chief got cornered for this asinine stunt, someone would have to be the scapegoat. And he wanted to make sure that it wasn't him.

The moment he was off duty, after booking Corey Dobias and assuring his partner that they'd done the right thing, he drove to the Dobias estate, where the "stolen" BMW had just been towed. There had been a party, he noted, and everyone was leaving. Only a few limos and Rolls-Royces still lined the snow-smattered drive, and a team of valets stood around the tow truck discussing the curious turn of events.

Flashing his badge at the valet who met him at his car, as if it afforded him admission to this huge estate, he began to question him, searching for one single bit of evidence that he could hold over the head of the commissioner, just in case he needed it. Something he could use to hang him if the noose started swinging in his own direction. Something that could assure him that he wouldn't lose his pension.

For one of the first times in his life, he stumbled quickly onto what he was looking for, and by the end of the evening, he thanked his lucky stars, or whatever divine force there was guiding him, that Gary the screenwriter/valet had been in the right place at the right time.

He didn't even know if the kid knew how valuable his information was.

chapter

4

THE TELEPHONE TRILLED THROUGH THE NIGHT,
cutting through the layers of Adam Franklin's sleep like
the subtle approach of a power drill. Levering himself up
onto his elbow, he squinted at the clock. One-fourteen.
His muscles ached, rebelling against the late hour like
those of a man much older than forty-five. That's what
forty-eight hours without sleep did for you, he thought.
He wondered if this was what it felt like to be old.
The phone squealed again, and muttering, "Shit!" he
snatched it up. Flopping to his back and clutching
the cursed product of technology to his ear, he said,
"Yeah?"

"Did I wake you, Adam?" a sultry voice that lacked con-
text asked. "I thought guys like you didn't wind down till
four or five in the morning."

"Who the hell is this?" he grumbled, vexed by the
characterization—mistaken or otherwise—of "guys like
him."

"Sylvie," the woman said, her voice already taking on
that don't-you-remember-me pout that made him glad
he didn't.

"Sylvie . . . Sylvie who?"

An indignant rush of breath whispered over the line.
"Damn you, Adam. Sylvie Ascot. Who do you think?"

Adam opened his eyes and vaguely tried to put a face
with the name. Sylvie Ascot, the sleazy little actress who
preyed indiscriminately on men whose net worth was
in the eight figures. So far, he'd managed to escape her

claws. Not that she didn't keep trying. "Oh, yeah. What do you want?"

"Well, for starters, you could pretend to be happy to hear from me."

Indignation didn't work well when delivered with a whine, Adam mused, rubbing his face with a rough hand. Someone should tell her so.

He heaved in a deep, impatient breath. His eyes were beginning to adjust to being awake, which would make it that much harder to go back to sleep. "Look, Sylvie, I just flew in from the West Coast, and tonight is the first I've slept in days. You have exactly thirty seconds to tell me why the hell you woke me up."

"All right!" she snapped. "Try to do a guy a favor and what does it get you? I thought you'd be interested in knowing what went on at Nik Dobias's party tonight. *Everybody* was there. Except you, that is."

"I wasn't invited," Adam said distinctly, as if that in itself warranted some degree of pride. "Frankly, I don't much care what went on there."

"You don't understand," Sylvie said. "It's news. All the papers will be reporting it sooner or later, anyway. You might as well get a jump on everyone else."

Adam kicked the sheet off of his legs and brought his feet to the floor. If there was anything he hated, really hated, it was some idiot calling him to report a story, as if he sat on call with his typewriter revved up ready to take dictation. "This may come as a surprise to you, Sylvie, but I have reporters who do that. Some of them were probably even *at* that party. I'm the wrong person to tell."

"The wrong person?" she blared. "You *own* the stupid paper!"

"Exactly! Now, if you have a story, call the city desk and tell the editor. I'm not interested in your gossip."

"For a man whose success is grounded in gossip, I would think you'd be real interested, Mr. Tabloid King. They do still call you that, don't they?"

"Not anymore, they don't."

"Well, in my book, no amount of respectable newspapers will ever whitewash what really got you to the top, Adam. So you can drop the too-good-for-gossip act with me. This story is for the *Investigator,* not the *Bulletin.*"

"I'm hanging up now, Sylvie."

"Adam, something important happened at the Dobias party tonight, and your reporters may not have hung around for all of it," she blurted before he could cut her off. "You know that three hundred million he was going to break up between his girls?"

Adam rubbed his stubbled face and wondered how much longer this might go on if he allowed it to. "Goodbye, Sylvie."

"Wait a minute! He didn't give it to them like everybody thought. He's giving his daughters a year to compete for it. Kind of cold-blooded, don't you think?"

Not surprised, or particularly impressed, Adam reached for the pack of cigarettes beside his bed and put one between his lips while he looked around for his lighter. It was on the floor, where it had fallen from his pocket when he'd tossed his slacks over the chair tonight. He reached for it and glanced at his clock again. "You're down to ten seconds, Sylvie."

"Corey Dobias refused to play it her father's way and stormed out," Sylvie said. "Next thing we know, as everybody's leaving the party, her BMW is being towed home and rumors are going around that Nik had her arrested for stealing it."

For the first time in the course of the conversation, Adam heard something that interested him. His spine stiffened and he leaned forward, bracing his elbows on his knees. "Wait a minute," he said, taking the cigarette out of his mouth. "Corey Dobias was arrested for stealing her own car?"

"Yes!" Sylvie's voice reeked with delight that she had finally evoked a response. "She's probably sitting in jail right now, unless that boyfriend of hers bailed her out. He didn't look like he could afford a six-pack of beer, though. Guess Nik has her where he wants her now, huh?"

Adam reached for the lamp next to his bed and turned it on as if light could add perspective to Sylvie's news. "Are you sure about this? Corey in jail?"

"Yes, of course I'm sure. I was there, wasn't I? The party fell apart after she ran out. It was a shame, too. You should have seen the expense that went into it. And the people who were there. I'll bet—"

Adam came to his feet and reached for the gray slacks hanging over the chair, and began to step into them. "Yeah, Sylvie. Listen, thanks. I gotta go."

He dropped the phone back in its cradle as Sylvie sputtered her protest, then snatched it back up and dialed the *Investigator*'s newsroom. Before the editor answered, he hung it up again and headed for the closet. As dog-tired as he was, he had to get down to the paper and make sure they nailed Dobias's ass to the wall. Chances like this didn't come along every day. Besides, he thought, he had more than a passing interest in this case.

If Nik Dobias's youngest daughter was sitting in jail tonight, for whatever reason, he wouldn't trust anyone else to stay on top of it.

The smell of stale urine wafted through the air from the sticky toilet in the corner of the cell, while the feeling of utter abandonment wrapped itself around Corey

Dobias like a damp blanket. She'd watched those in the cells around her disappear one by one during the night, when friends, relatives, pimps, and lovers came to bail them out. No one had come for her. Not even Eric.

Now at one-thirty, the only company she boasted was the junkie locked into the cell opposite hers, and the sound of guttural heaving as the woman vomited over her cot.

Where was he? She asked herself, as though she were two people—one sitting stoically stubborn and refusing to reveal that she grew more distraught by the hour, the other beginning to melt and tremble as dark reality seeped into her consciousness.

She had used her one phone call to call Eric's machine rather than her lawyer, for she had mistakenly believed that he would take care of both bailing her out and finding someone her father didn't have in his pocket to represent her. Maybe he's not home yet, and doesn't know I'm here, she thought without much conviction. Or perhaps he was testing her again, quizzing the determination of the pampered rich girl whom he thought was acting like a child.

Oh, God, she thought, she was tired of being tested by the ones she loved.

Funny, but even now, as she sat in jail fingering the simple locket on the tiny gold chain she wore, she found it hard to be angry at Eric, as if she didn't have the right. It was almost as if she expected to garner his disapproval. Was it because of the respect she'd had for him from the beginning? the awe? the admiration? Was it because he hadn't really cared that much for her until just recently, because he'd seen so clearly through her?

Nothing but a fraud . . .

She got off the cot and paced across the cell, scraping her fingers through her tousled hair, staring at the floor and wondering if somewhere deep in his subconscious, if he thought that of her now. She crossed her arms and peered through the bars, trying to conjure the image of his face, but all she saw was darkness. His words roving through her head, however, wouldn't be silenced.

You have too many options, Corey. Too many cushions. You'll never really grow up until you've learned how to jump without your father's parachute.

She pulled up her silk chiffon lamé skirt and slid down the concrete wall beside the bars, until she was sitting on the stained, sticky floor, facing the door that would open if anyone ever came for her. Shivering from the cold dampness, she brought the locket to her lips and wondered why he had bothered with her at all, when he'd found her so hollow, so useless. Perhaps it was because she had made it her mission to make him take her seriously.

She smiled slightly as a memory came back to her, of the day he had agreed to accept the *Life* magazine photo assignment to follow a mountain climbing expedition for Outward Bound, a program designed to mix a decidedly unmixable group from all stratas of society, for a six-week stint in the Adirondacks. "You'd be a good candidate for the program," he'd told her as he stuffed his things into a duffel bag smaller than his camera bag. "They need at least one debutante to make the group complete."

She had taken the comment more as a challenge than an insult, and as if she were stepping from one fairy tale into another, she had surprised Eric and signed up for the program, including herself among gang leaders and juvenile offenders whose probation officers felt the program would help rehabilitate them.

The first two weeks had been devoted to a tortuous unconditioning of their tightly molded characters. They had been rationed food and made to walk for hours with bone-crushing gear on their backs, with hardly a moment's privacy and no relief. She had guarded her rations from the street kids who watched her with contempt and suspicion, and had slept with a knife in her hands for fear someone would attack her in her sleep. She had suffered the stings of their insults and had kept close to herself, realizing that being different was not altogether bad. She had come to hate Eric Gray during those first two weeks as he scrutinized her quietly, waiting—ever waiting—for her to crack and flee for home. Because he expected her to do just that, she had excluded that particular option.

But like guinea pigs engaged in some grand experiment, she and the others on the journey had watched the tight boundaries separating them as individuals fade and blend, until they saw themselves as more alike than different. She had learned to trust them as she crept up sides of mountains on ropes held tightly by her camp mates, had learned to care for them as she offered them the same encouragement and support that they came to offer her. She had shed tears with them in their frustrations and failures, had laughed with them in their ecstatic victories. She had nursed their blistered hands and bleeding feet, and allowed them to nurse hers. And through it all, Corey discovered that options weren't worth a damn if one didn't take advantage of them.

But Eric had refused to acknowledge that the Boston heiress was becoming human, until the day she sprained her wrist catching herself in a fall. The pain had been excruciating and promised to get worse with each new climb she faced. But still she didn't exercise any of her options, and even refused the helicopter the team leader offered to call.

That night, however, when the temperature dropped below zero and her wrist swelled to the size of her knee, she remembered wondering at the confusing wisdom that had kept her here, when anyone else would have given up. She had gone off alone to a cove a few yards away from camp that night, started her own small fire, and wept as quietly as she could.

To her horror, Eric had caught her. Without offering a word of acknowledgment or comfort, he had photographed her in the firelight, her face wet with tears, red and chapped from the sun and wind, and as untainted by her options as she had ever been in her life.

A few days later, after he had returned from a trip to the nearest town to develop his film and send the first of it back to his magazine, she had found those photographs slipped under her tent flap, and had seen herself in a new light. On the back of one of them, Eric had written, "The substance beneath the surface."

It was probably then that she had fallen in love with him, but he hadn't seemed to notice. As elusive as the wind, he had been everywhere and nowhere for the rest of the expedition, ever hiding behind the camera that provided him with divine eyes into the human heart. It wasn't until the final night, when they had conquered the mountain, the cold and themselves, that she became his lover. The following week, when they were back in the throes of reality again, he had given her the locket she wore tonight, with the picture of herself in her basest state, and the word "substance" engraved on the back to remind her who she was and who she had the capacity to be.

The sound of someone's heels clicked outside the cell on the concrete floor, and she stood up expectantly. It was her turn to be released, she thought. Someone had come for her.

But just as quickly as the thought came, it was dismissed when another cell door down the way opened and closed, the sound reverberating over the wing.

Exasperated, Corey went back to her cot, leaned back against the wall, and pulled her knees to her chest. Her father was letting her sweat, she thought. He wanted her to sit in jail long enough to "teach her a lesson."

She shivered, and hugged her arms more tightly around her. The wool blanket tucked into the mattress was there to keep her warm, but pulling it off the mattress seemed too committal, as if she intended to stay.

Her father might never forgive her, she had to admit as the night wore on. She had destroyed his grand, theatrical surprise and ruined the party he'd waited his life for. The party that meant he was somebody, even if he wasn't from one of Boston's oldest families.

No, he would never forgive her. But she would never forgive him for pitting her against her sisters or having her arrested. It was a standoff that would, no doubt, alter the rest of their lives. Pride against conviction, love against blame.

The woman in the opposite cell stopped retching, and the sound of quiet filled the wing. Thick quiet, smothering quiet, poisonous quiet.

And suddenly Corey wondered if anyone would come for her at all.

I really should go for her, Eric Gray thought as he sat in his small Cambridge apartment over an all-night diner near Harvard, breathing in the scent of grease and stale coffee that he had almost grown accustomed to.

He sat on the windowsill, saw his reflection staring back at him in the glass. He looked too much like his father, though his dark hair was longer than the somber

Philadelphia banker would have tolerated, and his jaw was more shaded with neglectful stubble. The reflection gave him an eery sense of unease, so he leaned over to turn off the lamp beside him, erasing the image from the glass, and leaving only the lights of the street below him to focus his sights on.

He should go to bail her out, but something in the back of his mind made him resist. Nik Dobias wanted her in jail tonight, and who was he to cross the man who could have done him so much good, if she'd only had the sense to play his stupid little game?

He walked through the apartment into the tiny dark room and looked around him at the framed prints leaning against the wall, the prints that Corey had promised to buy for the lobby of her father's new casino. Now the deal would be off, and he was right back where he'd started.

Just months ago he had chided Corey for being exactly what he'd expected her to be tonight. But what was he supposed to do? Be glad that his one chance out of this hellhole was gone? Pretend that poverty was some noble state that he'd cling to for art's sake? He'd done enough suffering. It was time now that he proved his father wrong about him, by showing him that he could make his mark without playing the grateful bastard son.

He could marry a Dobias heiress.

Too bad he'd picked the sister too stubborn to see just what she had. Maybe he'd gone too far in hammering home that she had too much. Maybe he should have stopped once she got interested.

Maybe a night in jail, a night *without,* was just what she needed to realize that ten million dollars looked pretty damned good. He would wait until morning to get her out, giving her time to reevaluate those brick-wall principles that had landed her there. Maybe then she would change her mind, and accept her father's terms.

Maybe then Eric would have a shot at making something of his life.

At two A.M., the newsroom of the *Investigator* was all but asleep. Only four weary reporters sat at their word processors hammering out stories that had the bad timing to come in during the night. Downstairs, the presses rushed to get the morning edition out on time.

Adam Franklin, whose penthouse was on the top floor of the Franklin Tower, the building that housed the tabloid, the headquarters of his newspaper chain, his wire service, and various other interests, rarely got to this part of the building, and never at this hour. The quiet disturbed him. He never liked seeing anything he owned sitting idle.

The click of his heels on the tile startled the reporters slumped behind their computer monitors, and Joe Holifield came to his feet. "Adam, we didn't expect you—"

"Has anybody called in about the party at the Dobias estate tonight?" Adam cut in without greeting.

Holifield shuffled through the pages of the notepad on his desk. "Yep. Crain Goodall of the Society section was there. He brought some film by that his photographer had taken. Corey Dobias and her father screaming at each other. We're talking high drama. Also, Crain said there were rumors her father had her arrested for car theft. I checked them out and they're true. Can you believe that?"

"Yeah, I believe it." Adam eyed the thirty-year-old reporter who had come to him a year ago, unemployed after being fired from his job as a television news anchor for being caught patronizing a brothel the very night it was raided before a rival station's live cameras. To add insult to injury, he'd been found with a bag of cocaine in his pocket, for which he'd received a conviction with a suspended sentence. Throughout it all, Holifield had sworn that he'd been working on a story for his station, and that it was all just a terrible misunderstanding. His station had become a laughingstock in New Jersey, and no other station in the country would touch him after that. But the man had an instinct about him, Adam had noted when he'd reviewed some of his work. Once you got past the prime-time good looks that had taken him as far as they had, you could see that Holifield had a gut instinct for investigative reporting. Even if he was stupid and needed a few lessons on timing.

Still, Adam had instructed his editors to keep Holifield on the night shift, just to make sure he understood his place before they gave him anything substantial to sink his teeth into.

"I want to be careful with this," Adam said. "We can hint at some wrongdoing—police bribes, false arrest, that sort of thing—and still stick to the facts. Dobias would love to hit me with a libel suit."

Holifield rubbed a hand over his beard, the what-the-hell beard he'd grown after he realized that no one much cared how the blond wonder boy looked stuck in newspaper print. He referred to the computer that illuminated the article he'd been in the process of writing. "I understand that, Adam, but this might be pertinent. My source at the precinct where she was taken thinks she's still there. No one's bailed her out yet. Kind of strange, considering she's there on manufactured charges to begin with. I'm waiting to hear back before I write the article."

"She's still there?" Adam asked, not hiding the surprise in his voice. "How many hours ago did all this happen, anyway?"

"Happened about nine o'clock," Holifield said. "Plenty of time to have been bailed out by now. I mean, she must have friends or something."

The phone on Holifield's desk rang. The reporter turned his back to Adam and snatched it up. "Holifield."

Adam listened as the party on the other end of the phone confirmed the rumor that Corey was still in jail, making it more than obvious that her father was flexing his muscles. He felt his neck growing hot, and he stretched the V-neck of the sweater he'd thrown on. How could Nik Dobias have his youngest daughter thrown in jail? The bastard. He'd known for years the man was a fool. Ever since he'd seen how he'd neglected his wife in his dauntless pursuit of that elusive empire that meant so much to him. Ever since he'd lost sight of the riches he had in her.

Holifield hung up, drawing Adam's mind back to the young woman sitting in jail, and caught in the grips of a sudden decision, Adam started to walk away. "Go ahead and print the story," he said.

"You sure?" Holifield called after him. "Even the part about her being left in jail?"

"All of it," Adam said. He reached the elevator, punched the Down button. "Every last fact you've got. The worse you make that son-of-a-bitch look, the better."

"What about the libel suit?"

The doors opened, and Adam stepped on. "Tell him to stand in line."

"You bet," Holifield said with a dramatic punch at the air, then slumped back into his chair behind his computer, his fingers already rapping on the keyboard.

Corey Dobias was growing used to the scuff of heels down the hall, and the sound of the cell doors opening and closing. No longer did she expect them to come for her. She closed her eyes and wadded the thin pillow beneath her head, praying for sleep if she was, indeed, to spend the rest of her night here.

Eric had abandoned her, she thought as reality shuddered through her. He had ignored her plea for help, and the absence of her sisters spoke volumes about the degree of her father's anger. It wasn't often that Nik Dobias considered his own emotions over "how things looked." Ordinarily, he would have sent someone for her, along with word that he didn't want to speak to her or hear from her. After a day or so of that cold exile, he would expect her to approach him with her heart in her throat, wincing while he exploded about her lack of propriety and her self-centeredness.

So it had been when she came home from the six-week ordeal in the Adirondacks that had changed her life. He had wanted to hear nothing of her trials nor her victories. So she had never told him of them.

The clicking of heels on the concrete grew louder, but Corey had given up hoping that the guard would stop at her cell. Still, she lifted her head off the pillow and looked toward the bars, into the shadows beyond. The uniformed officer stopped at her door and jabbed a key into the lock. "Your bail's been posted," he said.

The door opened with an echoing scrape, and she got up slowly and went through it, wondering who had finally come. "Pick up your personal effects in there," the officer told her, handing her a receipt. "And then you're free to go." Not bothering to straighten her dress or her hair, she followed him away from the acrid stench she'd begun to grow used to, past the junkies and hookers who'd been brought in during the last hour and slept or paced in adjacent cells. The officer opened the door and motioned her into the lighted precinct, where other police officers, both uniformed and plainclothes, looked up from their work and watched the heiress, still clad in her eighteen-thousand-dollar gown, cut across the floor.

Adam saw her the instant she stepped into the room, with her mop of auburn hair disheveled and bound haphazardly at her nape by one long strand. She looked pale and tired, though her dress still shimmered, as if her fairy godmother had forgotten to retrieve it when her coach had turned into a pumpkin. Nothing about her resembled the fresh-faced, bright-eyed socialite he'd seen at an occasional party, flirting with yuppies and political figures, nothing like the child he'd often seen flitting around her mother, teasing and competing for the grace of Shara Dobias's smile.

Despite the weary droop to her posture, he saw no defeat there. There was almost a look of defiance in the way she held herself as she stood at the desk gathering her personal effects. Too much defiance to look around in search of her boyfriend or father or sister, or whatever savior had come to bail her out, after leaving her there most of the night.

He stepped forward, out of the obscurity of the waiting room where he had been standing, and saw the officer point in his direction. Her gaze cut through him without recognition, then darted back and forth to those beside and behind him. Then, as if she wouldn't waste another moment waiting for the anonymous bailor to appear, she started toward the door.

Adam stepped into her path, and she glanced up at him. Suddenly, she recognized him from the few social events at which they had met over the years. "Mr. Franklin . . ."

He saw her expression transform slowly from surprise to confusion, then to understanding as he remained standing in her path.

"Are you the one who—?"

"Yeah, I bailed you out," he said, taking her arm and escorting her through the door, away from the roomful of people gaping at her. "Now I'm taking you home."

"No." She hesitated on the steps of the precinct and withdrew her arm from his grip. "I'll take a cab." She looked up at the man she hardly knew and couldn't remember if they'd ever even spoken beyond a polite "hello."

"Suit yourself." Undaunted by her decline of his offer, Adam continued down the steps to the curb, stepping into a circle of light cast by a lone street lamp. Dark shadows defined the lines beneath his eyes, making him appear tired, though a pensive alertness seemed to reign in his guarded expression. Icy wind whipped through his hair and his clothes, and she realized she had never seen him dressed so casually. The tycoon usually wore thousand-dollar suits, not pullover sweaters and leather jackets that made him appear younger than she had once figured him to be. She groped for the facts she knew about the rugged tabloid publisher whose empire was virtually global. Mid-forties, self-made, changed women as often as he changed ties.

Quickly, her mind sorted through reasons he might have had to bail her out in the middle of the night. That he was not on the illustrious list of people her father counted as friends was no secret to anyone who knew Nik Dobias, for Adam Franklin had been vicious in the stories he'd allowed to run about her father in his tabloid.

"Do you expect some sort of exclusive interview for your paper?" she asked, confused.

"I have better things to do than interview debutantes," he said, stepping to the curb and attempting to hail a cab. "Frankly, nothing you say about tonight really interests me that much. Your daddy made you mad, so you showed him. But I guess he wound up with the last word, didn't he?"

Corey's face reddened with new fire, and she finished her trek down the steps until she faced him eye-to-eye. "It doesn't matter what you think about me, Mr. Franklin. And as for my father having the last word, it isn't really over yet, is it?"

"No?" he asked as the wind tossed the raven hair that matched the color of his eyes. "Sure looks like it to me. You'll go back now, with your tail between your legs, and 'reconsider' your father's challenge, because after all, a shot at everything is better than nothing, isn't it?"

Corey held her chin high, refusing to be made a fool. "I wouldn't take my father's challenge to compete with my sisters if I was starving in the streets, Mr. Franklin. I don't like playing games. Especially the kind where everybody loses."

Adam stared down at the young woman he would have bet—before tonight—was spoiled rotten and pampered like a princess. He still wasn't entirely sure she wasn't. "Nice little speech," he said, "but it needs work. Your delivery's just a little too well rehearsed."

Her teeth came together, and he noted the way her nostrils flared with the same indignation he'd seen often in her mother. "I mean what I say, and I don't give a damn whether you believe me or not."

He lifted his shoulder as if he didn't care one way or the other and looked up the street, squinting in the brisk wind. "You know, this is going to be all over the papers in the morning. My reporters have already written their stories about the rift in the Dobias family. It won't look good for any of you."

Fed up with his hard-nosed opinion of her, Corey stepped off the curb to catch a cab herself. She saw one a block away and lifted her hand to stop it as she gave Adam a disgusted look over her shoulder. "Will that run on the same page as the article on the woman in Kalamazoo who gave birth to a ninety-pound alien?"

Adam laughed appreciatively. "You know how it is, Corey. We cover what's newsworthy."

He watched as the car pulled to the curb, idled, waited for her to get in. Corey stood staring at him a moment, refusing to shiver against the dropping temperature. The angry energy in her pale eyes riveted into him with a directness and a perceptiveness that surprised him.

Finally, she opened the door.

Adam reached into his wallet and pulled out two bills, one of which he thrust through the window to the driver. The other he handed to her.

"I can pay for my own—" she started to object, but then her voice faded as she realized that the cash she'd carried tonight wouldn't get her two blocks down the road. The need for help from him, not once tonight, but twice, made her angrier. "I'll pay you back for the cab," she said, pushing his hand away and refusing the other bill. "But I don't need any more."

"Don't worry about it," he returned, a curious glint of amusement in his eyes. "It won't break me."

She got in, still refusing the bill, and Adam closed her door behind her. Through her open window she regarded him with a mixture of suspicion and grudging curiosity as he shrugged out of his jacket and thrust it through the window.

"At least take this. It's too cold to traipse around like that," he said. "You can return it later."

She looked down at the coat, longing to pull it on, but Adam knew she would freeze to death before she would let him see her wear it.

"I guess I should thank you," she said.

He glanced over the roof of the cab, his hooded eyes idly watching the passing cars. "Don't," he said. "I didn't do any of this for you."

The delicate brows over Corey's blue eyes—eyes that he'd seen on another woman before, eyes he had never forgotten—arched in question. "Then who?"

Adam looked down at the dirty concrete beneath his feet for a moment, then met those eyes again. "Let's just say it was a favor for an old friend."

Before Corey could glean more, he stepped back and gestured for the driver to pull away.

chapter
5

"WHAT DO YOU MEAN YOU LET HER OUT? I TOLD you to keep her all night!" Nik Dobias's fury thundered over the telephone line. Mitch Easterman switched the receiver to his other ear and heaved a deep, weary breath.

"Nik, someone met bail. What was I supposed to do? We're on thin enough ice arresting her for stealing her own car. I'll have hell to pay tomorrow."

The Boston police commissioner pushed out of the chair at his desk and strode across the room, rubbing his eyes and glancing at the digital clock glowing in the darkness. Four-thirty-two A.M. It was bad enough that he'd have to be at the office in three hours after being up all night, but it was even worse when he faced the fact that the press would probably be circling like vultures trying to get a statement about Corey Dobias's arrest. He'd spent hours tonight trying to come up with a suitable story: that the car had been reported stolen, so their overzealous officer—Murphy Johnson was his name—had arrested Corey, not realizing she was Dobias's daughter. A mistake, he would maintain. The charges were all being dropped. If allegations arose about bribes, he would divert the attention by saying that the officer was currently under investigation.

He'd found answers for every question that could possibly arise, but no matter how meticulously he constructed those answers, they still didn't wash. Of all the "favors" Dobias had demanded of him, this was the worst yet.

"Who bailed her out?" Dobias asked finally. "Was it that boyfriend of hers?"

"No. It was someone who could do us a lot more damage." He could almost see the old tyrant pacing across the floor, that vein on his temple throbbing and those silver eyes darting back and forth with alertness that no one should have this time of night. "Adam Franklin."

"Adam Franklin?" The name was repeated with absolute confusion. "What does he have to do with this?"

"Got me," Easterman said. "All I know is that the man isn't stupid. It makes me look bad, Nik. Real bad."

"Stop whining," Dobias snapped over the line. "If you get pushed against the wall, just go take a cruise on that yacht I bought you last year. It'll snap you out of it."

The phone went dead, and Mitch Easterman slammed it back in its cradle and cursed the day he'd ever met Nik Dobias.

Dobias leaned back in his chair and stroked his lip with a finger, trying to decipher some reason why Adam Franklin would have bailed Corey out of jail.

Did he want an interview? It was a possibility, he imagined, since Franklin hadn't yet missed an opportunity to write scathing things about him in hopes of toppling his empire. There was the tax evasion thing a couple of years ago, which had ultimately cost Dobias a mint. Before that, Franklin had gone on a vendetta about some of Dobias's shadier acquisitions, costing him a fortune in lost deals and investments gone bad.

Even then, Franklin had always had one of his sleazy reporters do the dirty work. So why now, after he'd finally thought he'd gotten the man off his back, did Franklin get involved in a family matter?

The question ate at him, and he pulled up out of his

chair and grabbed his glass of Scotch. Throwing back a drink, he went to his bedroom door and stepped into the wide corridor, lit by dim recessed lights strategically placed every few feet.

A portrait of his wife hung there, her face illuminated with angelic highlights, and he lingered, gazing up at those blue eyes that had always made him feel as if he could own the world, wrap it up in a package, and give it to her.

But tonight he felt her censure radiating from the portrait as if it were his own conscience. They never had agreed on how to handle the children. She had been too lenient, too generous, for things had always come so easily to her. He had known the other side, the side of life where struggle and compromise balanced against each other every moment of the day. The side of life that had driven his father to put a bullet through his own head to end the cyclic oppression of poverty he had inflicted upon his family. The side where other men's footprints scuffed his back, the side from which he'd looked up at the privileged few and sworn that one day he'd reach that state, surpass it.

His own methods had served him well, and they would serve his children, he'd told Shara a thousand times. But he'd never expected Corey to be the one to throw those methods back in his face, not as she'd done tonight. She was the one he'd gone easiest on. The one who'd always known how to slip through his barriers.

But that was his fault, and he'd learned that lesson well tonight. He'd been a fool to allow her that much power over him. He wouldn't make that mistake again. From now on he was in control, and she would learn just how powerful that control could be.

Abandoning the portrait of his wife, he went down the staircase to the study, where he picked up the telephone to call the guards at the front gate. "Corey is on her way home," he said, "but she is not to be let through the gates. Do you understand me?"

The guard hesitated. "Yes, Mr. Dobias. I'll tell the others."

"You do that," Dobias said. "She's to be turned away, and if she by any chance does get through—tonight, tomorrow, or any day after that—I'll have the ass of the fool who let her in, and yours too. Got that?"

"Yes, sir."

Dobias dropped the phone and rubbed his face.

He heard a sound at the door and swung around. Emily, his granddaughter, was standing in the doorway. Her hair was disheveled, as if she'd been in bed, and the quilted satin robe she wore lay open, revealing the ruffled gown she wore beneath it.

"Emily, it's four-thirty. What are you doing up?"

"I couldn't sleep," she said. "I was waiting for Aunt Corey."

Dobias turned away and went to the chair behind his desk, seeming to concentrate on a stack of papers there. "You'll have a long wait. She isn't coming back."

"But . . . Grandfather . . ."

"Go to bed, Emily."

Emily stood quietly in the doorway, not daring to utter another word, and finally, she slipped away.

Dobias sat back in the lamplight, staring at the doorway where Emily had stood. Slowly, his gaze gravitated toward the framed photograph on his desk, the one of Shara with the girls: Giselle standing on her right, Rena on her left, and little Corey, a saucy toddler who had the temperament of her Greek father and the beauty of her Irish mother, perched in her lap.

They'd had an argument that day, about his not sparing the time to join them in the portrait. Shara had never understood the amount of time and concentrated energy it took to build an empire such as his. She had never understood that he worked like a demon for her. She deserved more than the Greek upstart she'd married—someone more than the son of a fisherman and a seamstress, who had thrown their fortune away in the garbage bins of Wall Street. She deserved somebody who was somebody.

Somebody like Shara's movie-mogul father, who had disowned his only daughter after her elopement. No amount of gifts or trinkets from Dobias had ever chased away the melancholy over the loss of her family as a consequence for loving him.

But he had never stopped trying to make it up to her. When their firstborn child had come, he'd seen the maternal gleam in her eye and believed he had finally given her something that could make her happy. "I'm going to be worthy of you somehow," he'd told her. "You'll see. I'm going to be the richest, most successful man in Boston someday. I'm going to make you proud."

"I don't want you to make me proud, Nik," she had said. "I want you to make me happy."

But happiness wasn't something Shara would know for a while yet, for her father died the day after Giselle was born. Shara would never know if it was news of the baby that had lead to his heart attack, or if it was the grief over the daughter he had disowned. What she did know was that he still loved her when he died. He had left her in his will despite his vows not to, and his last words to her mother were to tell Shara that he loved her.

The sadness over her father's death after their long estrangement had never quite been quelled. The more melancholy Shara was, the harder Dobias worked to give her more, and the farther away she drifted.

It was a cycle he had never known how to break, for

its origins had always been such a mystery to him. But despite her quiet moods and silent musings about her past, she had always been there for him. Tonight, like a thousand other times since her death a decade ago, he wished he had her here with him to comfort and appease him, to calm him, to explain to him how his favorite daughter could have publicly humiliated him and become so ungrateful after a lifetime of pampering.

But Shara wasn't here. His fury was his to deal with alone. And he would vent it in the way he saw fit, no matter who suffered.

chapter
6

GISELLE PEELED HER GOWN OFF AND LET IT PUD-
dle around her feet, unaware of the man standing in
the shadows of her room, watching. She slipped on her
silk kimono, and sat down in front of her mirror to take
the pins from her hair.

She'd spent most of the night with her father, trying
to calm his fury, withstanding his swings from violent
rage to brooding misery, and telling herself that all was
not lost.

Despite the publicity his actions would create by
morning, she had to admit that she hoped her little
sister rotted in that jail cell.

She had ruined everything, marching into the party with that bum on her arm and flashing that ring
around as if he'd given her the crown jewels—that was
what had changed her father's mind, she was certain.
That was why Giselle, once again, had not gotten what
she'd spent a lifetime earning. Once again, Corey had
destroyed everything.

Her hair fell down around her shoulders, and she
picked up the brush to sweep out the tangles, staring
critically at herself in the mirror as she did. The tension was taking its toll on her eyes, she told herself. She
was beginning to look strained, frazzled. It never paid
to look as if she wasn't in complete control. Maybe tomorrow she'd insist that Henrique come to the office
and give her one of his famous facials. That is, if she
could work him in. She had a lot of work to do tomor-

row. There wasn't a day to waste.

"You're still the most beautiful of the Dobias women," a voice said from the shadows, and Giselle swung around.

John Keller, her sister's husband, stood leaning against the wall, smiling as if he had every right to watch her intimate bedtime ritual.

"What are you doing here?"

"I've been waiting for you. We need to talk."

She turned back to the mirror and indifferently slipped the brush through her hair again. "Go back to your wife, John. Rena's waiting."

"She's asleep," he said.

"Asleep?" Giselle uttered a laugh and shook her head, letting the full-bodied ebony hair tousle around her face. "How can she sleep after what happened tonight?"

"She took a pill," John said. "She always takes pills after your father plays his little jokes." He ambled across the floor to the cabinet where Giselle kept a variety of liqueurs, and poured himself a cognac. "You've got to hand it to the old guy, he never loses that sense of humor."

The bitterness in his tone was unmistakable, and Giselle laid the brush down and watched him finish the glass off in one gulp, then fill it up again. "What's the matter, John? Are you afraid of being a pauper?"

John laughed, but the sound was hollow and cold. "Oh, I don't intend to be a pauper, Giselle. That's what I wanted to talk to you about."

She leaned an elbow on her vanity table and looked up at him, her eyes cool and calculating as they swept over him, from his perfectly groomed blond hair to the piercing green eyes to the mouth set in a hard half smile. He hadn't changed all that much since the day her father had brought him home for Rena. Giselle had met him and despised her father for giving her sister the best when she had been left to fend for herself with a husband who lacked patience, understanding, or the romantic nature that Rena's flaxen-haired suitor so obviously possessed. She had liked that hungry look in his eye, that half smile that boasted sinful secrets, and that shrewd air about him that warned off anyone who would stand in his way.

It was scathingly clear that when he'd looked into Rena's myopic eyes, he'd seen only her father's dollar signs. The man was not a fool. Neither then, nor now.

"We don't have anything to talk about, John. You're not involved in this at all. It's between Rena and me."

"You know damn well that Rena hasn't got a chance."

Giselle grinned and tipped her head, letting the ends of her hair sweep across her shoulder. "So you thought you'd try and resume our little affair? Sort of lay the groundwork in case you have to change camps?"

She turned back to the mirror and opened a bottle of French hand lotion, poured some onto her palm, and began to massage it into her skin.

John came toward her as she knew he would, and taking her hands, finished kneading the lotion in. She looked up at him and he smiled. Indifference still gave him a rush, she thought. The challenge of her feigned disinterest still had the effect of an aphrodisiac on him.

She cocked her head, and he let her hands slip from his. Boldly, he reached out and pulled the silk robe down to expose bare flesh.

"I thought we could work together, Giselle. We always were a good team." His voice was still sexy, rich, bedroom breathless, inspiring fantasies she could fulfill with the slightest effort. As if he read those fantasies, he dipped his face down and kissed the base of her neck. His chin was rough against her bare shoulder.

"What's in it for me?"

He swiveled her chair around until she faced him, took a vial of perfume from her table. Slowly opening it, he trailed the wet ball of fragrance down her neck, her chest, and—pulling the silk of her robe farther back— wet a path across one bare nipple. "Use your imagination," he whispered.

A smile came to those vivid, almond-shaped eyes, and Giselle took the vial of perfume from his fingers and, peeling back the other side of her robe, slid the tip across her other breast as she smiled defiantly at him. "I'm going to win anyway," she whispered. "I don't need you."

The scent of Obsession wafted over the room, and John grinned. "All right," he said in the voice that always made her shiver. "If you want a war, you've got it, baby. I'll help Rena."

"I'll still win," she said.

Still grinning, John propped his hands on the arms of her chair, held his face inches from hers. "It's going to be a long year, Giselle. Think hard before you turn any allies away. You might need all the friends you can get."

He started out of the room, but stopped at the door and turned back. She hadn't covered herself, and she gazed up at him with a seditious look that never failed to arouse him. Shaking his head, he said, "I always knew I married the wrong sister."

"You married the only one who would have you."

John's grin skipped broader across his face. "Only because you were already married," he said. "But that didn't stop us, did it, Giselle?"

Giselle's smug smile faded by degrees, and she pulled the robe over her breasts and turned back to the mirror. "Go back to your wife, John," she said wearily as she confronted her reflection again. "And don't wake Emily. She's a light sleeper."

"Just like her father," John said.

Giselle watched the door as he closed it behind him, and a heavy breath issued from her lungs as the quiet settled around her again.

chapter
7

J. J. WESTON HAD ONLY BEEN DRIVING A CAB FOR two months, ever since he'd enrolled at Boston College, but he'd had enough celebrity fares to get pretty jaded. Last week he'd driven Stacy Keach to the Hilton. The week before that, Henry Kissinger had ridden in his backseat. Pretty famous bigwigs for a dirty cab with torn seats and a bashed-in fender, he'd thought, but he hadn't asked questions and had taken them where they wanted to go, keeping his curiosity to himself.

But tonight he couldn't help himself. It wasn't often he picked up a broad decked out like a *Vogue* cover girl, glittering like she could have paid for his cab with one yard of fabric from that sexy getup she was wearing. The fact that he had picked her up at the police station at four-thirty in the morning had piqued his interest initially, but when she had given him the Brookline address where she wanted to be taken, he couldn't help getting downright curious. It was in one of the ritziest sections of town, just a hop, skip, and a jump from the Kennedys.

"You get robbed or somethin' tonight?" he asked over his shoulder, glancing at the woman in his rearview mirror as she sat huddled in the man's jacket that hung from her small frame. She looked up at him, the vivid blue of those eyes startling him. He'd seen eyes like that before, but only on a hooker who wore tinted contact lenses. He suspected there was nothing fake about hers.

"Why do you ask?" she asked cautiously.

He shrugged. "Comin' outa the precinct like that, I just figured."

Her eyes strayed out the open window as the wind tangled her dark hair. "Yeah, I got robbed," she said.

"Nothin' important, I hope."

She smiled and glanced back at him. "No, nothing important. Just a BMW and about a hundred million dollars."

A low, disbelieving whistle came from the cabby. "You carry that much around with you?"

Corey threw her head back and laughed, and J. J. couldn't help smiling. She had a way about her, he thought, unlike the other ritzy ones he'd driven, who acted like it was beneath them to ride in a cab when they could have the fanciest limos at their disposal.

"What's your name?" she asked, surprising him.

His eyes widened in the mirror. "My name? J. J. Weston."

"Nice to meet you, J. J. Weston," she said. "My name's Corey." She breathed in a deep sigh, and said, "I've had a hell of a night. Do you know I got engaged tonight?"

The cabby glanced in the rearview mirror again. "No kidding? Congratulations."

Corey laughed and looked out the window again. "Thanks. Thing is, I don't know where my fiancé is right now. Or if he's speaking to me. Or if I'm speaking to him." She set her elbow on the window and leaned her head toward the wind, stroking her hair back with her fingers. "And then there's my father. Good old Dad."

"You have a run-in with your old man?"

Corey didn't smile this time. Instead, she just narrowed her eyes as the wind whipped her hair, and stared out the window. "You might say that."

He kept quiet for the rest of the drive, frequently

looking in his mirror to see Corey still staring out the window, as if she relived the night as they drove. When he reached the road that wound past the gates of so many huge estates, some of which he'd seen featured on *Lifestyles of the Rich and Famous,* he glanced over his shoulder. "Which one of these you want?"

"A little farther," she said. "The Dobias estate."

"Dobias, huh?" The cabby grinned, wondering if she was a Dobias herself, or if her fiancé was a Dobias, or if she was friends with a Dobias. She must know them pretty well, he thought, or she wouldn't be pulling in here at close to five A.M. and expect to be let in.

"They keep the gates closed at that estate," he said. "You sure they'll let you in at this hour?"

"They'll let me in," she said. "I live there."

J. J's eyebrows shot up, and he searched his memory for the name Corey Dobias. Yes, he'd heard of her. Just yesterday, as a matter of fact. He'd read something about her and her sisters in the paper. Something about her father dividing his fortune. *A hundred million dollars.*

It began to snow as he slowed at the gates of her estate and turned into her drive. In the little building to the side of the gate, he saw two guards, watching almost as if they'd been expecting them. He waited for the gates to open, but instead, one of the guards started walking slowly toward his car.

"I'm sorry, but you can't go in there."

"It ain't just me, pal," J. J. said. "I got Corey Dobias back there."

Corey leaned forward in her seat and gazed at the guard. "It's all right, Harris. Let me in."

The guard averted his eyes, and through the shadows cloaking his face, she could see the unmistakable strain. "I'm sorry, Miss Dobias. I have orders not to."

"What?"

J. J. looked over the seat at the young woman whose expression revealed the hell she had lived through that night, and he began to feel sorry for her.

Quickly, she flung open the door and jumped out of the car, walked in front of his headlights, and faced the guard herself. "I don't intend to stay, Harris. I just want to get my things and get out of there."

The guard shook his head. "I'm sorry. If it were just me, I'd let you in, but your father . . ."

"I want to talk to him," she said. "Give me the telephone."

"But . . . he's probably sleeping . . . I could get fired—"

"Give me the telephone!" she shouted again. "I want to talk to him."

"I'll call him for you."

She watched him step into the small building in which he spent eight hours a day, and saw him put the phone to his ear. "Tell him that after what he did to me tonight the very least he can do is to let me in long enough to get a change of clothes."

"Yes, ma'am."

J. J. watched her stand there, shimmering in his headlights, her tangled hair falling wildly around her shoulders, and that big jacket draped over her. She looked anything but forlorn, he thought, and yet the very pride that held her so still and so unwavering was probably the element that made him sympathize with her the most.

His meter was still running, and he glanced on the seat at the bill the man who'd put her in the car had tossed him. It would just cover the trip to the estate, he thought. But if she didn't have any more, and they really did turn her away . . .

He reached over and cut off the meter.

He saw the guard hang up, and Corey started toward him. "I told you I wanted to talk to him. Did you tell him—?"

"He told me to turn you away," the guard said, almost wincing with each word. "He said he won't talk to you, and . . . if you try to get on the grounds without permission, he'll have you arrested again." The guard cleared his throat and tipped his head to the woman glaring up at him. "I'm really sorry, Miss Dobias. I wouldn't do this for the world."

J. J. expected her to rear back and slug the guard—he would have. But she didn't. Instead, she wilted a little, nodded, and muttered, "All right. Thank you, Harris." Then coming back around the car, she got in.

"Well, J. J. It looks like you're stuck with me a little longer," she said, her voice sounding hoarse.

"No problem, ma'am," J. J. said. "Where to?"

Corey thought for a moment, and finally, she drew in a deep breath. "Take me to the Monarch Hotel."

He began to back out of her drive, but she leaned forward and laid a hand on his shoulder.

"J. J.? I—I don't have any cash on me. I could use my credit card to get some at the desk of the hotel, if you wouldn't mind waiting—"

"No problem, ma'am," the cabby said. "Your friend back at the precinct gave me enough to cover it. Don't worry 'bout it."

Corey slumped back in her seat and looked out the window again. J. J. didn't try to make any more conversation for the rest of the drive into town.

The Dobias name carried a lot of weight in Boston, and just about every place else, so when Corey checked in at the Monarch Hotel, no one questioned the fact that it was five A.M. or that she wore a designer gown with a man's jacket, while her hair was as tangled as if she'd just been in a wrestling match. The politeness with which they accepted her and led her to her suite, with the fireplace crackling as if they'd been expecting her, and the bed turned down with orchids on her pillow, might have amused her if she hadn't been so utterly exhausted.

She immediately took a shower, using the shampoo and soaps the hotel had laid out on the Vermont marble, washing the memories of the filthy jail cell from her hair and skin. Stepping out of the shower, she pulled on the white terry robe that hung on the door and dried her hair with the complimentary hair dryer provided in every room.

Then, unable to squeeze out one more ounce of energy, Corey slipped under the covers and fell into a deep, turbulent sleep . . .

. . . the scent of her mother's mild perfume washed over her, and she nuzzled her face into the quilt that Shara had tucked around her. She heard her mother humming, her voice deep and soft, and felt the warmth of her as she sat beside her, waiting until she fell asleep.

And then she was gone.

It was cold and the quilt had fallen away and the distant sound of knocking stirred her from her sleep and she couldn't smell her mother's perfume . . .

Corey struggled to open her eyes, and the knocking grew louder. She sat up, looked around, and remembered where she was.

The clock beside the bed said 8:30. She pulled out of bed, grabbed her gown off of the floor, and quickly slipped it back on. Still groggy and bewildered, she stumbled to the door. "Yes?"

"I'm sorry, Miss Dobias," a man's voice said. "It's George Katz, the hotel manager. It's important."

Corey shoved her tangled mass of hair back from her face and opened the door.

A man of about thirty-five stepped inside, and she could tell by the way he avoided meeting her eyes that his mission was not one of welcome. He was there to prolong this nightmare, she thought. He was an emissary of her father, come to twist the knife. "There's a problem," he said. "Uh, with your credit card, it seems."

Corey squinted up at him, still too groggy to grasp what he wasn't quite saying. "My credit card?"

"Yes." He cleared his throat. "When we ran the card through this morning, we were told that the account had been closed. The card isn't good."

"Closed?" Corey shook her head and started for her purse. "There must be some mistake. I have others, if—"

"I'm sorry." His tone was unwavering, and Corey swung around, glaring at him across the opulent expanse of room. "I don't think they'll be any better than this one."

Corey stared at him, speechless, for a long moment, and finally it dawned on her what exactly he was trying to say. "It's my father, isn't it? He called you. . . . How did he know where I was?"

The man sighed as if he found the whole matter extremely distasteful. "That's none of my concern, Miss Dobias. And I hate to inconvenience you . . . that is to say—"

"You're throwing me out?" Corey asked, incredulous. "Is that what you're trying to say?"

"Well, I wouldn't put it that way," the man hedged.

"What if I could pay?" she bluffed, straightening and stepping toward him. "What if I had cash?"

He met her eyes directly for the first time, and she saw the alarm there. And she knew then that no amount of cash would make any difference, because her father had more. He would always have more. "That would be fine, Miss Dobias, except that my desk clerk made a mistake. You see, this room was already booked, and we really don't have any vacancies—"

"He threatened you," Corey cut in softly, her blue eyes glistening with fiery understanding. "He told you to throw me out."

The man cleared his throat again. "I'd— be willing to give you a little time . . . a few minutes to—"

"How generous of you," she said.

The man went to the door, as if he couldn't get out of there fast enough, but Corey caught up with him. "I won't forget this, Mr. Katz. If there's anything I inherited from my father, it's the ability to hold grudges. And the determination not to let my debts go unpaid."

The man didn't offer her the courtesy of a response before he hurried down the hall.

Corey closed the door and wilted back against it, trying to convince herself that all was not lost. So her father had closed her credit card accounts. So he had seen to it that the hotel wouldn't keep her. So he wanted to see her thrown into the streets.

She blinked back the tears in her eyes and went into the bathroom, found the toiletries assembled there. Quickly, she brushed her teeth with the complimentary toothbrush provided by the hotel, then washed her face. She brushed her hair and French-braided it down her back. When she felt as though she could face the world, no matter how cruel and cold it had become, she swept the complimentary toiletries into the clean garbage bag in her waste basket, removed it, and wrapped it up. She might need them, she thought, for she feared the worst was not yet behind her.

Stepping back into her suite, she reached for her purse and sat down on the edge of the bed, trying to reign in her emotions. There was too much ahead of her to cry now, she thought, but still the tears came, plopping down from her face to bead on the fabric of the gown she was beginning to hate with a passion. If only she had a change of clothes, she thought, the humiliation would not be so hard to endure. If only she had a pair of flat shoes, a twenty-dollar bill, a friend she could trust . . .

Emotion overtook her, and she found herself wilting into the sobs that racked her. Where was everybody? Where were her sisters? Where was Eric? She picked up the telephone again, dialed Eric's number, and listened numbly to his answering machine again.

She hung up the phone and dropped her face in her hands, but after a moment, she told herself that was enough. There wasn't time for this, she thought. She still had her dignity, her integrity. No matter whom her father knew or how far his influence reached, he could not take those from her.

Wiping the evidence of weakness from her face, she pulled on her high heels and Adam's coat, and taking the bag full of toiletries and her small clutch purse that carried only her worthless credit cards, she walked out of the hotel onto the sidewalk coated with a fresh blanket of snow.

The doorman smiled at her from the curb. "Good morning, Miss Dobias. May I get you a limousine?"

Corey lifted her chin high and settled her gaze on him. "You don't have to be nice to me," she said. "I don't have any money. Haven't you heard?"

Not waiting for him to overcome his fluster at her

rejoinder, she started off down the sidewalk.

It was the dress keeping her down in the mud her father had created for her, she thought bitterly as she carefully made her way down Newbury Street, trying not to slip on the ice. She had to get out of it. If she were attired as any of the others on the street, people would stop staring. They wouldn't know that she was the "ungrateful heiress" who'd thrown her father's gifts back in his face. They wouldn't know that she'd spent the night in jail or that her credit cards had become worthless or that she didn't have a penny to her name.

Her feet ached as she covered the blocks to the bank where she had an account, the bank that would be her savior. All she needed was cash, and the world would be hers again. She could fight her father if she just had a few dollars.

She passed a string of newspaper vending machines lined up in front of a hotel, and saw her face sporting the front page of Adam Franklin's newspaper, the *Boston Bulletin*. "Dobias Heiress Forfeits Fortune," the headline read.

She glanced at the *Investigator*, the tabloid his name was most closely associated with, and saw the even more scathing headline: "Dobias Daughter Dragged to Jail." And the subtitle: "Dad cries, 'Lock Her Up!'"

A sick feeling of nausea swirled up inside her, and she started to walk again, keeping her eyes cast down as she passed the gawking people on the sidewalk. This dress was like a banner, she thought. A banner that read, "Yes, it's me. I'm the Dobias heiress. I'm the one whose father threw her in jail. I'm the one that everyone will be talking about for the next year."

But the farther her spirits sank, the hotter her fury became. She would show them. She would show them all.

She reached the bank where her mother had opened

her account long ago, the bank that held the trust fund she would not be able to touch for eleven more years. It also held her checking account, the fuel for her fading spirit, so she quickly stepped up to the window.

At once, it seemed as though all eyes in the building were upon her, and the whispers started with one of the tellers, then shuddered through the building like strategically placed dominoes. It was the dress, she told herself, and the headlines, and she wished the earth would open and swallow her. But it didn't happen.

The teller at her window looked over her dress, and a startled expression seeped into her eyes, as if serving Corey was the most loathsome task she'd confronted all day. "Yes . . . ," she said tentatively. "May I help you?"

"I don't have my checkbook with me," Corey said, ignoring the fact that everyone watched her. "But I need to withdraw some money from my account. My name is Corey Dobias."

The teller glanced down the row of workers to the bank president who had now emerged from his office and regarded her across the room the way he might regard an armed felon. "Uh, excuse me a moment."

The teller left the window, and Corey watched her approach the president, Theodore Winthrop, a man she had met on several occasions when she'd been running Dobias Designs. She had never liked him when she *had* money. He was too short and too bald and wore the smug expression of a man much taller and hairier. His attitude had always made her uncomfortable, for he practically drooled over her and made even more of a spectacle over her father. Dobias loved it, however, which was why he kept so much of his fortune in this bank.

The man approached her, but this time he wasn't drooling. She waited for what she sensed he would tell her, watched the way the light glistened off the top of his head, and wondered if he ever sunburned there and, if he did, if it was disgusting when he peeled. The degrading thoughts propped her up and made her feel better about what was about to happen.

"Miss Dobias, may I see you in my office, please?"

A feeling of futility washed over her, and she drew in a deep breath. "Mr. Winthrop, I just want to withdraw a little money. Not even a lot. Please don't tell me that my father has gotten to you already."

But the moment she uttered the words, she knew he had, and she couldn't imagine why she hadn't anticipated it before. Seeing the stoic look on the manager's face, she preceded him to his office, where just a few months ago she had sat with her father as he'd deposited yet another million into the company account of Dobias Designs, the company she had set up and run single-handedly for three years. But that was just a drop in the Dobias bucket, she had realized, for the bank was financing much of Dobias's new Atlantic City casino, and they expected to earn a mint's worth of interest on the loan, not to mention winning the accounts of the casino, itself, once it became operational.

Winthrop closed the door behind him, and Corey didn't bother to sit down. "Go ahead, Mr. Winthrop. There's no use wasting our time."

"I'm afraid your account has been closed, Miss Dobias. I can't tell you how sorry I am . . ."

She felt that fury that often got her into trouble raging up inside her, and she stretched her lips across her teeth. "That was my account! I worked for that money. He can't close it without my signature!"

"I'm afraid he can," Mr. Winthrop told her. "You've had that account since you were a little girl, and your father has always been a signatory on it. I suppose it never occurred to anyone to have that changed now that you've come of age, but—"

Corey struggled to hold her hands at her sides, for she doubted taking a swing at him would change his mind in her favor. "Are you telling me that I can't get one cent out? Not any of it?"

"I'm afraid not, Miss Dobias," Winthrop said sullenly.

"All right," she said, trying to control her breathing. "What about my trust fund? I could borrow on that. It's four million dollars that was just my mother's—not my father's."

Winthrop shook his head. "I can't loan you money on a trust fund that won't be yours for eleven more years. Besides, your father is the trustee of that money. He would never sign it over as collateral. Until you turn thirty-five or your father dies, whichever comes first, that money stays right where it is."

"I'm not asking for the whole four million, Winthrop. Just a few hundred dollars."

Smiling with a smug look of mock-sympathy, he shook his head. "I'm sorry."

Numb with disbelief, Corey gaped at him.

"There is one other thing, as well," he said. "I've been asked to take your credit cards . . ."

Corey continued staring at him for a moment, unable to comprehend the full significance of his words. When he held out his hand, illustrating his intention to follow her father's orders, she tossed her sequined purse at him, hitting him in the stomach. It landed at his feet on the floor. "Take them," she said. "They're worthless, anyway. I don't need them. And I don't need my father."

The man stopped to pick up the purse and gave Corey a doleful look that made her hate him even more. "This is most unfortunate, Miss Dobias. Perhaps you could make amends with your father. Patch things up."

"My father has pushed this past the point of return," Corey said. "And so have you. I won't stay down for long, Mr. Winthrop, and when I'm back on my feet, I won't forget those of you who kicked dirt in my face. My money is still in this bank, and so help me God, one of these days I'll use it to make you regret what you've done."

Still clutching her plastic bag full of toiletries, the only things in the world she owned, she started from the room.

"Miss Dobias."

She turned back around, and saw him pull a bill from his wallet. "I— could loan you twenty dollars, if—if it would help . . ."

Corey turned back to him and settled her frigid blue eyes on his. Reaching out, she took the bill, looked down at it, then met his eyes with steely ones of her own. "Use it to buy yourself some balls, Winthrop. I can promise you you're going to need them." Then slapping the bill back into his hand, she left the bank.

The ineffectual sun that failed to melt the snow mocked the bleakness in Corey's soul as she made her way without direction back up Newbury Street, ignoring the stares of those she passed. That was it, she thought. She had nothing. No money. No friends. No family.

Nothing.

But that wasn't true, she thought. She had a fiancé, and despite how he had avoided her, abandoned her, and ignored her, she couldn't help the tiny flicker of hope in her heart that she'd read him all wrong. It had to be a misunderstanding. He still didn't know what she had been through, she told herself. If she went to him, he would take her in, reinforce her, get her back on her feet.

But she didn't want to go to him desperate and penniless, wearing this dress that grew more vulgar by the moment, when she considered how many cab rides it would buy her, how many pairs of walking shoes, how many nights in a hotel . . .

That was it! she thought. She could trade the dress for a change of clothes, maybe a little pocket change.

Her eyes came to life, and she scanned the stores lining the streets. Not one where they would know her, she thought. It had to be a less expensive shop, one where they would jump at the chance to own an original Roehm.

She began to walk faster and turned off to a side street, walked several blocks, and turned again. And then she saw it. A little boutique that specialized in casual wear.

And she knew that things were about to start looking up.

Hazel Kranton heard the bell and came down from the ladder where she'd been stacking the new shipment of Levi's. Feathering her fingers through her short, curly hair, she started through the store. "May I help you, hon—?"

The moment she rounded the rack and saw the woman standing before her, glittering like a Vegas star, she let her sentence hang. "Oh, my God, look at you. You're gorgeous. But you should really do something about your makeup, honey."

Corey smiled. "I know. I'm afraid I looked a little better when I got dressed last night."

"Last night?" Hazel said in her nasal voice, winking at Corey as if she understood. "An all-nighter, huh? Did you have fun, honey?"

The innuendo gave Corey an idea, and she grinned and played along. "A blast. But I'm in trouble now. My daddy, he's really strict, and as long as I live under his roof, I have to follow his rules. And if I go home this morning in this dress, he'll know I was out all night—"

"Say no more, honey," Hazel interjected. "I understand perfectly. You want me to fix you up in a new outfit, so you can prance in and act like you got up early and went out, am I right?"

"Well . . ." Corey sighed and glanced at the woman's name tag. "You see, Hazel, I have a little problem with money. I sort of lost my purse last night, and, well, I don't have any money . . ."

Hazel's red pencil-drawn eyebrows came together, and Corey started talking faster.

"But I was thinking. This dress is a Roehm original, and believe me, it cost a fortune. I'd be willing to sell it to you for three hundred dollars. Then I'd have enough to buy some clothes."

Hazel eyed the dress. "I can see that it's a knockout, all right, but, honey, I don't own this place. You'd have to talk to the owner, and she's out of town."

"Then you could buy it for yourself," Corey ventured. "We're about the same size."

Hazel gave the dress another covetous look, then shook her head. "I'm sorry, honey. I don't have that kind of money on me."

"All right." Corey took a deep breath, tempering her voice so as not to sound too desperate. "Two hundred dollars. That's as low as I can go."

Hazel gave the dress another covetous look, then reached out and touched the silk chiffon lamé. "Well, there is that party I was going to next week. . . . It would look great, wouldn't it?"

"Are you kidding? An original Roehm? You'd be the hottest thing there."

Hazel sighed, but Corey knew she had already made up her mind. "Just a minute."

She went behind the cash register and pulled her purse out of a cabinet. Checking her wallet, she said, "I could give you a hundred dollars. . . ."

Corey sucked in a panicked breath. If she spent part of it on clothes, she wouldn't have much left over. And she was determined not to go to Eric without a penny, just in case he wouldn't take her in.

"A hundred dollars *and* an outfit," she said. When Hazel hedged, she added, "You could turn around and sell this dress for thousands, and you know it. Just cover the cost of the clothes with a personal check and sell the dress later. The store's owner will probably pay you ten times as much for it."

Hazel eyed the dress again. "All right," she said with a beleaguered sigh. "A hundred dollars and some clothes. I hope I won't regret this."

Breathing off ten pounds of relief, Corey picked out her outfit and disappeared into the dressing room.

Corey's only regret as she left the boutique was that they didn't sell shoes, and Hazel's were a size too big for her. She'd checked.

But somehow she had to admit that the high heels with the tightly tapered jeans gave her the look of someone not quite so desperate, someone not hanging from her rope's end. She would make it through this. After all, it wasn't as bad as when she'd been stuck halfway up a mountain with a sprained wrist, freezing to death and half starving. That had made her a stronger person.

Now it was time to put the lessons she'd learned on that mountain to good use. She wasn't ready to concede defeat just yet.

chapter

8

HE COULDN'T AVOID HER ANY LONGER. ERIC stood at the window of his apartment and watched her prance up the sidewalk like a Calvin Klein model without a care in the world. She didn't look any worse for the wear, he thought, though he wondered where she'd gotten the clothes. He hadn't seen her in jeans since her trek up the mountain, and he'd never seen her in a man's coat that was several sizes too big.

He rubbed the weariness from his eyes, for he'd only gotten a few hours' sleep, and quickly racked his brain for an explanation as to why he hadn't come to her aid. She wasn't stupid. He knew that.

Deciding to take the offensive, he swung the door open the moment she knocked. "Where the hell have you been?"

Corey lifted her chin high and stepped over his threshold. "*I've* been in jail, Eric. Where have *you* been?"

Eric pulled her into the apartment and slammed the door behind her. "First I was out looking for you. You weren't at any of the places I expected. When I finally came home and heard the message that you were in *jail*, for God's sake, I went to bail you out, and they told me you were already gone. I finally just gave up and decided you must have gone home."

Corey looked at him, noting the thickening stubble on his jaw and the redness in his eyes. Maybe he was telling the truth, she thought. Maybe she had been wrong about him. "I tried to go home," she said. "My father wouldn't let me through the gates." She walked across the room and flopped sideways into an overstuffed chair, throwing her legs over the side. "So J. J. took me to the Monarch—"

"J. J.? Who the hell is J. J.?"

"The cab driver," Corey said, resting her head on the back of the chair. "But then, of course, my father cut off all my credit cards and they threw me out."

"Dammit, Corey, you've really done it."

Corey's eyes took on a dull glare as she stared at him across the room. "What's the matter, Eric? Worried about the prints we were going to put in the casino? Is that what all this is about?"

"It's not just my prints, Corey," he said, going to her and leaning over her chair. "It's your future. Our future. Where does this leave us?"

Corey dropped her feet to the floor and sat up, and the dullness in her eyes took on a sad understanding. "I didn't know our future depended on my father's money," she said quietly.

Eric dropped dramatically into a chair across from her and covered his face with his hands. "I don't believe this. I've never seen anyone so stubborn. What does he have to do to you to make you play it his way?"

"Oh, I don't know," Corey said. "He's done just about everything I can think of. Closed my bank account. Had me thrown in jail. Forced me out into the street with no place to go. I'd say he's about tapped out. There's nothing else he can do to me."

Eric gave her an indicting look and popped up from the chair again. She watched him stroll across the small apartment, looking at the matted prints leaning against his wall. "You just don't get it, do you? It's just going to get worse. Money doesn't fall out of the sky. And it sure as hell isn't that easy to earn. Not the kind you're used to. You have no idea what's ahead of you."

"What was it Nietzsche said?" she asked. "That which does not kill us . . .' "

"How the hell do *you* know what Nietzsche said?"

For a moment Corey was quiet, and he could see that he'd hit a nerve. Finally. Maybe this would be the thing that would make her snap, so she'd run back to her daddy and make him forgive her.

She got to her feet, and he could see that she strained to keep from crying. But she was pretty adept at not showing it. "I sold my dress to pay for my clothes," she said, looking down at the ring he had put on her finger last night. "I could have sold the ring, but I didn't. I figured you'd want to just take it back to the store. Maybe they'll give you a refund."

It was a graceful out, and he almost took it. But then he thought of all the other times in his life when his timing had been lousy, and he'd missed the boat by an inch. Not this time. He wouldn't let her break their engagement, only to send her running back into her father's good graces. When she went, he would be beside her.

Sighing deeply, he pulled her into his arms. She was stiff, unyielding, and he knew he'd have to work to make it up to her. "I don't want the ring back," he whispered. "I want you to wear it. We're still going to get married. We just . . . won't set a date yet."

Corey closed her eyes as he kissed her, and he could feel her failure to respond. That, too, would take time, he thought, but he was good at seduction. A real pro. He could handle it.

He looked down at her. "You said you sold your dress. How much did you get?"

"A hundred dollars and this outfit," she said, as if she had struck the bargain of the year.

He moaned. "You've got to be kidding me. How much did you pay for that dress?"

Corey saw where the questioning was leading, and rubbing her eyes, she looked away. "Eighteen, Eric, but that really doesn't—"

"*Eighteen* hundred dollars and you sold it for a hundred bucks?"

She smiled, but was not amused. "No, Eric. Eighteen *thousand.*"

His face actually turned red as he gaped at her, and for a moment she feared he'd start choking and clutching at his heart. "Do you have any idea how much money that is? Do you know what we could have done with that?"

Corey tipped her head up to him and snatched up her garbage bag full of toiletries. "Next time you decide to leave me in jail all night, Eric, you remember this. If you'd been there when I needed you, I wouldn't have had to sell it."

"So I'm the stupid one?" he flung back. "You sell an eighteen-thousand-dollar dress for a hundred bucks, and it's my fault?"

Shaking her head, she started for the door. "I'm not in the mood for this, Eric."

He put himself between her and the door. "Where do you think you're going?"

"I have an appointment."

"An appointment? Come on, Corey. Don't con me."

"I have an appointment," she said. "I had a life before my father threw me out, and I still have a life. I don't intend to shrivel up and die." She wondered what she had hoped to gain by coming here in the first place. "I have to meet with the owners of the building on Tremont Street," she said in a flat, dull voice. "I have a contract to buy one of their buildings, and I want them to know that I'm still going through with it."

"Tremont Street? You're not going ahead with that idiot deal in the Combat Zone, are you?"

Corey swallowed back the rising anger obstructing her throat. "You didn't think it was idiotic when I mentioned it to you before."

"That was when you had your father's money to back you up. It had possibilities then, but only if you bought a lot of other buildings there and started converting the whole raunchy area. But, Corey, be realistic. You don't have backing now, you don't even have your father's advice, and you don't have any money."

"I worked in my father's company for three years, Eric, and I've lived with him all my life. I think I've learned a few things. I can handle it."

He threw up his hands and slumped down into his threadbare chair. "God, you have got to be the most stubborn woman I have ever known."

Her throat constricted, and she attempted to clear it. "I have to go. I'll come back later, if you want."

"If I want? I was going to marry you, wasn't I?" He wilted at her look, shook his head, and spread his hands dramatically. "What the hell? What's mine is yours. At least until you and your father work things out."

"Hell isn't forecasting a freeze anytime soon, Eric," she said. "I'll find my own place."

"Corey, if you want to come back, come back. What am I supposed to do? Beg?"

"No, Eric. I wouldn't think of making you beg, any more than I'd consider doing it myself."

He watched her leave the apartment, with all the dignity of someone who really had a hundred million dollars in her back pocket, and told himself to bide his time. She was sure to break sooner or later. And when she did, he didn't want to be yesterday's heartbreak.

*   *   *

Corey stepped out into the unshoveled snow, blinking back the sudden tears bursting into the corners of her eyes.

It was the money, she thought. It had changed everything.

She dabbed at her eyes before the tears had a chance to fall, and recalled her father's words years ago, before she'd even started dating.

"Money can buy you all the love you'll ever need, Corey. But you have to shop carefully."

Corey, idealistic and naive even then, had argued with him. "You can't buy love, Daddy. It's not something with a price tag."

"Everything has a price tag," he'd said. "We all pay in one way or another. You try emptying your pockets for a month or two, and see if anybody of worth shows up at your door."

Her father wouldn't have considered Eric "anybody of worth," but ironically enough, he had fulfilled Dobias's prediction.

She drew in a ragged breath, looked around, and asked herself where in the hell she was going to go. She didn't anymore have an appointment than she had a home. But she wasn't about to sit in that apartment and listen to Eric whine, and she wouldn't dwell on his choice of words a few minutes ago. *I was going to marry you, wasn't I?* She wondered if he even realized he'd put it in the past tense.

She walked the few blocks to Harvard and found a bench on campus against a tree. Sitting down, she pulled her high-heeled feet into her seat and hugged her knees.

The frosty wind whispered through her hair, and she turned her face into it and squinted her eyes, trying to concentrate on the contentment it offered. There were things in life that were free, that didn't cost money, she'd learned on the mountain expedition. Things like wind and rain and satisfaction and contentment.

But she had to admit that as hard as she'd worked to sluff off her rich-girl image, she had always truly loved being rich. Occasionally a surge of guilt would shoot through her, but overall, she had more good feelings about it than bad. That was why last night had been such a disappointment to her. She'd had such plans for her portion of her father's money.

She closed her eyes and thought of the long hours she'd put into learning the business over the last three years since she graduated from college. It had occurred to her more than once that her choice to major in art history rather than business had been a frivolous rich-girl decision. For that mistake, she'd had to work over-time to know what one in her position needed to know to make responsible decisions. But as tough as it had been, she had done a good job. Her portion of the company was to have been her reward.

She sat up and dropped her feet to the ground, and leaned forward with her elbows on her knees. Anticipating the division her father had promised, she'd had plans to invest in an old building in Boston's Combat Zone, one of the seediest and most run-down sections of town. The building had sparked her imagination the moment she'd seen it, and she had plans for renovating it into a luxury office building, then buying up more of the property on the street, in an effort to squeeze out the bad element that owned the nude bars and pornographic theaters that occupied the area now. She'd signed a contract to buy the building for a song, and she was certain that she could renovate it and turn it around at a phenomenal profit. After all, she'd learned from the best.

She was supposed to have closed the deal this week, as soon as her money came through. She'd kept it all a secret from her father, for she'd badly wanted to impress him with her business acumen. But now it was all for nothing. As soon as the current owners of the building heard of her new status, they were bound to revoke their agreement.

If there were only some way she could still get the money and go ahead with the plan. But that was unlikely, when she couldn't even afford a hotel for the night.

Still . . .

It occurred to her that people made investments every day with other people's money. There were banks which loaned money to entrepreneurs, individuals always looking for good investments, even government aid for those needing help getting started in business. She had the connections, the sources, and the chutzpah, if her father didn't stand in the way. All she needed was the cash.

A new flood of energy burst through her as she jumped up and dashed to the nearest pay phone, and called the building's owners to arrange an appointment. They wanted to call off the deal if she couldn't close this week, they said, but they would meet with her to see what her options were.

Not wanting to look like a loser without even a purse to her name, she took the "T" to Filene's Basement, Boston's bargain capital, and bought a marked-down alligator briefcase, though she had nothing in it. She lingered over the shoes and skirts but finally decided she couldn't spend another penny since she didn't know how far she'd have to stretch what little cash she had. Then, not wasting any more time worrying how she looked, she walked the rest of the way to their offices, determined to convince them that she still had the resources to close the deal, if they'd only give her a little more time.

Andrew Hinton, Jr., was the senior partner in the HDRS Group, a group of Boston physicians who, for years, had been investing in properties around the area. Each blamed the others for the decision, years ago, to buy the string of properties on Tremont Street. They had all been delighted to talk to Corey Dobias about her interest in it when she'd come to them two months ago.

Today, however, Hinton met her with a little trepidation. He'd read the account in the newspaper of her rift with her father, which reduced her from the exalted state of a Dobias to someone with no money and no power. And he didn't have a lot of time to waste dealing with someone with a pipe dream and no one to finance it.

The moment she stepped into his office, he knew his fears were justified. She was wearing jeans and carrying a briefcase. He smiled. It was the first time he'd done business with a kid. He'd get it over with as fast as he could and try to find another buyer for the building at the first opportunity.

"Thank you for seeing me, Mr. Hinton," she said, walking toward him with her hand extended.

Reluctantly, he shook it.

"I read your unfortunate story in the paper this morning," he said, not wasting any time. "I take it they got the account right."

Corey took the seat opposite him and smiled, though he could see the weary shadows beneath her eyes. "I wouldn't know. I haven't read it."

"Then let me summarize it for you," he said. "It said that you've been cut off from your family. That you no longer have a position in your father's company, nor do you have his money or his influence."

Her smile didn't falter, but he noticed her pale eyes looking him over, as if he had some crucial accessory out of place. He suddenly felt awkward.

"I still have my plans, Mr. Hinton," she said. "I still intend to hold you to your contract. You gave me ninety days. I have another month to come up with the money."

"Yes, well." Mr. Hinton checked his watch, shifted his weight in his chair, and settled his eyes on her again. "You see, I feel it would be a charade to continue with this. It's possible we could find someone else who wouldn't have any trouble getting financing."

"The building wasn't even for sale when I came to you," Corey retorted. "You even offered to finance it yourself."

"Your plan interested us at that time," Hinton said. "We thought you could make a go of rebuilding the Combat Zone, wiping that disgusting element out of our city. We thought a Dobias—if anyone—had the resources to do it. But to do that, you'd have to buy up a great deal of property. You'd have to have a lot of money. You'd have to have the kind of experience it takes to enter such an endeavor."

"I have as much experience now as I did two months ago," she said.

"Perhaps," he said. "But you don't have as much money."

She met his eyes directly, and he realized that she had learned a great deal about intimidation from her father. "I expect you to honor your contract with me, Mr. Hinton. I have thirty days left. I can come up with the money. If you sell the property to someone else before our contract has expired, then I'll sue you. It's that simple."

He snickered, as if the threat were an empty one. "We've encountered lawsuits before, Miss Dobias. We're quite familiar with the legalities of a contract such as ours."

"Then you must know that thirty days is hardly worth the time or money that would be spent in litigation."

He stood up and buttoned his Bond Street coat, then paced to the window of his office. "All right. We'll give you thirty days, but that's all. Not one day more." He turned back to her. "Is that absolutely clear?"

"Absolutely," she said. She remained seated, making no effort to leave. "As for the financing—I didn't need it before, when I had my father's influence. But now—"

"I'm afraid that's out of the question," Hinton said. "You'll have to arrange your own financing. Otherwise, we have no deal."

"All right." She came to her feet, and for the first time he allowed himself to notice the long, thin legs encased in jeans, the fullness of her rich hair, the color of her eyes. Again, she reached out to shake his hand and he took it, thinking that she still carried the air of a woman who stood on top of the ladder, rather than one who hadn't yet made it to the bottom rung. "I'll be in touch with you, Mr. Hinton."

"I'm certain you will," he said.

chapter
9

THE PAPERS WERE READY TO BE SIGNED, THE
ones that spelled out the conditions of the scratch-and-
claw competition with Giselle; that created two new corporations—IDK, Incorporated and GCD, Incorporated; and
that stipulated in one short year it would most likely all
be taken from Rena.

Just as it had been taken from Corey. But Rena wouldn't
think about that. Corey was strong; she would make it.
It was her own plight that concerned Rena now.

Giselle sat across from her in their father's office, waiting for him to join them and make it all official. Giselle's
eyes were alive and fiery with purpose, and Rena knew
without a doubt that her older sister counted the fortune already won. One year from now, she would have
no problem sweeping Rena out of the way. Giselle had
always been strong like that.

Emily stood between them, her big eleven-year-old
eyes, as black as coal, looking tired and rimmed in
red. She hadn't slept well, Rena thought. How could
she, after the things Dobias had said in front of all
those people about Emily's father abandoning them
when she was six months old? How could the child
ever understand that her grandfather hadn't meant to
hurt her? It had been nothing more than one of his
performances. But Emily would learn his ways soon
enough.

She reached out and took the girl's hand, pulled her
down onto the divan next to her. Settling a nurturing

arm around the girl's shoulder, she asked, "What's the matter, Emmy?"

Emily watched the door, dreading the moment when her grandfather would enter. "I've been so worried about Aunt Corey," she whispered.

Giselle snapped a look at her daughter. "Emily, don't say a word about that to your grandfather, do you hear me? If you do, you'll be out in the street with her, and so will I."

"Giselle, don't frighten her like that! Dad would never throw Emily out."

"She's not a baby," Giselle argued. "She has the mental capacity of a thirty-year-old, and she has enough Dobias in her to understand the way the world works. It's no use lying to her." She regarded her daughter, saw the tears beginning to glisten in her eyes. "You know what I'm saying is true, don't you, Emmy?"

Emily nodded and looked at Rena, holding her eyes wide to keep those tears from falling. "People thought he'd never throw Aunt Corey out," she whispered. "Mother has always said she was his favorite, but even that didn't matter last night."

"They'll patch things up soon," Rena said with hollow confidence.

Emily shook her head like an adult who couldn't make another understand her own wisdom. "But it'll be too late," she said. "You and Mother are signing the papers today. She'll be left out. How could Grandfather do that to her?"

Giselle bent over her daughter and cupped her chin, bringing her shattered gaze up to her. "Corey is a Dobias," she said. "She'll get by. In the meantime, you and I have a lot of work to do, if we want to be the two richest women in Boston. There isn't time for worrying about anyone but ourselves."

Silently accepting the implication that she would lose the game, Rena dropped her arm from Emily's shoulder and carefully laid her hands back in her lap. So much for Giselle's maternal reassurances, she thought. As always, she tried to soothe Emily's deepest childhood fears with the promise of an extravagant future. She couldn't blame her, though, for she was quite sure that was what had always soothed Giselle.

Not for the first time, Rena nursed the wish that Emily had been her own. She would have been a good mother, and she had no doubt that Emily would have been a happier child. It was ironic, after all, that Giselle had been married less than two years and produced such a wonderful child, and Rena and John had been married for over thirteen and had yet to conceive. It was just one more disappointment she bestowed on her father, her husband, and, most especially, herself. The possibility that it might be some physiological problem with John never even occurred to her. She was certain that it was her own inadequacy that had kept her barren. One more flaw among so many.

The door to his office opened, and Dobias came in, followed by Robert Gloster, who cleaned his glasses on a handkerchief as he walked. Dobias dropped the papers on his desk and plopped down in his big leather chair. From the looks of him, no one would ever know that he'd been up all night, or that the circumstances of the last twenty-four hours had thrown a wrench into the life that had been so carefully etched out by his lawyers and top advisers. Steepling his fingers, he faced the three remaining women in his life, regarding each with a piercing scrutiny that made them brace themselves for anymore surprise blows.

"The papers are all ready," he said, "and we might as well get this competition under way."

Giselle smiled, and with great effort, Rena followed her lead as Robert Gloster began to enumerate the conditions one by one.

Thirty days. Corey mentally counted ahead, deciding exactly what day would be her deadline for closing the deal on the Tremont Street property. Even though the chances of her raising four hundred thousand dollars in financing and thirty thousand in cash by that date were slim, she wouldn't allow herself to entertain the possibility that she would fail.

Her father had bluffed his way through bigger deals, and so would she. She'd show him she could do it, too. She'd show them all.

Filled with a sense of hope that she hadn't possessed when she'd left Eric's that morning, she went to a deli, bought a sandwich and a drink, carefully counting out her money, and thought over her options. Eric didn't have a cent to his name, so he was absolutely no help. Most of her rich friends were still under their parents' thumbs—just as she had been—and their parents were involved in deals with her father. If she knew the politics of her father's world, none of them would touch her when it came to business. She'd have to find some unbiased source. Someone with a lot of money. Someone who didn't fear her father at all. Someone who might even have a vendetta against him. Someone like . . .

Adam Franklin.

The name fell into her mind like manna from heaven, and she felt her heart accelerating with renewed vigor as she abandoned her plate and rushed out of the deli. Adam Franklin would loan her the money. He might even consider a partnership. After all, he hated her father. Why else would he have bailed her out last night?

Wishing she had splurged and bought some flats so

she could throw these heels as far as she could see, Corey started up the sidewalk toward the Franklin Tower. Her luck was about to change, she told herself. After all, she was a Dobias. And she knew a few things about survival that her father hadn't taught her.

Adam Franklin rubbed his tired eyes and looked up to focus wearily on the presidents of his various companies sitting around the table in the glass-enclosed conference room. "The Knights of the Round Tabloid," rival newspaper chains had called them, belittling the decisions made in this room. But not so many jokes had been made at his expense lately. Not since he'd emerged as a serious publisher and a businessman with a vision.

The jokes hardly ever bothered Adam, for he was usually the one laughing the hardest. Twenty years ago, when they'd scoffed at the Oklahoma "boy" hocking everything he owned to buy the ailing tabloid, which at the time was nothing more than a dying rag that no one read, he'd been the one laughing. They had underestimated him. They always had. When he'd turned the *Investigator* into a daily paper distributed in more stores than Charmin toilet paper, the chuckles had been tinged with a dull note of envy.

When he'd bought the *Bulletin* and upgraded it to a newspaper that provided serious competition for the *Boston Globe,* the chuckles had all but died.

But Adam was a restless man, so he had begun work to set up his own wire system, the FranklinNet, which rivals claimed was a waste of time, for no one could compete with AP or UPI. Within a year every major newspaper in the country, as well as several thousand papers abroad, was using it.

But the *Investigator,* still housed in the Franklin Tower, though some of his other ventures were seated elsewhere, remained the trademark he could never quite escape. It was the bane of his acceptability, but in many ways it was also his baby. He would neither make excuses for it nor forsake it, for despite his empire, he remained grounded enough in reality to know on which side his bread was buttered.

"I guess that about wraps it up," Adam muttered, distractedly jotting notes on the papers spread out before him. "Set up those staff meetings and get back to Sarah this morning. It won't be easy, but I want to fit them all in this week. It looks like I might have to go back to Tokyo next week if they don't make any more headway without me this week. Those Japanese are trying to squeeze every penny out of us, but I think they want the FranklinNet there as bad as we do."

The presidents of the various companies disbursed in quiet conversation, and Adam leaned back in his leather chair and rubbed his eyes again. Damn, he needed some sleep. After two days without sleep, last night's interruptions hadn't done him a bit of good. But he supposed it had been worth it.

He looked up as his "knights" filed out through the glass door, and a figure standing aside caught his attention through the glass. A kid standing in jeans, staring in at him— No, he thought suddenly. Not a kid. A woman.

Corey Dobias.

Dropping his papers back on the table, he slung an ankle over his knee and tilted his chair back, reached for his cigarette pack, and motioned harshly for her to come in.

She waited until he was alone, then came in, closing the door behind her. "I tried to get an appointment, but your secretary has an authority complex and wouldn't give me one."

He smiled as he lit his cigarette. "That's why I pay her so well." He glanced her over, noting the lack of makeup on features that hardly needed help, the long French braid that gave her an innocent air of sophistication, the casual clothes that fit her like a glove, the high heels, and the brand-spanking new briefcase clutched in her hand. Over her arm, she carried his coat. He would have been amused at her cross between lady of leisure and CEO, a look that all rich kids seemed to pull off without meaning to, but something about the determination on her face reminded him of someone he was very close to. Himself.

She didn't wait for an invitation to sit down. Instead, she set her briefcase on the table and leaned one hip on it, ignoring the chairs.

"You could have left the coat with my secretary," Adam said, rocking back and forth in his swivel chair and dragging on his cigarette as he watched her, fascinated by her obvious lack of shrivel-up-and-die regrets. "You didn't have to thank me again."

"I didn't come to thank you," she said. "By the looks of the *Investigator*'s front page today, you should be thanking me. You probably doubled your sales this morning."

Adam grinned and opened his hands. "Like I said, you make the news, we report it."

Corey shook her head and tossed her braid back over her shoulder. "I didn't come here about the news, either," she said. "I didn't even read it. The pictures were sensational enough."

Adam's grin grew more demure. "I could get you a copy, if you want it. An eight-by-ten glossy?"

"Send it to my father," she said, losing the amusing edge to her tone. "He's the one who likes to keep score."

"Don't we all?"

"Yes, we do." She lifted her brows and settled her piercing eyes on him. "And that, Mr. Franklin, is why I'm here. I need a loan."

Adam didn't reveal any surprise at the statement, but his eyes sparkled with a hint of more amusement. "Everybody calls me Adam," he said. "Especially those who have the nerve to ask me for money." He reached into the inside pocket of his coat, withdrew his wallet, and reached in for a bill. "How much do you need?"

Corey's laughter stopped him. "A little more than even you carry around, Adam. I need somewhere in the neighborhood of four hundred thousand dollars."

"Four hundred—?" His words fell off on a laugh, and he shoved the wallet back into his coat pocket. "You've got to be kidding."

"It's no joke." She pushed away from the table and stood up straight to face him. "I had a deal worked out to buy a piece of property for a song and renovate it into a commercial office building. I was supposed to close as soon as I got my share of my father's money, but now the whole deal is jeopardized." She stepped closer to Adam, leaning toward him in his chair. "I convinced them this morning that I would close in thirty days. Now all I have to do is raise the money."

Adam's smile faded, and disbelief replaced it. "So why me? Why not a thousand other guys out there who loan money for a living?"

"Because you obviously aren't afraid of my father," she said. "Everyone else is. Everyone from the jerks who closed my accounts at the bank to the jackasses who used to call themselves my friends but are nowhere around when I need them."

Adam tapped his cigarette on an ashtray. Finally, he came to his feet and slid his hands beneath his jacket into his trouser pockets.

"And because . . . because I know something about your history," she ventured, "and I know that you've done things with all the odds against you, with people slamming doors in your face, with everyone waiting to see you fall flat on your face."

She was good, he thought. He had to give her that much. And she was clever. But not clever enough. Not yet.

"Honey, if the first person I went to with my hand held out had given me the money I needed, do you think I'd be where I am today?" he asked. "Do you think I'd still be so hungry?"

Corey faltered and looked up at him. "You're not the first person," she lied.

Adam turned back to the table and began slipping his papers back into their appropriate files. "Sorry, Corey. I'm in the business of making money, not lending it."

"Then we could be partners." She stared up at him with relentless eyes, though he seemed to ignore her. "You could be an investor, and earn a piece of the profit. It'll be huge."

Adam gave her a patronizing smile and shook his head. "I don't go into partnerships with little rich girls whose daddies are mad at them. If you need money, I suggest you tuck your cute little tail between your legs and go back to Daddy."

"I'm not going back to my father!"

Her eyes were two fiery sapphires full of heated conviction, and somehow, he knew she meant every word. "Then do what other people do when they feel the pinch. Get a job. Earn the money."

"Four hundred thousand in thirty days?"

"It can be done," he said. "All you need is the right kinds of investments to raise enough of a down payment to make a bank take you seriously."

"And something to start with," she added.

"That's where the job comes in."

Corey turned away and paced to the window of the tower, overlooking Boston's skyline, much of which was owned by Dobias Enterprises. "I've been trained in real estate development and interior design. For the last year of my life, I've worked on nothing else."

"What about before that?" Adam asked. "What about in college?"

She looked down at the floor, as if embarrassed by her own frivolity. "Art history," she said. "Who knew it would ever matter?"

"Art history," he repeated, but there was no humor in his voice. "Well, let's see. You could work in an art gallery. The pay's not bad for something like that. Or you could go into real estate. Selling it, instead of buying it. Or you could start your own decorating business. You've had a good education, no doubt, and probably some pretty good training. I can tell that you have a business head, though I'm not sure you're hungry enough yet. But somebody'll hire you."

She turned around and leaned back against the window, darkening her silhouette against the sun. "I don't want my father's whims to destroy my chance, Adam. I can start my own business. I can make my own money. I just need a little help getting started. Didn't you ever need help?"

"Sure I did." Adam leaned back against the table and looked thoughtfully at her. "And I'm willing to help you. But not by giving you money."

"Then how? A pat on the back and a pep talk? I don't need anybody for that."

"No," he said. "I can show you how to get the money you need to get off the ground. If you really want to listen and do what is necessary."

She sighed and he saw the weariness in her face. "I'm open to anything."

"Well," he said, "for starters, you must have *some* assets of your own. Money stashed away somewhere, trust funds, property, bonds . . ."

"No," she said. "Everything is in my father's name. Except for the trust fund my mother left me, which isn't one bit of good to me for eleven more years."

"What about jewelry?" he asked. "Your father has always been big on jewelry. It makes *him* look good for you to wear it. Don't you have anything at all—"

"Nothing in my possession," she said. "Last night I wore this locket my fiancé gave me, and my earrings aren't worth much. And this ring—"

Adam looked down at the engagement ring on her finger and noted that the diamond was hardly worth as much as its gold setting.

"But it isn't really mine," she said. "I have a feeling he's going to want it back. He's a little put out with me about all this."

"I would guess so," Adam said. "Quite a blow to lose a hundred million dollars."

"That wasn't why he was marrying me."

"Yeah, right." The hurt in her voice almost made him regret the insinuation. "Then think. Anything at home that one of your sisters could get out for you? a stock certificate? an antique? an heirloom?"

"There was the necklace," Corey said, whispering the words as she thought of it. "An emerald and diamond necklace that my mother left me. After she died, Dad had it appraised for over twenty-five thousand dollars. I remember because he was so surprised. She had bought it for herself, apparently, and it wasn't like her to spend so much. But she—she left it to me in her will. . . . I've never even worn it."

An image of that necklace flashed into Adam's mind, radiant rows of dazzling, fiery diamonds surrounding rich, luxuriant emeralds. It had been custom-created for the woman who was meant to wear it. But she hadn't worn it for long. . . .

He cleared his throat and looked out the window over her shoulder. "The necklace. All right. Then maybe that's your ticket."

"What do you mean?" she asked. "I could never sell that. Besides, it wouldn't be enough."

"It would be enough to invest in a quick turn-around profit," he said. "I might be able to show you how, if you had the money. But you'll have to get it on your own."

"But it's in my father's house," she said, "and he won't even let me through the gates. No way is he ever going to let me have that. Besides, it means too much to me. It's one of the only things of hers I have. My father has all of her other things boxed away. I want to keep it, Adam."

His eyes took on a frosty glare as he put his cigarette in his mouth and began stacking his files. "In the real world, sacrifices have to be made. The sooner you learn that lesson, the easier your life will be." He dropped the files into his briefcase and turned back to Corey. "When you come to terms with what you have to do, give me a call. Until then, I have real work to do. Just leave the coat on the chair."

Corey gaped at him as he left the room, and finally, snatching up her own briefcase, she added him to the list of people who had lessons to learn about her.

chapter
10

RENA ADJUSTED THE THIN-FRAMED READING glasses perched on her nose and tried, once again, to immerse herself in the paperwork her new corporation required, but it was futile. Finally admitting that she had reached her saturation point, she leaned back in her chair and slung off her glasses. "I've changed my mind," she told John, who sat beside the fireplace in their suite, reading of the Dobias saga in the *Investigator*. "I'm going to throw the towel in and turn to a life of prostitution."

"You'd starve to death, darling."

The barb, meant to be facetious, stung her. But she didn't say anything. She never said anything.

Silently, she got up and went into the huge bathroom that she had no way of knowing was bigger than most people's living rooms, and after stripping down slowly, she stepped into the water, carefully avoiding the massive mirrors that lined one wall as she did.

Rena went to great lengths to avoid the sight of her naked body. It wasn't fat, not by most people's standards. It was just that, in comparison to the svelte leanness of Giselle's and the athletic grace of Corey's, hers was ordinary. Average. And that was one of the greatest sins a Dobias could commit.

Reaching for the hair clasp she kept beside the Jacuzzi, she tied up her hair and sank deeply into the pulsating water.

As relaxed as the water made her muscles, it did nothing to soothe the hollowness in her heart. But she was growing used to that. She had felt it for years. Ever since her mother died. And for the life of her, she hadn't managed to make time heal it.

Maybe this competition would. Since she no longer had her mother's approval to prop her up, perhaps somehow she'd be able to earn her father's. And her husband's.

Perhaps this time she could make them both proud of her.

You have nothing to prove, sweetheart.

Her mother's words echoed through the chambers of her heart, taking her back twenty years, when she had really known peace.

But as warm and secure as her mother had always made her feel, she had never really understood.

"I have everything to prove, Mama," she had cried so many years ago, standing before the mirror in the same dress that had transformed her bean pole sister into a beauty, but that did nothing but make Rena look silly and awkward. "Daddy says Dobias women are all supposed to be beautiful, but I'm not beautiful. I'm short and I have this long nose and my hair does whatever it pleases!"

Her mother had pulled her onto her lap and held her like a toddler. "You're short because you're twelve years old, your hair is gorgeous, and you have your father's Greek nose. It's a proud, wonderful nose. It's one of the first things I fell in love with on your father."

"But I'm a *girl*," she had whined. "Girls are supposed to have pretty noses like Giselle's."

Her mother had continually reassured her about her nose and her hair and her way of wearing her clothes. But when puberty hit and those miserable anxieties still clung with desperate claws to her self-esteem, Shara had allowed Rena to have plastic surgery to correct what the girl was certain was nature's mistake.

Strangely, even though her nose emerged as beautiful as either of her sisters', she still saw herself with the big nose, the frizzy hair, and the clothes that were never quite right, no matter who designed them or how much they cost. Her mother's love had kept her from ever seeing the nose, even before the surgery, so her reassurances became less and less meaningful over the years. Her father, on the other hand, never let her forget it. Despite the difference in her new, improved face, he saw nature's mistake as a symbol of his middle daughter's ailing potential. She would always be an ugly duckling, whether she looked like a swan or not.

In the bedroom, she heard John pouring another Scotch—his third, she realized—and she wished, just this once, that the liquor would stir his libido and make him want her again. She opened the little music box on the marble floor beside the tub. It launched into a delicate rendition of "Send in the Clowns." Out of a satin pocket, she took a bar of scented soap and began to lather her legs.

"John, will you pour me another drink, darling?"

There was no response from the bedroom, so she closed the box and cut off the Jacuzzi. "John?"

"I heard you." His response was clipped.

Accepting the irritated answer as a reprimand, she sank deeper, letting the water turn her skin pink and flush her cheeks.

In a moment, he came into the steamy bathroom, his shirt off, his feet bare. He carried a glass in each hand.

He handed her drink to her and finished off his own. Closing her eyes, she took a long sip, then smiled up at him and began to lather the soap over her breasts. There was a time when water over bare skin had excited him. Now, he only stared at her without really seeing. She had lost her touch.

But he hadn't. He was still a beautiful man, she thought, almost mournfully. Women still found him fascinating and irresistible, and she wasn't fool enough to think that he didn't succumb to their seductions now and again. It was only her seductions that he could defy. That was just one more thing she had resolved not to dwell on, for it got her nowhere.

He raked a hand through his blond hair and leaned back against the marble sink across the room.

"Come in with me, John," she said softly.

He shook his head. "Not now, Rena. I told your father I'd come back down."

"It doesn't have to take that long."

He snickered. "It always takes too long."

She felt her face reddening and hid it behind her glass as she took a long sip.

"Your sister's created quite a scandal," he muttered. "You should read that article. It's priceless."

Rena closed her eyes and rested her head on the edge of the tub. "I don't know what's gotten into her."

"I had a few calls today about her. It seems she's been going around to art galleries asking for a job. A job! Can you fathom that?"

Rena opened her eyes. "Did she get one?"

"Of course not. Nik made a few calls himself and made sure that no one would hire her." He took a drink and chuckled quietly, as if immensely enjoying Corey's fall from grace. "He's really going to make it tough for her."

"Why?" Rena sat up in the water, letting it bubble around her shoulders. "I don't understand why he won't just let her alone. He threw her out, left her penniless. Isn't that enough? She has to make a living to survive."

"Let that be a lesson to you," John said. "Don't ever cross your father. It isn't worth it. As for Corey, your father is a threat to a great number of people. They won't cross him if they don't have to, and they know that hiring Corey would ignite that famous Dobias fury. No one wants it turned on them."

"Then what will she do?"

John laughed with a glee that Rena found disheartening. "Maybe you should drop her the idea about prostitution," he said. "She'd at least have a better shot at it than you."

He watched her face fall, and laughing, he started from the room. "Oh, stop pouting. Sometimes you act like a little child."

"And sometimes you make me feel like the most unattractive woman on earth."

"If the shoe fits, darling."

Her eyes filled with tears.

"I was kidding, Rena. You take everything too seriously. I married you, didn't I?"

"Yes, you married me."

"And I'm still married to you, aren't I?"

"Yes."

"And whose bed do I sleep in every night?"

"Mine," she whispered, not adding that they did far too much sleeping there and not enough of anything else.

"And who's going to help you become the richest woman in Boston?"

The mention of money aroused him more than the sight of her lounging naked in a steaming Jacuzzi, and she knew it. The thought disgusted her, but even so, if he had discarded his clothes and come into the spa with her, she would have accepted him willingly.

He didn't.

"My father said you couldn't help—"

"To hell with your father. No way am I going to stay out of this and watch Giselle run away with it all." His eyes took on a lusty gleam as he bent down to her and cupped her breast, running a thumb over her turgid nipple. "No, my love. We're going to win at this game. I'll see to it."

The fact that he knew she couldn't do it on her own didn't even cross her mind as he drew back his hand and wiped it on the towel hanging over the bar. Then, smiling like a man with a scheme and a purpose, he left her lying alone in the bath.

Emily wasn't afraid of being discovered in her Aunt Corey's rooms, riffling through her things in search of the gold-gilded book of telephone numbers she had seen Corey use. No one ever noticed her slipping around the house, quiet as a mouse. No one ever really looked for her. No one ever asked where she was.

Just the same, she jumped when the door to Corey's bedroom opened, and she saw her mother standing there, looking startled and a little surprised.

"Emily! What are you doing here?"

Emily closed the drawer she'd been going through and gave her mother a contrite look. "I was . . . looking for something."

"For what?" Giselle asked. She closed the door at her back and stepped farther into the room. "Have you been in touch with her, Emily? Has she put you up to something?"

"No! How could I be in touch with her when I don't even know where she is? I heard Rebecca talking to her on the phone this morning, but she wouldn't let her speak to you or Rena or me or anybody! She didn't even find out where she's staying!"

"She was obeying Dad's orders," Giselle explained. "That's her job."

"Well, it's a stupid job," Emily said. "When I grow up and take over this house, I'm going to fire her. And anybody who calls can speak to anybody they want."

Giselle grinned, as if her daughter had a lot to learn. But that smug grin only made Emily bristle more. She hated being treated like a kid.

"If you didn't know I was here, what are *you* doing here?" she asked.

Giselle thought of lying, but she looked at her only child and knew that Emily could see right through her. "Well, I guess you could say I was spying. I wanted to take a peak at Corey's papers in her briefcase. I heard she was working on some deal she'd planned to close this week, and since she doesn't have any money to do it now, I might be interested in it myself. I'm sure Corey wouldn't mind if she were here to ask."

Emily stood up and went to Corey's window, overlooking the pentagonal courtyard below. All of their bedrooms overlooked it. Her grandmother had carefully designed it that way.

"What if she still wants to do it herself?" she asked. "It wouldn't be right, your just taking it like that."

Giselle began to look around the room for the briefcase. "Well, sometimes what's right isn't the wisest choice. We do what we have to, to get the edge. You never told me, Emmy. What were you looking for?"

"Her phone numbers," Emily said, lifting her chin defiantly, the way she'd seen her mother do so many times before, especially when she was cornered. "I was going to call some of them. Try to find her."

Giselle flung around, and the alarm and anger in her eyes frightened Emily. "Call her? Are you crazy? Do you know what your grandfather would do to us if he found out you'd spoken to her?"

"No, what?"

"I told you! He'd disown us, too," Giselle said. "Rena would wind up with every penny to herself and that meandering husband of hers. And we'd have nothing."

Emily followed her mother into the massive closet to scan the shelves for the missing briefcase. She found it on the top shelf and pulled it down with a look of utter delight in her eyes.

"So we wouldn't have Grandfather's money," Emily said quietly. "You're smart. You could make your own money."

"Not the kind my father has." Giselle took the briefcase back into Corey's suite, laid it on the mahogany secretary, and opened it. Withdrawing the stack of paperwork, she began to scan the documents there. "No, darling, with his money, I could do almost anything. And so could you. With his money and my brains, I could make us the two richest women in the entire world. Wouldn't you like that, sweetheart?"

Emily didn't answer. Instead, she watched the avarice in her mother's eyes as she pored over Corey's papers, a look that made her shiver.

"This family says good-bye too easily." The whispered observation made Giselle look up.

"What do you mean, sweetheart?"

"I mean that it doesn't even bother you that Corey's gone. It's like she's just dead. Erased. Just like my father."

Giselle's face paled instantly, and she dropped the papers on the bed and locked her gaze on her daughter. But Emily turned away and looked out the window again. The wind was billowing up, rustling the bare limbs of the oak trees outside.

"We didn't erase your father," Giselle said, her voice notably shakier now. "We just . . . we couldn't make our marriage work out."

"So he left, never to look back. He lives in Boston, just a few miles away, and he never even wonders about his daughter."

Abandoning Corey's papers, Giselle went to her daughter. Gently, she closed her arms around her and pulled the child's head against her shoulder. She was growing so fast, she thought. In two or three years, they'd be the same height. She hadn't seen it coming at all. Just like she hadn't anticipated this talk about Emily's father, a subject that was on the child's mind more and more lately.

"I'm sure he thinks about you all the time," she whispered. "I'm sure he wonders what you're doing."

"Bullshit." The word startled Giselle, and Emily slipped out of her arms and went across the room, picked up Corey's hair brush, examined it.

"Emily! I've told you—"

"If he ever thought of me, then why hasn't he once tried to see me? And that time last year when we went to the inaugural ball, and I saw him there, he didn't even look at me. It was like he wasn't the least bit curious what his daughter looked like. And the way he looked at you, well I could tell he despised you!"

Giselle wilted back on the bed and struggled for the words that might soothe her daughter's feelings. But she'd never been good with words. "Emily . . . it's complicated. You just don't understand. . . . There are things that adults go through . . . things that aren't just black or white. . . . They have rifts. They go their separate ways."

"Like Grandfather and Corey?" Emily asked, meeting her mother's eyes.

"It isn't the same thing," Giselle said. "You're making too much of this. Dad was very, very hurt by what Corey did last night."

"What about what *he* did? The things he said about all of us?"

"He can say and do whatever he wants, Emily, as long as he holds the checkbook. But I can swear to you that it won't always be that way. I'm going to turn things around."

"Will Corey come back?"

Giselle issued a weary breath, and her gaze drifted back to the papers on the bed. "I don't know. I can't say for sure."

Emily looked down at the brush in her hand, stroked her fingertips across the soft fibers.

"Things are going to be all right, darling," Giselle whispered. "You'll see. I'm going to make us so rich that by the time you're sixteen, princes and dukes and movie stars will be lined up from all over the world trying to get a date with you."

Emily closed her eyes and tried to picture herself adorned in a gorgeous gossamer gown, dancing with one handsome suitor after another in a fog of glamour and glitter. But they all looked like her father, just as he'd looked that day she'd met him a year ago, when he'd gazed right through her as though he had no connection with her at all. They were all just as handsome, just as tall. But there was a difference.

In her fantasy, she was the center of all their worlds.

chapter
11

THE OVERSTUFFED CHAIR IN ERIC GRAY'S LIVING
room felt like heaven, and Corey kicked the shoes off her
aching feet and propped them on the table. She looked
like hell, she thought, even though she'd spent the rest
of her money today on a twelve-dollar skirt at Filene's
Basement, a thirty-dollar blouse, a pair of panty hose
and some underwear, so that she could search for a job
looking halfway presentable. Though she had desperately wanted new shoes and a warm jacket, she decided her
heels would make her look more professional, after all.
And a little cold never hurt anyone. Besides, her money
was running out. But what she'd worn to her interviews
hadn't mattered at all, for not one of the fifteen places
she'd tried today would give her the time of day, for fear
that her father would exact retribution.

And where did that leave her? For the first time in
her life, she honestly didn't know. She had swallowed
her pride and come back to Eric's, thankfully found
him at home, and asked if she could "bunk" at his
place tonight. He'd found the choice of words amusing,
and she immediately saw the change in his mood. He'd
gotten some sleep, he told her. He'd had time to think.
Things were going to be okay. She would see.

But the pep talk hadn't really helped, and as he showered in the bathroom, Corey sat in the dusky apartment
and stared into the shadows, trying to find some clarity
in the haze her life had become. She was on her own.
For the first time in her life, she really had no one to

turn to. Except for Eric, everyone else had abandoned her. And she didn't know for sure how much longer she could count on him.

She had to find a job, she thought. She had to find one immediately, so that she could save something and get Adam Franklin to show her the best way to invest it. But where could she go that her father didn't know anyone?

"Maybe I'm just shooting too high," she muttered.

"What?"

The response from the bathroom was muffled, and Corey glanced toward the partially open door. She saw the steam escaping, and the masculine fragrance of soap wafted into the room. This place wasn't big enough for one person, she thought. Let alone two. Her closets at her father's were bigger than this whole apartment.

"I said, maybe I'm shooting too high. Maybe I need to stop looking for good jobs. Maybe I need to lower my standards a little."

"To get out from under your father's influence, Corey, you're going to have to lower them a lot. Change your name. Dye your hair. Take on a new identity. Everyone in Boston knows Nik Dobias, and no one wants to cross him. If he doesn't want his little girl to get a job, then she won't get one."

Corey bristled. It was crazy, she thought, the way he swung from total support to sarcastic reminders of how impossible her ordeal was. He still thought she'd run back home and fall on her knees in apology. It made her wonder where he thought all that "substance beneath her surface" had gone, or if he'd really ever seen it at all.

"The only people afraid of my father are those who stand to lose something," she said. "But there are people out there who have nothing he could take from them. A lot of people. I just have to find them."

Eric emerged from the bathroom, a towel around his waist. He'd shaved, a rare act for him, and he looked as brooding and beautiful as he had the first time she'd seen him. "It's gonna be a long search. If those people really do exist."

Corey's melancholy gaze fell from his hazel eyes to the flat stomach that he worked hard to maintain, to the white towel draped around his hips. "I used to think you were one of those people," she said.

"Used to? What do you mean by that?"

"I mean . . ." Her words trailed off on a sigh, and she shook her head and let her gaze drift back to the shadows. "I don't know."

"No," he said. "I want to know what you mean."

Corey stood up and turned her back on him, and went to sit on the windowsill. "What I mean is that I think we both learned a few surprising things about each other last night. I think my father's money affects you a lot more than you want me to think. I don't even guess I can blame you."

She looked over her shoulder and saw the flash of anger in his eyes, but oddly, he didn't act on it. Instead, he reigned it in, took a deep breath and started toward her. "If your father's money affects me," he whispered, "it's because I care about you. And for all your independence and pride, I don't think you have a clue yet just how shitty the real world can be without money. I hate to see you find out."

She felt tears pushing to her eyes, and hated herself for them. Blinking them away, she turned back to the window and looked out onto the night descending over Cambridge.

Eric slipped his arms around her and pulled her back against him, and dipped his face to her neck. "You're tired," he whispered against her skin. "And so tense."

"I didn't sleep but a couple of hours this morning before I got thrown out of the Monarch," she whispered. "And the day's just been"—those tears won their battle over her, seeping over her lashes, and she tried to swallow back the emotion—"unbelievable."

"Come here," he whispered, turning her around.

She went willingly into his arms, and for the first time that day didn't let her mind do the thinking. She needed to feel the touch of someone who loved her, needed to rest in the knowledge that she wasn't completely alone.

If it was all a lie, well, she'd deal with that later. She was beginning to realize that now was all that mattered.

The steady rhythm of her breathing would have comforted him as Corey slept beside him, but Eric was beyond comfort. Quietly, he pulled out of bed and stepped into the jeans crumpled on his floor.

The blue light in his darkroom glowed from the work he'd been doing earlier, and he went in and pulled up the stool to check the prints that hung drying on the line. A corncob and a tomato, side by side, for some asinine advertisement that Humphrey and Jones Advertising had hired him to do. He should be grateful, he supposed, to have the work at all. It wasn't as if art galleries were knocking his door down to exhibit his prints.

No, there wasn't much chance of that. Not unless he could get Corey back together with her father. Not unless he could somehow help to mend the rift between them.

He sloshed his hand in the water tray, then shook it off. It wasn't just for himself that he was concerned, he told himself. Corey needed her family. She needed her father. And as soon as she admitted that, she could collect her ten million and start the competition for the even bigger jackpot, and he'd fight tooth and nail to see that she won. When she did, oh, when she did, he'd know that it had all been worth it.

He heard movement in his bedroom and left the darkroom. She was out of bed, standing in front of the mirror staring at herself. Did she wonder what madness had gotten her here?

"You up?"

"Yeah," she muttered. "Is it morning? I didn't realize I was so tired . . ."

"I let you sleep," he said. "You needed it."

He went to the closet and pulled out a shirt, shrugged it on. "I have a shoot in the Gardens today. I'll probably be gone all day."

Corey shoved her hair back from her face and nodded.

"Okay."

"So you gonna call your dad?"

Corey's grogginess faded as she looked at him directly. "No, I thought I'd look a little more for a job."

Eric unzipped his pants and tucked in his shirt. "Whatever. One way or another, you've got to do something."

"What do you mean?"

He stepped into his tiny bathroom and squeezed toothpaste onto his toothbrush. "I mean that I barely make enough to support myself. I can't support you, too."

"Oh." She sat down on the bed and hugged the corner bedpost as she watched him brush, and he could see that he'd been a little too harsh. He'd have to watch himself. He spit out the toothpaste, rinsed his mouth, and turned back to her. "I just mean that I'm short this month, and I don't know how—"

"It's okay," she said. "I'm going to find something. Don't worry. I won't be here for long."

He wiped his mouth on a hand towel and slung it over his shoulder as he stepped out of the bathroom. "Come on, Corey, you don't have to leave. You can stay as long as you want."

She looked down at her hands, and he could see that she struggled with those tears that she seemed to view as such a monumental weakness. He stepped toward her and raised her face with a gentle hand. "I don't want you to go, you know."

"Thanks." Her gaze met his only for a second, before it moved back down to her hands. "But I think it would be best. Just—just let me get on my feet. I'll pay you back as soon as I can."

"I don't want your money. I just hate seeing you so down. I want to see you smiling again. I want to see you happy."

"I'll be happy," she said, "as soon as I know what I want to do. I'll make myself happy."

The determination in her eyes and the quiver in her voice told him that she meant it, and for the life of him, he didn't know if that was good or bad.

Slowly, he knelt in front of her and slipped his fingers through the back of her hair, and pulled her into a soft gentle kiss that he felt her melt into. Then, pressing his forehead against hers, he whispered, "I have to go. At least call your sisters. They're probably worried sick about you."

"Maybe," she said.

He started for the door, and she stood up.

"Maybe I'll come by the shoot later. We could have lunch."

"Maybe. We'll see."

As he left the apartment, he almost cursed himself for feeling the way he felt. Angry, defeated, cheated once again out of everything that should be rightfully his but never had been. Why couldn't he just roll with the punches? Why couldn't he just be happy that one of the most beautiful women in Boston was sharing his apartment? Why couldn't he just relax?

Because relaxing only made you poorer, and fate stalked those who let their guard down. He didn't have time to let fate have its way, because it had always been his archenemy. This time, he was going to be in control. This time, he would come out on top.

Corey sat in the shadow-laden apartment for a while after he'd left, staring at the walls and trying to make some sense out of what was happening to her. She felt herself slipping into the oblivion of despair, but it went against the grain to waste time feeling sorry for herself.

She had to make a list, she thought. A list of things to do. Number one, she would get a job. Any job. Number two, she would find a place to live. Number three, she would save her money until she could get Adam Franklin to tell her how to turn it around for a quick profit. All she needed, after all, was four hundred thousand dollars.

Four hundred thousand? It was incredible that a week ago it had seemed like such a paltry, accessible sum, and now it was a ridiculous dream. If she got a meager job typing or waiting tables, there was no way she could pay for living expenses and save up enough to put even a dent in that amount. It was hopeless. Unless . . .

The memory of her mother's necklace came back to her like a symbol of life's cruel choices.

"In the real world, sacrifices have to be made."

Adam Franklin could help her, but first she'd have to help herself.

She shoved her long, tangled hair back over her shoulder and made the decision even as she picked up the telephone. Rena was her best bet, she thought. She would be worried about her and perhaps would want to help. Maybe she would bring the necklace to her. Maybe she'd even have other ideas for raising the money.

She dialed the number to Rena's private rooms at the Dobias estate and sighed a breath of relief when her sister answered.

"Rena? It's me, Corey. I—"

The quiet click took her by surprise, and she sat dumbfounded, holding the phone to her ear, telling herself it must be a mistake. "Rena?"

But her sister was gone.

The heat of fear and fury beat to her face, and quickly, she dialed the number again. This time it rang unanswered.

Determination rushed like fire through her veins, and quickly, she called Giselle's number. Harboring no hope that her older sister would help, she prayed that Emily would answer, instead. Maybe the girl could get to the necklace and send it to her.

But it wasn't Emily who answered the phone. "Hello?"

"Giselle." The word was steeped in disappointment, but Corey tried nonetheless. "I—I need to talk to you."

"Who is this?"

She could hear the pleasure in her sister's voice, but she didn't let it stop her. "You know damn well who it is, Giselle. It's Corey."

Click.

The idle dial tone hummed like a mockery in her ear, and tears sprang to her eyes. "Damn you," she whispered, not certain if her curse was directed toward the phone itself or the sisters who had turned their backs on her.

Furiously, she punched out her father's personal number, and began to pace as it rang.

"Dobias," he said on the third ring, and she could hear the typical impatience and anxiety that pulsated in his voice on a regular business day.

"Daddy, it's Corey."

He didn't hang up, but he didn't answer, either.

"Why are you doing this to me?" she demanded. "Do you hate me so much that you'd turn my own sisters against me, that you'd rather see me destitute than independent, that you'd humiliate me in front of the entire city?"

"You made your choice," he bit out, and before she could utter another word, he cut off the line.

"Bastard!" She threw the phone against the wall and watched it land in an unbroken heap on the floor. "What did I do to make you hate me so much?"

The scream was impotent and unheard. After a moment she realized the futility of tears, and an almost hysterical laughter took over. Forget the necklace, forget help from her sisters, forget any chance of utilizing any of the Dobias opportunities that had previously been at her disposal. She was completely, absolutely, on her own.

Forcing herself back to her feet, she went to the shower, turned it on, and stood beneath steaming hot water, as if it could wash away the person she had been. She was a new person now, she decided. She was a person who would do what she had to do. Starting with first things first. Before this day was over, Corey Dobias was going to have a job.

And she was going to have at least some idea how in God's name she would get her mother's necklace.

chapter

12

ADAM CHECKED HIS WATCH AND CLAMPED THE phone between his ear and shoulder, then picked up the folder of facts on his desk and balanced it in one hand. "Get back to me on that in thirty minutes," he told the managing editor of the *Bulletin*. With his free hand, he waved for Joe Holifield to come in and take a seat, instead of floating in the doorway like a spirit without a resting place. "Okay, Rick. I'll be here."

He dropped the phone back in its cradle and studied the contents of his file once more before acknowledging Joe's presence. "So what brings you here?" he asked. "Better make it quick. I have a meeting in ten."

"It's about my job," the golden boy said, dropping into the Chippendale wing chair across from Adam's desk. "I think it's time I got moved out of the trenches."

Adam shook his head and dropped the file onto a pile on his desk. "I repeat my original question. Why are you here? I'm not the person responsible for your promotions or your assignments. You report to his—"

"I don't want a promotion within the *Investigator*," Joe cut in, slinging an ankle over his knee. "I want more."

"More?" The man's audacity almost amused Adam, and he went around his desk and sat down. "All right. I'm listening."

"The cable station you just bought. You'll need an anchor once you get the news team beefed up. I want the job."

This time Adam laughed out loud. "Yeah, you and

about a million other guys." He grabbed another file and flicked it open.

"No, I mean it." Joe dropped his foot to the floor and leaned forward. His cobalt eyes held an intensity that always demanded Adam's full attention.

"I'm sure you do," Adam said. "Just what in hell makes you think you have something to offer me as anything but a reporter?"

Joe came to his feet and leaned over Adam's desk, taking complete control. Adam liked that aggressiveness and made a mental note of it.

"I'm a damn fine investigative reporter, Adam, and you and all those bastards who call themselves my bosses know it, too. I've been tucked away in the basement of your tabloid for a year now, and by God, it's time you let me do what I'm good at. You're wasting me, Adam. Do you want a pretty boy who can read your news for that station, or do you want someone with brains behind the good looks, someone who can write a story as well as he can read one?"

Stroking his chin, Adam sat back in his chair and gazed up at the man leaning over his desk. "To tell you the truth, Joe, I've never once considered you for that job. I have two network correspondents interested, and I've narrowed it down to them and a handful of others. Why would I hire you?"

"Because I belong on television. I got shoved out because of a lousy break. A stupid mistake."

Adam snickered again, and Joe straightened. "Okay. All right, if you won't consider me for the anchor, at least think about me for a correspondent. I could do it, Adam. I don't belong on the midnight shift at a tabloid covering UFO sightings."

"You have no credibility, Joe. When a rival station catches you patronizing a brothel with a pocketful of coke, it doesn't look good for the guy who signs your paycheck. I don't want to take the heat the next time you're caught with your pants down."

"Dammit, Adam!" He banged his fist on Adam's desk and spun around, putting his back to the man who had so much power to change his situation. "The coke was a plant. I don't know how it got there."

"Yeah, right. And Elvis is still alive and living in Slap-out, Texas."

Joe turned back around and jabbed a finger at Adam. "Adam, it's true. As for the brothel, you gonna tell me you haven't dipped your own wick a time or two?"

Adam's grin twisted the knife. "I don't have to pay for it, Holifield."

Joe slid his hands into his pockets and regarded his boss for a moment. "We all pay for it in one way or another, Adam. You've been around enough to know that."

Adam looked down at one of the files on the corner of his desk. The Dobias file. The facts he'd accumulated over the last ten years. Slowly, he picked it up. "I'll tell you what, Joe. I'm gonna give you a chance."

The defeat on the reporter's face melted into surprise. "No kidding?"

"No kidding. Not for the anchor job, but maybe something else. But you're going to have to earn it."

"Anything," Joe said. "I can do it."

Adam handed him the file. "If you can crack this story for me, expose that bastard for what he is, I'll give you a job at the network."

Joe opened the file and saw the aging clips of Nik Dobias, along with several lengthy documents put together at various intervals detailing deals Dobias was involved in. He smiled. "Nik Dobias is so publicity hungry, this ought to be a piece of cake."

"Not if he knows you work for me." Adam came to his feet. "I want facts. We know he must have paid off somebody in the police department when they arrested his daughter, but I want to know who else has been bribed. Some of his deals over the years have gone down a little too easy. And this casino thing he's working on . . . I don't know. It doesn't smell right. Things are moving too fast on it, and the red tape other men get tangled up in seems to disintegrate when he's involved. Somebody's palm's being greased. Maybe a lot of people's. His hearing with the Casino Control Commission is just around the corner. I want to know his strategy. Whatever you can find out."

"You'll cover me with Rick?" Joe asked.

"I'll cover you," Adam said. "I'll tell him you're working on a confidential story for me. And let's keep it that way, understand? I don't want Dobias alerted that I'm onto anything. Got it?"

"Yeah, sure."

Adam narrowed his dark eyes and regarded the man who looked as if he'd just been given the story of the century. "Don't waste my time, Joe. I want updates whenever you get something. Tell Sarah to put you on an expense account. You'll probably have to grease a few palms yourself."

The excitement in Joe's eyes was rabid, and Adam wondered if he'd just uncaged a monster. He wasn't sure. There wouldn't be any way to tell until the deed was accomplished.

Besides, if there was a monster to be let loose, he supposed it wouldn't hurt to set it on Dobias.

"I appreciate it, Adam," Joe said, shaking his hand across the desk. "Really, man . . ."

Adam nodded toward the door. "My meeting . . ."

"Yeah, I'm going. I'll be back in touch soon."

"Do that."

He watched Joe leave the office, and sat rubbing his chin for a moment. The wheels were in motion now, he thought. Nik Dobias would get his due just as soon as Adam had what he needed.

He picked up his phone and buzzed his secretary.

"Yes, Adam?"

"Are Sid Wheeler and his staff here yet?"

"Yes, sir. But Corey Dobias is waiting, too. Should I tell her you can't see her now?"

"Corey Dobias?" Adam glanced at his watch again. "Uh, no. Go ahead and send her in. Tell Sid I'll be right with him."

The door opened as soon as he hung up the phone, and Corey Dobias stepped in, looking like a prissy little schoolmarm with her hair pulled back in a French twist. He liked it better down, he thought, but that was none of his business. If her fiancé didn't have the good sense to tell her, that was his problem. Her face was still bare of cosmetics, a fact that he found intriguing, for most of the women he knew wouldn't have cast a shadow without a thorough Elizabeth Arden treatment.

"I'm sorry to barge in like this," Corey said, and when she walked toward him, he noted that she still wore those high heels she'd had on the other night, the ones that made her prance instead of walk. It softened the schoolmarm look, and almost made him smile. But he knew better.

"I'm due in a meeting," he said, motioning for her to take the chair that Joe had abandoned. "I can give you three minutes."

Corey smiled. "You don't like to waste any time, do you?"

"I don't have much to waste."

"Well, I guess I do. More than I ever wanted. Which

brings me to why I'm here." She paused a moment, crossed her legs, and looked down at her clasped hands. "I want a job, Adam."

Adam's laughter was not what she'd expected. "A job? From me?"

She set her lips, and he knew she hadn't appreciated his reaction. "You won't loan me money. You told me to get a job. Well, my father is putting up roadblocks everywhere I turn. No one in this town will hire me." She stood up and came around his desk, surprising him as he looked up at her. "But you aren't afraid of him, Adam. I can tell that you're one of the few men in Boston who isn't intimidated by my father. That's why I keep coming to you."

She smelled clean, untainted, unlike the other women who traipsed into his life doused in two-hundred-dollar-an-ounce perfume. He remembered seeing her fully made up, with her long hair flowing like a midnight waterfall over her tanned arms. She had been beautiful then, but he'd never noticed her as more than a kid who had a lot going for her. Something about her standing so close now, unadorned, made him uncomfortable.

"Even if all that's true," he said, "what makes you think that I'd hire you?"

"I'm not asking for chairman of the board, Adam. I could work for the newspaper. Preferably the *Bulletin*, since I have this thing against tabloids. Of course, if the *Investigator* was a last resort . . ."

Adam rubbed the grin forming on his face. "Corey, didn't anyone ever tell you not to insult a man when you're begging for a handout?"

Corey flashed him a coy grin. "Sorry. Anyway, I can file, I can answer the phone, I can run errands—"

"It would be a disaster," he cut in. "They'd be on you like vultures the minute they knew your last name."

TERRI HERRINGTON

"Then I'll change my last name. My mother's maiden name was Caine. I'll be Corey Caine."

The reminder of her mother's name made his face flush, and he looked down at the wood grain of his desk and traced it with a finger. "Corey, you've never worked under anyone else in your life."

"I've worked under my father. Simon LeGree couldn't hold a candle to him." A strand of hair slipped out of her twist, and she swept it back with an idle hand. Suddenly, her face was serious, and that confidence that had so amused and delighted him was fading fast as she realized she wasn't making any headway with him.

"Adam, please."

Adam stood up and looked down at her. Her eyes met his, and he didn't like himself very much for the way his heart hammered under his shirt. She was the Dobias baby, he told himself. Practically a kid. He had no business breathing in the scent of her or noticing that strand of hair slipping back out of its place. He reached for a cigarette.

She set her hand on his chest, and he could feel it shaking through his shirt. He wondered if she could feel his runaway heartbeat. For the life of him, he hoped not.

"I'm desperate," she whispered. "I need your help. I'm willing to do anything."

That "anything" she referred to was more than obvious, and the fact that he considered it—for the slightest fraction of a second—made him kick himself again. He swallowed and removed her hand.

"That's very tempting," he admitted, avoiding her eyes, and looking instead at the hand that still trembled within his. "But I don't generally take sex as a payoff for my favors."

Tears welled dangerously in her eyes, and her gaze

dropped to his lips, then climbed back to his eyes.

"And I don't generally offer it for that," she said.

He frowned down at her, trying to discern whether she was admitting to her seduction attempt, or denying it. He wasn't sure, and maybe she didn't know, either.

The fact that she'd almost gotten to him—was still getting to him—made him angry, and leaning back against the desk, he dropped her hand to her side and jammed the cigarette between his lips. He couldn't be attracted to Corey Dobias, he told himself. He had too much history with that family. Too much that she would never begin to understand.

Schooling his voice to sound stronger than he felt, he turned away from her and paced across the room. "I run my operation efficiently, Corey, and the last thing I need is driftwood cluttering up one of my staffs."

"Driftwood?" Those tears seemed to disappear with the word, and she lifted her chin higher. "I've never been called driftwood in my life."

"You've also never been thrown out in the street without a penny," he pointed out. "It seems to me that times they are a-changing."

"Then you won't give me a job?"

"No, Corey," he said. "You'll have to find one on your own. But the offer still stands to help you invest the money when you get it. Have you thought any more about the necklace?"

"The necklace," she repeated, crossing her arms and coming back around his desk. "You keep acting like I have it to sell. Adam, I can't get on the grounds of my father's estate, and my sisters won't take my calls. There's no way—"

"There's always a way," Adam said. "It's your necklace, after all. You could get a lawyer to get you a court order."

"That would take time, Adam. And the cost would

defeat the purpose. Besides, I don't want to feed the media's craving for Dobias news. I don't know if I want it that badly."

"Well," Adam said, dropping back into his chair. "I guess that's the big question, isn't it? Whether or not you really want it. Until you answer that, I don't think I can be of any more help to you."

She breathed out a helpless sigh, and shook her head. "I guess not. And I guess my three minutes are up."

He looked at his watch. "Actually, I gave you ten."

"No," she corrected. "I gave *you* ten. And an offer you just might regret turning down. See you later, Adam."

Adam sat back in his chair and watched as she pranced out of the room. Whether her reference was to her offer of herself for a job, or her offer of herself in his bed, he didn't know. He could only imagine.

And yes, he supposed he would regret it. He had to admit, he already did.

Corey was two blocks from the Franklin Tower before she allowed her tears to track down her face. What had come over her! Offering herself to him like a two-bit hooker! As if sex were the only resource she had available to her.

As difficult as he must have known it was for her to do that, he had thrown it back in her face. He had hoped she'd shrivel up and die with embarrassment, she thought, slapping the tears off of her cheek. But she had shown him. He hadn't expected her to do anything but cower from his rejection of everything she had offered him. She had surprised him.

But not as much as she had surprised herself.

She leaned back against a building and closed her eyes as the tears flowed more freely down her face, chapping her cheeks in the frigid wind. If he had been hunched over and had warts on his face, would she still have been desperate enough to offer herself to him?

The thought was almost funny, and a hint of a smile tugged at her lips. No, she thought. She wasn't that desperate. If Adam hadn't had those dark eyes that made a woman want to fall into them, and that hair that looked as if it could stand a trim, if he hadn't smelled like her favorite male cologne, though she knew very few men who would lower themselves to buy a supermarket brand, she wouldn't have suggested such a thing. But he had, and she did.

Then, as if the humiliation had played itself out, she felt a growing anger that he'd had the temerity to turn her down. She wasn't at her best today, she admitted, but she wasn't anything to blow his nose at, either. Some of the most sought-after men in the world had tried to get into her silk panties. The fact that her panties were now cotton and cost three-for-five-dollars shouldn't make a difference to anyone but her.

She wiped the remnants of her tears from her face and caught the scent of fried shrimp wafting out of the restaurant a few yards away, and remembered that she hadn't eaten since that piece of toast at Eric's that morning. She checked the pocket of her briefcase, saw that she only had enough for the trip back to Cambridge, and closed it again.

Covetously, her gaze drifted through the window of the restaurant, where diners sat idly passing away the lunch hour before they went back to their busy jobs.

For they all had jobs, she was sure. They all had families. They all had places to live.

As her gaze scanned the customers in the restaurant, she saw the sign posted on the glass out front: Help Wanted. Apply Inside.

Without a moment's hesitation, she hurried inside,

determined not to leave the premises until the manager had promised her a job.

The question of whether she would have offered herself to a hunched-over man with warts on his face was answered when Corey confronted the restaurant manager of Franotelli's Shrimp and Pasta House and saw that he fit that description exactly. While she would have done many things to get this job, sex never even figured into the picture. Thankfully, the man only required that she fill out an application, which she did as creatively as she could to hide her name, her past, and her predicament. When he hired her, she almost kissed him, but thought better of it.

Under the name of Corey Caine, she started working that afternoon, in full waitress uniform. Her first check wouldn't come for a week, she was told, but she could take home whatever tips came her way in the meantime.

She learned three important things that day. The first was that there was a vital difference between what she had previously called work and what she was expected to do now. The second was that whoever invented four-inch heels was a sadist and an idiot, and that anyone foolish enough to wear them deserved whatever pain they caused her. The third was that, despite the pain, if you looked good, you got bigger tips. She supposed life was a series of little trade-offs.

She earned forty dollars in tips that afternoon, and while she had to take off her shoes on the T and limp home barefoot, she couldn't help delighting in how good it felt to put that forty dollars in her pocket. It was a feeling she would never forget. If she could do that in half a day, she calculated, she could do twice that tomorrow. Maybe more if she got faster. She wouldn't have enough to buy her building, but she'd have enough to get her own place, buy a new pair of shoes, a coat, maybe even a tube of mascara. She wouldn't have to depend on Eric anymore, and she wouldn't have to go back to Adam and humiliate herself again.

Before it was over, she'd show them all that Corey Dobias was a survivor. On a frost-bitten mountain or the streets of Boston, she could make her way.

It wasn't over by a long shot.

chapter
13

DOBIAS LURCHED FROM THE CHAIR BEHIND HIS
desk and slammed his hand down, glaring at his son-in-
law relaxing in the chair across from him. "You tell those
bastards to get back to work or I'll fire every last one of
them and put Redding's men on the job. I'm not paying
them to piss and moan about substandard materials. If
they can't do it my way, then tell them to get the hell out
of the way and let someone else do it."

A knock sounded at the door. Rena cracked it and
stepped inside. Dobias offered her a distracted, cursory
wave and motioned for her to come in. Slowly, she went
to the chair beside her husband.

"You can't hire Redding's men," John Keller said, his
tone as relaxed as if they discussed the day's temperature reading on the old John Hancock Building. "Giselle
apparently has them working on something for her."

"Giselle?" Dobias looked back at his son-in-law, a perplexed sparkle in his eye. "Already? You have any idea
what she's working on?"

"Not a clue."

"No, I guess you wouldn't." He picked up a pencil,
bounced the eraser end on his desk, and gave his other
daughter an almost-disgusted look. "I don't suppose
you've even gotten out of the starting gate yet, have
you?"

Rena glanced down at her hands. "I'm—I'm working
on several things, Daddy."

Dobias blew out a disgruntled sigh and shook his

head, then returned to the original subject. "Okay, then, John. We'll get Henderson or LeGarret or any number of other contractors, but I won't put up with this shit. This is a multimillion dollar contract. If he wants to lose it over a question of empty ethics, then that's fine with me. You tell him that."

"I'll tell him," John said. "But let's face it, Nik. It's going to cost you a little more than you planned. The only reason they're complaining is that the city inspector is putting the heat on them. It ups the ante considerably."

Dobias dropped into his chair and rubbed his hands over his face. He hated his hands, he thought. They were too smooth. Too unscarred. There had been a time when he could have sanded a wall with these same fingers. But now all they did was push papers.

"Find out what it'll take. Another half a million here or there to keep morale up is better than increasing the cost of the casino by half just to keep those asinine city inspectors happy. If the man's worth his salt, he can make it look like we're up to code."

"And if he can't?"

"Everybody has a price," Dobias said, dismissing his son-in-law with a wave of his hand. "I pay you real well to find it."

"Right."

Without a word to his wife, John left the room, and Rena's gaze followed him to the door. When she turned back to her father, he was absorbed in a set of blueprints on his desk, as if he'd forgotten she was in the room.

"I'm sorry if I interrupted, Dad."

"What is it, Rena?"

She waited until he was looking at her, but when he did, her hand rose nervously to her hair, freshly coiffed by the hairdresser who stopped by the estate on appointed mornings. Despite the expertise with which Henrique styled it, Rena always felt she had a frizzy red halo of escaped wisps and wild strands that couldn't be tamed. She could see her father's disapproval in his eyes. "I wanted to ask your advice about an investment I'm considering for IDK," she said. "It looks like it might—"

"No. No advice," Dobias cut in. "It wouldn't be fair to Giselle."

"Fair?" Rena bit her tongue and didn't ask when fairness had entered into any of this. "But how will I learn?"

"That's the point," Dobias said. "If you haven't learned by now, you never will. That's what the competition is designed to determine."

Rena's cheeks mottled. "But Giselle has had years of preparation for this. I never knew I was going to have to be a developer. Purchasing is what you trained me for, and I was good at that. . . ."

"You weren't concerned about how well you could handle it when I was going to hand it over to you on a silver platter, were you?" Dobias asked. "Neither was Corey. It was only when I told you girls that you'd have to *work* for the money that all hell broke loose."

Rena blinked back the tears threatening her eyes, stood up, and stepped closer to her father's desk. "It's not the work that scares us, Dad. It's the race. The end result. The pressure of all we have to lose."

"Welcome to the real world." Dobias returned to his blueprint, once again locking her out. "Now if you'll excuse me, I have to figure out how in hell I'm going to build this casino without losing my shirt."

Rena swallowed her further arguments and cleared her throat. She glanced down at the blueprints, then back up at her father. "What you and John were talking about when I came in—why do you have to resort to bribes? You can afford to build the casino to code."

The naive question made him look up at her, amusement dancing in his eyes. "Rena, if you know what's good for you, you'll learn to swallow a little of your own moral fortitude and do what has to be done from time to time. If the blood of the battle with your sister doesn't bring that out in you, then I don't guess anything ever will."

Rena wet her lips and tried to come back with a rejoinder, but somehow she found that there was nothing she could say. Maybe he was right, she thought. Maybe she did need to stop worrying about how things would look and how things might turn out and just concentrate on the here and now.

Without saying good-bye to him, she got up and started for the door.

"Be home for dinner tonight," Dobias ordered before she closed the door behind her.

She stopped and looked back at him.

"I'm sick and tired of everybody running their separate ways every night. Tonight we're eating together. Like a family."

Rena nodded. "All right, Dad. I'll be there."

She wondered if he even heard, he was so absorbed in the blueprint spread out over his desk. Figuring that it didn't really matter whether he had or not, she closed his door behind her and decided it was time she ducked out of this building and got some air. Besides, she thought, she needed a drink.

Tough job, Joe Holifield thought as he threw back the last of his beer. Expense account, a good story, and so far everything was falling into place. It hadn't taken him long to discover that Rena Keller stopped in at the Yankee Doodle Club about this time every day. All it had taken was watching the family for a couple of days, tailing each of them with hopes of gaining some insight into which one he had the best chance of chumming up with, and being in the right place at the right time.

Rena was the obvious choice, he thought, because she seemed to have the most weaknesses. He had no doubt in his mind that they would hit it off just fine. The main thing was not to push it. To get what he needed from her, he'd have to take it slow and easy. Revelations like the ones he sought didn't come overnight. Fortunately, he was very good at his job, and knew exactly what it would require.

Rena noticed the blond man sitting in the corner of the booth the moment she walked in, mainly because he seemed to have noticed her. Self-conscious under his intense scrutiny, she ordered her drink at the bar, then took a stool and glanced at the man again.

He was staring into his glass, she saw, and he had one leg pulled up on the seat and an elbow propped across his knee. Idly, he tapped his finger on the outer edge of his glass to the beat of the Guns and Roses hit blaring from the speakers in the back. What was he drinking? she wondered. Scotch, gin? Beer, she guessed when he raised it to his lips and took a drink. Absently, she realized she had never seen John drink beer. Only Scotch and cognac and the most expensive wines. Only drinks that befitted his station, whatever that was.

He looked toward her again, and this time raised his glass. His lips curled into a flirtatious smile. She turned away.

"Put it on your tab, Rena?" the bartender asked.

"As usual," she said. The cool, sour sustenance of her drink relaxed her, taking her mind from the million details that whirled around her head, and allowing her to forget the pressure she was under. She should be happy that she had something to occupy her time, just as John and her father and Giselle always did. You never saw them wasting time feeling sorry for themselves. Even Corey was probably busy with something or other, not giving a thought to what her father had done to her. Rena was the only one who wasn't invincible. She decided that was her greatest flaw.

From the corner of her eye, she saw the man walk across the floor toward the pinball machine in the corner. Still holding his glass, he began an intense game that allowed her to watch him unnoticed.

He was taller than John, and the slanting lines of his back told her he worked out and took care of himself. She let her eyes run down his back to the hard, fit buttocks beneath his jeans. The idea that she would look at him like that made her skin flush with heat, and she moved her gaze back to the bar.

Drinking the rest of her drink—too quickly, she knew—she ordered another, a double, and smiled at the bartender, an ex-pianist she called Archie. Laughing softly to herself, she recalled the time she had learned that his real name was Virgil, but that he'd inherited the name Achie, not Archie, after Liberace, who happened to be one of his idols. Over the years, it had evolved into Archie. Ever since, she'd learned that, she'd felt a giggle when she'd said his name, but usually only after she'd had a couple of drinks.

"I read about you in the paper, Rena," Archie said, leaning on the bar as she brought the glass to her lips. "So you're a CEO now, huh? Workin' up there with the big boys."

"Guess so," she said. "Walking the tightrope and hoping the wind doesn't blow too hard."

"Tightrope hell," Archie said on a chuckle. "If I had

a shot like that, I'd be dancing on that tightrope. You give 'em hell, babe. You'll be all right."

"Shit!"

They both looked toward the pinball machine and saw the stranger turn around and offer a grand shrug. "Sorry."

Rena smiled.

He dug through his pocket again, inserted another quarter, and started another game just as intense as the one before.

Rena made herself look away. "So how's your wife, Archie? She still taking that macramé class?"

"You know it," he told her. "I got mac-traps all over the house, hanging from hooks on the ceilings, doorknobs, you name it. She claims they're plant hangers, but God-help-me, they look like nooses to me."

Rena laughed and brought her glass to her lips. "Well, if you turn up missing, I'll pass that information on to the police."

She finished her drink and shoved the empty glass out again. Archie filled it without question.

A thud sounded on the pinball machine, and she looked over her shoulder again and saw the blond man shaking it, his face turning red.

"Damn thing's rigged," he muttered. Then, noticing that she was watching him again, he broke into a wry grin. "I hate being beaten by a box full of chrome and plastic. I'm telling you, it's fixed."

With a fresh drink in her hand, Rena felt her self-consciousness slipping away. "Archie, are you back to stealing quarters from strangers again?"

Archie offered an exaggerated shrug. "What can I say? That machine is what pays my mortgage."

Rena laughed as the man walked toward her, still wearing that grin, and took the stool next to hers.

"I've seen you here before," he said. "You must work nearby."

She stirred her drink with her finger, then put the wet tip into her mouth. "Funny, I've never noticed you."

"Ouch." He laughed then, and she met his eyes—blue eyes.

She wondered how his beard felt, if it was soft as cotton, or if it had the same strong texture as his hair.

"Well, maybe you'll remember me next time."

"The high-roller done in by the pinball machine. How could I forget?" She bottomed her drink and slipped off her stool.

"You aren't leaving, are you?"

"A girl's gotta make a living," she said, cocking one side of her lips in a seductive grin. "Later, Archie."

Then, to Joe, she said, "Hold onto those quarters, Pinball Wizard."

She picked up her step and saw the blond man grinning over his shoulder as she started out of the bar.

So nothing had happened, she told herself, and that was good. But something about the way he had singled her out, even though there were more attractive women in the bar, made her skin tingle. It had been a long time since she'd turned a head. A very long time since anyone had noticed her. She had to admit that she liked it.

Somehow, that little spark of flattery, along with the drinks she'd just downed, gave her the energy she needed to get through the rest of the day. Dinner with her father would be another story.

Giselle found Emily in her study room, her hair stringy and tousled around her face as she strained over the trigonometry problems on her computer screen. On the television across the room, *The Brady Brunch* blared.

"Emily, I told you to do something with your hair,"

she said, coming in and turning off the television. "And you're not to watch television when you're studying. Least of all that trash."

Emily touched her hair self-consciously and looked up at her mother. "What's wrong with my hair?"

"It looks like it hasn't seen a brush all day," Giselle said. She leaned over her daughter's shoulder and studied the screen in front of her. "So what are you doing? Trigonometry? Oh, Emily, this problem is wrong. You've got to pay more attention."

"I'm not even supposed to be taking Trig, Mother," the girl said. "It's too hard, and it's not required. . . ."

"I've told you, sweetheart. A Dobias does more than what's required. You have to be better than the others your age. It doesn't matter what everyone else's pace is. Yours is what counts. By the time you come into the business, you're going to be so well-prepared that the world out there won't know what hit it. And I don't care how much it costs me."

"There might not even be a business by the time I grow up," Emily said, turning off the computer. "Rena might win, and it could all belong to her."

"Not on your life," Giselle muttered. She started back for the door, talking as she went. "Now go get ready for dinner. Dad wants us all there. And whatever you do, don't mention Corey. Lord knows we want to be able to digest our food without any more explosions from him. Remember, not one word."

"She might as well be dead. We can't even talk about her."

"Right, darling. You remember that if you ever think of defying your grandfather. Do something with your hair and meet me downstairs in half an hour. Oh, and wear your new yellow dress. Dad likes that one."

Emily fixed her brown gaze on her mother's face. "After

the year's up, if you win the competition, will anybody
care then if my hair isn't brushed or if I eat in my
jeans?"

The question caught Giselle's full attention, and she
smiled, thinking how perceptive her little daughter was
becoming. That was good. It never hurt to see reality so
clearly. "All that you have to be concerned with, Emmy,
is that it matters today. If you can get through that,
tomorrow is in the bag."

She watched Emily swallow that with as much enthusiasm as the asparagus that Rachel, the cook, often
prepared. Emily pushed past her toward her bedroom.
Giselle stood in the doorway, smiling to herself at the
potential of that shrewd little mind. It would take a lot
of cultivation, she thought. But it would be worth it.
By the time Emily was her age, she'd have the world at
her feet.

The file clutched in Dobias's hand set a somber mood
at the dinner table that night, for everyone seated there
knew that when he brought work to the table, it always
concerned each of them and it usually ended in tears
and humiliation.

He dropped the file next to his plate and pulled out
his chair. His expression was sober and controlled, but
beneath it was a volatility that no one could ignore.
"She's gone to work as a waitress," he muttered through
his teeth.

Giselle set down her wineglass and regarded her father
through a frown. "Who?"

"Who the hell do you think?"

"Corey?" It was Rena who dared to mutter the name,
but she regretted it the moment she did.

As if he hadn't heard, Dobias opened the file and
referred to a detailed account of Corey's every move for

the last twenty-four hours. "It says here that she placed phone calls to each of you this morning."

Rachel began to serve dinner, ignoring the conversation, and no one at the table noticed her.

"What did you do, Dad? Tap our phones?"

Dobias brought his seething eyes up to Giselle. "If I found it necessary to know what was going on in my household, I would take necessary action. I won't tolerate deception from my daughters."

"But there wasn't any deception, Dad," Rena said, her voice shaking, even though she knew she had done nothing wrong. "I didn't talk to her. I hung up immediately."

"He knows that," Giselle said, still fixing her father with disbelieving eyes. "Since he does, I have to wonder why he brought it up. Just to let us know that we're being watched, Dad? Are you so sure we're going to turn on you, too?"

Dobias closed the file and offered them all an amused yet threatening smile. "I brought it up just to make it clear that if one of you speaks to her, I'll know."

Silence filled the dining room, punctuated only by the sound of silver clinking against china as they tried to eat. After a moment, Emily looked up from her plate.

"I thought we weren't allowed to mention Aunt Corey."

The question was not a naive one, but one designed to make a statement. Giselle gave her daughter a visual reprimand, but no one answered.

"So we can talk about her, as long as Grandfather brings her up?" she asked, feigning innocence.

Dobias pulled the napkin from his lap and slapped it onto the table.

Acting on his scathing look, Giselle said, "Emily, go to your room."

"But I haven't eaten—"

"Now."

The girl scraped her chair back and flung her shoulder-length hair back from her face. "Then I'll order a pizza," she said. "Tell Rachel to send it up when they deliver it."

"You'll do no such thing," Giselle said. "I'll have her bring you a tray, but you will stay there for the rest of the evening."

Emily bit her tongue and pranced the rest of the way up the stairs.

Once again, complete silence engulfed the dining room.

"You did the right thing," John said after a moment. "She can't go around saying whatever she pleases."

"She just misses Corey," Rena said through tight lips. "You can't blame her. They were very close, and this whole thing is confusing for an eleven-year-old."

"An eleven-year-old with the brain of a twenty-year-old," Dobias added. "Don't underestimate the child, Rena. She knows exactly what she's doing."

"And what is that?" Giselle asked, daring to challenge her father against her daughter.

"Rebelling," Dobias said. "If you don't nip it in the bud now, it'll cost you a great deal when she's older. Trust me. I know."

Again they ate in silence, but after a moment, Rena spoke. "Those phone calls Corey made. Did you trace them?"

Dobias nodded.

"Where is she staying?"

"With that boyfriend of hers. That unemployed vagrant who thinks he'll come into a fortune if he holds onto her long enough."

Giselle's interest seemed piqued again, and she frowned. "What was his name?"

"Eric Gray," Rena said. "And he isn't unemployed. He's a free-lance photographer."

"Eric Gray." Giselle memorized the name in case she ever needed it. "Wonder what he thinks of his prize catch now? The threat of poverty is the best test of true love, they say."

"That's enough," Dobias said, cutting the conversation off as he slid back his chair. "I'll be in the study."

The three of them watched him leave the room. Giselle finished her wine and offered a satisfied grin. "So much for that nice family dinner he demanded."

Rena sighed. "He's depressed. He's taken a stand he can't back down from, and he's bound to regret it."

"The only regret your father has, darling, is that Corey isn't wandering the streets barefoot and in rags yet," John said. "He won't be happy until his private eyes find her sleeping on a park bench."

Rena glared at her husband. "I don't believe that, John, and I hope you don't, either." She looked at Giselle. "Why won't she apologize to him? Come back on her knees if that's what it takes? He'd forgive her, if she just demonstrated how sorry she is."

"I guess she's not sorry enough yet," Giselle said. "But I don't agree. I think Dad's made up his mind. Nothing Corey ever does will make him forgive her for embarrassing him in front of all those people. The pie's ours now, Rena, and you'd better stop pining away and start fighting for it. Because once it's mine, I don't intend to cut it at all."

Rena shoved her plate away and scraped back her chair. "Somehow I've lost my appetite. I'm sure you'll both excuse me."

"Certainly, darling," John said. "It won't hurt you to miss a meal or two."

He smiled over his glass at Giselle as Rena started out of the dining room.

Dobias sat in his study for a half hour or more, neglecting to turn on the light as twilight seeped into the room between the thick, drawn brocade drapes. Corey working as a waitress. Somehow, that held poetic justice. He should be happy.

But that was never what he or Shara had planned for her. He cupped his hand over his weary eyes, rubbing the cracks and wrinkles there, and wondered where in God's name the time had gone. Just yesterday, she was a baby, tucked snug and happy in her mother's arms. She was the first and only of his children whose birth he had witnessed. She was the one who had shown him what he had missed with the other two.

From the past, Shara's voice, quiet and shadowy, beckoned to him, reminding him how close they had come to losing her. Shara's water had broken at home, and the pains had been so intense that there hadn't been time for an ambulance.

"Help me, Nik!" Shara had cried. "Help me!"

He remembered feeling woefully inadequate in the face of such a crisis, though he solved crises every day at his office. "Just hold on. Just hold on."

"I *can't!* Something's wrong, Nik! I know something's wrong."

He had called the doctor frantically, trembling at the pain in his wife's voice, at the panic in her face. The doctor had come quickly, but by that time, the baby, who wasn't due for another six weeks, was already crowning.

"Stay here," the doctor told him. "I'm going to need you."

The prospect had sickened him at first, but as the miracle began to occur, and as Shara's pain intensified, he found himself drawn into the event that he had denied himself twice before.

He had held Corey even before his wife, and had marveled so at her beauty and perfection, that it wasn't until hours later that he realized he didn't even harbor the same disappointment he'd felt upon discovering that his other two had not been boys.

That little girl had changed his life in many ways, for he had learned with her to be a father for the first time. He'd begun to spoil all of them as a result. Giselle had been the first girl in her school to own a sports car. Rena had been given the grandest birthday parties anyone in town had seen. And Corey had gotten all the love and attention that one man could give to a child. Despite how Giselle had excelled since the age of nine at one of the country's finest boarding schools—though Shara had refused to send Rena for fear that her shyness and fragility would hinder her there—Dobias never suggested letting Corey go. Instead, he had kept her home, under his wing.

While they had rarely agreed on the proper discipline for any of their children, or the achievements Dobias expected of them, he had to admit that Shara's talent as a mother couldn't be questioned. Her time with her children finally began to fill the void he saw gaping wider in her each day, the void that he had never been able to fill in all his years of loving her.

When she died of ovarian cancer ten years ago, he had felt the desolation of an empty soul. He had failed her in many ways, for she hadn't lived long enough for him to realize what it was that she had wanted— needed—most from him. But she had loved him. He never doubted that.

Despite the ingratitude and betrayal of his favorite child, despite the stings of disloyal friends, despite the boredom of being on the top, no one could ever take his memories of his innocent Catholic debutante, eloping with him and sacrificing a lifetime of her family's love. He knew that families could turn on you, but that true love between a man and a woman, that burning passion that had carried him through his marriage, could never be taken from him. Nothing would ever mar the memory of his twenty-three years with her.

Not even his conscience.

She would have understood his banishment of Corey, had she lived. She would have been as angry as he. She would have expected him to teach her how far it was from where she had lived to the bottom, where she was going.

He was sure of it.

But as the vaguest hint of doubt surfaced in his mind about what Shara would have thought, would have said, would have done about his treatment of Corey, he forced it out of his mind.

He had never been able to teach Shara that some sacrifices were necessary. Sometimes a man's honor and pride were far more important.

Upstairs, Rena went to the medicine cabinet where she kept the wide array of prescription drugs that helped her through the day. Pouring a Scotch, she reached for the pain pill she kept for her headaches. This one was a killer, she thought. But she could handle it. She always did.

Washing down the pill and finishing off the Scotch, she left her suite of rooms and went out into the wide, plush-carpeted hallway. Her father was upstairs now, sitting on the bench across from her mother's portrait, staring at it as if it would come to life.

Quietly, she approached him and sat down beside him. "You miss her a lot, don't you, Dad?"

He didn't answer, and she wondered if he heard. When a moment passed and there was still no answer, she started to get up.

"I may have been wrong earlier today," he said, finally moving his gaze from his wife back to his daughter. "About giving you advice. There's still a lot I have to teach you. An awful lot you need to learn."

Rena felt like a little girl being noticed by the man of her dreams. "Really, Daddy?"

He smiled. "We'll have lunch tomorrow. We can talk then."

She breathed in a shaky, surprised breath. "All right. Tomorrow. I'll look forward to it, Daddy." She leaned over and pressed a kiss on his temple, but his eyes grew vacant again and settled back on the portrait.

Annotelli's Shrimp and Pasta House wasn't at all like the restaurants Dobias usually frequented, but it bustled with hungry business men and women on their lunch hours. Rena didn't mention the fact that they wouldn't be able to discuss her business problems with any degree of success since the noise level in the restaurant was so high with the golden oldies blaring from the speakers overhead.

She was especially confused when he demanded a specific table, as if he'd been here before. He seemed distracted, as if he waited to see someone he knew, and Rena touched his hand to bring his attention back to her. "This is nice, Daddy," she said. "I'm glad we came. But why did you want this table? The one they had for us looked better."

"I wanted this table because of the station it's in," he said.

She saw that he had spotted what he was looking for, and turning her head, she followed his gaze.

Corey, donned in a brown uniform and apron, was stacking a tray in a corner of the room.

Rena snapped her head back to her father. "You knew she was here, didn't you? You brought me here on purpose!"

Dobias smiled and patted her hand. "I told you still had a lot to learn. I thought it would be good for you."

"But, Dad, this is cruel. She'll see us—"

"She'll not only see us," he said, his smile fading to a strange dullness, "she'll serve us. And you, my dear, will treat her like any other servant. Is that understood?"

Rena groped for her drink and emptied it as perspiration dotted her neck. Breathless, she whispered, "I need another drink."

"Don't worry, Rena. She's on her way. You can order whatever you want."

Corey stopped dead in her tracks when she saw her father and her sister sitting at one of her tables. It was a coincidence, she thought at first, and they didn't know she was here. She started to back away and find someone else to take over that table before they saw her.

But then her father's dull eyes met hers, and she knew it was no mistake. It was calculated, deliberate, and humiliating, and she knew he'd planned every moment of her torture.

She glanced at Dee-dee, one of the other waitresses who'd helped her out since her first day, and for a split second considered swapping tables, anyway. It wouldn't give her away. No one there knew she was a Dobias—at least, not until her father told them.

No, she thought, chastising herself for her cowardice. She wasn't going to back down.

Straightening, she approached them with cool composure.

"Hello, Dad. Rena."

Rena didn't take her eyes from the menu in her hands.

"She'll have another Scotch," Dobias said. "And we're ready to order. If you think you can handle it."

"I can handle anything," Corey said. And for the first time, she realized she meant it.

They stayed for an excruciating hour and a half, during which her sister drank six drinks and ate nothing. It was difficult to say if her father had eaten anything, for he kept sending his steaks back, complaining that they weren't cooked right. Finally, when the game had grown wearisome, and she'd demonstrated that she was no more willing to crack and grovel now than she had been before, the two of them left.

They left a dollar tip.

It was then, as she stuffed the hard-earned dollar into her pocket, that Corey made a decision.

She was going to get that necklace. And if it meant physically breaking into the house to do it, she was more than willing now.

chapter
14

THE WIND WHINED AND THE MOON SEARCHED
the snow-covered ground, and on the other side of
the stone wall skirting the Dobias estate the Dobermans
began to growl and bark. Slipping her flashlight into the
waistband of her jeans, Corey positioned the crates she'd
brought in the trunk of her rental car, and balanced on
them until she could get a grip on the top of the wall.

"It's me, guys," she told the dogs in a low voice. "It's
just me."

Confused at her familiar voice and even more familiar
scent, the dogs hushed for a moment. She reached into
the pocket of the black bomber jacket she had borrowed
from Eric's closet and withdrew a handful of milkbones.
She dropped them onto the ground, and the dogs whim-
pered and scurried for their share.

She jumped from the wall with a thud, and immediately the dogs descended on her, licking her face and
sniffing her pockets and her backpack for more treats.
But she had none.

"Hi there, Caesar," she whispered, scratching their
heads. "Brutus, you almost scared me. You can't have
forgotten me already. Polonius, tell him it's me."

She got to her feet, and the dogs jumped up, still licking and whining, but she ordered them to stay. "I'll see
you guys when I come back," she whispered. "Right now,
I have a house to break into. So for God's sake, be quiet."

Three of the dogs stayed behind to sniff for any forgotten treats, but two of them followed her as she cut like a shadow across the lawn. She could see that the light was still on in her father's study, and she wondered if it had been left on by mistake or if he could still be up at two in the morning. Maybe his conscience was bothering him, she thought, for what he'd done to her today.

For a moment, she stood still in the shadows, trying to decide whether to wait for the light to go off or take the chance of getting to the safe before he came up. If she waited, someone might discover her rental car parked under the trees outside the northern edge of the estate. They would see the crates she'd left, and they'd know that someone was breaking in.

She couldn't take that chance. If she got caught, he was likely to have her thrown in jail again. This time, who knew where it would end?

No, it was now or never, she thought. She had to get into the hallway and to the safe, take her necklace, and get the hell out of there before she lost her nerve. If she didn't get it tonight, she wasn't sure she'd be able to try it again.

Besides, her time was running out.

She went to the trellis on the side of the house and mentally measured the distance to her own bedroom. If there was a chance of getting in without being heard, it would be through her own suite. That way, she could take a moment to gather some of her things. Maybe a good coat, an outfit or two, some shoes.

The trick would be getting past the security system that her father had paid such a grand sum for. If a window was broken, an alarm would go off. If a lock were picked, the sirens would blare. But there was something that her father hadn't counted on when he'd planned it all out so carefully. She had a key, and it unlocked her balcony door. And because she and her sisters often opened those balcony doors at night, the alarms weren't activated if the right key opened them.

Careful not to let her feet slip in the flat pumps she had to wear, since she hadn't been able to afford tennis shoes, she scaled the trellis and made her way slowly up past her father's darkened suite, sideways past Giselle's window, and then to her own suite. The balcony was four feet from the trellis. A little too far to step onto easily, so she stepped onto the ledge shielding the first floor.

Her foot slipped beneath her, and a trickle of sweat ran down her temples and into her eyes. Quietly, she leaned over and took off her shoes, stuffed them beside the flashlight into the waist of her jeans, and tried to make it the rest of the way barefoot.

She reached the railing of the balcony and found that it was just within her reach. Holding her breath, she grabbed one of the rails and tried to pull herself up, but her right hand where she'd sprained her wrist last year was too weak. Compensating with her left hand, she tried to swing her body until she could get her foot over the edge. But just as her foot caught and she pulled her knee up to the balcony, one of the shoes slid out of her jeans, bounced off the ledge, and landed with a soft thump in the bushes below her.

"Damn," she whispered. But forcing herself to ignore the fallen shoe, she pulled to her feet on the outside of the rail, then easily stepped over it.

For a moment she only sat there, staring down into the courtyard from the place where she had idled away so much of her time, never dreaming that one day it would offer her a means of breaking in. When her breath was normal again, she fished in her jeans pocket for the key, then carefully slipped it into the lock.

The door opened easily, and holding her breath, she stepped inside her bedroom. She pulled the flashlight from her pants, and shone it around the room.

Home! It was the most wonderful concept she had ever known, and breathing a sigh of sweet relief, she dropped onto the feather bed and closed her eyes, savoring the feel of her own mattress, her own scents, her own possessions.

But it felt too good, and knowing that she couldn't cling to it, she forced herself to get up and shine the light around for things she had room for in her backpack. Slipping into the bathroom, she grabbed the few essentials she could manage: a framed picture of her mother, her address book, her makeup bag of Elizabeth Arden necessities. Then she went to her dressing closet, bigger than Eric's entire apartment, and grabbed three pairs of shoes, including a pair of tennis shoes which she slipped immediately onto her feet, two pairs of unworn jeans, a blouse, and two dresses.

The backpack gaped open with the contents, refusing to be zipped, so she decided she'd leave it partially open and take the chance of losing something along the way. Besides, she had one more thing to find before she got the necklace. Some of the papers from her briefcase.

Still in her closet, she looked on the top shelf where she had left it. The briefcase was gone.

Not entirely surprised, she stood staring at the empty shelf for a moment before she closed the door. Had her father taken it as another weapon to use against her? She hoped she was wrong, for the last thing she needed was for him to pry into her activities and jeopardize her deal.

There wasn't time to worry about that now, she told herself. She had the things she'd come for, but those weren't the most important things. The most important thing was the necklace, and that would be the hardest to get.

Even though the night was cold and the house was set to a comfortable seventy-four degrees, Corey still perspired beneath Eric's heavy shirt. Checking her clock, she saw that it was approaching two forty-five. She wondered if her father had come up yet, or if he still sat downstairs in his study.

Leaving the backpack on her bed, she went to the door, cracked it open, and peered into the hall. Recessed lighting illuminated the paintings and portraits that lined the passageway, making it impossible for her to slip into shadows and make her way to the portrait of her mother, the one that covered the safe where her necklace was hidden.

Besides that, the alarm system that guarded the safes was located at the other end of the hall, close to her father's wing. She would have to go there to shut off the security system first, before she dared to open the safe.

Her heart hammered at a dangerous rate, and her breathing grew labored and shallow. Wiping the perspiration from her brow, she stepped out of the room.

Not wasting a moment, she went up the hall to her father's wing, removed the painting that hid the security system controls, and punched out the code that would turn the alarm system off. The LED indicator flickered for a second, and her heart froze. What if he'd changed the code? What if he'd anticipated her coming here?

But after a second, the readout indicated that the system was disengaged. Closing her eyes, she let out a deep breath, then carefully replaced the painting over the controls.

She heard music in one of the rooms, indicating that someone was still awake. Slowly, she started up the hall, listening at each door until she could tell that the music came from Rena's room.

Her stomach began to rock with queasiness, and she

told herself to hurry up and get this horrible thing over with. It could be her beginning, or it could land her even worse off than she'd been before. It was up to her.

She came to her mother's portrait and looked up at it, at the gently smiling face that had meant so much to her. Her mother would have understood this act, she thought. She would have been appalled at the way her father had cast her out, and she would have been rooting her on. It was that knowledge that redeemed her.

With trembling hands, she moved the heavy painting, careful not to scratch the gold leaf of the frame. She set it gently on the floor, then stepped up to the safe she had opened countless times to remove her favorite, most expensive pieces of jewelry that were common property among herself and her sisters.

Her fingers quickly worked the combination, and the safe popped open. She reached inside, shuffled around the velvet-covered boxes, until she came to the pouch that held the emerald and diamond necklace. A swirl of excitement traveled up inside her as she slowly withdrew it and emptied the necklace into her hand.

And then she heard the footsteps on the carpet beside her.

Slowly, she turned around and saw Rena standing in the hallway, staring at her in utter disbelief.

Their eyes locked and held for a small eternity, and Corey braced herself for her sister to call out and end it all. They would all come running: her father, Giselle, John, even Emily. They'd see exactly how far she had fallen. From heiress to thief. It was a fitting end.

But Rena made no move to call out. She stood stock-still, her gaze falling from Corey's to the necklace she held in her hand. Finally, not knowing what else to do, Corey slipped the necklace back into its velvet pouch, closed the safe, and replaced her mother's portrait.

When the evidence of her theft was gone, she turned back to her sister. They stared in silent supplication, and tears half-mooned in both their eyes. Regrets and anxieties washed forward, but no words were exchanged.

Corey stepped forward and pressed a kiss on her sister's cheek. Then, not looking back, she hurried to the door to her own suite of rooms, stuffed the velvet pouch into her backpack, and lit out over the balcony. Climbing down the trellis, she reached the ground and broke into a run, with the rambunctious dogs on her heels, waiting for another treat.

Before Rena had even moved from the hallway, Corey was in the car, heading back to Cambridge.

Rena backed across to the bench opposite her mother's portrait. Her mother's gentle smile told her she'd done the right thing.

But if her father ever found out that she had let Corey escape with that necklace, she'd be reduced to stealing herself. She closed her eyes as tears seeped out between her lashes, and telling herself that she had no time for tears, that she needed to be tougher, she got up and went back into her suite. John still wasn't home, and his excuses about late business meetings were growing tiresome. But there was really nothing she could do.

She went to the medicine cabinet and stared at the brown pharmaceutical bottles that lined the shelves. She had hoped she wouldn't need something to help her sleep tonight, especially after all she'd had to drink. But the drinks didn't help anymore, and if she didn't take a pill, she'd lie awake all night and think.

And those thoughts were a little too potent to deal with now.

She washed down two pills with a half-empty glass of Scotch she'd left upstairs earlier, stepped out of her clothes, and climbed under the covers of her bed. She wondered if he'd come home at all tonight, or if she'd wake in the morning and find that he was still gone.

If it was a woman, she hoped it was someone she didn't know. Someone who didn't know her. Someone he'd met that day and would never see again. That was the only way she could stand it.

Numbness and heaviness washed over her, pulling her under the drunken haze of sleep. Tomorrow, maybe she wouldn't remember how she felt tonight. If she was lucky, she'd awaken with John beside her and have no memory of finding Corey standing at the safe in the hall. Tomorrow it wouldn't hurt so much when she remembered how Corey had served her father and her that day, or the way Corey had kissed her cheek tonight in tender thanks and forgiveness that she didn't deserve.

As sleep crept over her, pushing the thoughts away, she didn't care anymore about any of those things. Nothing really mattered, right now, except getting a good night's sleep.

chapter

15

ERIC GRAY WOKE THE MOMENT COREY CAME
back into the room, for the smell of cold and outdoors
created a subtle change in the apartment. Squinting his
eyes, he looked at the clock, saw that it was almost four
o'clock. She had already taken off her shirt—correction,
his shirt—and was stepping out of her jeans.

"Where the hell have you been?"

"Out," she said.

"Out." He sat up, letting the sheet fall around his hips,
and rubbed his eyes. "Just out? Don't I deserve more
than that?"

"Don't whine, Eric." She went to his drawer and withdrew the T-shirt she'd been sleeping in since she came
here. "I went to my father's to get some things."

"Oh." He glanced down at the contents spilling out of
her backpack and hope quivered through him. "So he
let you back in? You're speaking to each other?"

"No, he didn't let me back in," she said. "He didn't
know I was there. I just went in and got what I needed.
No one saw me."

Eric got up and picked up the backpack. "So what's
so important that you'd go there in the middle of the
night?"

He pulled out some shoes, a rolled up pair of jeans, a
makeup pouch.

"That," she said. "My makeup. I'm sick and tired of
walking around here with nothing on my face."

"Your makeup," he repeated, as if those two little words

validated every opinion he'd ever had about her. "Right."

"I'll get better tips if I look good," she said, snatching the case away from him.

She took the case and disappeared into the bathroom. Eric sat on the bed, watching the closed door, and wondered why someone shallow enough to sneak into a house in the middle of the night for a wand of mascara wouldn't come off her pedestal and apologize to her father. She was a nut, that was why. Only a nut would throw ten million dollars—more if she'd won the competition—down the drain.

She came out of the bathroom, her hair loose and falling around her shoulders, her legs bare beneath the bulky T-shirt, and crawled into bed.

His groin stirred to life, and he laid his hand on her satiny thigh and slid it into the leg of her panties. He missed the silky ones, he thought, but he supposed he could get used to these.

Her hand closed over his.

"Not tonight, Eric," she said. "I'm beat, and I have to work a double shift in a few hours."

He moved his hand and cursed the fact that for all he'd done for her, he couldn't even depend on her when he needed her. "A double shift? You? How'd they rope you into that?"

"I volunteered," she said. "I need the money. Good night."

Eric flopped to his back and laid his wrist over his eyes, wondering if he had missed something. This wasn't the same woman he had asked to marry him. Or was it? he wondered. On the mountain, she had exhibited this same ridiculous martyred stubbornness. He supposed he should find it moving.

Regretfully, he found it inconvenient and aggravating.

Corey was asleep in minutes, and Eric cursed her for

waking him up in the first place. Now he was ripe and restless, dog tired, and unable to satisfy either his libido or his fatigue.

Already he felt like a married man, and he didn't like it one bit.

Despite the fact that she'd only had a few hours' sleep, Corey sprang up the next morning and dressed for work, tucking the emerald necklace, which had previously been hidden in her makeup bag, into a pocket in her brief case. Stepping into one of the Bill Blass dresses she had taken from her room the previous night, she smiled as the image came to life. Something that fit right, she thought with relief, though she'd dropped an inch or so from her waist since this whole ordeal had begun.

She was out of the apartment, looking like a business executive rather than a poorly paid waitress, before Eric woke up.

She didn't have to be at work until ten, so she took an hour to pay a visit to some of the jewelry shops near the restaurant and try to sell the necklace. By the end of the day, she reasoned, she would have twenty-five thousand dollars in her pocket. Then she'd be able to wave it in Adam Franklin's face and show him that she wasn't dead weight.

But by ten o'clock, as she was changing from her Bill Blass into the cotton uniform she kept in a locker at the restaurant, she wondered if Adam hadn't been right. What had ever made her think that anyone would give her what the necklace was worth? She'd had one offer of a thousand dollars, and she'd laughed in the man's face. Another offer had come in at five thousand, but by then she hadn't felt like laughing. She'd used all her energy to keep from crying.

She worked like a demon through the lunch and early afternoon shift, then took off from two to three-thirty before her second shift would begin. Too tired and too rushed to change out of her uniform, she grabbed her briefcase and raced to Franklin Tower, to confront the man who had seemed so certain that the necklace was her ticket.

Adam Franklin, she was told, had already left the office for the day. He had retired to his penthouse in the tower and did not wish to be disturbed.

But that had never stopped Corey before, and she vowed that it wouldn't stop her now. Clutching her briefcase in her hand and prancing like a sophisticate who'd just decided that waitress-wear was this year's hottest trend, she buzzed the penthouse and waited for Adam to answer.

Adam closed his eyes and moaned as the masseuse moved her slippery hands over his back, kneading out the muscles that had been balled up as tight as knots for the past week. His birthday present, he thought with a smile. Until his office staff had entered his office snickering and chuckling, acting like conspirators in a covert operation, then sprung this surprise on him, he had forgotten that today was his birthday.

Forty-six, he thought. Damn. If the truth had been known, he would just as soon have forgotten his forty-sixth birthday. His father had been dead before he'd reached that age, and his mother had died even before that.

Still, he couldn't complain about a blond Swedish masseuse who barely spoke English, smelled like a teenager's starkest fantasy, and touched him in a way that made him forget about all the work he had piling up on his desk.

His intercom buzzed, and he tried to ignore it. He was too relaxed to move a muscle, except of course the one that responded every time her hand slid across his skin. He was greasy and naked beneath the towel that absurdly lay across him, considering that she had already seen and touched almost everything the towel covered. He couldn't wait until she turned him over.

Idly, he wondered where she got her training and thought he'd have to donate money to their program. Training like this was well worth a pat on the back, or whatever part of the anatomy applied.

The buzzer sounded again, and Adam cursed. "Hand me that telephone," he told the masseuse.

Wiping her hands on a towel, she reached for the telephone. He took it and put it to his ear. "Yeah? What the hell is it?"

"Adam, it's Corey Dobias. I need to talk to you."

He frowned and looked up miserably at the masseuse. "Not now, Corey. I'm busy."

"So am I," she said. "I have to be back at work in an hour. Come on, Adam. Let me in. Just for a minute."

"You'll take ten," he said.

"Only if you let me."

He smiled at her tenacity and admitted that he'd love to see her face if he did let her in. Maybe next time he told her he was busy, she'd believe him.

"All right, Corey, but I warned you. I'll send the elevator, and you just come on in. The door's open."

He punched out the computer code that allowed her entrance to the elevator, handed the phone back to the masseuse, and chuckled as he waited.

Muttering something in husky Swedish, the masseuse gestured toward the door, asking if she should go.

He grinned up at her and thought of turning over and instructing her to work on his chest and thighs while

Corey made whatever pitch she'd come to make this time. With a sigh, he decided against it. "No, honey. Just go right ahead with what you were doing. It won't bother me a bit."

The woman smiled, oozed some more warm oil over his back, and slid those firm, strong hands over his shoulders. Damn, she was good.

He heard his door open in the living room, and that grin grew broader.

"Adam?"

"In here, Corey," he called. "Just come on back."

In a moment, she appeared in the doorway, and he raised up on his elbows and grinned at her. "Told you I was busy."

Instead of withering like he expected, Corey only returned his grin and shook her head. "Oh, that's all right. I have a theory about conducting business with naked men. I've been wanting to test it."

"And what might that theory be?"

"That it puts me at an advantage."

"Well, that wouldn't be fair, would it? Maybe you should take your clothes off, too."

Corey grinned. "You had your chance, Adam. Besides, I'm not one to even things out. I like the odds this way."

The fact that he hadn't gotten the reaction he expected didn't daunt him. He liked this one better, anyway. "This is Helga. She doesn't speak English," he said. "She's my birthday present."

Corey stepped up to the table, reached across him and shook Helga's greasy hand. "It's your birthday? How old are you, Adam?"

"None of your business."

"That old, huh? I thought so."

He bristled and raised up again, and Corey winked at the masseuse.

It was only then that he noticed the uniform that sported the Annotelli's Shrimp and Pasta House logo—a cartoon shrimp in a chef's hat and mustache, brandishing a hot plate of spaghetti.

"So where'd you get that getup you're wearing?"

Corey smoothed down her short brown skirt and set her hand on her hip, as if the outfit made a rare fashion statement. "It's my waitress uniform," she said. "I happen to be gainfully employed now."

"Really? I'm impressed."

"Wait till you see this." She reached into her briefcase and withdrew the velvet pouch that held the necklace.

"What's that?" He propped himself on one elbow and took the pouch.

"Only twenty-five thousand dollars' worth of the most beautiful necklace you've ever seen. And if you want it—for your masseuse friend or whomever—I'll take a check. I think you're good for it."

Adam's playful smile faded, and clutching the towel around him, he sat up completely and opened the pouch. The necklace spilled out into his hand, and for a moment he only stared at it, his eyes pensive and serious as he studied every stone. Something about the way he frowned down at it told her that she had come to the right place. Adam wanted that necklace, and she was going to make him pay for it.

"Have you tried to sell it?" he asked quietly.

"I've gotten a few offers."

"Low ones, huh?"

She shrugged. "A little lower than I liked."

"What's the highest offer you've gotten?"

Her heart rate accelerated, and she knew better than to tell him five thousand dollars. "Twenty-three," she lied. "I told him he was crazy. Emeralds like that, and the diamonds alone—"

"Don't shit me, Corey."

She met his harsh eyes and saw that, to him, this was nothing to joke about.

"How much? Four? Five?"

She lifted her chin. "All right, I'll be honest with you," she lied again. "I was offered eight. But it appraised for twenty-five, and that was a few years ago."

"Nobody cares what it appraises for," Adam said. "And frankly, I don't believe anybody offered you eight."

Corey's face drained of its color. "What are you saying? That I won't get that much?"

"You won't get any more than that. That's for damn sure. But if you want me to help you invest it, that would be enough to start you off."

She looked away, her lips tightly compressed. Finally, she turned back to him. "All right, what will you give me for it?"

"I'll give you eight," he said. "Not a penny more."

Corey took the necklace out of his hand and dropped it back in its pouch. "I should have known I was wasting time coming here. I could have eaten lunch before my second shift, for God's sake! But no, I had to come here and watch some Swedish bimbo put her hands all over you while you insult me with that kind of offer!"

"Aw, now. You don't want to hurt Helga's feelings, do you?"

"How can I hurt her feelings? She doesn't speak English!"

"Oh yeah." Adam nodded toward a bowl of grapes on the table next to him. "You're welcome to some grapes, if you're really hungry."

"Do I eat them, or feed them to you?"

Adam's chuckle was insufferable. "Either one would be fine with me."

She started out of the room, and Adam came to his

feet. "Where are you going?"

"Back to Annotelli's," she called over her shoulder. "Some of us have to work for a living."

The door slammed before he had time to tuck the corner of the towel in at the waist and go after her. Shrugging, he decided to lie back down and let Helga finish what she was hired to do. The extent of his birthday present wasn't clear to him, but he figured he'd find out soon enough. All he had to do was lie still and enjoy it.

But two hours later, when he felt drugged from the power of the massage and lay cursing the staff for hiring a legitimate masseuse who didn't go beyond the call of duty, he cursed himself for letting Corey get away with that necklace.

He stepped into the shower, the hot steam fogging the room, and recalled the perfect cuts of full carat emeralds, eight of them, surrounded by diamonds. Corey had no way of knowing that he'd seen that necklace before, or that he'd known it intimately. He had designed it himself and paid to have it made. But that was another life ago.

A life he hadn't entirely let go of yet.

He lathered the soap on his skin, washing away the oil the masseuse had left there, and told himself he could do without that necklace. She could sell it to someone else, someone who would wear it in public and feel like a million bucks. It belonged in the light, around a beautiful neck, rather than tucked away in his memory somewhere.

But that wasn't really where he wanted it. He stepped out of the shower, dried off, and began to dress in a pair of gray cotton slacks and a pullover shirt. Where had she said she worked? That Italian seafood place—Annotelli's something or other.

He chuckled at the thought of her waiting tables,

taking orders from anyone else. The idea had a special appeal to him. He'd have to see it for himself.

Maybe then he could talk her into selling him the necklace for eight grand. That was the highest he could go, or he'd seem too anxious. And he was certain no one else would offer more.

She'd take it, he thought, if he just waited her out. But meanwhile, he was hungry. Shrimp sounded real good right about now. After all, it was his birthday.

chapter
16

COREY SAW HIM THE MOMENT HE STEPPED INTO the restaurant, and she almost dropped the tray of frog's legs she was carrying to table fourteen.

"He's mine," Dee-dee, the waitress behind her whispered in her Biloxi, Mississippi, accent. "Honey, he wouldn't even need to tip me. I might just tip him if he asked me real nice."

Corey grinned. "I know him. He probably wants to be at my station." She glanced at the little blond dynamo she had come to like a lot over the past few days, and noted the girl's disappointment. "See, I have something he wants."

"Yeah, I just bet you do," Dee-dee said. "Well, take good care of him. Don't let it make you feel guilty that you just may be diverting my prince charming. I'll find another one. Somewhere."

"You're breaking my heart."

Dee-dee tossed her wiry blond hair back from her face and sashayed away.

Corey watched as the host—that was what they called him, since calling him a maitre d' in such a low-budget establishment would have sounded ludicrous—ushered Adam to one of her tables. Schooling her expression not to appear too pleased, she approached him.

"I hope I don't read about this in the *Investigator* tomorrow. Everyone here thinks my name is Caine."

"Your secret's safe with me," he said with a grin.

"So you suddenly had a taste for Italian food, did you?"

"You might say that. That cute little shrimp on your pocket there made me hungry."

"Oh yeah. One of Boston's greatest advertising coups. Well, don't think I'm going to give it to you on the house, just because it's your birthday. Don't want anybody thinking I'm dead weight, you know." She offered him a cocky grin, and he set his elbow on the table and propped his chin.

"How did your massage turn out? Was it a birthday to remember?"

Adam grinned. "I'm still tingling."

"Yeah, I'll just bet you are. It must have been awful trying to get all that oil off."

"Helga helped me. She's what they call a full-service masseuse."

"What other kind is there?" She pulled her waitress pad out of her apron pocket and poised her pencil, wishing she had some gum to pop. "So what'll you have? Our seafood is, well, Italian. And the pasta dishes smell like fish. But it must taste all right, because this place is always packed."

"Can you join me?"

She stopped and narrowed her eyes down at him, almost angry that he expected her to take this job so lightly. "Adam, I'm working. I can't just take off any time I want."

"But you must take breaks. Don't they let you rest once in a while?"

She looked around at the crowd standing in the doorway, waiting for tables. "Well, yes. But not until around nine or so. Then I get a half-hour break."

"Okay," he said. "I'll wait. Bring me a bottle of the house wine."

"You'll wait?" She dropped the pad back in her apron and gaped down at him. "Why? It's your birthday. You could be out with Hilda—"

"Helga," he corrected with a grin.

"Whoever. You could be doing all sorts of things on your birthday. Why would you want to sit here and drink cheap wine by yourself?"

"Because," Adam said, his face sobering a degree, "I've been thinking about that necklace. I want to talk you into accepting my offer for it."

She smiled, but she feared her disappointment shone in her eyes. "I see. Got a little lady with a naked neck waiting in the wings?"

"Hardly." His smile faded completely now, and she could have sworn the shutters over his eyes closed out all his previous amusement. "My reasons for wanting it are personal. You need the money, and I'm willing to help you by buying it."

She glanced around, then shrugged and let out a grand sigh. "All right, Adam. I'll take off at nine and have dinner with you. You'll have thirty minutes to convince me why I should take seventeen thousand dollars less than it's worth. And if you think putting the FranklinNet deal together was tough, you ain't seen nothin' yet."

She pranced off, knowing he was watching her, but didn't bother to look back. It felt too good to be on top for once in what seemed like such a long time.

Adam didn't remember when he'd enjoyed a birthday more. His last four had been spent with money-hungry vixens who wanted to be seen with him in fancy restaurants and hoped to wind up with their pictures in the society section of one of his papers. Before that, he'd tried solitude but found that it just reminded him how dismal his life had become.

He'd left too much out, and he supposed it was too late to fix it.

But tonight he sat in the center of this crowded restaurant, where hundreds of people came and went, where the tables were always full.

For most of the night, Corey was a blur. She whizzed here, leaving a trail of smoke in her wake, then barreled over there, balancing a tray of meals as if she'd done it all her life.

He was impressed. He never would have expected her to last one day at a job like this, but here she was working the second of a double shift and handling it all as if she didn't mind a bit.

She reminded him of himself.

He'd been a hard worker all his life, always willing to get his hands dirty. He'd spent his summers in high school working on a sanitation truck for the city of Tulsa, picking up dead animals left to bloat in the street. Some people said he still did that, when he went after ailing communications businesses and newspapers. The difference was that he always brought his businesses back from the dead.

The year he graduated from college with the enthusiasm of someone ready to conquer the world, the arrogance to believe he could do it, and the finances of someone who didn't have a chance, he discovered that the jobs awaiting him weren't what he'd had in mind. They were boring, nowhere jobs with pitiful salaries offered by nowhere companies. Rather than seal his fate and accept something that had little appeal, he chose a different route altogether.

A friend of his had told him about an opportunity to work as a steward on Ari Onassis's yacht. At first he'd thought that being a steward was beneath a college man with a fresh degree in his hand. Hell, in a few years, with a little luck, he'd be able to *buy* the *Christina*. But the more he thought of being around the rich, listening to the tips they passed around like hors d'oeuvres, and getting in covertly on some of their investments, the more the idea appealed to him.

He'd worked there for a year, time enough to pick up enough morsels of information to make a killing on the investments he'd made. That was where he earned the money to buy the *Investigator*. From there, his success had spiraled upward. He had already been smart before he'd worked on the *Christina*. But working for Onassis had made him lucky. And luck was something he'd never taken for granted since.

He sipped his wine and leaned back, slinging an ankle over his knee, and checked his watch. It was almost nine. He hoped Corey had enough energy left in her to conduct an intelligent negotiation. Then again, maybe if she was as tired as he suspected, she'd be a little easier to convince to sell him the necklace.

Then he would teach her how to be lucky.

Corey's feet ached, her head throbbed, and her muscles reminded her of how little sleep she had gotten the night before. It was tough, this double life: thief by night, waitress by day.

And there was Adam, waiting patiently, probably half drunk from all the wine he'd put away while waiting for her. She wondered if he was having a good birthday.

Then she decided that it wasn't her problem.

"It's slowing down," Al, the manager of the restaurant, told her as she started to punch the time clock for her break. "You've been here all day. You can go on now."

She caught her breath. "Really?"

"Yeah, sure. Go on home."

She only stared at him for a moment, wanting desperately to kiss him, but she was too tired. Finally, she offered him a mild salute and started back to the locker room.

Slowly, she changed back into her Bill Blass, a dress her aching body didn't want to wear. She'd kill for her jeans and tennis shoes, she thought. And a big sweatshirt that had some ridiculous phrase on it. Idly, she realized she'd never owned a sweatshirt like that. She would have to buy one.

She slipped into her high heels, though her feet objected vehemently. Then, barely able to walk, she grabbed her briefcase and went back into the dining room.

Adam looked up, surprised, when she reached his table. "You changed."

"Yeah," she said. "Let's get out of here."

"You got fired?"

Corey smiled. "Hey, I'm a good waitress. Why would anybody fire me?"

"Well, I just thought—"

"I got off early for working so hard. Do you want to eat or not?"

"Well, sure, but—"

"Then take me some place decent," she said. "I want prime rib and cheesecake and a baked potato stuffed with butter and sour cream . . ."

"Can't you settle for something here?"

She gave him a disgusted look. "If you're worried about the price, we can go dutch. I'm about to come into a lot of money."

Adam pulled back his chair and got up with a grin. "I think I can handle it. Let's go."

They were halfway down the block before he noticed she was limping. "Are you okay?"

"Fine," she said. "But I wouldn't have suggested another place if I'd known you were going to make me hoof it."

They neared the Franklin Tower, and Adam slowed his step. "Look, we could go up to the penthouse, order something delivered, whatever you want, and talk in peace and quiet. Meanwhile, you could put your feet up and relax."

Corey's slow smile disarmed him completely. "You're a prince, Adam Franklin. A real prince."

She took off her shoes when they were just inside the door, hooked them under her fingers, and padded barefoot across the lobby to the private penthouse elevator.

The doors closed, and as the car rose, she gave him a dry look. "I'm no fool, you know. You want my necklace. That's the only reason you're being so nice to me. Just a few days ago I wasn't good enough to work on your staff. And you would have died before loaning me two hundred dollars. But for some reason, you really want my necklace. You'd better be careful, or I might have to drive the price up."

Adam grinned. "Don't overestimate my interest. I happen to be a bleeding heart, and I have yet to turn away a hungry, exhausted woman who needs help."

"You know a lot of hungry, exhausted women, do you?"

"Maybe not as many as I'd like to."

"Maybe you're looking in all the wrong places."

"Maybe I'm not looking at all." He glanced at the ring she still wore on her left hand. "You're still engaged, aren't you?"

The doors opened, but Adam made no move to get off. Corey stood leaning back against the wall in her bare feet, looking into the luxurious penthouse beckoning her. "I thought I was, but frankly, I'm not so sure, anymore. A lot changes when you go from power to poverty.

It's not all bad, though. I think it gives you a lot more clarity. There's something to be said for seeing things clearly."

Adam touched her elbow and drew her off the elevator and into the penthouse. "Have a seat," he said. "I'll call for dinner."

She dropped into a soft, overstuffed recliner, one whose primary purpose was comfort rather than decoration. It wasn't something she would have chosen for her own home, for it wasn't chic or contemporary or even particularly pretty. But tonight it seemed like wrapped heaven. When Adam came back, she had propped her feet and closed her eyes. "This is wonderful," she said. "You know, I think the worst part of this whole ordeal is that I miss my home so much. My plush carpet in my bedroom, my comforter, my satin sheets. I miss my long, lingering baths, and the food Rachel made. I miss being rich."

Adam took off his coat and tossed it over a couch. "Oh, I don't know. Sometimes I wonder if it's all it's cracked up to be."

"It is," Corey said. "Trust me, it is."

"Then you'll just have to get rich again," he said. "Something tells me you've got it in you."

"Oh, I've got it in me, all right," she said. "I'll be rich again, and when I do it my way, no one can ever take it from me again."

Adam poured her a drink and peered at her from the wet bar. She looked so relaxed, so peaceful, so beautiful, but he told himself that it was all the wine he'd drunk tonight. "You remind me of someone I used to know," he said.

Her eyes opened—blue eyes that never faded with fatigue the way most people's did—and she looked at him. "Oh, really? Who?"

"Myself," he said. "You remind me of myself about twenty years ago."

"Well, you didn't turn out so bad," she said. "I was just telling Eric the other day, 'That which does not kill us makes us stronger.' He didn't hear it, though. He was too surprised that I could quote Nietzsche."

Adam grinned. "Nietzsche said that? I thought it was Conan the Barbarian."

Corey laughed. "Yeah. Him, too."

The laughter faded, and Adam's eyes sobered a degree. "So will you take my offer for the necklace?"

Corey closed her eyes again. "Let's see. What was it again? Twelve thousand?"

Adam chuckled. "It was eight."

"No, I think you're wrong," she said. "I distinctly remember—"

"You're right," Adam cut in. "It was six."

Corey's eyes opened, and he saw the amusement glistening there. "Adam, come on. What's a measly twelve thousand dollars to you? You tip more than that in a month."

"Corey, the day I lose sight of the value of money is the day I don't deserve to be rich. I didn't get where I am by throwing it away. I'll give you nine and not a penny more."

She brought her hands to her temples and began to massage. "Catch a girl who's just come off of a grueling double shift, a girl who didn't sleep more than three hours the night before—"

"You shouldn't have played so late."

"I wasn't playing. I was taking care of business. Looking out for me."

"Hmmm. That sounds intriguing. Are you going to tell me more?"

"No, it's none of your business. Now, about the necklace. I'll take ten thousand, but only because you've worn me down, and I honestly don't think I can take many more days like this one. And there are so many things I need. So many things I want. I don't want to wait for them."

He sat down on the arm of the sofa across from her and pulled his cigarette pack out of his shirt pocket. "Like what?"

"Like a place of my own. A room where I don't owe any explanations. A little integrity."

He watched her for a long moment, and she waited for him to tell her how stupid that particular wish was, how shallow, how insignificant.

"Lady, you've got more integrity than anybody I know."

A slow smile played across her pale face, and he thought it had to be the most beautiful smile he'd ever seen. Even prettier than—

The bell rang, and he reached for the phone to make sure it was the delivery of the dinner he had ordered.

But Corey leaned forward and made him look at her again.

"Thank you for that, Adam," she said. "I really needed to hear it."

He winked at her and grabbed the phone, punched the intercom code, and instructed the caterer to bring in their meal.

Corey fell asleep before she got to the cheesecake. He had gotten a phone call that he'd had to take, was in his study for ten minutes, and when he came back, she was out cold.

It occurred to him to wake her, but then he realized that that asshole she lived with didn't deserve to have her come home to him. She could stay here, he thought. If she had to work tomorrow, and he felt sure she did, she could go from here. And she would have the rest she obviously needed so badly.

He went to his linen closet and dug through the sheets his maid kept there for the satin ones that he preferred not to use. Then going to his bedroom, he stripped the percale sheets off his bed and replaced them with the shiny almond-colored ones. It had been a long time since he'd changed his own sheets. Not since he was broke and unemployed, a wandering entrepreneur with empty pockets and too many dreams.

He finished the task that he realized he hadn't missed in all these years, then replaced the comforter.

Quietly, he went back into the living room and bent down over her.

She looked so innocent, sleeping there with her blistered bare feet propped on the ottoman, and her hair splayed and tangled across the back of the chair. He had seen her sleeping once before, but she'd been only thirteen then, curled up on the backseat of her mother's car, barefoot and tousled after a day of riding horses in the country. They had dropped by his place for only a moment, not nearly long enough. It had never occurred to him then that the sleeping girl would grow into a woman whose beauty would outshine even her mother's. It was that familiar beauty that made her appear more fragile, filling him with the fierce need to protect her.

Just as he felt the protectiveness, an even more powerful anger toward the son-of-a-bitch who'd thrown her out of his house burst through him. He'd hated Dobias for years. Now he was ready to see him pay.

He hoped Holifield came back to him with something soon.

Gently, he slipped his arms under Corey and lifted her. She stirred to life and slipped her arms around his neck. "I fell asleep," she whispered. "Need to go home."

Adam didn't answer. He took her into his room, laid her down on the satin sheets, and watched her curl into them and fall back to sleep. A gentle sigh fell from her lips as he covered her.

He backed away and realized that his hands were shaking. This couldn't happen, he thought. He couldn't be attracted to her. Not a Dobias. Not again.

But life didn't always follow logic, he reminded himself. And neither did emotions.

He turned the lamp off and left the room, and told himself that tomorrow, after he'd paid for the necklace and had it back in his possession, he'd get control over these feelings again. Some things just weren't meant to be.

Having Corey Dobias for his lover was one of those things.

chapter
17

THE CLOCK'S BLARING ALARM WOKE COREY WITH
a start, and she looked around her, disoriented at the
bedroom she had never seen before, the luxury she'd
thought she would never know again, and the feeling
of complete rest that she hadn't known since she'd left
her father's home.

She saw a shirt tossed over the chair next to the
bed—the shirt Adam had been wearing last night—
and suddenly it all came back to her. She was still in
Adam's penthouse, lying in his bed, on his satin sheets,
listening to his alarm.

Slamming her hand down on the clock to turn it off,
she sat up, shoving her hair back from her face. She
couldn't remember anything past eating the best meal
she'd ever eaten, getting more relaxed than she'd ever
felt.

Had they gone to bed? Had something happened that
she'd like to remember someday? A slow, regretful smile
dawned across her lips, but quickly faded the second it
occurred to her that she was still fully dressed in that
damned Bill Blass dress she'd worn here last night.
Pulling out of bed, she looked grudgingly at her reflection
in the mirror, her rumpled silk making her wince with
disgust. For a woman who couldn't afford a roof over
her head, she sure managed to sleep a lot of nights in
designer originals.

A note on Adam's dresser caught her eye, and frowning, she picked it up.

Corey,

Didn't know if you had to work this morning, so I set the clock just in case. Check's on the dresser. Leave necklace there, too.

Give me a call when you're ready to invest, and we'll see what we can do.

Adam.

She looked at the check lying on the dresser, picked it up, and saw that it was made out to Corey Dobias for ten thousand dollars. Her heart sank, and she wondered if the disappointment came from giving up the necklace or from the fact that he hadn't said anything more personal in the note. So he'd let her sleep in his bed. He probably would have done that for anyone. It was no big deal.

Once again, she regarded her image and frowned at the tangles in her hair and the pale cast to her complexion. She was lucky that Adam hadn't been here to see her like this. Not that he would have noticed her appearance, anyway. Adam seemed to have eyes only for her necklace.

Realizing she had no choices left, she went out to the living room and found her briefcase, dug through it for the necklace wrapped in its velvet pouch. She took it out and held it in her hand one last time, watching the light shimmer off the brilliant gems. Her mother had left it to her for a reason, not so she could sell it for a third of its value.

Tears crowded her eyes as she slipped it back into its pouch, went back to the bedroom, and laid it on his dresser next to a pair of onyx cuff links and a scattering of change. The necklace was his now, she thought. Bought and paid for.

Feeling as if she'd just sold a vital piece of herself, she went into his bathroom. He had laid out a new toothbrush for her, a woman's hairbrush, and a bottle of pink bubble bath. She smiled and wondered if he had female company often. Of course he did, she told herself. A man like Adam Franklin probably had a different lover for every night of the week.

Why, then, had he tucked her into his bed like a child and done nothing but allow her to sleep?

Perplexed and a little dejected, she brushed her hair, gargled with his mouthwash, then left the apartment to go home. She still had a little time before she had to be at work. Time enough for a shower, she hoped, and a change of clothes. Time enough to have it out with Eric, if that became necessary. After all, she'd stayed out all night. He would be angry, she was certain, and she'd have some explaining to do. But she'd get through it. The sooner she got it behind her, the better.

It was the first decent night's sleep Eric had had since the ordeal at the Dobias mansion. Corey hadn't come home last night, and he had convinced himself she was at her father's. By today, she'd be back in his good graces, and Eric's future would be back on track.

The door opened, and he sat up in bed. Corey came into the room, dropped her silly little briefcase on the floor, and began stepping out of the crumpled dress that, at this point, looked like a discard on the racks of Goodwill.

"Have you been at your father's?"

"My *father's*?" The very idea of such an assumption made her angry, and she shook her head and tossed her dress over a chair. "You're incredible, Eric. You don't ever give up."

"Then where the hell were you? You were out all night."

"No kidding." She went into the bathroom and closed

the door behind her. The shower came on, ending the short-lived conversation. Her abruptness incensed him, and slinging the sheets back, he got out of bed and went to the bathroom door. "Corey, open this door!"

When she didn't answer, he opened it himself. She flung around, naked from her waist up, and shot him a fiery look. "Can't you give me a little privacy?"

"No," he yelled. "I can't. It's *my* apartment, Corey. I don't like having doors slammed in my face in my own fucking apartment!"

Muttering under her breath, she stepped out of her panties. Without another look at him, she got into the shower and yanked the curtain shut.

Eric clenched his hands into fists. "You come flouncing in here at nine A.M. after being out all night, and you don't think you owe me an explanation?"

"Not when you assumed I was at my father's," she said, pouring a handful of shampoo into her hair. "Not when you thought I'd buckled like you hoped and gone back with my hands out. No, Eric. If that's what you thought, I don't owe you anything."

"All right, I'm sorry." He threw up his hands, then clenched another fist and punched at some invisible force in the air. "Excuse the hell out of me for trying to convince myself you weren't dead on the street somewhere. Excuse me for hoping for the best."

When she, once again, didn't answer, he flung back the curtain, letting the hot steam roll out of the shower. She jumped slightly, but casting him a searing look, began to rinse the shampoo from her hair. His groin reacted at the way her breasts perked up beneath the spray, and the way the drops of water rolled down the flat plane of her stomach. "You gonna tell me where you were or not?"

"I had a business meeting!" she shouted. "I worked

a double shift yesterday, and then I had a business meeting. I fell asleep!"

The idea that she had spent the night in the company of some unnamed "business associate" fed his tumescence. "You mind telling me if this business associate was a man or a woman?"

"A man," she taunted, meeting his eyes directly. "I slept, Eric. That's all. I fell asleep and he let me stay there."

"Where?" His voice cracked with anger, and he stepped back and watched her get out of the shower, dripping on the threadbare rug beneath her feet.

"Don't worry about it, Eric! I came home with a fat, juicy check this morning. Just the head start I needed to get my own business affairs started."

"He *paid* you?"

Corey faced him, dripping wet and completely naked, and suddenly her hand swung out and landed so hard on his face that it knocked him off balance.

"What the fuck—?"

"It was a business deal, you bastard! A *business* deal! My body isn't up for sale! Ten thousand dollars wouldn't be enough!"

Eric lowered his hand from his face, revealing the handprint she'd left there. "Ten thousand? You made ten thousand dollars last night?"

She grabbed her towel and began chafing it over her skin. "Yes, Eric. I made ten thousand dollars. That makes everything all right with you, doesn't it? As long as there was money involved." She started back into the bedroom.

"What do you want me to say? What?"

"I don't know, Eric! You're an intelligent man! Think of something!"

He grabbed her arm before she'd gotten too far out

of reach and slung her down on the bed. Before she could react, he was above her, pinning her down with his body.

His kiss was punishing, greedy, and the hunger in his hard groin strove against her. He'd always known how to incite lust, how to fill it. He just hadn't known how to go beyond that.

Lady, you've got more integrity than anybody I know . . .

The memory of Adam's words from the previous night cooled whatever lust she still felt for Eric, and she turned her head away from the kiss.

"Come on, baby," Eric said against her ear as he reached to lower the briefs he'd slept in. "You know I can't stay mad at you when you're standing there soaking wet and looking like a teenage boy's dream."

"I don't want a teenage boy," she said, trying to push him off of her. "I want a man."

"You got it." His breath came shallower, and she struggled to pull her legs together.

"No, Eric. I'm not in the mood. Stop it."

The hazed ardor in his eyes turned to hooded anger, and he snapped her face back to his. "You're jerking around with me, Corey. I'm not going to let you do that."

"I'm not a toy that turns on and off when you say, Eric. Now get off of me."

His hand moved down between her legs, and he forced his hips between them. "You're living in my house, Corey. You're eating my food. You're sleeping in my bed. I have to get something out of this."

"You bastard!" Her fingernails clawed at his back, but suddenly he thrust himself into her.

He grabbed her flailing arms and held them over her head, but she continued writhing and kicking. "I hate you, you son of a bitch!"

The fight only heightened his pleasure, however. He didn't let her go until he was finished, and then he rolled off her and left her lying on the bed.

He expected another furious string of expletives, of well-deserved names, of fists flying and fingernails scratching. He figured he probably deserved at least some of it.

But Corey didn't do any of those things. Instead, she slowly got up and showered again, washing his scent from her skin. He dressed while she pulled on her own clothes, biding his time and bracing himself for the explosive reaction that would make him regret what he had just done. But she had nothing to say. Without a word, she packed all of her things in her backpack and briefcase, and not looking at him once, left the apartment.

Eric didn't worry. She would be back tonight when she got tired and remembered that she didn't have a place to stay. She'd be back, because when it came right down to it, she'd probably enjoyed it after all. He hadn't heard any complaints yet in all the time they'd known each other.

Ten thousand dollars. He wondered what she planned to do with it. He had a few ideas, but he supposed he'd keep his mouth shut for a few days, until she got over being mad at him. He wondered how she'd made it and if there was more where that came from.

He grabbed his camera bag, checked the address where his assignment for today was, and reached for his car keys. The key he'd given her to his apartment lay on the dresser where she had left it. He picked it up and looked at the door.

For the first time since she'd left, he wondered if he'd made a mistake.

*　　　　*　　　　*

Corey held herself together long enough to ride the T back to Boston, open a bank account in the name of Corey Dobias at the same bank where Adam's account was—so they wouldn't have to hold it until it cleared, and make it to the Public Garden, not far from her restaurant. It was only then that she allowed the tears to come.

She wouldn't go back to Eric now or ever, for if there had been any doubt before about his feelings for her, there was none now. She dropped her face into her hands and let the tears glide between her fingers.

It wasn't the way he'd made love to her that had made her feel so defiled, she decided after a moment. It was the way he'd used her. First for her promise for his future. Then for her potential wealth. And when all that was lost, for sex. She was an instrument for him, and he would use her in whatever way he needed her.

But no more.

She wiped her tears and shoved her hair back from her face as the unseasonably warm wind frittered through the bare branches, melting the snow and ice in a brief preview of the spring to come. She told herself that she'd have to find a place to live today. She had the money now, and she had the will. All she had to do was find the place.

She checked the watch she had stuffed into her back-pack at her father's the other night. It was ten-thirty, and she didn't have to be at work until eleven, so she leaned back and tried to get hold of herself. There were people in the world a lot more forsaken than she. People a lot lonelier. People a lot more confused.

Her eyes strayed from one person to another in the garden, children laughing and running around the Ether Memorial, where the Good Samaritan helped his enemy. On the other side of the statue sat an old man, slumped on a bench all alone, feeding the pigeons and looking as melancholy and abandoned as she. She watched him lean down and offer a crust of bread to the pigeon. It fed from his fingertips, then lifted up and fluttered away. The old man's eyes followed it until it disappeared.

For a moment, he reminded her of her father, and her heart ached, as if he were the one cast out into the street, homeless and hungry, without a friend in the world.

But her father would never be caught wearing baggy pants with a hole in the knee, and he would never have shared his lunch with birds. He wouldn't look that vulnerable, as if he, too, had lost his family and his home and all the security he'd ever known in his life. People like her father created victims but never became one themselves.

She grabbed her backpack and her briefcase and stood up, feeling the sudden surge of despair that her father would forever after be the man who threw her out without mercy. Gone were the memories of him doting over her, spoiling her, loving her. The funny thing was, he still didn't realize what he had lost. Giselle would use him, and Rena would cower from him. But no one would really love him.

As it occurred to her that she still cared for him, no matter how much she wanted to hate him, she cursed herself and thought that maybe he was right about her not being tough enough. She supposed she was on her way to being just that.

One day maybe she'd learn to hate, as he did. Maybe that one emotion would finally make her into the woman her father wanted her to be.

chapter
18

THE YANKEE DOODLE CLUB WAS ALWAYS ABUZZ with activity in the early afternoons, when business lunches moved from restaurant to bar and dragged on sometimes for hours. Many of the faces here were familiar to Rena. Many of them she knew by name. Most of them knew her.

She wove through the crowd, waving at an occasional acquaintance, speaking to an associate, and made her way to the bar. She hadn't eaten all day, but somehow her stomach seemed too unsettled for food. What she really needed, what she had come for, was a good stiff Scotch. Then she could cope with the pressures piling up on her.

She ordered and closed her eyes as she took a long sip, and remembered the deal she had closed today. It was a stupid deal, and she hadn't given it enough thought. She had acted impulsively to buy a piece of property that probably wasn't worth what she'd paid, and she hadn't even gotten proper estimates from contractors on what it might cost to renovate it. She knew all that, and yet she'd gone ahead anyway. Why? She asked herself now. Because doing something wrong was better than doing nothing at all. At least it was moving forward. She just wished she'd had someone to talk to about it. Her father had turned his head, Giselle had turned her back, and John—well, John just hadn't been there when the decision had been made.

She finished off the glass and felt the gentle buzz of

relaxation taking over, and gestured for Archie to get her a refill.

Rena studied the older man who'd been pouring her drinks for the past year now. Idly, she realized that he had probably given her more advice than anyone else in her life ever had.

"Archie, do you know anything about real estate development?"

Archie laughed and reached for a glass to fill an order. "I know that the asshole who bought my building wants to tear it down and put up a skyscraper. I know that I'm going to fight like hell to keep him from it."

"But do you know anything about investing in it? Do you know a good deal when you see one? A good opportunity?"

Archie shrugged. "I know that if you got the money and you put it in property, you're bound to come out with somethin'."

Rena took another drink and grinned. "That's it? That's all the wisdom you can offer me?"

Archie laughed. "Whadda you want, babe? I'm an ex-piano player and a bartender. What do I know about real stakes?"

Rena smiled and thought that she wouldn't mind such a simple occupation, where so much money didn't ride on your whim, where all you had to do was pour the drinks. For the first time, she realized that Corey might not have it so bad, after all. She was out of the rat race. Rena had just left the starting gate, as her father had so delicately put it, and she didn't have a clue where she was heading.

Archie went to fill another order and offer some more advice, and she swiveled on her bar stool and scanned the crowd.

And she saw the man again. He was sitting in the same

booth, with that same foot propped nonchalantly on the seat. And he was smiling at her.

Lifting her hand in a half wave, she turned away and bottomed her glass, and tried to remember if it was her first or second. She decided that it had been her first, so she could afford to have another. She held out the glass, motioning for Archie to fill it again.

But someone reached around her and took the glass.

She glanced over her shoulder and saw the man standing behind her. His eyes were even bluer than she'd remembered, and his smile was more mesmerizing. "Mind if I buy this one?" he asked.

Rena gave him a self-conscious smile. "Well, if it isn't the Pinball Wizard himself."

Grinning, he slipped onto the stool next to her and extended a hand. "I have a name, you know. Joe Baker."

She shook his hand, not missing the way he held hers a moment longer than necessary. "My name is Rena."

"I know," he said. "I asked Archie after you left the other day."

"Did you?" A warm heat colored her cheeks, and when Archie handed her the refill, she all but grabbed it.

She looked down at her Scotch, took a sustaining sip, and told herself that the man's interest had piqued only after he'd learned she was a Dobias. It had happened before, and she wasn't such a fool that she hadn't learned to watch for it.

"Rena Keller," he went on, taking his own drink and dropping the cash onto the bar. "I knew some Kellers in Missouri. Are you by any chance related to Michael Keller in St. Louis?"

A gentle frown tugged at Rena's brows as it occurred to her that he hadn't made the Dobias connection at all. Could it be that he really found her attractive, without her name or her financial might? "No," she said. "My husband's family is all from New York."

"Husband, huh?" he asked, apparently surprised. "Damn. I should have known."

The disappointment in his face made her smile, and she felt her barriers dropping by degrees. He really didn't know who she was. She had caught his attention on her own.

"Then . . . I don't suppose you'd want to go for a bite, would you? I haven't eaten, yet. There's this great little deli right around the corner."

She hesitated, but the smile in his twinkling eyes coaxed her. "I'm a terrific conversationalist, you know. You really don't know what you're missing."

She glanced at her glass, saw that it was almost empty, then looked at Archie, as if he could tell her what she should do. Archie gave her a grin and a wink. Finally, she brought her gaze back to Joe's. "Do you promise not to beat up any pinball machines?"

He held up his hand in a mock vow. "Swear to God."

She cocked her head and considered him for a moment longer. It was just lunch, after all, and she could use someone to talk to. If he had designs on her, well, that wouldn't hurt her ego any. Even she could admit that.

"All right," she said, slipping off her stool. "Just a bite. But then I have to get back to the office."

Joe flashed his charmed smile and took her arm as she started toward the door.

Rena hadn't expected to run into Giselle at the deli around the corner, for she'd foolishly believed that her sister only dined in black-tie restaurants where the maitre d' drooled over the name Dobias. She'd seen the surprise on Giselle's face when she saw Rena laughing at some remark Joe had made. She wasn't sure if it was the pleasant, but platonic, lunch they'd shared, the guilt at having enjoyed it so, the extra drinks she'd had with him, or his request to see her again that had prompted her to go to see Giselle when she got back to her office. All she knew was that she felt it deserved explanation, for she didn't want her sister to think she was cheating on her husband.

But the moment she stepped into Giselle's office she realized that she could no more confide in her sister than she could compete with her.

"I heard about the deal you closed this morning," Giselle said as if the incident with Joe had never occurred. From the way she pored distractedly over some blueprints on her desk as she spoke, Rena wondered if she even remembered it. "What on earth could you have been thinking?"

Rena dropped into the chair across from her. "What do you mean?"

Giselle looked up, and Rena wondered how her sister managed to work such long, hard hours and still look as if she'd just stepped out of Henrique's chair. "Well, let's face it, darling. It isn't exactly the deal of the century. It could turn into a major embarrassment."

Rena's spine went rigid. "Your opinion doesn't have a lot of credibility, considering the circumstances."

Giselle cracked a wicked half grin. "Still, you really do have to start thinking. You can't go off on a whim and make investments like that. You weren't given that big a budget."

"I'll manage," Rena said, not sure she would. "Don't worry about me. Besides, I didn't come in here to talk about that."

Giselle went back to her blueprint. "What then? That guy you were tucked away with at lunch?"

Rena let out a ragged breath and glanced at the wet bar. She wondered what Giselle kept stocked there. Idly, she got up and went to it. "We weren't tucked away. If we had been, you wouldn't have seen us, would you?"

Giselle looked up and grinned across the room. "Nice looking, if you like blonds with beards. Is he the one who suckered you into that ridiculous deal?"

Rena grabbed the first bottle she came to and poured herself a drink. "No. He had nothing to do with it. I don't even know what business he's in. I just met him."

Giselle sat back in the chair and watched Rena close her eyes as she brought the glass to her lips. "Well, you can bet that he knows what business *you're* in. And exactly how much that could be worth."

Rena swung around. "He doesn't even know I'm a Dobias. He bought me a drink and invited me to lunch. No ulterior motives. No aces up his sleeve."

"Oh, my God. You'll believe anything, won't you?"

Rena's face mottled, and she told herself just to walk out, that this wasn't worth a fight. But she'd had enough to drink to feel a courage she rarely felt around her sister. "Would it be so preposterous that such an attraction could exist?"

"Attraction?" Giselle asked with a deprecating grin. "Or lust? Men lust for a lot of things, you know. Money, power, prestige. They're not so different from us."

Rena finished off the glass, and felt more courage pumping through her. "What about passion, Giselle? Couldn't that be all? Why does it all have to go back to money?"

"Passion," Giselle repeated, as if it were a fairy-tale word that someone had invented to make people look stupid. "God, you are naive, aren't you?" She sighed and glanced back down at her desk.

"Oh, Giselle, why does everything have to be such a big deal? What would be so bad about a man being attracted to me for *me*, and my enjoying it for a few minutes?"

She started back to her sister's desk, but stumbled and caught herself on the chair.

Giselle shook her head. "Rena, how much have you had to drink today?"

Rena glanced back at her empty glass and shook her head, and suddenly she felt like crying. It was stupid, she thought, when a few moments ago she'd been exhilarated. "Not enough," she said. "Not nearly enough."

Giselle came around her desk, took her shoulders and forced her to look at her. "Do yourself a favor, Rena, and stay away from the bottle for a while. You can do yourself a lot more good thinking about business instead of fantasizing about some gold digger who's pretending he doesn't know who you are."

"Oh, right. If someone comes on to me, it's a con, but if they come on to you, it's only natural, right?"

"I'm not married. You are."

"Marriage never stopped you," Rena said, meeting Giselle's eyes directly.

She didn't miss the alarm that flashed across Giselle's brown eyes. "What are you talking about?"

Rena smiled then, suddenly filled with a fleeting sense of power. So fleeting, that she knew she'd better use it before it was gone. "I'm talking about last year, when you had that little fling going with Louis Marks, three months after his wedding. And the time you disappeared with J. R. Roje at the corporate Christmas party, when his wife was right there. Don't play sanctimonious with me, Giselle. I'm not stupid."

The alarm she thought she had seen on Giselle's face seemed to fade, and a half smile touched her sister's lips. "It's only the wives who are stupid, Rena. The ones who sit by, faithful and patient, while their husbands sample what can never be theirs."

Rena uttered a mirthless laugh and shook her head

at the futility of reaching her sister. "I'm glad we had this talk," she said. "It reminded me how different we are. And how glad I am of that."

"Anytime, sis," Giselle returned. "Remember me when you take that roll in the hay."

"I'll remember you when I'm in bed with my own husband," Rena said. "I'll remember what my alternative is. I could be as bitter and self-serving, and as utterly alone, as you."

Giselle stood staring at the door for a few minutes after her sister had walked out, then picked up the telephone and dialed John's office. She needed some legal advice, she told him. He said he'd be up in fifteen minutes.

While she waited, she pulled the pins out of her hair and let it fall around her shoulders, the way he'd always liked it. Slipping the scarf off her collar, she opened the top few buttons of her blouse, and dotted fresh Obsession on the pulse point of her neck.

Not once questioning her motivation, or her sudden desire for the man she'd been rejecting since his revived interest in her lately, she decided that she would show her sister just how dangerous it was to be smug. Maybe the jolt was what she needed to knock Rena out of the game.

If there was one quality that Giselle found most valuable in a man, it was stupidity. Not the run-of-the-mill kind of stupidity, but the kind where he thought he was playing both sides against the middle and actually believed that no one would realize it.

She smiled and stretched like a cat, and watched John pull his hands behind his head and stare up at the ceiling, his eyes full of ideas and greed and optimism about what had just occurred right here on the sofa in her office. He actually thought he was laying the foundation for the possibility that Rena would lose the competition. He thought Giselle would fall so head over heels for him that she would offer him part of her half if she won. If she lost, which wasn't even a logical possibility, he'd still have Rena.

What he hadn't anticipated, however, was that she was smarter than he was.

"You've been practicing, darling," he muttered, turning on his side to look at her. "You've had some fine teachers since we were last together."

"So have you," Giselle murmured. "Obviously, my sister wasn't one of them."

John reached for his drink and started to laugh. "You're as wicked as always, Giselle."

She stood up and stretched again, knowing that the fine-tuned shape of her body would arouse him all over again. She didn't care if it did. She'd had enough for today. Now there was work to be done.

"Poor Rena," she said, reaching for the hairbrush she kept in her top drawer and gliding it through her hair. "So misguided. So floundering. Did she tell you about that deal she made today?"

"Come on, Giselle. You aren't jealous, are you?"

"Jealous?" She snapped her head around and gave him an incredulous look. "You've got to be kidding. She bought a property that no one else would have touched in a million years. Even if she built an architectural marvel there, it'll never work. And the time it took her to make the decision. What did she do? Close her eyes over the map and buy the first property her finger touched?"

"Well, no one ever accused her of having a business head," he said, getting off the couch. "But that Dobias instinct has to be worth something."

Giselle made a disgusted sound. John stood up and nuzzled her neck, but she moved past him. "Speaking of the Dobias instinct, I think it's run amuck. I found out about the deal that Corey was working on before she left. You can't imagine. It's in the Combat Zone, of all places. What was she going to do? Build luxury condominiums in the seediest area of town?"

"Who knows what's in her head?" John said, watching Giselle dress. "Maybe she had some philanthropic idea about housing wayward prostitutes and drug dealers."

"Well, the point is moot now, I guess."

John laughed. "No, I don't think Corey will be investing in anything for quite a while. Here, I'll get that."

He moved her hands from the buttons on her blouse, but instead of closing it, he began opening it again.

Giselle grinned as he slipped it off. "Don't you ever get enough?" she whispered.

"Not ever," he said, pulling her against him. "And neither do you. That's why we're so good together."

His kiss sent a fresh hunger surging through her, and for a while, she put her sisters and their business and the money at stake out of her mind. And she concentrated on filling her own needs.

chapter

19

THE LUNCH CROWD WAS THINNING OUT, SO COR-
ey slipped into the back room and grabbed the paper
she had been trying to scour for places to live. It would
have to be cheap enough that she could afford it on a
waitress's pay, since she didn't want to touch the ten
thousand dollars she needed to invest. The problem was,
there weren't many places she could afford that weren't
infested with rats, thieves, and crack-heads.

She dropped a quarter into the pay phone and dialed
one of the numbers she had circled. The gruff man's
voice on the other end of the phone took her slightly
aback.

"Uh, hello. I'm calling about the ad I saw for an apartment?"

"Yeah. I rented it out this morning."

"Damn." Corey balanced the phone between her jaw
and shoulder and crossed out the ad. "Don't you have
any more apartments for the same price? It sounded like
what I'm looking for . . ."

"If I had more, don't ya think I'd tell ya?" the man
barked out.

"Well, yes. I guess so. Thank you."

She hung up the phone with a grand sigh, and saw
Dee-dee watching her with a sympathetic smile. "No
luck, huh?"

"No luck," Corey said. "I can't believe this. I knew it
was miserable being broke, but I didn't realize it was
dangerous, too. To get a place I could afford, I'd have

to pack a weapon all the time and share a room with rodents."

Dee-dee chuckled. "So this surprises you? Where'd you live before?"

"With my fiancé," she said evasively, looking back at the paper. "My *ex*-fiancé."

"Boy, you are down on your luck, aren't you? You sound as bad as me."

"What do you mean?"

Dee-dee sighed, sat down, and slipping off her shoe, she began to massage her foot. "I came to Boston with *my* boyfriend for a vacation, but he dumped me and sorta left me here."

"Sort of left you? How do you get sort of left?"

"Well, I got real left. Anyway, I figured I'd make the best of it, and I got this job and just stayed. But Lordy, it was scary there for a while. So see? We have a lot in common."

"Yeah," Corey whispered, glad she'd never told her exactly how different their backgrounds really were. "Well, I guess I'll have to find a hotel tonight . . ."

Dee-dee stood up and started unbuttoning her uniform. "You know, honey, I hadn't brought this up before because I didn't think you'd be interested. But if you're really looking, there's an apartment in my building that's vacant. It's no luxury condo. Matter of fact, it's a real dump, but it's safer than some other places."

Corey's eyes filled with potent hope. "Really? If you live there it couldn't be that bad."

"Trust me. The paint is peeling in places, the floors are warped. Sometimes you can hear mice in the walls, which really gives me the creeps. In the winter the heating system doesn't work too good. And the vacant apartment is just a studio. You know, one room with a kitchenette."

"I'll take it!" Corey said. "It's perfect."

Dee-dee shook her head. "I really suggest you look at it first, Corey. It might not be for you."

Corey smiled and sat down on the bench as Dee-dee stepped into a threadbare pair of jeans and a knitted cardigan with a hole in the elbow. "Listen, I'm taking lunch in an hour. I could come over and look at it then."

"Fine," Dee-dee said. "I'll tell the manager as soon as I get home. Her name's Agatha. She used to skate in the Roller Derby, till she hurt her knee. She's built like a Viking but has the heart of a pussy cat. She keeps the crack-heads and dealers out. You'll hit it off just fine." She got her purse out of her locker and pulled the strap over her shoulder. "Besides, it'll be great having a friend living upstairs."

"Thanks, Dee-dee," Corey said. "You may have just saved my life."

An hour later, Corey discovered that the place in question was much, much worse than Dee-dee had told her. But it was also within her waitress budget, which made it marginally appealing. She could clean away the dirt, she told herself, and fumigate. Meanwhile, it had a stove and a bed and a bathroom—though she couldn't boil water, was afraid to sleep with mice scurrying about, and nearly gagged at the smell of the toilet. But if she took it now, she wouldn't have to go back to Eric's at all. And that had its own value.

Gritting her teeth, she paid Agatha, the Roller Derby Queen, her first and last month's rent, necessarily cutting into her ten thousand dollars to do so. But it couldn't be helped. As she was leaving the building to hurry back to work, Dee-dee stopped her in the hall.

"So when are you moving in, neighbor?"

"Already did," Corey said.

Dee-dee frowned and glanced up the broken, rotting stairs toward the apartment. "All you took in there was a backpack and a briefcase."

"That's all I have," Corey said cheerfully. "I like to travel light."

"You can say that again," she murmured as Corey dashed out of the building. "Stop by after work and I'll loan you some disinfectant and a set of sheets!"

"I will," Corey shouted, but she was already halfway down the block.

Corey arranged to take her first day off on the day Adam was to take her to an estate auction, at which he'd told her, in strictest confidence, that she would have the opportunity to buy a painting by the recently deceased artist Jobere, whose work had tripled in value since the publicity of his gruesome suicide. He let her in on the secret—known only in publishing circles—that a book about the painter's colorful life was in the works. When it was released, the value of the paintings would escalate. The owners of the estate had gone bankrupt, and the auction had been poorly publicized. There was not much of value being sold, he said. And the paintings, which had been tucked away in the attic, had been treated like outdated accessories rather than valued pieces of art. He didn't think that anyone was yet aware how valuable they could be.

She left the auction with two Joberes and no money, but consoled herself that it didn't matter. She had a place to live now, a job and a goal. That was more than a lot of people had.

"So, do you have buyers for me?" she asked Adam as he drove her back to her apartment.

"Buyers? Of course not. That's your job."

"Oh." She stared out the window for a moment, then

looked at him again. "That shouldn't be so hard. I know a lot of art buyers in town. The fact that they all turned their backs on me when I needed a job should help me go right for their jugular. I'll let them all sweat first, then milk them for everything they're worth. That is, if their fear of my father doesn't outshine their desire for the paintings."

"If they don't bite," Adam said, "maybe you should try a different avenue. Sometimes the people willing to pay the most for a painting are private individuals. Not museums and galleries."

"I'll keep that in mind. Thank you, Adam."

He glanced over at her, and she could have sworn that the smile in his eyes sparked to life each time their eyes met. And yet, he'd never made a move to be more than her mentor.

He turned onto her street, and she pointed to the building she lived in. "It's there. Park the car and come on in. Your hubcaps should be safe, but I'd lock the doors."

Adam smiled. "I wouldn't miss this for the world. Corey Dobias's first apartment."

"Don't expect much," she said. "The same decorator who did my jail cell had her hand in this. I call it modern decrepit."

Adam snickered as he took the paintings out of his backseat. "I can't wait."

They took the two flights of stairs carrying the bulky paintings, carefully stepping over the splintered and warped boards that threatened to cave in beneath their feet. When they reached her door, she dug through her briefcase for her key.

Adam's face, the moment she opened the door, went from curiosity to absolute amazement. He set the paintings down, leaning them against the wall, and stepped farther into the small room. "You weren't kidding, were you?"

She gave him a feeble smile. "Nope. I told you."

"What about furniture? You don't even have a place to sit."

"I have the bed," she told him sarcastically, lavishing a hand in that direction. "But look at the upside. There's nothing to pick up. It'll be a cinch to clean if I ever get the scum scraped off of the stove and the bathroom tile."

His bewildered expression teetered on the edge of amusement. "You know, I probably would have let you stay at my place until you could afford something a little . . ."

"Better than this?" she provided. "That would be like taking three steps backward. The last thing I needed was to trade in one keeper for another."

"Then your engagement is off?"

Corey laughed at the quick, astute question, and went to the small refrigerator. She got out a bottle of wine she had salvaged from one of her customers' tables. It had hardly been touched, so she'd slipped it in her locker and taken it home before it was poured out.

Reaching into the cupboard, she pulled out two plastic cups she'd picked up at the supermarket the day before. "What there was of it," she said. "Looking back, I don't know what got into me. I guess I never saw him clearly when things were going well."

Adam took the proffered glass of wine and leaned against the bar of the narrow kitchenette, staring at her with pensive eyes.

"I saw an old man the other day," she said, recorking the bottle and returning it to the refrigerator. "Sitting alone in the Public Garden, feeding the pigeons. For a minute, he looked just like my father, and even though it wasn't him, I felt this rush of sympathy, because I can't help believing that he's more lonely than I am right now."

"After all he's done to you?"

Her smile was weak and strained, and she walked across the room to the window that looked out onto another building with peeling paint and torn shingles. Lifting the dirty pane of glass, she sat down on the windowsill. A breeze stirred her hair. "He's still my father," she said. "Despite everything, I think I'd like to make peace with him somehow. But I guess that's impossible."

"Call me dense," he said, ambling across the room to join her at the window, "but I can't understand that. The man has ruined you. He's literally thrown you into poverty. He had you put in jail. He turned all your friends and business associates against you. Most people would vow revenge. What does he have to do to make you hate him?"

Corey looked up at Adam and took a sip of her wine. "I don't know. I asked myself the same thing."

Quiet settled between them, a thick, thoughtful quiet that filled the room with warmth. After a moment, he sat down on the windowsill beside her.

"I really appreciate the things you've done for me, Adam," she whispered without looking at him.

It occurred to him that her bravado had slipped a little, and now she was like a shy, vulnerable child, stripped of all the trappings that had carried her for so long. "I haven't done anything *for* you," he said. "I've just helped you do it for yourself." His voice was hoarse, but he didn't clear his throat.

"No," she said. "I mean . . . the kindness, when everyone else has been so cold. I had friends before, lots of them. They weren't all even rich friends." She stood up and set her glass on the windowsill. "I made some close friends in the Outward Bound program—you know, we climbed a mountain. Spent weeks together in the Adirondacks. But I guess those were like wartime friendships or something. You think you'll have a bond all your lives because of what you've been through, but then when you get back to the real world, well, nothing seems to stick."

"So you're not in touch with them anymore?"

She shook her head. "No, not really. And the other friends—the ones I grew up with, went to school with, told my secrets to—I don't know. Now that I'm in such bad shape, I honestly don't think I could count on them. They're fickle. They don't have a lot of tolerance for people whose lives aren't all worked out. They like things nice and neat."

"I think you're selling yourself short, Corey. Maybe you aren't giving them enough of a chance."

"Maybe not," she said. "I don't know. All I was getting at is that you've been there for me, and I'm not sure why. That night you bailed me out of jail, you mentioned that you considered it a favor for a friend. What friend, Adam?"

He looked down at his glass, and when he brought his eyes back to hers, they were troubled. "Just someone I knew a long time ago. Someone you remind me of."

She smiled, realizing she had gotten as much of an explanation as he was going to give. "Well, anyway, I appreciate all you've done. Whatever this mystery person's part was in all this, I'm grateful for it."

"It's been a pleasure. I just hope I haven't led you wrong."

"About the paintings?" She looked at the Joberes, and a flash of alarm shot through her. "I trusted you about them, Adam. You better not have led me wrong."

Following the new direction of her thoughts and

thankful she had abandoned the subject of his secret "friend," he grinned. "You know, you should have doubts. I talked you into letting go of that money entirely too easily."

"Well, what can I say? I figured you had more than one chance to ravage my body, and you declined. And your check didn't bounce. I've looked, Adam, but so far I can't find any deep-seated motive for your being nice to me. All I can deduce from that is that you're drawn to my magnetic personality."

"And don't forget the good looks."

"Yes, of course. That, too."

They looked at each other for a long moment with gentle smiles, and finally those smiles faded into serious contemplation.

Corey wet her lips, and her gaze dropped to his, soft and moist and set in a somber line. "I think I could really fall for you, Adam Franklin."

Adam stared at her for a moment, and finally, he drew in a deep breath, stood up, and finished the last of the wine in his glass. "I'd better be going."

Corey's heart plummeted. "Don't worry, Adam. I said I *could* fall for you. I won't, though."

He set his empty cup on the bar, studied it for a moment. "So you're going to start tomorrow trying to sell the paintings?"

She nodded mutely.

"I'll keep my ears open. If I hear of a potential buyer, I'll let you know."

"Thanks."

He was out of the apartment before the tears made it all the way to her eyes.

The quest for a buyer of her paintings proved more difficult than she'd imagined, for no one she'd contacted so far was willing to offer her much more than she'd paid for them. Kindly rejecting these offers, she spent most of her free time at the library, digging up names of people who'd made large art purchases lately, as well as those who had shown particular interest in Jobere. The search was long and hard, but she enlisted two librarians and an acquaintance at Sotheby's to help.

Meanwhile, she thought it wise not only to hold onto her job at the restaurant, but also to grab a double shift whenever she could get one. The extra money she was able to save couldn't hurt, she told herself.

She had seen Eric only once since she'd left him. He had found her at the restaurant a couple of days later, demanded to know where she'd been, and warned her that if she left him now she couldn't ever come back. She let him know that she could live with that ultimatum. Before he left, full of hot air and indignation, she gave him back his ring with a few suggestions of where he could hock it if the store wouldn't refund his money.

It was on one of a series of double-shift days, when her feet ached and her stomach growled, that she glanced toward the door and saw her niece, Emily, dressed in her navy-blue school uniform and a short red leather trench coat, watching her wait tables with a look of horror mingled with pity on her face. That look made Corey laugh, for she realized that was just the way she would have looked at someone in her family had they ever sunk so low. Biting her smile, she headed for her niece with her arms outstretched. "Emily!"

The girl fell into her embrace, clinging to her with all her strength.

"I've missed you," she blurted, "and we've all been forbidden to talk to you. I had to sneak away from school to come here. I heard Aunt Rena say you worked here. Is it awful, waitressing tables, I mean?"

Corey glanced over her shoulder to the dining room. "Not really, no. There's something about being ordered around, pinched, and insulted that builds character." She checked her watch, saw that it was almost her break time, and decided to take it now to spend some time with Emily. "Come on. I have an hour and a half off. I'll change and we'll go get a soda or something."

"Really? They let you leave whenever you want?"

Corey laughed. "Only when I have it coming to me." She pushed through the door to the locker room and started unbuttoning her uniform.

When she looked over her shoulder, she saw that Emily lingered at the door, assessing the floor with a worried look. "Are there rats here?" she asked. "Uncle John said Boston was infested with them, that they're in all the restaurants . . ."

Corey rolled her eyes. "I haven't seen any, Emmy." She stepped out of her dress and into her jeans, hoping the breach in fashion didn't further traumatize the girl. "Now, tell me about your skipping school. How did you get here?"

"The T," Emily said. "It was fun. Jeremy—you know, the gardener's son?—he told me how to use it. You could go practically anywhere on it."

"But you'll get caught, Emmy. You can't just leave school. Besides, a child your age shouldn't ride the T alone. It's dangerous."

"I'm not a child," Emily protested. "And as for school, I'm covered. I paid Jordan Hood to write me a dismissal slip. He works in the office during his study hall, and he has a crush on me."

Corey gave her niece a wicked grin. "Oh, Lord. You're a Dobias through and through. Already giving bribes."

She tucked her shirt into her jeans, then pulled on her tennis shoes. "So what do you think?" she asked, striking a pose. "The new improved me."

Emily obviously didn't approve. "I think you look a lot like you did when you came back from that mountain thing. Before Grandfather brought you to your senses and made you start dressing like a civilized human being again."

"Oh. So you don't think I look like a civilized human being?"

"I think you look cool," Emily said on the edge of a laugh.

Corey smiled and messed up the girl's carefully braided hair. "This may come as a surprise to you, kiddo, but a great segment of the population doesn't know the meaning of the words *haute couture*. Come on, let's get out of here."

Locking arms, they left the restaurant and walked a block, stopped in a deli, and bought sandwiches with Corey's tip money, then strolled to the Public Garden to eat.

Renewed winter nipped at the air, and new icicles formed on the naked branches of the trees. They found a bench near the pond, where ice skaters glided across the frozen surface, their cheeks red and chapped in the wind. Sitting down, they unwrapped their sandwiches. "So Dad has laid down the law about contacting me, huh?"

"Yeah. He's turning into a monster. He blows up at the slightest little thing. He goes around threatening people. Every time I speak to him he sends me away."

Corey stared ahead at a father skating with his toddler on his shoulders, screaming with glee for her daddy to go faster. "You're taking a big chance coming to see me."

"I know, but I missed you. They act like you don't exist anymore. Guess I just wanted to see for myself that you do."

The pronouncement of her existence brought Corey's spirits lower, and she stared down at the sandwich in her hand. Suddenly, she wasn't hungry anymore.

"How *is* Dad? I mean, besides the raving lunatic aspect?"

"I don't know." Emily bit into her sandwich, shrugged. "That's all I see."

"Try to see more."

Dabbing at her mouth with her napkin, Emily met Corey's eyes. "Why? What do you mean?"

"I don't know. I haven't seen him, so I don't know how he is, but I would imagine he's. . . ."

"Bitter? He is bitter. He's as mad at you as if you'd murdered his best friend."

Corey sighed. "I know. When I walked out on him at that party, it was like throwing everything back in his face. I don't regret it. I'd even do it again. But still."

Emily looked up at her. "You aren't mad at him? After all he's done?"

A breeze whipped Corey's hair against her lips, and she combed it away with her fingers. "Do you remember when my mother died, Emmy?"

Emily shrugged. "Not much. I was only three then."

Corey nodded, and wished Emily had had a little more time to get to know her grandmother. "It was a bad time," she said. "Dad was like a basket case for six months. So broken . . . I tried to be there for him, help him through it. At first he didn't want me there all the time, hovering over him, taking care of him. But after a while, I think he started to like it. I think it helped to pull him back out, you know? It helped me, too. I think we came to depend on each other. And now . . ."

"Now he won't even say your name. You can't feel sorry for him, Corey. This time no one died. He hated what you did, so he threw you out."

"I don't feel sorry for him," Corey said. "But I can't help feeling . . . maybe grief is the word. . . . It's like I've lost someone really important in my life, and there's no hope of ever getting him back. But I haven't forgotten what he's done to me. I'll never forget that."

"Will you ever forgive him?"

Corey looked down at Emily, searching her heart for an answer. But she came up with nothing.

"He's still my father," Corey said finally.

"And you're still his daughter. But that doesn't mean anything to him."

Corey thought about what Emily had said later that night when she was all alone in her apartment, trying to sort out why she was so confused about her feelings toward the man who had done everything he could to humiliate and ruin her. But he hadn't been able to, she thought, for the very strength she had used to fight him was the strength he had given her. She supposed, in a way, she should thank him for that.

She fell asleep in her clothes that night, and the next morning when she woke to the sound of mice scampering between the walls and realized she was fully dressed, she wept with loneliness and despair for all she had loved and lost. She had fallen into a rut of mere survival, when all her life survival had been something she rarely considered. Her father was right. Before he'd thrown her out, she hadn't had the slightest idea what it really meant to survive.

As she racked her heart for the strength to make it through one more day, she heard a knock at her door.

"Just a minute, Dee-dee," she called.

"Ain't Dee-dee," an unfamiliar voice called through the door. "It's a delivery for Corey Caine."

"Delivery?"

Peering through the peephole, she saw the man carrying a huge chair on his back. The chair had a big white bow tied around it. "There must be some mistake. I didn't order anything."

"Either you open the door, or I leave this in the hall, lady. I ain't humpin' it back down."

"Fine," she said. "Good. Leave it there."

She heard a string of expletives and watched through the hole as he dropped the recliner to the floor. Then, pulling his clipboard from the waist of his jeans, he slipped it as far as it would fit under the door. "You gotta sign this, lady. The card's on top."

She bent down and signed her name with the pen he'd left on top of the clipboard, took the card and shoved it back through. Getting back to her feet, she read the card.

Thought you could use a little housewarming gift.
Adam

A soft smile curled her lips as she realized it was the very chair she'd fallen asleep in at Adam's penthouse the other night.

Suddenly, the day seemed a little brighter than it had before.

Seeing the delivery man limping away and panting like he'd just run the Boston Marathon and won, she stepped out into the hall.

"Wait!"

The man turned around. "Yeah? What now, lady?"

"Your tip." She disappeared into her apartment, grabbed a bill out of her own tip money, and rushed back to the door.

He took the money and stuffed it into his pocket with a grin. "Thanks."

"Thank *you*," she said as he started back down the stairs. "And have that back checked. It could get real bad."

She looked down at the chair, bit back her smile, and began to push it into her apartment. When she closed the door behind her, she let out a small squeak of delight and fell backward into the plush chair.

Her laughter rolled through her like adrenaline, making the day so much easier to face. She was rich, probably for the first time in her life. For now she understood that luxury wasn't satin sheets and handwoven rugs. Sometimes it was just having a place to sit.

chapter
20

GISELLE HATED TO BE KEPT WAITING, PARTICU-
larly for her father, but it was common knowledge that
when he was meeting with his advisers about his testimony before the Casino Control Commission, he was
not—under any circumstances—to be disturbed.

She paced his waiting area, arms crossed with impatience, and Grace Copiah, who had been his secretary
for the last twenty-five years, asked, "Can I get you a cup
of coffee, Giselle?"

Giselle bristled at the use of her first name by the staff.
The aging woman had known her since she was a child,
however, and could never remember to call her Miss
Dobias. "Yes, Grace. Black. Is he going to be much
longer?"

"I don't think so," she called behind her as she went to
the coffee pot. "He has another appointment in twenty
minutes, so he should be winding it up soon."

She took the coffee from the woman and checked
her watch. Just as she was about to give up, the
door opened, and the men inside—John Keller among
them—began filing out, each speaking to her in turn.

Dobias paused at the door to have a quiet word with
Gloster, and John winked at her and whispered, "Tonight? Eleven, your room?"

Giselle gave a discreet nod and made a mental note to
find out what had gone on in the meeting, just in case
it should prove useful to her later. One never knew when
something might.

Dobias rubbed the circles under his eyes, and she knew the meeting hadn't gone well. The frown lines between his thick brows were heavily defined, indicating his deep fatigue and deeper anxiety. Dismissing Gloster, he gave her a cursory glance. "Are you here to see me?"

"Yes." Without waiting for his invitation, she stepped into his office. "It's about Corey," she said. "I got a call from an old friend at Christie's. It seems Corey's in possession of two Jobere paintings, and she's been trying to sell them."

"Jobere? Who the hell is Jobere?"

Giselle swallowed back her irritation that her father, who tried so hard to be cultural and polished, knew so little about so many things. "An artist, Dad. He's become very popular, and his paintings have had a substantial increase in value over the last year."

"How did she get hold of any valuable paintings?"

"That's what I wanted to ask you. Paintings like that would cost several thousand dollars each, even if she got a real bargain. Where would she get that kind of money?"

"Not waiting tables," he said, going back to his desk and dropping into his chair, as if the day was growing too wearisome for him to stand. "So she's trying to sell them, is she?"

"Yes," Giselle said, still standing. "The rumor is that she's been very selective and very hard-nosed about the whole thing. My friend offered her six thousand apiece and she passed."

Dobias rubbed his chin and stared down at the papers strewn across his desk. "I'll make a few phone calls later. See if I can find out what she's up to."

"Let me know."

Her father flashed a look her way. "Why? What do you care?"

"I have a right to know what she's got up her sleeve. You know, I could have kept this to myself, but I didn't. Now I want to be kept abreast."

"All right," Dobias mumbled, pulling up out of his chair. "I'll keep you informed. Your sisterly concern is very moving."

The blood rushed from her face, and her eyes cut into him. "No more moving than your paternal concern."

He waved a hand, dismissing her. "I have a meeting. No doubt you have work to do, too."

"I'm on top of mine," she informed him as she started back to the door. "I always am."

"That's what we pay you for," he said, just before he closed the door behind her.

Late that night, after the fiasco of dinner, during which Dobias had railed about Corey's purchase of the paintings and her hidden source of money, Rena went up to her rooms and had a stiff Scotch to quell the headache gnawing at her temples. When that didn't work, she took some codeine from her well-stocked medicine cabinet, took a bath, and waited for John to come up.

He never did.

Finally, at half past twelve, she climbed into bed and told herself that he was busy, that her father's casino was taking up all of his time, that he was probably down in the study with him right now, scheming and planning their strategy for getting that license, though the odds were leaning against them. They would come up with something, she knew. They always did.

She snuggled into bed, closed her eyes, and conjured the image of Joe Baker. A warm, exhilarated feeling blushed through her, and she wondered if there would be any harm in seeing him again. Platonically, of course. Just have a drink with him, maybe a bite.

Then came the fleeting thought that her allegiance to John was not really earned, since he had cheated on her more times than she wanted to know. Maybe it was her turn to taste life on the other side. Maybe it was her turn to savor the taste of temptation.

Downstairs in the study, Dobias sat at his desk beneath the bright glow of a lamp, sorting out the allegations that the Casino Control Commission were expected to level against him, in a feeble effort to keep him from getting his license. It couldn't happen, he thought, for he had spent six hundred million already on the construction of the casino. It would be finished in a few months, but if his license was turned down, it would be a gigantic white elephant, one that his peers would laugh about, then offer to "take off his hands" for a fourth of what it had cost to build. He wouldn't let that happen.

The first thing he would do was insist that Giselle, Rena, and John go with him to Trenton for the hearing and take their turns on the witness stand, extolling his virtues and doing whatever was necessary to get things moving. Sometimes solidarity presented a cozy picture. Perhaps the family element would even make him look more human than his image as the big corporation head trying to pull one over on Atlantic City. Positive publicity about his family—for a change—could only help him, after all.

The Back Bay Bugle Boy was a couple of notches below Joe Holifield's usual level of tolerance, but this was where the cop said the kid worked. He hated dinner theater; the only thing worse was old musicals starring Shirley Jones. But he'd suffer any agony, he supposed, for a good story and a shot at a network job.

He saw the cop, Murphy Johnson, come into the doorway, and hoped he wasn't around when the buttons on that shirt over his paunch popped off. The impact could be lethal.

The sergeant waved at him across the room and wove through the diners to his table. "Sorry I'm late," he said. "I got tied up on a case." Slipping into his chair, he gave a self-conscious look around him. "I wanted to change before I came here. Don't want it to get out that I talked to you. My pension—"

"Your pension isn't worth anything if you're the scapegoat for Corey Dobias's arrest."

"I'd like to see that bastard Easterman nailed to the wall for dumping this shit in my lap," Murphy muttered. "Thirty years I've been with the force, and he blows in, takes a few bribes, gets fat and happy—"

"Proof," Holifield cut in. "You're not the one with the proof of those bribes."

"The kid'll tell you. He got it straight from the horse's mouth."

Holifield dropped his forehead against his palm. "Do I have to sit through another show before I can see him? If I do, I'll just throw the story right now. It's not worth it."

"Just hold on. I sent a message back to him when I came in. He'll be right out."

"This better be good."

"I'm telling you. You'll get a direct quote. He was there."

The door beside the stage opened, and a kid no older than nineteen or twenty came out, scanned the diners, and started toward them.

"There's your man," Murphy said.

The young man, Gary was his name, wore an intense look, the kind that had the potential to be a reporter's worst nightmare. It sometimes meant loyalty, morality.

People who wore anxious looks like that often clammed up when it came to the bottom line.

The kid introduced himself, and hoping to relax him, Holifield shook his hand. "Great show," he said. "You really wrote that?"

"Yeah." As if the comment opened the plug allowing his anxiety to deflate, the kid dropped into his chair. "I thought I'd never get it produced. My screenplays are going nowhere." He looked at Holifield, narrowed his eyes, and asked, "Did you really like it? What about the grandmother? She wasn't too clichéd?"

Holifield decided it wouldn't be wise to tell him that the grandmother looked a little too much like Morgan Fairchild in a gray wig to be believable with any script, let alone this one. "Just clichéd enough. I liked her."

"So tell him," Murphy cut in impatiently. "Tell him what you told me the night of the Dobias party."

Holifield gave the cop a scathing look, and thought of telling him to lay the hell off and let him handle the interview. But he didn't want to shake the kid any more.

"I was a valet there that night," Gary volunteered, "and when she—that is, Miss Dobias—came out of the house, she was frothing mad." He paused and looked pleased with himself for the choice of words.

Joe refrained from rolling his eyes.

"She drove off, and a few minutes later, all hell broke loose. Everybody was leaving the party, they all wanted their cars at once. . . . It was a real mess. And that was when they told me he wanted to see me."

Holifield began scribbling notes on his legal pad. "Who?"

"Dobias. He was up in his bedroom, ranting and raving. He asked me who she left with, and I told him she left alone in her BMW."

"And then what?"

"Then he turned to one of the others in the room and told the guy to 'haul her ass to jail' for car theft. It was crazy. Somebody, I'm not sure who it was, told him you couldn't arrest somebody for stealing her own car."

Murphy leaned forward, coaxing the kid on. "Tell him what Dobias said, Gary. G'ahead."

"He said—I swear, these were his exact words—'Call Mitch Easterman and remind him of that yacht anchored in the harbor,' and then he went on about how nobody'd believe he bought it on a police commissioner's salary."

Holifield's pen moved more quickly across the page, getting every word.

"Didn't I tell you?" Murphy asked Holifield.

Joe smiled and drew a gigantic star in the margin of his notepad. "Yep. You were right."

"Then this'll be in the paper tomorrow?"

Joe shook his head. "Not for a while yet. This information is good, but Mitch Easterman's just a drop in the bucket. This is a story on Nik Dobias, and I plan to dig a hell of a lot deeper than this before I'm done."

"But if you wait, it could be too late. They're saying *I* took a bribe. I could get the ax before my pension—"

"That's not my problem," Holifield said, closing his legal pad. "The story will come out when it's ready. I can't rush it."

"What the hell am I supposed to do in the meantime?" Murphy asked.

Holifield pushed back his chair and got to his feet. "Just relax and watch the show, Murphy. It starts in ten minutes, and you're gonna love the grandmother."

Then, shaking Gary's hand and muttering a barely audible note of thanks to the kid who had provided his first quote for the story, he left the dinner theater before he had to sit through a second show.

*   *   *

Giselle left John satiated and asleep in her bed, pulled on her robe, and walked down the hall to Emily's room. Her daughter lay asleep, cuddled up like a toddler with a fist pressed against her chin.

She had been pouting ever since she was sent from the table the other night, hardly speaking to anyone. Giselle would have to make it a priority to toughen her up and teach her to stop waiting for her grandfather's approval. Giselle had wasted most of her life waiting for it, only to reconcile herself to the fact that it would never come. Despite the grim satisfaction she'd known in seeing Corey excluded from her father's plans, she had to admit that she was nonplussed at how easily he was able to turn his back on the one he'd loved more than any other. It told her that she and Rena, even lower on his priorities, very likely meant less than nothing to him.

But she still had Emily, and whether she really wanted him or not, it looked as if she had John. She leaned over and pressed a kiss on her daughter's warm cheek. Emily stirred and half opened her eyes.

"Good night, sweetheart," she whispered.

Emily muttered good night and turned over, and Giselle went back to her bedroom.

John was up, his hair mussed, his clothes half on. He gave her a groggy look as he zipped his pants and shrugged into his shirt, leaving it unbuttoned. "Better get back to my own room," he said. "Have to keep up appearances. We don't want Rena to get suspicious."

He slipped his tie around his neck. Giselle grabbed it and pulled him closer. "Are you sure you can't stay just a little longer?"

"No," he whispered. "She knows I'm home. My car's in the drive."

"She's probably drunk or unconscious," Giselle said.

"I'll bet she doesn't know where *she* is, let alone care where you are."

"Just the same. There's enough trouble in this house without that." He slid his hands down her shoulder, then around to her back, and pulled her hips against him. "But I'll see you tomorrow."

"Will you?"

She felt the embers within him stirring back to life, and sliding her hand between them, did her part to urge him further on.

"Don't," he whispered on a chuckle. "I really have to go. Really."

"Then go," she challenged.

But he didn't go. Instead, he backed her to the bed, slipped the robe off her shoulders, and took her again, this time quickly, lustfully, greedily.

And then he fell asleep in her bed, and didn't wake until the sun had already come up.

The alarm blared with scathing finality, forcing Rena awake to confront the stabbing pain in her temples, and her empty bed. John hadn't come up last night. And yet, he was home, for she had checked more than once to make sure his car was still in the drive.

She stumbled out of bed and into the bathroom, clutching her stomach as it roiled within her. She wanted to throw up. She wanted to die. She wanted to go back to bed. She wanted another drink.

But common sense prevailed, and instead of taking refuge in any of those options, she forced herself into the shower and stood beneath the icy jet until she felt sharper.

It was one of the maids, she thought with certainty. He was sleeping with one of the maids. He couldn't have been with her father all night, for even with Dobias's driving ambition and obsessiveness when it came to business, he was too old for marathon sessions. No, there was only one answer. It was one of the house-keepers. Probably that new one—the little redhead—what was her name? Janie. Yes, that was it.

The certainty of her conclusion made her tremble, and she stepped out of the shower, trying not to fall apart. Clutching the towel bar to keep from falling, she stood for a moment, dripping on the ceramic tile floor and try-ing hard to talk herself out of believing what she knew to be true.

After a moment of trying to stay upright as her world collapsed around her, she grabbed her silk robe off the hook and pulled it on, ignoring the fact that she hadn't dried herself or that her wet hair soaked a stain onto her back.

She had to do something, she told herself. They were probably laughing at her—the housekeeper, the garden-ers, the cook—they probably all knew that she was being made into a fool while her husband meandered all over the house, sleeping with anyone with breasts!

It was rage more than courage that drove her out into the hall and down the stairs to the kitchen, where the staff sat around the table, drinking coffee before starting the day. She thought of firing them all for those damn-able innocent faces, just so they'd know she wasn't an idiot.

"Where's my husband?" she asked them all, as if they had hidden him in one of the kitchen pantries.

"I haven't seen him, Mrs. Keller. Has he—"

"Where's Janie?"

"In the laundry room. She's—"

Ignoring the housekeeper who had worked in the house for ten years, Rena ran through the kitchen into the laundry room and found the girl in question, already bent over the ironing board. "You're fired," she said, wiping her wet hair out of her eyes and struggling to keep her tears from surfacing. "Get your things and get out within the hour."

"But Mrs. Keller! What have I done?"

"Don't play stupid with me," she shouted. "Despite what my husband thinks, I'm not a fool."

"But I didn't—"

"I said get out!" she cried, plunging toward her and grabbing the hot iron out of her hand. "Now!"

The girl backed out of the room, her face a study in terror, and for the slightest of moments, Rena wondered if she'd made a mistake.

She set the iron back on its plate, then slowly, as if in the fog of a daze, went back into the kitchen. Mysteriously, all of the servants had disappeared.

She went back up to her bedroom, and her hands trembled harder in anticipation of the drink she so desperately needed. She closed the door behind her and saw John's shoes beside the bed. That rage filled her again, and she dashed into the bathroom and saw that he was in the shower.

"How dare you?" she asked, flinging the doors open and letting a cloud of steam fill the room. "Right here in the house. Did you think I wouldn't notice?"

His wet face went pale, and whatever doubt she may have had of his guilt instantly vanished. "I was with your father. I fell asleep—"

"I fired the little bitch!" she cut in. "It won't be so convenient for you from now on."

"Fired?" He grabbed the towel from its rack and cut off the shower. "*Who* did you fire?"

"Janie! She's gone now, so you'll have to go outside the house for your sleazy affairs!"

"Janie?" He stepped out onto the tile floor, fixing her

with a look of absolute bewilderment. "Who the hell is Janie? Rena, what are you talking about?"

The genuine puzzlement in his expression took her by surprise, and she felt her tears bursting fully to her eyes. "How could you do it right under my nose? I've never cheated on you, John. Never. And with one of the servants! I'm so humiliated." Her tears plopped down her damp cheek and left more wet spots on the silk robe.

Relief flooded his face, and a smile tugged at his lips. "You thought I was having an affair with some maid named Janie? Rena, I didn't even know we had a maid named Janie. I swear to God, I was with your father. He's worried sick about the hearing next week. We were up all night trying to decide if you or Giselle should testify. At some point during the night, he went up to bed, and I stayed to finish my notes. I guess I fell asleep."

More tears spilled over her lashes, and she felt her lips quivering. "John, you wouldn't lie, would you?"

"Of course not, darling."

Her face twisted, and she pressed both fists against her eyes. "Oh, God. I fired her, and she didn't do anything!"

"Come here." He pulled her into his arms and held her the way he had when they'd first fallen in love, when she had believed she was the very core of his existence. He was still hers, she thought. After all these years, he was still here.

"I've been neglecting you," he whispered. "Tomorrow night, we'll have dinner at the Aujourd'hui. Just the two of us. I'll romance you like I used to, and you won't have any doubt that I'm still crazy about you." He kissed her, so deep and sweet that she knew at once he told the truth.

"Can you forgive me?"

"Of course," he whispered. "I can forgive you anything."

His innocence and gentle understanding of her silly
insecurities meant more to Rena than John could have
ever known, and melting in his arms, she let him carry
her back to bed.

Tomorrow she'd worry about the injustice she had
committed against the maid. For now, she would bury
herself in her husband's love.

As precarious and short-lived as it was, it was all she
had.

chapter
21

COREY FOUND WHAT SHE WAS LOOKING FOR IN A backdated issue of the *Connoisseur*. It seemed that a Dr. Arthur H. Abernathy of Long Island, New York, had purchased two Joberes at an auction six months ago. He'd paid ten thousand apiece for them and had indicated that he was always in the market for more.

Corey called him from the phone booth in the library, told him of her two paintings, and asked him if he was interested. He immediately made an appointment to meet with her in his suite at the Copley Plaza the next day, which told her just how strong his interest in the paintings was.

After arranging to take a day off, she went to the hotel, where she had dined many times before. It was only now, from the perspective of one who had nothing, that she truly saw the elegance of the place, from its mosaic floors to the Waterford crystal chandeliers hanging from the gilded ceilings. It was extravagance at its best, she thought with a smile. It was wealth at its most polished. It represented what she had been and, she vowed, what she was destined to be again. But this time it would be on her own terms.

She rode the elevator to Abernathy's floor and found him waiting for her with an elaborate lunch of lobster and champagne, and at once she decided to raise her bottom-line price by a thousand dollars. When he showed her photos of the rest of his Jobere collection, she tacked on another thousand.

"Art is an excellent investment," the man said in an accent that was hard to place. New York with a trace of Britain, she thought, as if one or the other was absorbed at the cost of the other.

"Yes," Corey said, becoming more at ease as the champagne seeped through her senses. "Rumor in the art world has it that Jobere's paintings are going to triple in value as soon as the biography of his life hits the stands next April."

"Biography?"

Corey seized the moment. "Yes. Several of the gallery owners have been interviewed for the book, and it's creating a lot of excitement."

"Is that so?" He frowned deeper and looked at the paintings with even more curious eyes.

"It's my guess," Corey said, "that anyone who can get his hands on a Jobere before the book is released stands to make a sizable profit afterward. For a short-term investment, you really can't lose."

She watched the wheels turning behind his eyes and saw the new interest she had cultivated. Silently, she thanked her stars for letting Adam leak the information about the book when he had. For good measure, she added another four thousand onto her price.

"I'm prepared to offer you ten thousand for the pair," the man said when the dinner was almost done.

Corey flashed him an amused, if sympathetic smile. "Oh, Dr. Abernathy. You must know that I've had offers much higher than that."

"Have you now?" he asked skeptically. "Just what do you have in mind?"

Corey kept her unblinking eyes directly on him. "Well, for the pair I'd have to have at least twenty-eight thousand."

"And for them individually?"

"I'd rather not sell them individually," she said, "but if I did, I would have to get at least sixteen."

Abernathy shifted in his seat, and she could see that the inflated price chagrined him. "That's just out of the question, I'm afraid."

Corey didn't let her calm smile fade. "I am sorry, Dr. Abernathy. I know how you wanted the paintings." She drew in a deep sigh. "It's just that I've been going back and forth about whether to sell them at all. I know that if I were to hold onto them for a year, I'd stand to make quite a bit more than I can make now. They're such rarities . . ."

She came to her feet and took one long, lingering look at each of the paintings in turn, then shook her head and extended her hand to him. "Again, I'm very sorry, Dr. Abernathy. I wish we could have done business."

"Wait a minute."

He didn't seem happy about being backed against the wall, but he played her game nonetheless. "What if I gave you twenty for the pair?"

Again, she tipped her head and offered him that amused smile. "No, Dr. Abernathy. I really don't think so. I have to consider what they'll be worth after the book. Everyone will want a Jobere, and as you know, there aren't that many."

The man's face flushed to a bright red, but she turned away and began returning the paintings carefully back into the crate she'd brought them in.

"All right," he said at last, though his tone was anything but affable. "I'll give you twenty-five for the pair. But not until I've confirmed what you've said about the book. Who is the publisher?"

She gave him the name of the small New York publishing house that had bought the book, and waited, holding her breath, while he retired into the bedroom to make the phone call.

What if the rumor wasn't true? she asked herself on a note of panic as the minutes ticked away. What if Adam had gotten it wrong? What if he found out and called off the whole deal?

But if the rumor checked out, he would actually pay her twenty-five thousand dollars for something that had cost her less than ten!

She heard him come out of the bedroom, and steeled herself for whatever was to come.

"It appears that you were right," he said. "The book is due to be released next April. I phoned my banker, and he's on his way over with a cashier's check for twenty-five thousand dollars." Something in Corey's heart leapt, but she kept her voice calm.

"I hope I'm doing the right thing," she said.

As if to get them out of her sight before she changed her mind, he lifted both canvases and moved them into the other room. When he returned, he signed the appropriate paperwork. The banker brought the check just moments later, and Abernathy handed it over to her. "It's been quite a pleasure doing business with you, Miss Caine."

She tried to school her smile not to look quite so victorious. "The pleasure's been all mine, Dr. Abernathy. Thank you very much."

It wasn't until she was safely tucked away in the elevator that she danced the little jig that she'd wanted to dance since he'd handed her the check. Twenty-five thousand! It was a miracle!

Her heart pounded with excitement as the doors to the elevator opened, and she felt she would burst if she didn't share this with someone right away. Dee-dee? No, she thought. Dee-dee still didn't know who she was, and the shock of that sort of easy money might only make her feel more downtrodden. Eric? No, he was the last person with whom she'd want to share her joy, or her money.

Adam Franklin. Yes, he would understand what this victory meant to her. He might even be proud.

Besides, she hadn't had a chance to thank him for the chair, beyond a phone call with a message left on his machine. And she wanted very much to see him again.

Feeling as if she walked on top of the world, she deposited the check, then hurried to Adam's office.

Adam was on his way out when his secretary buzzed to tell him that Corey Dobias waited to see him. Hanging his coat over his shoulder on a hooked finger, he went to the door himself and opened it, and leaned out into the waiting area.

Corey wore the brightest smile he'd ever seen, and from the dancing in her eyes he knew this was one visit he couldn't put off. "Corey? Come on in. I was just on my way out, but—"

"You're always on your way out," she said, prancing past him. "And you always only have ten minutes. But this is worth it."

She twirled around as he shut the door and raised her hands high in the air as if she would take flight at any moment. He couldn't help the smile creeping across his face.

"What is it?"

"I sold the paintings," she said, her voice bubbling on the edge of a shout as she threw her arms around him. "Twenty-five thousand dollars."

"Twenty-five thousand—"

"Yes! I held out, Adam. I even walked away from several pretty fine offers. I held out, and I got it!"

She let him go and pirouetted around the room. Adam

leaned back against the edge of his desk and raked a hand through his hair. "Wait a minute. You're telling me that you sold those two paintings for twenty-five grand? The two paintings that you bought for peanuts at that auction?"

She stepped flirtatiously close to him, putting her face inches from his. "What's the matter, Adam? Sorry you didn't buy them yourself?"

"Hell yes, I'm sorry. Lady, you must drive a hell of a hard bargain."

"I was nothing short of brilliant," she conceded. "And to celebrate, *and* to thank you for my lovely and thoughtful and much loved housewarming gift . . ."

His grin widened.

"I'm taking you to dinner tonight. Seven sharp. I'll meet you here."

He hesitated a moment and thought of turning her down, but somehow, he wasn't able. "Don't bother. I'll pick you up at home."

She hesitated. "Well, okay. But not in a limousine or anything. Your own car is okay, but park it a little way down the street, so it doesn't look like it's at my building."

"Since when did you have a problem with expensive automobiles?"

"Since I moved into a place where people can't afford decent shoes to walk in, much less extravagant cars. I don't want them to have an inkling that I'm a Dobias, or that I'm soon going to invest this twenty-five thousand and make untold profit, and be as rich as my father or my sisters—"

"Hold it now. Twenty-five thousand is hardly untold riches. Don't go overboard."

"Oh, don't worry, Adam," she said. "I'm not going to spend a penny of it, except on you tonight. The rest goes to buy my building. All I need is someone to finance it and the renovation, and I'll be all set."

Adam laughed. "That's all? That doesn't seem like a lot to you?"

"Piece of cake," she said. "And I'll have done it all myself, with no help except for the sage and valuable advice from geniuses like yourself."

Her ecstasy was contagious, and he had to admit that he wanted more of it. Still, he held back. "I'll pick you up at seven," he said, "but we'll have to make an early evening of it. I have meetings all day tomorrow. I'm getting ready for a trip to Tokyo in a few days."

"Tokyo!" Her face fell. "How long will you be gone?"

"Only a week, with any luck."

That smile found its way back to her face. "Good. That should give me enough time to make my first million."

He laughed for the first time in . . . how many years? He honestly couldn't remember. And despite his resolutions and all of his misgivings, he couldn't wait until seven tonight.

chapter
22

RENA HAD BELIEVED JOHN LAST NIGHT WHEN he'd sworn he wasn't cheating on her, but she wasn't self-deceptive enough to believe that he never had, or that he never would again. As soon as his reassurances wore off, she had little doubt that his mind would wander again. Just as her own thoughts kept drifting to the blond-haired blue-eyed man she knew next to nothing about.

Joe Baker.

It was for him, rather than the drinks or the ambience or the people, that she increased her number of visits to the Yankee Doodle. That her intake of alcohol increased as a result was only a perk.

He hadn't been there during her first two visits today, and by midafternoon all thoughts of work had muddled into a pleasant haze. On her third visit, she had a drink and talked to Archie for a while, her gaze continually scanning the room. The yuppy crowd that came in and out swelled and deflated as did her spirit as the hour wore on, and finally she got her tapestry bag and stood up to leave.

"Hi, gorgeous."

She swung around to see Joe Baker standing behind her, holding a yellow daisy that he'd no doubt snatched from a vase on one of the tables he'd passed.

She smiled at the silly gesture and took the flower. It smelled like springtime in the country, and it made her feel young, a feeling she hadn't experienced in a very long time.

"Don't you ever work?" he asked.

"All the time. What about you?"

Joe was prepared for such a question. "I'm a computer programmer," he said. "I'm cooped up in my office all day, except when I can sneak out and come here. Believe me, I make up for it later, but it's a break I need from time to time."

He slipped onto the stool next to hers, and she let her gaze linger on his face—so strong and perfect, so Robert Redford handsome. She wondered what he saw in her.

"And what do *you* do?"

The question shook her a bit, and she looked down at her drink and tried to decide how much to tell him. "I work at a company called IDK. In the Dobias Building."

Archie handed Joe a beer. "What do you do there?" Joe asked.

She thought of lying, saying that she was a secretary, but it seemed so stupid. Maybe it was best to go ahead and tell him who she was, before he found out anyway. Besides, her title made her look important, and that wasn't a luxury she enjoyed very often.

"I'm the president."

He choked on his drink. "Of the company?"

"Yep. For now, anyway."

"What is it? Temporary?"

She shrugged. "It's kind of a long story."

He tipped his head, and the interest in his eyes made her feel as if she'd known him all her life. She didn't remember the last time she'd had anyone's undivided attention. "So what does I-D-K stand for? Indestructible Kid?"

"Hardly," she said. "Actually, it stands for Irena Dobias Keller." She watched his face carefully, waiting for some sign of change, but he looked rather unimpressed.

"Your initials, huh? Makes sense." He took another drink and grinned over the rim of his glass. "No wonder you're the president. What else could you be in a company named after you?"

From the nonchalant way he accepted the explanation, she wondered if he even knew who the Dobiases were, or if he cared. She wondered if he'd heard of the competition raging between herself and Giselle, or if he knew of Corey's exclusion from the family.

"So what does IDK do?"

The question was almost amusing to her, for everyone in Boston knew that the Dobias family dealt in real estate development and acquisition.

Giving him a deadpan look, she said, "We manufacture tutus." She waited for a reaction, but he only rubbed his beard and gave her a skeptical look. "I come from a long line of tutu manufacturers," she said seriously. "My father made his fortune in dancing tights, but tutus is really where his heart is."

Joe didn't crack a smile. "Tutus."

"Tutus." She hid her grin behind her glass and watched as he frowned down at his drink, nonplussed. He really didn't know.

"Okay, you're pulling my leg, right?"

She couldn't hold back her smile. "Maybe a little. You're not from Boston, are you?"

"No," he lied. "I've only lived here about a month."

She finished her drink and set the glass down a bit too hard. "I thought so."

"Tutus." He shook his head and chuckled again. "I almost believed you."

The laughter edging up inside her felt good. "Truth is, I'm in real estate."

"Like buying and selling houses?"

"Something like that," she evaded. "It's really not very interesting."

"Well, maybe you can help me find a decent place when my lease is up."

They talked for another hour before Rena's speech began to slur and she realized she had to go back to the office while she could still make it. He walked her to the door of the Dobias building, steadying her when the world tipped a little too much.

She leaned back against the glass before she went in, and shoved her hair back from her face. "Thanks for walking me over, Joe. You're a real gentleman."

"How about dinner tonight?"

The question took her by surprise. "No, I have plans. My husband's taking me out to dinner."

"Tomorrow night, then?" he asked, undaunted. "It wouldn't be cheating, you know. Just dinner. Nothing else. I just enjoy being with you."

She looked down at her embroidered suede pumps, shook her head. "I don't think so."

Joe moaned, but his grin didn't fade. He pulled a pen out of his shirt pocket, frisked his pockets until he found an old receipt, and jotted his phone number on it. "Call if you change your mind. You won't regret it."

She took the paper and smiled. "I'll see you later, Joe."

"Yeah," he said. "Later."

She felt him watching her as she pushed through the revolving door into the building, and when she made it to the elevator, she saw him still standing there smiling at her through the glass. He lifted his hand in a wave.

The sheer joy of his attraction melted her inside, and she looked down at the phone number crumpled in her hand. As good as it felt to tingle at a man's smile again, it wasn't anything she would consider acting upon. She could never cheat on her husband.

She blushed with shame at the thought of even considering such a thing. John would be so hurt if he knew. Especially today, when he was planning an elaborate, romantic dinner at one of the city's most exclusive restaurants. Already she looked forward to it.

But two hours later, as she sat at her desk feigning interest in the fabric swatches for the casino, John's secretary called. "Mr. Keller asked me to tell you that he has a late meeting tonight, and he won't be able to take you to dinner."

"But we have reservations! He said—"

"I'm sorry, Mrs. Keller. He did say that you should go ahead without him, though."

A lump of helpless emotion planted itself in her throat. "All right. Tell him I will."

She hung up the phone and picked up the wadded receipt with Joe's phone number scratched on it. She wondered if he'd still be interested.

Her hands trembled as she dialed his number.

"Hello?"

She cleared her throat. "Um, Joe? This is Rena Keller."

"Rena!" She could hear the joy in his voice, and that restored the warmth that John's cancellation had taken from her. "Have you changed your mind about dinner tomorrow night?"

"I've changed my mind," she said. "But how about tonight, instead?"

"Great. Where do you want to meet?"

"The Aujourd'hui," she said. "At the Four Seasons. And don't worry about the expense. My husband will get the bill."

He was quiet for a moment. "No. I can't agree to that."

"Why not?"

"I just don't like it. If we go, I pay."

She sighed and twirled the cord around her finger. "All right, then. We'll go somewhere else."

"No, we'll go there. I can handle it, okay? I make good money, and I don't have anyone else to spend it on. Besides, I've been meaning to try the Aujourd'hui."

"All right then. I'll meet you there at eight o'clock. The reservations are already made."

"Eight o'clock," he said. "See you then."

She hung up the phone and closed her shaking hands beneath her chin, and told herself that she was doing nothing wrong. She wouldn't have more than dinner with him, but she would enjoy it. It was her right.

If John got wind of it, perhaps it would put him on his toes. It would serve him right to learn that his wife had admirers of her own.

Adam arrived at Corey's door at seven sharp, and found Dee-dee in the apartment, performing some service that he couldn't pinpoint. She was a small woman with a wiry blond perm, a smile that was a little too big for her face, and green eyes that seemed on the verge of laughter. He liked her instantly.

It was Corey, however, who drew his attention across the room. She was bustling around her kitchenette, as if doing a quick house-cleaning before her dinner date, and she wore a bright red dress with a short ruffled skirt.

He let out a low whistle.

Corey did a pirouette that ended in a curtsy. "I take it you approve," she said. "It's Dee-dee's. She let me borrow it."

The small woman threw her hand over her forehead. "Corey, you aren't supposed to tell anyone it's borrowed!"

"Oh." She shrugged, and Adam couldn't help laughing.

"You both have excellent taste."

"How do you like the hair?" Corey asked, spinning around to exhibit the French twist. "Dee-dee did that, too."

Dee-dee shook her head as if the whole situation was hopeless. "Corey! He's supposed to think you just threw it up with no effort at all."

"Oh, he knows better than that," Corey teased, winking at Adam.

"I'm leaving before she tells you all her deepest secrets," Dee-dee said. "Sheez. You'd think the girl had never borrowed a dress in her life."

When the door was closed, Corey cocked her head and shoulder and smiled at Adam. "I haven't, you know."

"What? Borrowed a dress or had a friend do your hair?"

"Either. Can you imagine borrowing someone else's clothes? It's incredible. And so much fun. For someone who's practically living on the poverty level, Dee-dee has a couple of really nice things. Don't worry. I'll pay her back when I get back on my feet and get my wardrobe up to par. I might even make her an executive in my company."

"You know, most people don't consider 'on your feet' having a seven figure bank account and a wardrobe that costs more than the average American's annual income."

"So I have high standards," she said. "But until I reach that point, I'm going to have a good time. Starting with tonight."

Adam leaned against the stained bar of her kitchenette and crossed his arms. "So, where is it you're taking me tonight? Someplace expensive, I hope. You know you have me to thank for your windfall."

She grinned. "I know. I don't know about expensive, but I have an evening planned that'll knock your socks off. That is, if you're the man I think you are."

A small frown cracked between his brows. "Sounds intriguing."

"Oh, it is," she said, grabbing the small handbag and black fake-fur coat she'd also borrowed from Dee-dee and lifting the picnic basket that waited beside the door. "You just wait."

Adam did as he was told when she asked him to drive to the waterfront and didn't bother asking what was in the picnic basket. He couldn't imagine that a Dobias could cook, so he bore no illusions of fried chicken and corn on the cob tucked in tin foil within the basket. Not unless she'd borrowed them from Dee-dee.

Besides, he'd taken the basket from her to put it in the car, and found that it was surprisingly light.

He reached the waterfront area and looked over at her. "Which restaurant? The Durgin-Park or Romagnoli's Table?"

"Neither," she said with a coy smile. "Just park anywhere you can find a place, and we'll walk."

He had to admit he was curious, but something about the mystery and the fun she was having with it made him want it to linger. He couldn't remember ever being out with a woman like Corey, one who fascinated and astonished him, and always kept him smiling.

They left the car in a pay parking lot. Adam carried the picnic basket and Corey latched onto his arm, making him feel a disturbing heat in the center of his being, a heat that had stirred to life many times over the years but had never been so intense. It frightened him even as it exhilarated him.

They entered the throng of tourists and night people at Quincy Market, and Corey stopped, brandishing a hand in the direction of the booths that lined the marketplace. "Anything your heart can desire," she said. "Pizza, bagels, turkey sandwiches, chow mein, franks, tacos, shish kabob, shrimp, clams. It's all right here."

Adam grinned down at her. "I don't believe it. I thought you wanted to go to some extravagant restaurant."

"I've been to extravagant restaurants," she said. "You may not believe this, Adam, but I've led a pretty sheltered life. Dee-dee told me about how delicious the food was here, and how nice it was to sit on the steps facing the harbor. There's a blanket in the basket."

Considering the smile on her face and the dancing light in her eyes, he determined that there was no way he could deny her anything. But it did pose a serious problem. All day, he'd vowed to keep his distance. Not to let her charm override his common sense. Not to let his heart slip away when his guard was down. It was too dangerous.

But sitting in the frosty night air watching the lighted ships making their way across the harbor, and hearing the distant sounds of street musicians, and listening to Corey's dreams about building her own business from scratch and being independent and free of all the trappings her sisters had inherited, breathing the untainted scent of her hair and laughing to the sound of her voice, he feared he'd made a dreadful mistake in coming with her.

But even that knowledge didn't hamper the magic of the evening she had created for him.

Later, as they strolled the sidewalks lined in cobblestone, granite, and brick, lit with nautical lights that gave the place a magical flair, she stopped and smiled up at him. The wind whipped the fallen strands of her hair into her face, and he thought he'd never seen a more beautiful sight than Corey Dobias standing in the night, smiling up at him.

"I've had a good time tonight, Adam," she whispered.

The memory of her words a week ago, the words that

had driven him out of her apartment as fast as he could move, flitted through his mind again, as they had done a hundred times in the last few days. *I think I could really fall for you, Adam Franklin.*

He swallowed, and told himself that he was getting into something from which there was no escape. Falling too fast and too hard, and if he allowed it, he would take her down with him.

Still, she wet her lips and looked up at him, and his heart beat with the force of a sledgehammer destroying his neat, well-ordered conscience. And without his conscience, he was left with only a burning desire and a stirring feeling that based itself in his heart.

"You're a treasure, Corey. I hope you realize it." His voice sounded distant, hoarse, dry.

Her eyes absorbed her smile, and he realized she could make a Jesuit priest forsake his vows. And he was no Jesuit priest.

He drew in a deep sigh and slipped his hand behind her neck, and before his mind could stop him, he pulled her into the kiss that had been burning into his mind with incessant regularity. She tasted of all that was cool and fresh and young, all that was bright and colorful and hopeful. She tasted of life and fulfillment and need and desire. Even as he tasted her, he craved more. Even as he drew her into his arms and felt her body melt against his, even as he breathed her breath and gave it back to her, he knew that it would never be enough.

The sharpness of that painful, joyous feeling was foreign to him, for he hadn't felt it in years. Not since . . .

The joy died, and the exhilaration faded as his conscience reinstated itself on his heart.

Quickly, he pulled away and let her go.

An icy breeze whipped up around them, and she hugged her arms around herself and looked up at him with sad, glistening eyes that didn't understand. "Why?"

"Because," he whispered, trying to catch his breath against the flood of emotions that had winded him. "We're too different. I don't want to see you get hurt."

"Who said I'd be hurt?" she asked, but already he could see that she was.

"It's inevitable." He turned away from her, trying hard not to let her sweet look break through his barriers again. "There are things you don't know, Corey. Things you wouldn't understand."

"You might be surprised."

He turned back to her, saw her shivering, and he wondered if it was from the cold or the pain he saw in her eyes. "Trust me," he whispered.

She let it go at that, though he could feel the tension radiating between them as he drove her home. The humorous teasing had faded, there was no room for that now. All that was left was the yearning and craving that echoed within the empty chambers of his heart, and the knowledge that it must never be.

He walked her to her door but kept his distance as she unlocked it. She didn't even bother to ask him in.

"When do you leave for Tokyo?"

"In three days," he said.

"Will you call me when you get back?" she asked. "You can reach me at the restaurant, or just drop by here."

He thought of saying no, but couldn't manage it. "Of course."

"If you don't, I'll call you," she said. "Or I'll show up at your office unannounced and throw your whole schedule off."

He smiled. "I'll call."

He watched her go inside, watched the door click shut behind her. It was a moment before he was able to over-

come the urge to open it and follow her in, and play
out the fantasies that he feared would keep him from
sleeping tonight.

But if there was anything he prided himself on, it was
his strength. So bridling every ounce of it he possessed,
Adam walked away.

Because the maitre d' knew he was dealing with one
of the Dobias daughters, he seated Rena and Joe near a
floor-to-ceiling window overlooking the Public Garden.
Joe seemed duly impressed.

They talked and dined for three hours. Loosening up
because of the diminishing bottle of wine and the new
one that replaced it, Rena found herself telling him odd
details about her life, things that no one else had ever
been interested in, things that came from her heart.
The strangest part of it was that he listened with deep
interest.

She told him about her mother's death and the dev-
astating effect it had had upon her father. She told him
about her father's decision to divide his estate and dis-
tribute it among his children before he died. And she
told him about Corey's defiance, her father's fury, and
the competition she was engaged in with Giselle.

Still he listened with fascination. And his fascination
so fascinated her, that she didn't see when he reached
inside his coat pocket and flicked on the tiny tape recorder he carried wherever he went.

"He really had your sister arrested?"

Rena leaned back in her chair, enjoying the wine-
induced buzz in her head. "Sure did."

"How could he do that? I can't believe the police would
go along with it."

"They wouldn't have," she said, "but Dad has friends
in high places. They owe him."

"Owe him for what?"

Rena laughed. "I could make a list. Barbados vacations, a condo in Denver, a yacht sitting out in Boston Harbor . . ."

Joe laughed and pretended to be more amused than curious. "But why? People in the police department— why would he need to keep them in his debt?"

Rena shrugged. "From time to time, it's helped him to get business associates out of trouble, or into it."

"So when your father wanted your sister arrested, they accommodated him?"

She nodded. "That's about the size of it. But it was okay. The next day they had a press conference and claimed that Corey was arrested by mistake. They dropped all the charges, so I guess no one really got hurt, except maybe the poor cop they blamed the whole thing on."

He grinned. "Remind me never to cross your father."

She smiled. "I remind myself everyday." She picked up her glass, waved it toward the center of the restaurant. Some of the wine sloshed over the side and trickled down her fingers. "All this could crumble in a second with one slipup, and I'd be waiting tables like Corey."

"Corey? Waiting tables? Where?"

She told him of Corey's job and the cruel lunch date she'd had there with her father. And she drank more.

When they had exhausted the possibilities of the Aujourd'hui, they stepped over to the Bristol Lounge and drank more and danced and drank and danced.

"So what did you do before you were president of your tutu company?" he teased when they'd come back to their table after a particularly fast number.

Rena, still breathless, gestured to the barmaid for another drink. She'd changed from wine to Scotch, and he had seen her down at least five. "I ran Resources, Incorporated," she said with a slur. "We did all the purchasing for my father's properties. Kept all the money in house, you know. And it helped us out a little with taxes."

Joe slipped his hand inside his coat to reactivate his tape recorder. "How do you mean?"

"Well, you know." She propped her chin on her hand. "It cost a lot of money to furnish and decorate the house we live in, not to mention the five other residences we have. One in the Virgin Islands, a condo in Palm Springs, and the others. Daddy likes to charge all of our personal expenses off to his other buildings. That way they become business expenses. Even his personal cash—well, all of ours, really—comes from Resources."

"You just draw out of it what you need?" he asked.

She laughed. "Oh, no. That would be too obvious. No, we just have invoices sent there for the amounts we need. Say I need five thousand dollars. I draw up an invoice for some furniture for the hotel. When I bill them for it, the cash comes from their account. The paperwork is nice and neat, and I get some tax-free income. It works like a charm."

"Doesn't your father have partners, investors?"

"Sure," she said. "He never uses his own money."

"Doesn't that come out of their profits? If their buildings are paying for things they never get—"

"Oh, they don't know about any of this," Rena said. "Besides, it's just a little here, a little there. It's not enough to make a difference. My father makes sure they don't notice it."

"Your father sounds like a brilliant man," Joe said.

Her smile faded, and she lifted her chin with a peculiar kind of pride. "Oh, he is. My father is the most brilliant man I know." She looked at him for a moment, then dropped her face in her hand. "I'm sorry. I must be boring you to death. I've done nothing but talk about myself all evening."

Joe hooked a finger under her chin and lifted her face back to his. "Don't apologize. I've loved every minute of it. I could listen to you talk all night." He pushed a stray wisp of hair back behind her ear, traced the shell of it with the tip of his finger. "As a matter of fact," he whispered, "I was just thinking. We could get a room. Stay the night."

He saw the pretty way her face blushed in the candle-light, and he thought that the perks that went with this job weren't bad. He wouldn't mind a bit spending a night with Rena Dobias.

"No, Joe. I couldn't."

"Why not?"

She struggled for the right reason, but came up empty. "Because. I just . . . couldn't. Please understand."

"Another time, then?" he whispered, his finger still feathering the curve of her ear.

She swallowed and looked down at her empty glass.

"Just give me a maybe," he whispered. "Just a maybe will make me happy."

"All right. Maybe."

He walked her outside and waited for the limousine he had called for her in the lobby. "When can I see you again? I have to see you again."

"I don't know. I shouldn't see you again. You're dangerous."

"Dangerous?" he asked on a soft laugh. "I'm perfectly harmless. My motives are very simple and very selfish."

She smiled. "I'm going to Trenton next week, and I'll probably be there for a few days. My father's building a casino in Atlantic City, and he has to testify before the Casino Control Commission. I might testify, too."

"When will you be back?"

"I'm not sure yet."

"Fine," he said softly, slipping his arms around her.

"Then I'll come, too. I'll get a room in the same hotel, and at night you can sneak away and we'll do the town."

Rena succumbed to the gentle warmth of his arms, and wet her lips as she let his eyes mesmerize her. "I couldn't do that. My husband will be with me."

"I'll be there, anyway," he whispered. "If the opportunity arises, you'll know where to find me."

"But why?" she whispered. "Why would you go there on the off chance—?"

"Because I'm becoming obsessed with you," he whispered. "Because I'm not going to be able to rest until that 'maybe' becomes a 'yes.' "

Her heart pounded with the force of her desire, and she opened her lips and watched his face descend slowly to hers.

His kiss was lustful, powerful, and it melted her rationale and almost made her change her mind and rush back up to one of the hotel rooms where she could feel his body next to hers and writhe in the pleasure of him.

Instead, she pulled away completely, separating herself from him, and looked up the street toward the limousine coming toward them. "All right," she whispered breathlessly. "If you come to Trenton, maybe I can get away one night. Maybe we can talk or . . . have dinner . . ."

Her voice trailed off, and he pulled her back against him. "Or maybe we'll think of something else to do by then."

She swallowed the great obstruction blocking her throat. "Maybe."

The chauffeur got out of his car and opened the back door. Joe let her go. "I'll see you in Trenton," he whispered.

Rena only smiled and got into the car.

chapter

23

"YOU RAN UP A FIVE-HUNDRED-DOLLAR BILL AT the Aujourd'hui and expect *me* to pay it?" Adam stood in the center of his office, staring down at the receipt in his hand.

"Adam, she's practically in the palm of my hand," Joe said. "But I had to get her to trust me. They're not a very trusting bunch, you know."

Adam thrust the receipt back at him. "Did you find out anything?"

"A lot. I found out that Mitch Easterman has a yacht sitting in Boston Harbor. That kid—that Gary what's-his-name—told me he heard that from the horse's mouth, and last night Rena practically confirmed it. Then she tells me, without realizing I know she's talking about Easterman, that Dobias also gave him use of a condo in Denver and some vacations in Barbados. I'm going to try to track down some documentation on those today, and see if I can dig up what Easterman has done for him in return."

"Do that," Adam said, unimpressed. "It isn't worth a damn without proof. What else have you got?"

Holifield's eyes brightened. "Resources, Incorporated, one of Dobias Enterprises' subsidiary companies, seems to be one of the key elements in a major tax evasion scheme."

"Tax evasion?" Adam shook his head. "He was under investigation for tax evasion years ago. There wasn't enough evidence. He got off."

"But maybe they didn't know about this," Holifield argued. "We're talking dummy invoices sent to this company, cash paid out to petty cash accounts that the Dobiases draw from, and bills sent to various Dobias properties to cover them. We're talking decorations and furnishings for their personal residences, all written off as business expenses. I think the IRS would be real interested in this."

Adam frowned and rubbed his hand across his shadowed jaw. "Yeah. I think you're right. But we need some of those dummy invoices. Talk to some of the contractors who've done work on his houses. See if you can find names of disgruntled ex-employees. Maybe some of them can substantiate it."

"You got it," Joe said. "I also found out that the whole kit and caboodle is going to Trenton next week, and that Giselle and Rena might testify for their father. I figure emotions will be flying high. If the commission is tough on him, he'll be saying things. Maybe even doing things."

Adam set his hands on his hips and paced across the room. "I guess you're right. If he's going to slip up, it'll be then. So are you going to be there?"

Holifield gave him a grin that reminded him of the high-school studs bragging in the locker room. "Staying in the same hotel. We've made plans to get together . . . after hours."

"And you think she'll tell you what her father's up to?"

"She drinks a lot, Adam. And then she rambles. And she's not that careful about what comes out of her mouth. Besides, she trusts me."

"You're enjoying this, aren't you?"

Holifield laughed. "Hell, yes, I'm enjoying it. I could do a lot worse."

"Just do it fast and leave as few casualties as possible,

Holifield. Act like you have a conscience."

Holifield's smile faded. "It doesn't pay to have a conscience, Adam. Not when you work for a tabloid."

The comment disturbed Adam, but he didn't reply. The phone on his desk buzzed, and Adam picked it up. "Yeah, Sarah? Okay, tell him I'm on my way." He hung up, reached for his briefcase, and gave Holifield one last look. "Give the receipts to Sarah. If you get anything substantial, call me."

Holifield followed Adam out of the office. "Oh, Adam. Something else. Rena told me that her younger sister, Corey, is working as a waitress since her father threw her out. I thought I might visit her and see what she knows. She probably has a vendetta, so she might be more than willing to talk. Besides, I hear she's a real piece—"

Adam swung around, the lethal look on his face silencing Joe at once. "You leave Corey Dobias alone," he said through his teeth. "You lay one hand on her, or follow her, or so much as speak to her, and I'll find out about it. And when I do, You'll have a hell of a lot more than your job to worry about."

Surprised, Holifield raised both hands. "All right, Adam. I swear, I won't go near her. Bad idea."

"A real bad idea," Adam agreed.

Holifield watched him, astounded, as he stepped onto the elevator.

The diner beneath Eric Gray's apartment was the quintessential greasy spoon, and Giselle had to wonder if her mission was really worth eating here. Deciding to compromise, she ordered coffee. She would eat breakfast when she got back to the office.

She checked her watch and noted that he was late. Typical, she thought. He had feigned uninterest when she'd called him last night to set up the meeting, until she'd mentioned her intention to pay him for any information he could give her. Suddenly, he was all cooperation.

She saw him step into the doorway, look around. She lifted her fingers in a fluttering wave. He had shaved, she noted, and she wondered if it was for the meeting. Did he think she would find him as attractive as her sister had?

The idea, while it brought a smile to her lips, suddenly fixed itself within the realm of possibility as he walked toward her. There was a certain something about him. A masculine indifference. A brooding virility. She wondered if he was good in bed.

Without fanfare, he slumped into the booth opposite her and gave her a dull look.

"I almost gave up on you," she said.

He gestured toward the waitress to get him a cup of coffee, then settled his green eyes on her. "Let's get to the point. What do you want to know?"

"Several things, actually." She waited, running the tip of her finger around her cup as the waitress poured his coffee. "My father has kept up with Corey's progress. We understand she's gotten her own place."

Eric leaned back in the booth and propped his arm on the back. "If you know all that, why do you need me?"

"I wondered if that meant the two of you weren't an item anymore. The last I heard, you were engaged."

"She gave the ring back. It didn't work out."

Giselle smiled. "No, I didn't think it would. Not after Corey lost everything."

She had insulted his integrity, and he bristled. "Is that all you wanted to know?"

"No," she said. "What I really wanted to find out is what she's up to right now. I understand that she's recently acquired some Jobere paintings, and that she sold them for a pretty big profit."

"Joberes?" She could see from the puzzlement on his face that Eric knew nothing about the paintings. "Where would she get those?"

"More specifically, where would she get the money to buy them?"

He stared down at his coffee, and she could see the irritation drawing his weary features. "She told me she didn't have a cent. I checked—she had maybe thirty dollars." He looked up at her, his eyes a degree brighter. "Could she have gotten it when she went back to your house?"

Giselle didn't like being confused, but she made no effort to hide it now. "What do you mean? She hasn't been home since the night of the party."

"Wrong," Eric said, flashing her a smug grin. "She went home in the middle of the night a couple of weeks ago. Came home at the crack of dawn, with a backpack full of makeup and clothes."

"That can't be. No one would have let her in, and she couldn't have gotten in without us. We have one of the most elaborate security systems—"

Eric laughed. "Looks like she did."

Giselle fixed him with a sharp look. "What else did she take?"

Eric shrugged. "I told you. Makeup. That kind of shit. You know Corey."

It occurred to Giselle that neither one of them really knew Corey.

"There had to be something else. A person doesn't go to that kind of risk without taking something."

"Was anything missing?"

Giselle shook her head. "I don't know. I'll have to check the safe when I get home."

"Well, if she did take something, that would explain how she got the money."

"Yes," Giselle said, leaning toward him, her face more intense. "But what I really need to know is what she plans to do with it. Do you have any idea?"

Eric smiled, and she knew she'd hit paydirt. "Yeah, as a matter of fact, I do. She said she still wanted to close the deal she'd been working on before all this happened. She got them to give her thirty more days. Plans to buy some dilapidated building in the Combat Zone and renovate it for offices."

Giselle nodded. "I know about that deal, but I can't figure out how she thinks it'll possibly turn her a profit. It's the worst area of town."

"Got me," Eric said. "The original plan was to buy up the whole area, but now she doesn't have that kind of capital."

Giselle let her vacant gaze drift out the window, to the busy Cambridge street. "The thirty days," she said. "When is it up?"

Eric shrugged again, and Giselle determined that that was his most frequent gesture. "Can't you count?"

She met his eyes again and saw the challenge there. "I meant when did the thirty days start? Before or after her fallout with my father?"

"After, I think. It really should be up soon."

"I see."

He smiled at the sparkle lighting her eyes, and she wondered if he could read what she was thinking. The idea didn't even bother her.

"It's been a pleasure doing business with you," she said, reaching into her purse and withdrawing an envelope.

Eric took it, flipped it open and counted the ten hundred dollar bills. The first truly genuine smile she'd ever seen on him flashed across his face, and she saw instantly why Corey had fallen so hard for him. "The pleasure is all mine," he said. "But it isn't your money I want."

He shoved the envelope back across the table, and taking it, she gave him a suspicious look. "What then?"

His smile didn't waiver, and the sparkle in his eyes warned her that she hadn't gotten off that easily. "I'll find out whatever you want to know about Corey and report back to you, but I want more than money to do it."

"I'm listening."

He leaned back, tapped his fingers on the table. "I have some prints that would enhance the lobby of your casino—prints that were carefully selected to go with the color scheme and the furnishings there. Corey had planned to use them. Now I want you to."

A slow smile spread across her lips, as if she liked the fact that he'd seized an opportunity. He was smarter than she'd imagined. "Why don't you show me what you've got?"

For the first time since the Dobias party, Eric saw light at the end of his tunnel.

chapter
24

EMILY AND HER GRANDFATHER WERE THE ONLY
two at dinner that evening, but she tried to smile and
make the most of it.

"Looks like it's just us, Grandfather."

"Where's your mother?" he asked, spooning up a
mouthful of soup.

"I don't know. I thought she was upstairs. She didn't
say she was going out."

"It's a damned ghost town around here. Sometimes I
wonder why I bother to come home."

Emily tried to remember what Corey had told her
about how she should try to see past the gruff facade
and the distractions that always kept them from talking.
"I'm glad you come home, Grandfather," she said. "If you
hadn't tonight, I'd be eating alone. I really hate to eat
alone."

He looked up at her, and a soft smile broke through
his hard facade. "So do I, Emmy. So do I." He took another spoonful of soup. "You know, you're turning into a
very polished young lady. That's important, you know.
It'll take you far."

It was so rare to glean a compliment from her grandfather, that Emily beamed. "What do you mean, polished?"

"I mean your manners, the way you dress, the way
you carry yourself. It makes all my work worthwhile."
He considered his soup for a moment, then brought his
gray eyes back to his grandchild. "Emily, it took me forty

years and over a billion dollars to get this family listed in the *Social Register*. My money was considered new money, so it wasn't any good, no matter how much I had. You have to inherit it for it to mean something, you know."

"But it has to start somewhere, doesn't it, Grandfather? I mean, even the Rockefellers haven't always had money."

"That's the logical way of thinking, but that's not the way it is. In the beginning there was God, but the Astors were here long before that. The 'right' families didn't have a beginning. They just always were. It takes at least three generations of money to be taken seriously in this town. That puts it all on your shoulders. You're the third generation in this family. You're the first who'll be really respected. You have to be ready for that responsibility."

Emily set down her spoon, unable to eat more with such a burden facing her. "They respect you, Grandfather. Mother said you could buy most of the Boston families and sell them into slavery."

Dobias laughed softly. "Your mother would say something like that. But that doesn't matter so much. Your grandmother was raised in one of the finest families of Boston. She wasn't deleted from the *Social Register* until she married me. She never lived to see the Dobias name listed."

"But did it matter to her? Aunt Rena said Grandmother wasn't that interested in society."

"She may have pretended not to be, my dear, but I could see the disappointment on her face every time we were excluded from a function because I didn't talk like I had a pencil stuck between my teeth, and I couldn't brag that my great-great-aunt's cousin was an in-law of Queen Victoria. I spent my whole life trying to make the Dobias name worthy of her, and now I have. And you have to live up to it."

He frowned and regarded her with a scrutiny that made her uncomfortable. "How old are you now, Emily?"

"I'm eleven, Grandfather. My birthday is in October."

"Eleven," he repeated. "Seems like only yesterday that you were a little toddler sitting on Shara's lap. Now you're all grown up."

In a moment of impulse that she knew her mother would not approve of, she leaned over and hugged Dobias. He accepted the embrace with surprise, and she looked into his eyes and saw the mist glistening there. For the first time, she realized that he was getting old, this man who had been such a constant in her life, who seemed as strong as a mountain and as big as a sea. This man who frightened and flabbergasted her.

She heard footsteps outside the dining room, and sprang back, as if she had done something wrong. Giselle came dashing into the dining room, breathless. "It's gone. Dad, she took the emerald and diamond necklace that Mama left. She came in here, and she took it!"

Dobias shot up. "What are you talking about? Who?"

"Corey! I saw her ex-fiancé today . . . that photographer. He told me she had been to the house and come back with a backpack full of things. So I checked the safe, and it's gone! She broke in here and robbed us!"

Emily came to her feet, her face a study in bewilderment. "But . . . I thought it was hers. I thought Grandma left it to her."

Giselle turned on her daughter. "That's not the point. Don't you understand? She broke in! She went through our safe!"

Abandoning his meal, Dobias started out of the dining room, and Giselle followed close on his heels. Emily trailed behind.

He took the stairs by twos and rounded the corridor until he came to the safe, where his wife's portrait was propped against the wall where Giselle had left it. Quickly, he opened the safe and sorted through it.

"Is everything else here?"

Giselle sat down on the bench across from the safe and raked her fingers through her hair. "Yes. I checked. She just took the necklace."

Dobias stared into the safe, then without warning, grabbed the heavy steel door and slammed it shut. "Dammit! She had no right." He turned back to Giselle. "That must be how she got the money for the paintings."

"Right," Giselle said. "She sold my mother's necklace. Can you fathom that? That she would stoop so low as to steal from us and then sell something that belonged to our mother?"

He leaned over and picked up the portrait, hung his wife's face back over the safe. His hands were shaking when he brought them back to his sides.

Emily's cautious voice broke the quiet. "Are you all right, Grandfather?"

"I want that necklace back," he said in a smolderingly low voice. "It belonged to my wife, and I want it back. We have to find out who she sold it to."

"There's probably some bag lady lying in the gutter right now with a twenty-five-thousand-dollar necklace around her throat."

"No," Dobias said, still not taking his eyes from his wife's portrait. "Corey isn't stupid. She took the necklace for a reason. I'm going to find out what it is and make sure she's stopped."

Emily started to cry, but her tears were quiet, and neither her mother nor her grandfather had the presence of mind to notice.

"Don't worry, Dad. I've already started the wheels in motion. I know what she's up to, and believe me . . . I'm going to be the one to stop her."

But it wasn't Giselle who showed up at Annotelli's the next day and grabbed Corey's arm, making her drop the tray of shrimp she carried.

The crash hushed all of the diners in the packed lunch-hour crowd, and all eyes turned to Corey as she fell to her knees and looked up at her rabid father. "Dad!"

"Where's my necklace?" he demanded, not concerned that all eyes were upon him, and that from a corner table a tourist's camera flashed.

Corey threw the shrimp haphazardly back onto the tray and stood up. "I'll speak to you in the back room," she whispered. "Please!"

"You'll speak to me here!" he shouted. "You broke into my house and stole the necklace from my safe!"

Horrified, Corey looked around her. "You're making a scene," she said through her teeth. "I'll lose my job!"

As if on cue, her boss came out from the kitchen and made a beeline to her. "Is there a problem?" he asked Dobias.

"Hell, yes, there's a problem!" he said. "She's a thief!"

Corey slammed the tray down on a vacant table with another crash, and swung back to her father. "Dad, stop it! You've taken everything else from me! Why are you doing this?"

"Where's the necklace?" her father demanded again, his breath coming as heavy as if he'd just been in a scuffle. "I want it back."

"I don't have it!" she said. "It was mine, Dad. She left it to me! She probably never dreamed I'd have to hock it for survival, but she left it to me just the same. It's in the will!"

"Where is it?" he shouted again.

Unnerved by the whole disaster, the manager of the restaurant took Dobias's arm and tried to escort him out of the dining room, but Dobias shook it off with a power that frightened the man.

"I sold it!" she cried. "It's too late. You can't have it back!"

Her father started toward her, but she didn't back away. He had never struck her before, and while she didn't doubt that he was capable of doing so, she didn't fear it, either. "Who? Who did you sell it to?"

"None of your business!"

"Then I'll have you thrown in jail!"

"You've already done that, Dad," Corey cried. "There's really nothing else you can do to me! But in case you've lost enough of your faculties to try again, I swear to God I'll get a lawyer and sue you and every one of those police officials you have in your pocket! You won't get away with it again!"

"I'd appreciate it if you'd both leave," the manager said, being more forceful in taking Corey's arm than he'd been with her father.

Corey's attention shifted to her boss, and a look of fear played across her face. "But . . . I was supposed to work a double shift."

"Not anymore," he said in a low voice. "I can't have someone working for me who's just been accused of breaking and entering, theft, and God knows what else. Leave the uniform in the locker."

"But Al . . . please! I need the money. I've worked like a dog for you!"

"I'm sorry, Corey. I can't have these volatile scenes upsetting my customers."

Corey turned to her father, who stood impassive, staring at her with hate-filled eyes. "How could you keep doing this to me? Why?"

"I won't tolerate betrayal," he said.

"I'm not the one betraying you, Dad. Don't you see? You're doing it to yourself."

"I asked you a question," he bit out. "Where is the necklace? Who bought it from you?"

"Adam Franklin!" she shouted finally, lifting her chin defiantly. "And he's not afraid of you, Dad. Why don't you go see if you can bully him out of it? But I'll warn you. You may have met your match with him."

"Adam Franklin?" The momentary surprise was replaced with smoldering rage.

"Yes, Adam Franklin. Have at him, Dad. I think he can handle it."

As if to accept the challenge, her father turned and left the restaurant.

Slowly, she turned back to her boss, who had had the mess cleaned up but still waited for her to leave. "Al, please . . ."

"You lied about who you are," he said. "I don't like being lied to."

"But if you had known, you wouldn't have hired me. I needed a job, Al. I still do."

"I'm sorry, Corey. I'm trying to run a business. I can't take the chance of any more scenes like this one. Come back tomorrow and I'll have your check ready."

Wilting, she went back to the locker room.

She had hung the uniform back in her locker and gotten back into her jeans, when Dee-dee pushed through the door. Her friend only stood looking at her, expressionless.

"So you're really Corey Dobias."

"Yeah," she said.

"You're rich."

Corey shook her head. "No, I'm not. I don't even have a job now."

"What's going on, Corey?"

Corey swallowed the tears in her throat and wiped her face. "It's a long story, Dee-dee. I'll tell you about it when you have some time. But for now, let's just say that being a Dobias is doing me a hell of a lot more harm than good. As for the money, well, it isn't mine. It never will be again."

"Then it wasn't all some kind of sick joke? The poverty bit? The job? The borrowed clothes?"

"It was for real," she said. "I haven't lied to you about anything except my name. I swear."

"I believe you."

Corey glanced toward the door and wiped her face again. "Well, you'd better get back in there. I don't want you to lose your job, too."

"Yeah. Listen, when I get off tonight, I'll come up and check on you. Maybe then you'll want to tell me that long story. I have to say, the curiosity is killing me."

"It's sure giving a lot of people something to talk about," Corey conceded.

Dee-dee left her alone. She tied her tennis shoes and looked around the restaurant one last time. She had hoped to earn at least five thousand dollars in tips to add to her twenty-five thousand down payment, which she hoped would impress the bankers she approached. So far, she'd only managed to come up with two thousand. It was okay, she thought as she held her breath and walked out into the brisk air. She'd find another job. And get more tips. And she'd hope that her father wouldn't appear there one day to badger and humiliate her and get her fired.

She wondered if Adam would regret the day he'd helped her, when her father got finished with him.

    *   *   *

When the door to Adam's office burst open and Nik Dobias cut a path across his floor, Adam almost smiled. A confrontation, he thought. He'd wanted one with the bastard for a long time now.

"Where's my necklace?"

Adam slung an ankle over his knee and tilted his chair back to look up at Dobias. "Did I miss something here?"

"She told me she sold it to you. Did you know it was stolen goods? Are you prepared to deal with the consequences of that?"

"Now, wait a minute." Adam came to his feet and walked around his desk, so that nothing stood between him and the tycoon. He stood half a head taller than Dobias, and the difference in height gave him a decided advantage. "Corey told me her mother left it to her in her will. It was her necklace."

"That's a matter for the courts to decide," Dobias flung back. "Are you the one who told her to break into my house to get it?"

"Break in?" That smile he had tried to keep in check began to seep into his eyes. "She broke in and took it?"

"Stole it," Dobias corrected.

Adam grinned as he reached for the pack of cigarettes on his desk and shook one into his mouth. "Well, I'll be damned."

"I want it back," Dobias said. "It belonged to my wife."

The statement knocked the grin from Adam's face, and slowly, he lit the cigarette. "It's mine."

"The hell it is! I'll have you arrested, if I have to. Or I can sue you for buying stolen goods. Don't think I can't do it, Franklin."

Adam took the cigarette from his mouth and laughed lightly. "Oh, I don't think even Mitch Easterman would be stupid enough to mess with me, Dobias. I could do him a lot more harm than you ever could."

Dobias's face lost its color. "Easterman? What's he got to do with this?"

Adam took another long drag on his cigarette, considering Dobias through the smoke. "You tell me."

Dobias took a few steps back and shook his head. "If you're threatening me . . ."

"Threatening you?" The idea amused him. "Now why would the mention of our esteemed police commissioner threaten you?"

Dobias stared at him, a disgusted scowl curling his lips. "I don't know what you're getting at, Franklin, but your scandal-sheet tactics won't work on me. I want that necklace, and I'm prepared to fight you for it. Is it really worth it to you?"

That murderous certainty sharpened Adam's eyes as he took the cigarette from his mouth. "Hell, yes, it's worth it."

"Why?" Dobias shouted. "What do you want with it?"

Adam unclenched his fists and settled his eyes on Dobias's hard, angry ones. "I could ask you the same question. You probably never gave that necklace a second thought until someone else wanted it. But then, that's the story of your life, isn't it?"

"My life has nothing to do with you," Dobias said. "But I'm warning you. If I don't have that necklace back in my possession by the weekend, I'll make sure you pay."

Adam stubbed his cigarette in the ashtray on his desk. "You won't have time, Dobias. By then, you'll be too busy covering your own ass."

"What do you mean by that?"

"I mean that you'd better look over your shoulder, pal, before you make any of those brilliant decisions of yours. You never know who you can trust."

"The day I trust anyone is the day a nobody like you can best me," Dobias muttered. "And that day will never come."

He started from the room and turned back at the door. Adam still smiled.

"I'll get that necklace back if it's the last thing I do," he said. "You're going to regret ever laying eyes on it."

"It'll wind up where it belongs," Adam said. "I have no doubt about that."

Dobias didn't take the time to consider that. Instead, he marched to the elevator with the regal posture of a man who owned the world, though he didn't know it was perched on the sharp end of a pine needle.

chapter
25

IT WAS THE FIRST TIME IN HER LIFE THAT COREY could remember sharing her tears with another human being, without feeling awkward or embarrassed or angry at herself. The surprising thing was, after she'd told Dee-dee her miserable story, her friend had cried with her.

"So what are you gon' do?" Dee-dee asked, her lazy Biloxi drawl making her seem more real and alive than most of the people Corey had known all her life.

"I don't know," she said. She strolled across the bare floor to Adam's recliner, which she kept beside the window. Sitting down, she curled her feet beneath her. "I just don't know. I was hoping to have at least thirty thousand dollars to put down so I could have a remote shot at getting financing. But I only have a week left, and so far I haven't even found a bank that'll talk to me."

"Maybe the building's owners will give you an extension," Dee-dee said. "Maybe if you just explained—"

"That I can't come up with the four hundred thousand I agreed to pay because I lost my waitressing job? I don't think so."

Dee-dee wiped the dampness from beneath her eyes. "I'd help you out myself if I could, Corey. You know that, don't you?"

"I know, Dee. And I appreciate it."

Shoving back a frothy mass of blond curls, Dee-dee stood up from her perch on the bed. "Well, I can't offer money right now, but how about a cup of tea?"

"I don't have any," Corey said.

"I have some. I'll run down and get it and be right back."

Corey watched as Dee-dee rushed out of the apartment, leaving her door open to the hallway. And she smiled.

But that smile quickly faded. Hugging her knees to her chest, she leaned her head back and gazed out the window, to the dark, unsightly view of another brick building and a filthy alley between them.

She didn't like this feeling of helplessness, she thought, and she didn't intend to hold onto it for long. Tomorrow, first thing, she would set out to get financing. If she had to go to another state, she would do it. If she had to get down on her knees and beg, she was up to it.

She closed her eyes and thought of Adam, and wondered if he was disgusted with her by now, since her father had confronted him. She didn't even want to know how the scene had turned out. The idea made her nauseated.

Propping her chin on her hand, she stared out into the darkness falling over the city. If he wasn't disgusted with her, maybe he could help her, she thought. But as quickly as the thought occurred to her, she banished it from her mind. When she'd met him, she had been broken and helpless and confused. Now she had a goal, a means of reaching it, and her self-respect. She thought she had his respect, too.

No, she wouldn't ruin it by begging him for money or a job again. That respect meant too much to her, even though she knew that was about as much of him as she could ever hope to have.

The kiss of the other night shivered through her memory, and her heart melted. He had felt the magic, too. His embrace had been as hungry as hers.

Then he had pulled away.

Trust me, he'd said.

Trust him with what? she'd wondered a thousand times since. With her honor? Her heart? She honestly didn't know, and yet she didn't feel she really had a choice. He was as far from her reach as her pampered past.

Adam didn't trust himself as he stepped into the dilapidated building that Corey called home, and yet he had come.

He started up the steps, avoiding a hole in one of them, and looked up when he heard a door open on the first floor. Corey's friend Dee-dee stepped out with two steaming cups of tea in her hand.

"Oh, hi."

He stopped and looked at her over the rail. "I was just going up to see Corey. Do you know if she's home?"

Dee-dee's hair bobbed with her nod. "Yeah, she's there. I was just taking her a cup of tea, but here, you take it. She'd probably rather see you, anyway. She's real down."

He took the hot cup and frowned down at her. "I went by Annotelli's first. They said she got fired."

"Yeah," Dee-dee said. "That jackass father of hers started calling her a thief right there in the restaurant. It was unbelievable. Just because he's rich, he thinks he can treat people anyway he wants. Boy, I'd love to see him get his."

Adam stood still for a moment, studying Dee-dee's face. "Corey told you who she is?"

Dee-dee nodded solemnly. "Yeah, she told me. Pretty incredible, huh? Wish I could help her."

Adam glanced up the stairs. "Well, I'm gonna go on up. I'll take her the tea."

She nodded and sipped her own, and he left her standing there.

Corey's door was open when he reached her floor. He raised his hand to knock, but then he saw her curled up in the recliner he had given her, staring pensively out the window with tears glistening on her cheeks.

Suddenly he didn't give a damn what kind of promises he'd made to himself.

Quietly, he stepped inside.

Corey looked up and caught her breath. "Adam!"

He closed the door behind him. "I brought you Deedee's tea."

She took it, but didn't drink.

He sat down on the windowsill facing her, and reached out to wipe the tears from her cheek. "So how are you doing?"

"I'm fine," she said. "Really. What about you? No scratches or bruises?"

He smiled. "Your father can't hurt me. It's you I've been worried about. You lost your job."

"Yeah," she whispered, warming her cold hands on the coffee mug. "It's okay. I'll find another one. I don't give up easily."

"No. I know you don't."

She sipped the tea, then set the cup down on the sill beside him and wiped her tears with both hands. "I'm sorry you caught me like this. I must look awful."

He smiled and leaned forward and stroked her wet cheek with the backs of his fingers. "When I came up here and saw you sitting here in that chair, crying, I can't tell you what it did to me. No, Corey. You don't look awful." He stopped, breathed a deep, ragged sigh.

She met his eyes, and he memorized the lengthy sweep of wet lashes surrounding the bluest eyes he could imagine, and the moist set of full lips slightly parted. He could taste her from memory, the warm velvety texture of her tongue and her mouth, the shape of her lips, the crush of her body against his. And yet the memory wasn't strong enough when he had her within his reach.

It was Corey who made the first move, so slowly, so quietly, so naturally, that he had no time to remind himself of that conscience that would haunt him in the night, or the vows he'd sworn to uphold. The power of her kiss was stronger than any fortress he'd built and hidden himself within. It was stronger than either of them.

She came to her feet and slipped between his knees and into his arms. She splayed her hands through his hair, and a yearning dread grew inside him at how helpless he had become. "No, Corey," he whispered. "I didn't come here for this."

She didn't break the fragile contact of their lips as she asked, "What then?"

"To see if you were all right," he whispered. "I was worried about you."

"I'm all right now," she said. She opened the kiss again, and with a resigned and shuddering sigh, he closed his hands around her hips and pulled her against him as the kiss grew deeper, hungrier, more urgent.

She felt his arousal despite his denial of it, and knew that he was hers for now. She dropped her lips to his neck, nuzzled, and he sought her mouth again and pulled her back into a searing kiss. His hand trembled as it rose to her breast, and as if that bold touch set off an electrical impulse, she began to unbutton his shirt with an urgency that neither of them could slow.

Her lips trailed down his neck to his chest, and she traced her tongue across his nipple and felt him quiver.

The reaction gave her an intense sense of power, a power she intended to use.

At once he was opening her blouse, pulling it off one shoulder, tasting the fragrance of her flesh, feeling her bare breast against his chest.

When he lifted her and took her to the small bed in the corner of the room, she shed the shirt completely. In seconds they had rid each other of their clothes as they fell into the cadence of obsession that neither could escape.

Afterward, she lay in his arms, watching the way the moonlight from the window played on his features, and she saw the sad regret sparkling in his eyes.

"Was it that bad?"

He smiled. "Are you kidding?"

"Then what is it?" she whispered, propping herself on an elbow.

Adam lay staring up at the ceiling, his hands behind his head. "I just don't want you to get hurt, Corey."

"Well, I don't think you'd hurt me, would you?"

He didn't look at her. "Not intentionally."

She laid her arm across his chest and turned his face to hers. A poignant light sparkled in his eyes.

"You're really beautiful, you know that?" he whispered.

The sadness in his eyes broke her heart. "What is it, Adam? Tell me. Why are you beating yourself up for making love to me?"

"How do you know I am?" he asked. "How do you know I'm not beating myself up for not doing it sooner?"

Her smile broke through the worry on her face.

He moved his arms around her and pulled her head to rest on his bare chest. "Go to sleep," he whispered.

"Will you be here when I wake up?"

There was a pause, and she knew he was wrestling with whatever ghost was plaguing him. "Yes," he said finally. "I'm not going anywhere."

It was four-thirty when Corey awoke and saw that Adam had left her bed. Groggy, she sat up and looked around the room.

She saw him sitting on the windowsill, staring out into the night, and that tormented look was back on his face as he brought a cigarette to his lips. Something told her not to approach him, for whatever dragged him down was too big for her to conquer just yet.

She lay in the dark watching him until, finally, he put the cigarette out. When he came back to bed, she closed her eyes. He slipped in beside her, laid his arm gently over her, and pressed a kiss on her warm forehead.

And she knew that whatever it was that loomed between them, it was growing smaller all the time.

The morning sunshine filtering in through the window didn't lighten Adam's mood, for Corey still saw the self-deprecation straining his face as he shared breakfast with her. She didn't know why, but somehow she felt that sleeping with her had complicated his life beyond explanation.

Just before he left her to go back to Franklin Tower, he handed her a note with the name of a New Jersey banker he had jotted down. "Try calling him today," he said. "I don't think his bank owes your father anything, and I've already put in a word for you. I think he can help you out."

Corey's eyes widened. "Really? Do you think he'd finance my building?"

Adam dropped another gentle kiss on her lips but pulled away before it could grow into anything more.

"If he has half a brain, he will. And I told him so."

"You did?"

She had come to equate that sad look with his own desire, and while she didn't understand it, she reacted with a fresh surge of longing.

"I did."

He started through the door, but Corey stopped him. "Adam?"

He looked down at her, as if he knew already what she was going to say—and dreaded it.

"Will I see you again? Soon?"

He nodded. "I'm canceling my trip to Tokyo. I have some things here I have to take care of."

"Tonight?"

He looked toward the door, as if he couldn't get through it fast enough. "I don't know, Corey."

Dejected, she wilted and stepped back. "I see."

"No, you don't see." He turned back around and drew her into his arms. "I'll call you. I will."

She swallowed. "Adam, you know I don't have a phone. Don't just tell me things I want to hear."

"I'm not doing that," he said. "Anyway, you should get a phone. The bankers will need your number."

"I will," she said, making the decision even as she spoke. "But this isn't about my phone. This is about us. What are you afraid of?"

He pressed a kiss to her forehead. "Regrets," he whispered. "I'm afraid you'll be the one with regrets when it's all over."

"Then don't let it end," she whispered.

He kissed her again, a kiss that foreshadowed the ending he spoke of, and left her feeling tragically abandoned even before he'd let her go.

Then, as if he couldn't put her away from him fast enough, he opened the door and left her alone.

chapter
26

STEPHEN ASTLEBERRY RESEMBLED POPEYE'S
Wimpy—minus the hamburgers—but since he was
a friend of Adam's and executive vice president of the
New Jersey bank, Corey credited him with intelligence.
He was instantly likeable, and the longer she sat in his
office, the more she realized that he had something all
the other bankers she'd visited didn't have.

He had the word *yes* in his vocabulary.

"I told Adam I'd look out for you," he said, leaning
his overweight frame back in his chair and clasping his
hands over his stomach. "If you have him vouching for
you, you can't be all bad."

She smiled. "Have you known him long?"

"Since he bought the *Investigator*. He was practically
a kid, traipsing in here with his head full of dreams.
Everyone else had turned him down, but he hadn't given
up. Something about him won me over, and I haven't
regretted it since." He leaned forward on his desk and
studied her through sharp eyes. "He seems to think you
have that same something."

Corey sat straight in her chair in the linen suit she'd
bought that morning to look as professional as she needed to, and met his eyes directly. "If that something is
determination, you bet I've got it. I was raised a Dobias,
Mr. Astleberry. Whether or not that means anything to
me right now, it did give me a kind of business education that you can't get in school. I know how to make a
deal, I know how to cut costs, and I know how to make

a lot out of very little. I helped my father renovate his mid-Manhattan hotel, and up until a few weeks ago, I had been helping with the decorating of his new casino in Atlantic City."

"But buying and selling," Astleberry said. "Have you done much of that yourself?"

"Under my father's supervision," she said. "My father has negotiated some of the most creative deals of the decade. I've picked up a few things. I know what I'm doing. If you'll give me the money I need for this project, you won't regret it. And there will be many, many more where that came from. But time is of the essence. My contract to buy expires the day after tomorrow. I need the money by then."

Astleberry frowned and shook his head. "I'm afraid that would be impossible. We couldn't possibly make this kind of loan to you that quickly. Two of our board members are out of the country, and we have to have their approval on a loan this size."

"Then how soon?"

He thought for a moment, cleared his throat. "Well, our board meeting is next Tuesday. That's a week from now. I suppose it could possibly come about then if everyone agrees."

"That's the absolute soonest?"

"I'm afraid so," he said. "But you can probably negotiate an extension. Have the owners call me, and I'll assure them that things look good."

Two hours later, after she'd met with several other bank executives, as well as the president and two board members, she left the building with more energy in her step than she'd had in a long time. It was going to work out. They were going to give her the money.

Feeling confident that the HDRS Group would give her

another week, considering that she practically had the financing lined up, she took the train back to Boston, then rode the T to Beacon Street and hurried to Andrew Hinton's office. He was on his way out when she walked in.

"Please, Mr. Hinton. I need to speak to you."

Issuing a long-suffering sigh, he turned and led her back into his office. "I don't have a lot of time," he said, dropping into his seat behind his desk. "What is it?"

"I need an extension," she said, trying to ignore his abrupt tone. "Just another week. I have the financing lined up, but it won't be available until Tuesday at the earliest. But you could call the bank and talk—"

"I'm sorry, Miss Dobias." The words cut her off before she'd even finished talking, and she let her sentence die. "You see, we've had a better offer for that building. If you can't close the deal by your deadline—let's see, I believe that's the day after tomorrow, isn't it?—I'm afraid we'll have to proceed with another buyer."

"But there wasn't anyone interested in it when I came to you. It was just sitting there, boarded up and dilapidated. No one else wanted it!"

"But all that has changed."

Corey came to her feet and leaned over the desk, her gaze direct and threatening. "Who is the other buyer?"

Hinton cleared his throat and diverted his eyes. "Well, I don't suppose it's a secret. After all, you'll find out anyway." He looked up at her and adjusted his glasses. "I'm afraid it's your sister."

She knew without a doubt which one, but the reality of it knocked the breath from her. "Giselle?"

"Yes."

Corey dropped into her chair and raked her fingers through her hair. "Why? What does she want with it?"

"That's not my concern," Hinton said. "My only interest is in selling the property. What goes on between you and your family is your business."

"Mr. Hinton, don't you see? She doesn't really want that property. She just doesn't want me to get it. It'll probably continue to sit there, untouched, just as broken and decrepit as ever. I could have helped change the face of the Combat Zone, and that would increase the value of all the other property you own on Tremont Street."

He opened his big hands, as if to offer her an unspoken apology, though the smile on his face belied it. "What can I say? You still have two days. Bring us the money and close the deal, and the building is yours."

"Yeah, right." Then, not bothering to say another word, she grabbed her briefcase and left his office.

Corey stopped at the first pay phone she came to and dialed Giselle's personal number in her office, the one used only by the family.

"Hello?"

"Giselle, this is Corey," she bit out. "I want to know why you bid on the Tremont Street property. I want to know what you plan to do with it."

She could almost hear Giselle smile over the phone. "Oh, I don't know," her sister said in a lazy voice. "Maybe something, maybe nothing. Haven't decided yet, you know? Some things are just nice to have."

"A junk building on Tremont Street is nice to have? It must be contagious, Giselle. You've caught Dad's insanity!"

Giselle's laughter made Corey's blood curdle.

"Listen to me, Giselle. I never wanted to compete with you, but if you want a war, you've got it. I can play with the best of them, and when it comes right down to it, you have a hell of a lot more to lose than I do."

"Is that some kind of threat?"

"Hell, yes, it's a threat," Corey said. "Just stay out of my way!"

The phone clattered into its cradle, and Corey backed away from it. Not knowing what to do with her anger, she set out walking.

She should have known, the moment she discovered her briefcase missing from her bedroom the night she'd broken in to the estate, someone had been looking for information. The fact that Giselle was interested in anything she had going on was beyond her, and yet she saw the competition keenly sketched out, as if she'd never walked away from it.

Well, she thought, there might not be a multimillion dollar pot of gold waiting at the end of her victory now, but she intended to knock Giselle out of her game, anyway. And maybe her father while she was at it. After all, they'd seen to it that she had nothing else to lose.

She found herself heading down State Street, peppered with tourists taking the Harborwalk to the ocean. Idly, she followed them, having no place else to go.

Most of the wharves on the waterfront had been rebuilt, and buildings that had once been warehouses were now expensive restaurants and office buildings and apartments. The area that had been one of the eyesores of Boston was now a chic, exclusive area. She wished she'd been here years ago when all the rebuilding had started. It would have been exciting to be one of the pioneers who bought the first dilapidated property and vowed to make it a showplace, a beginning to transforming the entire area. She could have done that with the Combat Zone, she thought. She could have turned it around just like this. It wouldn't have been easy, but it could have been done.

She could have restored some of the buildings, leveled others, built skyscrapers for offices, blending modern necessity with elegant old. She would have changed the face of it, and the clientele, and subsequently, the reputation. It would have done Boston good.

But now Giselle was in the way, throwing up yet another obstacle in her path. Vengeance was as potent for inspiration as unrealized dreams, so Corey caught a cab to Tremont Street and walked up into the Combat Zone, where the building she had come so close to owning stood. She looked across the street, saw the gaping building that had a neon sign outside that boasted Girls, Girls, Girls, and next door to it the adult theater where porno flicks played throughout the night.

Her visionary's eyes imagined in its place a Victorian facade to a thirteen-story skyscraper that blended contextually into the decor of the rest of the city. A building that would house luxury offices, perhaps her own when her business got underway. Then she could buy the surrounding properties, and renovate the ones that could be salvaged, and tear down and rebuild the rest. And Giselle would have to follow suit and do something with her building, something to help Boston, rather than just own it to spite her sister.

But what about money? she asked herself. It would take millions. Hundreds of millions. But that had never stopped her father when he was starting out. One of his primary philosophies in life was never to use his own money. That would be hers, too, if she could find investors and infect them with her excitement.

She had time now, she thought. Ironically, Giselle's bid on her property had bought her that. She would go back to the New Jersey bank and convince them to put the money on some of this other property rather than the one she had originally chosen. She would use their names and their commitments to inspire other banks to follow suit. It would be a long process, and a

time-consuming one. But she had no doubts that she
could do it. She had a lot of her father in her. The biggest
obstacle would be getting around his influence.

Quickly, she jotted down the addresses, found another
cab, and went to city hall to search the records for owners
of the buildings she wanted most. As she worked, she
discovered the swirling thrill of having a challenging
goal, a vendetta, and the knowledge that she had nothing left to lose.

chapter

27

THE SUITE AT THE TRENTON ARMS RESERVED for Nik Dobias was large and pampering, but with himself, Giselle, Rena, John, and Robert Gloster crammed in to advise him, he was getting downright claustrophobic. The fact that he'd been caged in that hearing all day didn't help matters any.

"I can't believe how hostile those people were," he muttered, pacing the room with a Scotch in his hand. "It was incredible. That question about tax evasion. They acted like I'd been convicted of a crime. I was acquitted, for God's sake!"

Robert adjusted his glasses and tilted his head to scrutinize his old friend. "Nik, I have to tell you, that's not the question that worried me the most. It was the one about the code violations. Those construction workers they got to testify might have delivered our kiss of death."

"The building passed the code inspections! They can't come back now and claim it's not up to par."

"That's not all they're claiming," John said, slinging an ankle over his knee. "It sounds like they've got some evidence of bribery."

Dobias waved off the comment. "Name me one person who lets the chips fall where they may and doesn't get buried beneath them. I'm not one to just sit around and trust fate. I make things happen."

Giselle smiled. "I wouldn't say it in those words to the committee, Dad."

"Why not? Maybe that's exactly who I need to say it

to. One on one. Maybe I need to pick out a couple of the ones whose votes could sway the committee in my favor, and see what we can do for them."

Rena covered her face with her hand and shook her head. "I can't believe this."

"Believe what?" Dobias asked, striding toward her and daring her to tell him.

She looked up at him and thought of keeping her mouth shut, but she couldn't sit still while her father dug his hole deeper. "Dad, you can't buy these people off. Just trust yourself. Giselle and I can testify for you, and you have some of the best legal minds in this part of the country working with you. You'll be fine."

"I'd rather make sure of that," he said. "This could drag on six or eight weeks. I've seen it happen." He rubbed at the burning in his stomach. "Dammit, I shouldn't have started construction until I had the license in my hand. If I don't get that license, it's six hundred million down the drain."

Rena emptied the glass in her hand and headed for the wet bar again. The staff must have restocked it, for she could have sworn she had polished off what was left of the Scotch at lunch. "Don't worry, Dad. You did it the best way. When the license comes through, you'll be almost ready to open. Just be patient."

Dobias laughed, but the sound was brittle and hard. "Patient! When the *Titanic* was sinking, I seriously doubt anyone told those people to be patient!"

He strolled to the round table in the corner of the suite, where Gloster sat behind a mountain of paperwork. "Who should we approach, Robert? You have dossiers on all of the committee members."

"I don't have enough information to be sure that any one of them would take a payoff."

"It depends on the bribe," Dobias said. "It always does.

Give them the title to a Sabre liner and a couple of Jaguars, and they'll come around."

"What if airplanes and sports cars don't mean anything to them?" Gloster asked with a note of weariness in his voice. "What if you're just buying yourself a hell of a lot more trouble? Think about it, Nik. These men have dealt with some of the richest men in the world. Don't you think they've been offered bribes before?"

"I'm prepared to pay whatever it takes," Dobias insisted. "They'll take it. They *have* to." He took the profiles out of his lawyer's hands and scanned the pages himself. "This one . . . Sid Ranger. He likes me. I can tell he's impressed by money. We'll try him. And how about Alan Bayson? Says here he has five kids, four of them in college. The man is bound to need some help. I think we can help him."

Gloster sighed and jotted some notes on his legal pad. "All right, Nik. I'll arrange a meeting."

"Make it tonight," he said. "I don't want to wait. Tomorrow could do us in completely. We want them to push toward an end to this ordeal. I have better things to do than answer questions for a bunch of hypocritical bureaucrats." He checked his watch. "It's six now. Get one of them here at seven-thirty. Tell him we have some information that might shed light on the hearings. Anything to get him here. We'll meet them one at a time, just in case one of them doesn't bite. If they're together, they're more likely to stay clean."

"I'll sit in on the meetings with you, Dad," Giselle said. "If things don't go well, I can use some persuasion of my own."

Dobias gave his daughter a long, scrutinizing look. "All right," he said finally. "And you, John. I'll need you and Robert here."

The fact that she'd been excluded didn't hurt Rena as

it might have, for all day she'd seen Joe Baker waiting for her around various corners of the hotel when she had come and gone. He had slipped her his room number earlier, and she had been astonished to discover that he had gotten a room on the same floor as the entire Dobias contingency. The sheer bravado of his pursuit of her was titillating. If she didn't have to attend the meeting, she could see him.

She stood up and began rubbing her temples, a habit she'd picked up without realizing it in the last few months. "I guess I'll just go back to the room and order room service," she said.

"You can stay if you want," Dobias said as an afterthought.

Rena shook her head. "No, I have a headache. I think I'll just go lie down, get some rest. If I have to testify tomorrow, I want my head to be clear."

No one answered, for by then they were all caught up in studying the dossiers of Sid Ranger and Alan Bayson, trying to find their Achilles' heels. She was glad she wouldn't be a part of it.

Quietly, she slipped out the door and went down the hall into her own suite, kicked off her shoes, sat on the bed, and pulled the telephone into her lap. She punched out Joe's number.

The line was busy, so she hung up, dialed the hotel operator, and left a message for him to call her. The operator would turn on the message light on his phone, she hoped, and he'd get the message immediately.

While she waited, she poured herself a drink, started a hot bath in the marble tub, and fantasized about how the night was going to be.

I'm obsessed with you, he'd said.

She feared she was becoming obsessed with him, as well. She only hoped that, if tonight led to what she thought it would, she wouldn't disappoint him.

A new swell of anxiety pulsed through her, and she went to her makeup case on the bathroom counter and dug for her Valium. If she was more relaxed, she'd do so much better, she thought. Her inhibitions would be gone. She could be what he thought she was. She could be herself.

But then she thought again and decided that might not be such a good idea. Maybe she should be someone more exciting. Someone like Giselle . . . or even Corey. But not Rena. Never Rena.

She washed the pill down with her drink, then stared at herself in the mirror. She had a lot to do to get ready to see him, she thought. She only hoped there was enough time.

Joe Holifield balanced the phone between his chin and shoulder and jotted furiously on the notepad that was almost full, as the ex-Dobias Enterprises VP spilled his guts about Dobias's tax-evasion scheme.

It was a gold mine, he thought, and he had Adam to thank for it. It had been his idea to contact the man who had been fired three months earlier. He was hostile, he said, and might talk.

And talk he did. He supplied names of others who had been screwed by Dobias, men who would love the opportunity to see the man castrated.

Even after all that, he had a whole list of people who had testified against Dobias in the hearing today, people who might prove invaluable as contacts.

"I need tangible proof," Holifield told the ex-VP now. "Can you get me copies of invoices? Phony bills? Anything?"

"I still have some friends who work for him," the man said. "I could try."

"I have to have them," Holifield said again. "I can't print the story without some kind of proof. If you can do it, I'll make it worth your while."

The man was quiet for a moment, and finally he said, "Yeah, I think I can handle it."

The red light on Holifield's phone began to blink, and he closed his pad. "If you need to speak to me in the next few days, I'll be at this number. Otherwise, try me at the *Investigator*. I'll meet you wherever you say."

Once again, the man expressed his urgent desire to see Dobias get his, and hung up the phone.

Still reeling with excitement from all the information he'd gotten, Holifield dialed the operator. "Message for me?" he asked. "Room twenty-three twelve, Joe Baker."

"Yes, Mr. Baker. There's a message for you to call Rena in room twenty-three oh five."

He grinned and mouthed the word *bingo*. Hanging up, he quickly punched out the number.

"Hello?"

"You called," he said in a soft, bedroom grumble, as if he'd done nothing all day except fantasize about her. "My heart might not be able to take this."

"I can meet you tonight," she said. "Seven-thirty all right?"

He frowned. "What about your husband? I thought we'd have to sneak around after midnight or something."

"No," she said. "He has an important meeting with my father in his suite tonight. I expect it to go on pretty late."

He reopened his pad and jotted, "meeting—important."

"So how did the hearings go?"

"Not good. He's really upset. But as usual, he has a plan. Either it'll blow up in his face tonight, or tomorrow things will go a lot smoother. Who knows?"

The scraps of information swirled with tornado force through Joe's head, and he tried to put it together. In bold letters, he scrawled, "Plan." "Uh, what time does his meeting start?"

"Seven-thirty," she said. "Why?"

"Well, maybe it would be better if we waited until eight. I don't want to trip over your husband in the hallway."

"All right, then," she said. "Eight sounds good."

He smiled. "Hey, Rena? Let's don't leave the hotel. I want you all to myself tonight. We'll order room service."

He could hear the shiver in her voice when she answered. "Okay, Joe. Whatever you want."

"You," he whispered. "I want you."

He hung up the phone and smiled at the image he had of her still holding the phone to her chest, her little heart pounding in fear and apprehension. He doubted she'd ever cheated on her husband before. That fact gave him a strong, strange sense of power over her.

He had no doubt that he would, indeed, get what he wanted tonight.

At seven o'clock, Holifield loaded the wristwatch camera that Adam had provided him with—a gadget that no self-respecting tabloid reporter could do without. He stepped into the corridor and began to pace the length of the hall, passing the elevator as he did. Each time the elevator doors opened, he checked his "watch" and took a noiseless, flashless picture of the person getting off.

He watched, pretending to wait for the elevator, as John Keller, Giselle, and Robert Gloster approached Dobias's suite one by one.

At seven-thirty-five a man got off of the elevator, and Holifield snapped his picture. When he saw that he was headed for Dobias's suite, Holifield pulled his code card from his pocket and went to the suite next door to

Dobias's. Pretending to have trouble with the lock, he poised his watch and waited until Dobias opened his door. The second he did, he clicked two pictures.

"Mr. Bayson, thanks for coming," Dobias said in a low voice as he ushered the man in.

The door closed, and Holifield wilted with relief. Bayson. Memorizing the name, he hurried back to his own suite and flipped back through his notes until he came to Bayson's name, listed as one of the members of the Casino Control Commission.

Quickly, he dialed Adam's number. It took a few minutes to get past the secretary, but when Adam answered, he was gratifyingly attentive. "What have you got, Joe?"

Joe grinned. "You'll never believe this. Alan Bayson, one of the head guys on the Casino Control Commission, just got off the elevator and went into Dobias's suite. And according to Rena, her father has plans for a meeting tonight that will, quote, 'either blow up in his face or make things run a lot smoother tomorrow.' That wrist camera you gave me was a godsend. I got him and Dobias on film, Adam."

Adam's slow, quiet laugh almost took Holifield by surprise. "Well, I'll be damned. I think we've got the son-of-a-bitch."

"Meanwhile, I've got gads of other info ready to be written up." Holifield checked his real watch, the one lying on his bedside table. "I'm meeting Rena in a few minutes. Man, this story is about to bust wide open."

"That's what I want to hear," Adam said. "Let me know if you find out anything else. And remember. We can't print without enough evidence. Before you write the story, I want you to meet with the attorneys and go over everything you've got. I've decided to run this in the *Bulletin*. It'll pack a bigger punch if it isn't in the tabloid."

Holifield mouthed the words *thank you* to the ceiling

and flopped back onto his bed.

"Did you hear me?" Adam asked. "I'm finally pulling you out of the trenches."

Joe sat back up and tried not to sound too pleased. "That's good, Adam, but I don't want you to forget our deal. You get the story of your life—for whichever paper you want—and I get back on the tube."

"You deliver what you're promising, Joe, and I'll have a job waiting for you."

As Joe hung up, he couldn't wipe the smile from his face. Looking in the mirror and stroking his beard, he drew in a long, deep, proud breath. "You old son-of-a-bitch," he told his image. "You're a fucking genius."

He poured some cologne into his hands, slapped it onto his beard, and checked his clothes one last time. Not that they would matter, he thought. He'd be out of them before he knew it.

The perks with this job were getting better all the time, he thought as he left his room and knocked on Rena's door. But he figured he deserved them. It was about time things started looking up.

The moment the door closed behind Alan Bayson at eleven-thirty that night, Dobias turned back to John, Giselle, and Robert and stretched his arms out above his head, as if he were a god who'd come to claim his world.

"We did it," he whispered with barely controlled glee. "We did it. I told you he could be bought. I *told* you."

Giselle looked more drained than she had when she came in that night, and she poured herself a stiff drink and downed it. "I can't believe you gave him all that. It'll cost you millions! *I'd* love to have some of what you gave him."

"This license is worth millions!" Dobias said. "I've poured six hundred million into that casino already, and it isn't even finished yet! If I don't get the license, the banks will go nuts trying to get that money out of anything and everything else I have. It could bankrupt us."

"But you have a meeting with Ranger tomorrow night. You'll have to offer him the moon and the stars, too."

"Whatever it takes, Giselle. I'll do whatever it takes."

He turned to John and Robert, who sat at a round table, making notes about the various things they had promised the hard-nosed commission member tonight. If this didn't get the license approved, Dobias thought, nothing would.

"John, call Stan and tell him to get right on this tomorrow morning. I want everything Bayson asked for delivered where he said by this weekend."

John picked up the phone and punched out the number of one of the managing directors of Dobias Enterprises.

Dobias sat down by his daughter as John spoke into the phone, and patting her knee, he gave her the happiest look she'd seen in years. "It's going to happen!" he said. "In just a few months, I could have the casino operational. We'll be raking in the cash faster than we can count it."

"Uh, Nik?"

Dobias glanced toward his son-in-law, who held out the phone with a worried look on his face. "I think you'll want to talk to Stan yourself. It seems that some reporter from the *Investigator* has been snooping around today. He's contacted a couple of our people and drilled them about phony invoices and personal expenses being charged to the buildings. And Stan says there were a few questions about bribery of public officials."

"Give me that." Dobias grabbed the phone. "Stan? What the hell is going on there?"

Stan, who'd been at Dobias Enterprises for ten years, cleared his throat. "His name was Holifield. I cut the conversation short when I realized where it was leading, but I thought you should know. I understand he called quite a few people around here today, and Nik, from the questions he was asking, I'd say he already has a good bit of information."

"Shit!" Dobias switched the phone to his other ear, and his face turned a dangerous shade of red. "You call a meeting first thing in the morning, Stan. Tell the employees that if one of them is caught talking to that bastard, they're out on their asses! Do you hear me?"

"Yes, of course. I'll take care of it."

Dobias slammed down the phone and turned back to the other three in the room. "We've got to nip this in the bud. Robert, call Adam Franklin. Tell him we'll sue him for everything he's worth if they print any of this. Try to find out what they've got and when they plan to print it. Dammit, we've got to stop him! If this comes out before my license is approved, we're sunk!"

He dropped into a chair in the corner of the room and covered his face, as if waiting for the roller-coaster ride to end. But he suspected it was just beginning.

Joe and Rena didn't bother to order dinner for hours after she had come into his room, for it seemed that the moment the door was closed, the urgency of what had built up between them for days, and the secrecy and forbidden aspect of her sneaking here right under her husband's nose, made the wait too much to bear.

He undressed her with the trembling hands of a man who'd waited a lifetime to touch his treasure, and she fought to get his clothes off just as quickly.

Before they'd even accomplished the task, he had taken her against the door of the hotel suite, then brought her to the floor and fulfilled her with such expertise that she shivered and pleaded for more.

As she lay in his arms afterward, naked and feeling more cherished and beautiful than she'd ever felt in her life, she began to get philosophical. "Joe? Do you believe that everyone has a soul mate out there, someone that's meant exclusively for them?"

"Yeah, I can buy that."

"Me, too," she whispered. "I think I've found mine."

She had never said words like that to John, for he would have laughed them off and made her feel like a stupid romantic. But Joe drew his arms tighter around her, kissed her slowly and sweetly, and made love to her again.

And Rena thought that she had never been happier—or more cherished—at any time in her life.

Joe's phone rang just after midnight, and he squinted and reached over Rena to answer it. Her eyes came open, and he heard her gasp at the time glowing on the clock in the darkness.

"Yeah?" he growled into the phone.

"Holifield, this is Adam. Are you alone?"

Joe glanced at Rena, who had slipped out of bed and was pulling on her clothes. "No, I'm not."

"All right," Adam said. "Just be quiet and listen. I just got a call from Robert Gloster, Dobias's attorney. They got wind of your snooping around today, and they want to meet with us to discuss our allegations. This might be just what we're looking for. If they confirm any of what you've come up with, we can go with the story. Even a strong reaction might be enough for us."

"I think you're right."

"They're bringing a team of lawyers themselves, and I'll have my own. I want you here, too, to confront them with your story. Can you have it ready to print tomorrow, so we can go to press immediately if we get what we need?"

Joe couldn't suppress the smile inching across his face. "You bet your ass I can."

"Then get back here tomorrow. I'll see that someone else covers the committee hearings, but you've got some more work to do from this end if we're going to be ready."

"You got it," Joe said. "I'll see you."

He hung up the phone and turned on the lamp, and saw that Rena was almost dressed. "That was the guy I work with. Do you have to go?"

She checked her hair in the mirror, searching for signs of infidelity. They were all over her, from the whisker-chafed spots on her face, to her swollen lips. "Oh, God. I didn't mean to fall asleep. Look how late it is. John's probably back by now, wondering where I am."

"Tell him you were in the bar having drinks."

"I will. Yes, that sounds good." She came back to the bed, leaned over him, and gave him a deep, lingering kiss. "I'll call you tomorrow when I can get away."

"You do that." He pulled out of bed and escorted her to the door.

She stopped before opening it. Her eyes were misty with emotion as she looked up at him. "Joe? This night meant so much to me. You have no idea."

"Me, too," he whispered. "You just may have changed my life."

Her smile was beautiful as she opened the door, checked the hallway, then slipped out. When the door closed behind her, Joe wore a smile of his own.

Quickly, he began to pack to meet his ship that was on its way in.

chapter
28

"WHERE HAVE YOU BEEN?" DEE-DEE WHISPERED as Corey stepped into their dilapidated apartment building. "He's been waiting for over an hour. God, where did you get those clothes? You look fabulous!"

Corey looked up at Dee-dee from the newspaper article she was reading about her father's progress with the Casino Control Commission, and closed the front door behind her. "I was meeting with one of the owners of a building I want to buy. Who's waiting? Is it Adam?"

"No. Some other guy. He looks like Mark Harmon, only sexier. I tell ya, some girls have all the luck."

She took the newspaper out of Corey's hands and pointed toward the staircase. "Go on! He's been sitting up at the top of the stairs waiting for you."

"He didn't give a name?"

"No."

Corey started up the stairs but stopped when she realized that Dee-dee was following her.

"I won't go all the way," she said in a stage whisper. "I just want to see who he is. And, you know, make sure he isn't an ax murderer or something."

Corey smiled and hurried up the stairs.

She saw Eric as she rounded the landing. He was sitting on the top step, leaning back against the wall, his camera bag lying on the floor beside him. He looked good, she thought, as good as he had the first time she had seen him. But her heart didn't flip the way it had then.

"What are you doing here?"

"I came to see you. I miss you."

"Yeah, right." Corey looked over her shoulder and saw that Dee-dee had stayed back, out of sight. She brought her gaze back to Eric. "I still haven't made up with my father, if that's what you came to find out. It's not going to happen, Eric."

She stepped over his legs, and he grabbed her hand. "Come on, Corey. You know that's not why I'm here."

Corey withdrew her hand. Stepping over a cracked plank in the floor, she unlocked her door. "All right, Eric, come on in. I don't have a lot of time, so let's just get to the point."

"What's gotten into you? You're getting downright bitchy."

"I've always been a bitch, Eric. You just couldn't see it for all the dollar signs."

"Give me a break. I'm here, and you're not worth a penny now."

Corey gave him a saccharin smile. "You've always had a way with words, Eric." She dropped her briefcase on the bar in her kitchen and opened the refrigerator. All she saw were a few cans of Diet Coke, a bottle of Perrier, and an apple.

Eric shoved the door closed and took her hands, making her face him. "Look at you, Corey. You look like a million bucks." He glanced down at the neckline of her dress and feathered a finger down the base of her throat. "You aren't wearing the locket. I've never known you to take it off since I gave it to you."

"That was before I found out that the substance beneath my surface amounted to my daddy's bank account."

"Hey, don't do this, Corey. What do you want me to

do? Get down on my hands and knees and beg you to forgive me?"

"For what, Eric? What would you want me to forgive you for? I wonder if you really know."

He shrugged and turned away, and paced across the small floor to the window. "For being a first-class bastard, I guess. For not having more patience. For being selfish."

"You've been practicing," she said. "How about that?"

He dropped into her chair, threw a leg over the arm, and looked back at her. "Look, I thought we could be friends."

Corey went to the only other place to sit in the room— the bed—and sat down. Suddenly she felt very tired. The day had been a long one. She'd spent the first part of the morning buying an outfit that would make her look like a successful Dobias when she went to talk to the owners of the building she wanted to buy on Tremont Street near Boylston, far enough on the outskirts of the Combat Zone where she could start and work her way inward, until the sleazy theaters and pornographic retail stores were squeezed out. She'd spent hours in their offices, then met with an architect she'd known in college, going over ideas she had for contextual designs for the building that already had thirteen floors and only needed a renovation that wouldn't take more than a few months. There were more meetings scheduled for tomorrow, meetings with her New Jersey banker and her architect. She was proceeding as if she had unlimited capital, for that was how her father had always postured himself. She only hoped she could pull everything together as well as he'd always done.

But despite the fact that she'd had a phone installed and had left her number with Adam's secretary, she hadn't heard from him since the night they'd spent together. She wanted to share her plans with him, thank him for his help, feel his arms around her, and hear his reassurances that she could pull off whatever she set her mind to. What she didn't want was to sit here swapping barbs with Eric.

"Corey, don't shut me out now. We've meant too much to each other."

"A lot of people have meant something to me, Eric. I've lost all of them. Every last one."

"Then don't alienate me," he said, dropping his foot back to the floor and leaning forward. "Let me back in. There's nothing says we have to live together, or be engaged."

She pushed her hair back from her face and looked down at her hands. It had been a long time since she'd had a manicure. Now she kept her nails short and unpainted, and her hands seemed rougher and less cared for than she could ever remember them being. She wondered if her spirit was becoming calloused, as well. She looked up at Eric, saw the sincerity on his face, and knew that he couldn't hurt her anymore. She was immune. "All right, Eric," she said. "You want to be friends? We'll be friends."

He got up and came to sit beside her on the bed, and leaned over to kiss her neck. She allowed it for a moment, sitting cold and stiff beside him. But his arms slid around her, and that was more than she could stand.

Slipping away from him, she stood up.

"Let's go have a drink," she said. "There's nothing to do here."

"Couldn't we think of something?"

"No, Eric. Nothing comes to mind."

He let out a deep sigh and came to his feet, slapping his thighs. "All right. We'll go have a drink."

Eric looked around before he followed her out. "God,

this place is a dump. How do you stand it?"

"It's home now," she said. "And that's a hell of a lot better than living under someone else's rules. I make my own rules now. And I like it."

Eric's smile was strained. "Independence looks good on you, Corey."

"You always knew the right thing to say, Eric. Too bad you never knew how to mean it."

The emerald and diamond necklace felt cold weaving through Adam's fingers. He brought the strand to his mouth, felt the smooth cut of one of the stones. Just as he remembered.

But the memories were fading.

He thought of Corey, and the night he'd spent with her, entangled in a twin bed in a one-room apartment. He'd spent many nights with women in the past few years—beautiful women, intriguing women, women who stirred his embers to life—and those nights had been spent in sexual opulence and convenience.

But he couldn't remember ever knowing the extent of luxury that he'd known in that tiny, dilapidated room with Corey. And despite his need to put it out of his mind and write it off as a mistake—a colossal weakness on his part—it haunted him.

Just as his hatred of Nik Dobias did.

He dropped the necklace back into its velvet pouch, poured himself a drink, and walked across the Aubusson carpet to the sliding doors onto his balcony. The wind ruffled through his hair and sifted through his shirt.

He downed his drink and turned his back to the lights of the city below him, and stared, unseeing, at the glass doors to his apartment. In the next few days, Corey would know that he had done her father in. She would know that he'd nailed the man he had hated for so many years. He wondered if it would offer her the slightest satisfaction. He wondered if it would offer *him* any.

He should tell her, he reasoned, because he owed her that. He didn't want her to hear it from someone else. But the time wasn't right. He would wait a little longer, until the deed was already done.

He went back into the penthouse, set down his glass, and decided that he had to see her, anyway. He would ask her what the bank had said, see if she needed anything. It would be a casual visit, nothing more. He would see her smile, feel her warmth, then flee like a kid afraid he'd gone too far. And no matter what happened, he would not wind up in bed with her again.

He drove to her apartment and saw her coming up the street in the darkness the moment he parked in front of her building.

But she wasn't alone.

It was too late to pretend he hadn't come or that he hadn't seen her. His car was impossible to miss in a neighborhood like this, and she had seen him probably even before he had spotted her. He got out and waited for her to come closer, and regarded the man walking beside her.

"Adam!" Her voice was effervescent as she approached him. "I didn't expect you."

The man's brooding eyes accosted Adam as they came face-to-face.

"Looks like I picked a bad time to come."

Corey glanced awkwardly at Eric, then back at Adam. "No. Really, we just had a bite. Eric was walking me home. He's leaving now, aren't you, Eric?"

The question seemed to take the photographer by surprise, and he gave Adam a searing look. "Do I know you?"

Adam thought of extending his hand, but decided he didn't have much desire to shake the hand of the man who had played for her money and lost. From the looks of things, however, his interest had been rekindled. "Adam Franklin," he said in answer to Eric's cold question.

A slow, stiff smile dawned across Eric's lips. "Ah, yes. The knight in shining armor who keeps coming to her rescue. I should have known."

"I've been called a lot of things, but that isn't generally one of them."

"No," Eric conceded. "I don't suppose it is."

A moment of awkward silence fell, and finally Corey stepped between them. "Thanks for coming by, Eric."

Eric gave Adam another scathing look, then threw his glance Corey's way. "Yeah. See you later."

She didn't watch him as he walked away. Instead, she looked at Adam, her soft eyes revealing how happy she was to see him, and suddenly he didn't give a damn what he had promised himself about staying out of her life—or her bed. Eric was weaseling his way back into it, and somehow that changed everything.

Slipping his hands into his pockets, he followed her in.

"You didn't call," she whispered as they started up the steps.

"I've been busy," he said. "So have you."

"Not that busy."

He didn't say anything, for there was too much guilt waging war inside him. Not the guilt for his failure to call, but guilt for the secret that grew bigger the closer he got to her. He had never expected to confront these feelings again. But now he had to admit that it was beyond his control.

Corey Dobias had gotten under his skin, a fact that complicated his life.

And he knew that, when she left him, she would leave even more scars than her mother had ten years ago.

chapter
29

IN RENA'S MIND, JOE BAKER WAS A CANDLE BURN-
ing in a cold, dark hole, a candle that could warm her if
she could just get close enough. The moment the hearings broke for lunch, when she was sure that her testimony was over, she went back to the hotel and called his
room, hoping for another chance to bask in the affection
she had done without for so long and now, having found
it, didn't want to do without again.

A stranger answered the phone.

"Uh, I'm calling for Joe. Is he there?"

The man's voice was accented with heavy Italian. "No.
No Joe here."

"Is this room twenty-three twelve?"

"Yes."

Frowning, she hung up and dialed the front desk. "Yes,
this is Rena Keller. Could you tell me if Joe Baker is still
registered? He was in room twenty-three twelve."

She waited, and after only a second, the desk clerk
returned. "No, Mrs. Keller. He checked out this morning."

"He did?" Her surprise caught in her throat, and she
swallowed it back. "Um, did he leave any messages?"

The desk clerk paused to look. "No. No messages."

Rena set the phone carefully back in its cradle and
stared down at it. If he'd known he was leaving, he would
have told her last night, wouldn't he? He wouldn't just
run out on her, now that they'd finally come together.

Maybe he had been called away, she told herself. Maybe there'd been no time to leave a message.

She blinked back the tears in her eyes and told herself not to jump to conclusions. It had been years since she'd felt as loved as she had last night. It wasn't an act. There was something wrong, and when she found out, she would understand. Everything would be all right.

She went to the bathroom, found her Valium, and dropped three pills into her mouth. She washed them down with stale Scotch and waited for the pain to numb over. Then she could have hope again, she thought. That pattern struggling to reassert itself on her life was just in her imagination.

The assemblage that Dobias brought with him to Franklin Tower was more for intimidation purposes than for any help they could offer him. Only John Keller and Robert Gloster were really necessary, but it made him feel better to have a team of extra lawyers, two CPAs, and Giselle and Rena as part of his entourage as they went to meet his accusers.

The room that Adam Franklin had reserved for them was big enough to accommodate his group, as well as the team Adam had assembled himself. Two lawyers for his papers, three editors, and the moronic reporter who, as far as Dobias was concerned, needed to be taught a lesson or two about snooping where he wasn't welcome. After the last two grueling days of testimony in Trenton, and the efforts last night to win over the second of the commission members—who had finally succumbed, but only after Dobias dragged a skeleton out of Ranger's closet that could ruin him personally and professionally—he was in no mood for this fiasco. But it couldn't be helped.

He walked into the room, his entourage in tow, and sat down at the head of the table directly opposite Adam

Franklin, who grinned as if he'd finally skewered his biggest catch yet.

"I don't have a lot of time, Franklin," Dobias said. "I trust you'll get right to the point so my lawyers can explain to you the consequences of slander, defamation of character, and libel, and we can put this matter behind us as quickly as possible."

Adam's grin widened. "Before they do that," he said, taking his cigarette out of his mouth and tapping it on an ashtray, "perhaps you should have them explain to you the consequences of bribery, tax evasion, and embezzlement."

Gloster set a hand on Dobias's shoulder and quelled his rebuff with an infinitesimal shake of his head. But Dobias didn't need the warning, for already he could see that he stood on shaky ground.

Rena and Giselle were the last ones to take their places in the room, and as they rounded the table to the empty seats, Rena scanned the faces at the opposite end of the table. Adam Franklin, several men she'd never seen before, and—

She sucked in a strangled gasp and staggered as she met the eyes of the man she had begun to fall in love with.

Joe Baker.

Their eyes met, seared together, and finally, he looked back down at the papers and photographs stacked in front of him. No one in the room noticed the exchange. No one except Giselle. Roughly, Giselle pulled her down beside her, but Rena didn't take her stricken gaze from him.

Adam was introducing his lawyers, his editors, and the others on his side of the table, and finally he came to the man who had pursued her, the only man she had ever made love to besides her husband, the man Giselle had warned would only use her.

"And this is my reporter, Joe Holifield," Adam was saying. "He's already written the story in question, and we intend to publish it on the front page of tomorrow's *Bulletin*."

Rena wilted onto the table as if the breath had been knocked out of her, and covered her face with both hands. It couldn't be. He hadn't wanted her just so he could get the dirty facts he needed for his story. He had been obsessed with her. He'd told her that and . . .

And she had believed him!

She looked up at him as the room seemed to spin around her, as the voices seemed to grow louder and more distorted, and for the life of her, tried to remember if she'd told him anything significant. Nothing she could remember, nothing more than the fact that she'd found her soul mate in him. Nothing more than how important her night with him had been.

But there must have been other things!

Whatever she had told him, it must have been enough. She had obviously given him everything he needed to nail her father. And she was the only one to blame.

She scraped back her chair and came to her feet, and mumbling something about not feeling well, dashed from the room, stumbled into the bathroom, and wretched into the toilet.

When the nausea had passed, she splashed water on her face and dropped into the chair next to the sink. She needed a drink. She needed an alibi. She needed a friend.

But she was unbearably alone, and there was no one who could help her. No one.

She stumbled out of the bathroom and into the elevator, and made her way to the first bar she came to after leaving the building.

She would stay there until the alcohol filled her with strength and absolution. But she knew it might take the rest of her life.

Back in the Franklin Tower boardroom, Rena's quick departure had been written off to fatigue and failure to eat breakfast, and forgotten almost as quickly as it had occurred. Only Giselle had realized the significance of Rena's reaction to Joe Holifield, but she pushed the knowledge aside for now. There were much bigger things to worry about.

Dobias looked over the copies of the invoices Holifield had gotten his hands on, and without betraying his surprise or intention to find out who the hell in his organization had given them to him, he studied them carefully. They were damaging, he knew, and it would be difficult explaining his way out of them. He pushed the stack to Gloster. Trying to conceal the trembling in his hands, he turned to the other documents they had presented and, finally, to the photograph of Alan Bayson entering his hotel room.

Clasping his hands under his chin, he brought his hard gaze to Adam Franklin.

"I think we should address the invoices first," Gloster said, taking off his glasses and looking down the table.

Dobias cut him off. "Obviously, someone in my organization is plotting to steal from me." Gloster touched his arm to shut him up, but he moved it away and continued. "These invoices prove that money is being funneled out of my buildings and is going into someone's pocket. When I find out who that someone is, they'll regret the day they ever heard my name."

He saw Adam glance at his lawyers, and from the nods they returned to him, he knew he'd just put his foot in his mouth. Gloster leaned over and cupped his hand over

Dobias's ear. "Shut up, dammit," he whispered. "You just gave them the confirmation they were looking for that these invoices are phony!"

Dobias mouthed a curse and tried to look unruffled.

Gloster cleared his throat, shuffled his papers, and tried to repair the damage. "Gentlemen, you have nothing here. These invoices, in truth, could have been manufactured by anyone. As a matter of fact, I have to question the integrity of Mr. Holifield. It's come to our attention that his reputation leaves a lot to be desired . . . and I have to wonder just what he might do to get the story of his career."

"They came out of your files!" Holifield said, leaning forward on the table. "And there's more where they came from."

Adam stopped Holifield with an outstretched hand. "As I told you on the phone, we have ample proof of these allegations. But I was particularly interested in what you might say about the photograph of Mr. Bayson going into your suite," he said. "We'd love a quote for the story."

"Quote this," Dobias bit out, coming to his feet.

Gloster stopped him and forced him to sit back down. "This photograph proves absolutely *nothing*. It's sensational garbage, Franklin, and you know it. It's tabloid trash, and if you print this in the *Bulletin*, you'll be lowering it to the sleazy level of the *Investigator*."

Adam shook his head and took another long drag from his cigarette. "I don't know. We might have some readers who would disagree. I think we'll print it. Right next to the quotes from the contractors who claim the casino is being built under code, even though certain building inspectors have given it a passing grade. I think the allegation of bribing building inspectors ties in nicely with your visit with Bayson, don't you?"

"Who did you talk to?" Dobias demanded. "I want names!"

"You'll get them," Adam said quietly. "They'll be in tomorrow's paper. We might consider giving you an advance copy, however, since we've arranged to get one to the U.S. attorney."

"You *what*?"

Adam pushed his chair back. "I think we have everything we need. Unless you have any further quotes you'd like to give us."

Gloster tried to rally. "The casino is built *above* code, despite what some bitter contractor who lost out may have told you, Mr. Franklin. And if you come up with allegations of bribing public officials, you'd better have a hell of a lot of proof, because you're going to get lawsuits from every angle. I'll see to it."

"Proof." Adam shifted the papers stacked in front of Holifield and picked up another photograph he'd been saving for just such a threat. "Hmmm. Let's see. This might be proof. A yacht docked in Boston Harbor . . . the *Dick Tracy*." He chuckled. "I like the name. I'll bet Mitch Easterman likes it, too."

Dobias's very silence was all the confirmation that Adam needed, but Gloster wouldn't leave it at that. "You won't find one shred of proof of that boat's ownership."

Adam chuckled again. "No, you're right about the documentation being carefully concealed. Of course, if we had verbal confirmation . . ." He shifted through the paperwork again, found the notes Holifield had scribbled with Rena's exact words. "Oh. Looks like we have it. And I quote, 'Barbados vacations, a condo in Denver, a yacht sitting out in Boston Harbor.'" He looked up, gauging Dobias's reaction. The man's face had gone pale, and he'd slumped back in his chair. "This is from a very reliable source, Nik. Someone very, very close to you."

Dobias's lips trembled. "I want a name! I want to know—"

Holifield shook his head. "This particular source is confidential."

Dobias flung forward in his chair, his face as red as the blood pulsing through his veins. "You won't get away with this, Adam Franklin! I'll get you for this!".

"Where you're going, Dobias, you won't ever be able to hurt anyone again."

He left the room, followed by his own people, leaving Dobias floundering for the right threat, the right explanation, the right weapon, to save him from this horror that he'd in no way expected.

But Adam knew Dobias wouldn't get out of this one. This time he had the bastard.

chapter
30

RENA STUMBLED FROM THE BAR STOOL, KNOW-
ing she'd stayed too long and that she had to face up
to what she had done, and somehow atone for it. But
she was too weak. She didn't have the strength.

Steadying herself, she made her way through the pa-
trons of the bar and out into the brisk afternoon. Maybe she couldn't atone, she thought. But she could fight
while she still had some fight left in her.

Her gait grew steadier as her goal clarified itself in her
mind, and she found herself heading for the Franklin
Tower. She wondered if they had told her father, her
husband, her sister, that she had been sleeping with
the reporter who was going to bring them down. She
wondered if they knew, yet, that she was the traitor.

She took the elevator to the floor she had left hours
ago, and realized that her stomach was no more stable
now than it had been then. A cold sweat broke out on
her face, but she forced herself to go on.

She headed up the hall, back to the conference room,
and found it empty. Undaunted and determined to find
them, she went to the first secretary she came to.

"I want to see Joe Baker—I mean Holifield. Joe Holifield. Where is he?"

"In Mr. Franklin's office, I think," the secretary began,
pointing down the hall. "But you can't go in there!"

Rena was already halfway down the hall and didn't
waiver when the secretary left her desk and started after
her.

"I'm sorry! Please! Do you have an appointment?"

"I don't need one." She stopped at the door to Adam's office, arousing the protests of the other secretaries on the floor.

Ignoring them, she burst into the office, found Holi-field sitting in the midst of a team of other men, and made her unsteady way to him. "Did you tell them?" she demanded. "Did you tell my husband how stupid I was to put my trust in you? Did you tell my father? Did my sister gloat and say how she told me that a man couldn't really be interested in me for myself?"

Embarrassed by the outburst in front of all of his superiors, Joe came to his feet.

"Did she?" Rena screamed. "Did they disown me, like they did Corey? Am I going to be waiting tables now, Joe? Was that the conclusion to this wonderful, divine plan of yours?"

"Rena, they don't know."

It was Adam Franklin who broke into her tirade, Adam Franklin who touched her and turned her away from Joe.

"What do you mean they don't know?" Rena cried. "Do you think it'll take a genius to figure it out? My sister saw me having lunch with him. If she hasn't put it together yet, she will! God knows, it's just a matter of time!"

She slapped at the tears on her face, and her voice broke. "How could you do it, Joe? When you ruin my father, you ruin me. How could you ruin me, Joe? I never did anything to hurt you. All I did was trust you."

"This isn't about you," Joe said quietly. "It's your father, Rena. He deserves to pay for the things he's done."

"And who's going to pay for the things you've done, Joe? Me?" She sucked in a sob and nodded her head. "Yes, I thought so. I'm the one who's going to pay."

She swung around to Adam Franklin, who had his hand on her arm, and the touch was so gentle that she almost believed he held some degree of compassion for her. But she didn't let herself go that far. She would never believe that again.

"You were a friend of my mother's," she said. "I remember her talking about you sometimes before she died. I wonder what she would think of what you're doing now."

Adam, who always seemed to know what to say, how to act, how to react, didn't have an answer for that. And knowing that no one ever would, Rena left the room with all the dignity she could manage, considering that her world had just shattered into a million tiny pieces.

As if she'd prepared her whole life for just such an emergency, Giselle filled the gulf that her father's shock had created, and completely in control, she paced Dobias's office in front of him. John Keller sat to the side, watching her handle the situation.

"So what have we got here? We have an article coming out tomorrow, and we can't stop it. The second thing is that it's going to the U.S. attorney's office tonight. In which case, we can expect a grand jury investigation soon. And let's be realistic. If that happens, there's every possibility that there will be an indictment."

Dobias rubbed his face, the way he'd been doing since he'd come out of Adam Franklin's office, so hard that she expected the skin to peel away at any moment.

"Dad, we have to keep our heads clear and try to salvage what we can. The first thing they're going to do is freeze your assets. If they do that, it could bankrupt us. So that's the first thing we have to act on."

Dobias looked up at her, his frown chiseling crevices into his features. "What do you mean?"

"I mean that our only choice is for you to sell everything to Rena and me. Just until this all blows over. It would be yours again when it's safe."

Dobias gaped at her as if he couldn't believe he'd heard her correctly, and for the slightest moment, she felt a surge of guilt. But there was no time for that.

"Dad, it's the only way. A few weeks ago, it was in all the papers that you were dividing everything among us, anyway. Everything else that's come out has been based on rumor. We could prove that you intended to do this all along, that we just didn't close the deal until now. That way, no matter what happens to you, your interests are safe. It's the only way to salvage as much as we can."

"Sell it to you." It came out as a statement, but it was bitter, accusing. "And what of the competition?"

"Dad, there are obviously more important things right now. We could resume the competition when it's all over. This is an emergency. Emergency measures have to be taken."

Dobias's accusatory expression turned to despair, and he dropped his weathered face into his hands. Giselle sat down next to him and put a hand on his shoulder. "Dad, I know how hard this is going to be for you. But we have to be strong. We have to think these things through clearly. We have to *act*. You've never been one to let things happen to you. You can't start now."

He nodded and patted his daughter's hand. "I know. You're right." He pulled up from his chair, and Giselle realized how old he looked. She had never seen him that old.

"John, get the paperwork that you and Gloster drew up before I changed my mind about dividing everything," he said. "Make the necessary adjustments, and let's close this deal tonight."

"And what should the price be?" Giselle asked carefully.

"A dollar each," Dobias said. The idea tickled him, and he laughed dryly, weakly. "Imagine that. A billion-dollar empire, sold for a dollar." He glanced at his son-in-law. "I want a clause added that I can buy it back for the same amount at any time between now and my death."

John jotted down the figure, not betraying any expression at all, as if he weren't pocketing a fortune in just a few moments. All they had to do was find Rena, so that she could sign the papers.

"Dad, we'll get you the finest criminal lawyer in the country."

"Criminal lawyer?" The suggestion seemed to throw him, and that despair returned to his face again.

"Yes. The charges are serious. But you'll come out on top, Dad. You always do."

Dobias leaned his head wearily back in his chair, and his mouth stiffened into a hard, set line. "I want to know who betrayed me," he said quietly. "And when I find out, I really will be guilty of a crime. Even if it's Corey."

"Do you think she's the one?"

"Probably," he said. "She's in bed with Adam Franklin, isn't she?"

He turned his hard, withered face to his oldest daughter, the one who had endured him the longest, the one who'd never been what he wanted her to be. "Giselle . . . ?"

"Yes, Dad?"

She hoped for a gentle word of confidence in her, that she could handle what he'd worked his whole life to build. That he could depend on her. That he was proud of her.

Instead, his eyes dulled to a hard, icy sheen. "Do as little damage to my company as possible. I want to have something left when all this is behind me."

The vague hope she had harbored dissipated to dust,

and she met John's eyes across the room. At once, her intentions crystallized.

Dobias was going down, but he would not drag his family down with him.

When this was all over, he would see who reigned victorious. Then they would all see.

chapter
31

"I THOUGHT YOU'D BE HAPPY." ADAM'S SOFT, NON-
plussed statement brought Corey's melancholy eyes up
to his.

"Because my father is facing the prospect of losing
everything he has . . . and prison?"

He knelt in front of her and set his hands on her knees.
They were bare beneath her skirt, smooth as silk, and
they made him want to slide his hands farther up and
pull her onto his lap. But he kept them still. "I'm not
doing anything worse to him than he's already done
to you."

She took in a deep breath and stood up, forcing his
hands to fall away. Slowly, she paced across her cracked,
rotting floor. "I know you're right. He did do all those
things to me."

"I'm not asking you to celebrate what's happening
to him," Adam said. "I just thought you should know
before the story runs tomorrow. I thought I owed you
that much."

She nodded. "It would have been awful to find out that
way."

He stood up and faced her. The tears glistening in her
eyes surprised him, for that was the last reaction he'd
expected. "What's the matter?"

She tried to smile. "I don't know. Really. He had me
thrown in jail, and now you're doing it to him. He took
everything I owned, and now his own empire is crum-
bling. He made sure there was no one I could trust, no one

who would be loyal to me, and now he's been betrayed. An eye for an eye. It all makes sense somehow, and yet . . ."

"And yet what?"

She blinked back the tears before they could fall. "Nothing."

He stepped closer to her, wanting to hold her, to wipe the confusion from her eyes. But she held back. "I guess I feel sorry for him. I wouldn't wish the things I've been through on my worst enemy."

"That's what he is, you know. Your worst enemy."

"He's also my father." Her voice broke on the word, and she went into Adam's arms, and he held her so tightly he feared he would crush her.

After a moment, she pulled back and looked up at him. "Why were you so anxious to bring him down? Was it for me?"

He hesitated a moment before he spoke, weighing his answer carefully. "I'm tired of seeing him hurt the people he loves."

Her embrace was gentle but cautious, caring but reserved, and he couldn't decipher the feelings he sensed in her. But still he held her.

A loud, urgent knock startled them both, and Corey pulled out of his arms and turned to the locked door. "Who is it?"

"Corey? It's me. Rena." Her sister's voice was shaky, panicked.

She rushed to the door and opened it, and her sister burst into the room. Her makeup was smeared an inch below her eyes, and her face was wet with fresh tears. Her breath smelled of whiskey and nausea, and her eyes possessed a wild terror that Corey had never seen before.

Rena looked at Adam, and as if his being here was the ultimate betrayal, began to shake her head. "I heard you two were an item," she said. "Are you in this together? Is this your idea of revenge?"

"Corey had nothing to do with this, Rena," Adam cut in. "She only found out about it five minutes ago."

"Rena, are you all right?"

Rena couldn't take her anguished eyes from Adam. "Did you tell her what you did to me, Adam? Did you tell her?"

Corey's eyes registered profound confusion. "Did to you? Rena, tell me. What is it?"

"He set me up!" she shouted. "He put one of his spies in my bed!"

She staggered with the force of her accusation, and Adam reached out to steady her. "Sit down, Rena," he said. "You've had too much to drink."

"I'm not drunk! I'm *ruined*!" She slung her arm out of his reach and swung around to her sister. "Ruined! And I won't be able to handle it like you, Corey. I'm nothing like you!"

Corey pulled her weeping sister into an embrace and held her tightly, fixing questioning eyes on Adam over her shoulder. Quietly, she whispered, "Tell me, Rena. What happened?"

"He told me his name was Joe Baker, but that wasn't his name at all. He was one of Adam's reporters," she cried in a hoarse, despairing voice. "I could talk to him, Corey. He listened. At first it had nothing to do with sex or money." Her shoulders shook with the force of her regrets, and finally she managed to go on. "I think I was falling in love with him. I've never betrayed John before, Corey. You know that. But this time it all seemed so . . . right."

Corey looked at Rena, wiped the tears from her face. She saw Adam lower himself to her bed, saw him drop his face into his hands. "Go on," she whispered.

"Don't you see?" Rena asked. "It's all my fault. Everything that's happened is because of me. I told him things . . . I don't even know why . . . I don't even remember all of it. But Giselle was right. He didn't want *me*. No one would want me. He wanted information! And I gave it to him. And Daddy may go to jail because of it, and he'll never forgive me."

Adam looked up at Corey over his fingers, his eyes filled with dread. She gave him a cold, searing look that cut into his soul, but she turned back to her sister. "Rena, I want you to listen to me. Are you listening?"

Like a little girl in desperate need of some kindness, Rena nodded and wiped at her tears.

"Rena, what's happening to Dad has nothing to do with you. Do you understand? He did it to himself. There are others who have talked, not just you. He has a lot of enemies."

"But I'm not his enemy!" Rena cried. "I never would have done it intentionally. I was so stupid."

"You were not stupid," Corey said through her teeth. "You were taken in. You were tricked. It was a sleazy, unethical thing to do, but you are not to blame."

She turned her sharp eyes to Adam. "Is her name going to be used in this article?"

"Of course not. I wouldn't allow that to happen."

"Oh, you allow plenty," she said. "One more question. Does my father know that Rena was instrumental in this?"

Again he shook his head. "We kept her completely out of it. She's our confidential source. Corey, you have to understand—"

"Shut up!" she bit out. She turned back to Rena, shook her slightly to make certain that she was listening and following every word. "Listen to me, Rena. You don't have to tell Dad that it was you. He never has to know."

"Oh, Corey, look at me. He'll take one look and know. His eyes are everywhere. He taps our phones, for God's sake. If he doesn't know already, he'll figure it out."

"He isn't God," Corey said. "He's human. He doesn't know and see everything. I know. I'm still here, aren't I?"

"But you're stronger than me," Rena said. "I'm transparent. He'll know. If he doesn't, Giselle will. And she'll tell him." Her dolorous eyes turned to Adam, beseeching, pleading. "You don't know what you're doing," she wept. "This article is the end of me."

"It doesn't have to be," Adam said.

She shook her head wildly. "You don't understand. Neither of you understand. You're not me. You can't feel what I feel. It's all so easy for you. Corey, you're brave and tough and stubborn. I'm different."

Adam came to his feet. "Corey, the article has already gone to press. I couldn't stop it now, even if I wanted to."

Corey had started to cry, but still she remained focused on her sister.

"I don't know why I came here," Rena muttered. "I— I don't know why I came."

"Rena . . ."

"I have to go," she said. "Have to face the music. I brought it on myself. Didn't we all?"

She slapped the tears from her face and started out of the tiny apartment. Corey went after her. But before she reached her, the door slammed in her face.

When Corey turned back to Adam, her face was crimson with rage. "How could you use my sister that way?"

"I didn't use her," Adam said. "I put a reporter on a story. She allowed herself to be used."

"Allowed herself? You saw her. She's insecure and lonely and vulnerable. You used that."

"If I had used that, then I would have used you! I wouldn't have shielded you from my reporters the way I did!"

"Maybe I wasn't the one who needed shielding, Adam!" she cried. "I could have handled it. But Rena—"

Adam's breath was heavy, and the air in the room seemed too thick to breathe. "Corey, if I could undo it all, if I could take it all back, go about it another way—"

"Then what, Adam? Would you change it? Would you really?"

Quiet settled between them like a live grenade falling in slow motion. "I don't know what I would have done," he said. "All I know is what is. The story runs tomorrow. People are going to be hurt. I'm sorry your sister is one of them."

Corey fell into the recliner he had given her, turned her face toward the window. "Just go," she said. "I want to be alone."

He started to argue that he needed her to understand, needed her to approve, but somehow his needs seemed insignificant in comparison to hers. This time there was nothing he could do to fulfill them.

Finally, with great effort, he left her alone in her apartment. As he did, it occurred to him that he might never hold her again. But that was unacceptable. He had betrayed his memories, had betrayed himself, by loving her. But now that the betrayal had taken place, he didn't intend to lose her. Not over this.

The wheels were in motion to bring her father down, and he would not let his pleasure in that fact be diminished. But that barren chamber at the bottom of his soul gaped wider than it ever had before. And Adam made a new vow to himself.

He vowed that he would not let Corey Dobias get away from him that easily.

* * *

By the time Rena took her limousine back through the gates of the Dobias estate and made her dreaded walk into the foyer, she had resolved to confess everything. First she would confess to her husband, beg his forgiveness for cheating on him, and plead for his understanding. Then she would go to her father and tell how she had been tricked and betrayed.

The consequences didn't even matter at this point. She had already beaten herself up much worse than anything her husband or father could do to her.

John met her at the bottom of the stairs. She had been missing for over twelve hours and looked as if she had been in a dog fight, but all he could think to say to her was, "Where the hell have you been?"

"I have to talk to you," she said. "There's something I have to say."

He shook his head and grabbed her hand. One of the servants appeared in the foyer, and he shouted, "Tell him she's here. We can get on with it now."

Rena felt that sick feeling overwhelming her again, and she resisted when he tried to pull her up the stairs. "John, I have to talk to you. It's important. Please, listen to me!"

"Not now, dammit," he hissed. "We've been looking everywhere for you." His eyes were wild, panicked, and for a moment she felt a sweet surge of relief that he had been panicked over her. But that hope was quickly dashed. "You're going to go upstairs and brush your teeth and wash your face, and then you'll march into your father's room and sign whatever I tell you. Do you understand?"

"Sign what?" she asked. "I'm not signing anything."

He jerked her hand up, making it clear that this was no time for games. "You'll sign whatever the hell I tell you to sign, and you'll keep your mouth shut until after you do. Do you understand me?"

"But we have to talk," she said. "I have to talk to Dad, too."

They were at the top of the staircase before he turned back to her. "If you're not in your father's room, with your mouth shut, in two minutes, I'll come after you, Rena. And so help me, if you blow this, you'll pay like you've never imagined."

More tears burst into her eyes, making her look even more weak and pathetic. "What is this all about?"

He let her go with a rough jerk. "It's about our finally getting what we're due," he said. Then he left her wavering in the hall and went to tell her father she was home.

Rena went into her room, stripped off the dress that was rife with sweat and spilled whiskey and tears, and washed her face over the sink. She brushed her teeth, as she had been told, and ran a comb through her hair. Then, slipping into another dress as quickly as she could, she concealed her trembling hands in silk pockets and went to her father's room.

Like an executioner's board, they were waiting for her, and weakly, she accepted the fact that they had already figured out her part in the disaster. She sat down, silent, and waited for the proverbial ax to fall.

"Finally," Giselle breathed out. "Let's get on with this."

"With what?" Rena asked.

The hollow, haunted shadows beneath Dobias's eyes told her that he was just as defeated as she. "I'm selling everything I own to you and Giselle," he said quietly. "To buy back when this is all over."

Rena recognized the soft, gentle note to his voice that wouldn't have been there if he had known of her deception. Instead, his anger seemed self-directed.

"Why?"

"Because if I don't, they'll freeze my assets, bankrupt me, and everything I own will be worthless for the duration of this nightmare."

John handed her a pen, and she saw the slight tremor in his own hand and realized that a fortune rested on her signature. "Everyone has signed except for you. Right here, Rena. Sign your name right here."

Rena frowned up at her father, saw the despair in his eyes. She had betrayed him, and now he was rewarding her with half of his billion dollar empire? "Daddy, are you sure? Is this what you want?"

"There's no other way. Just sign it, Rena."

She glanced at her husband again, saw the desperation in his eyes, saw the anxiety in Giselle's, and the resignation in her father's.

Corey's words whirled with dizzying speed through her head. *You don't have to tell Dad. He never has to know.*

But she would know. She would know.

A roiling surge of nausea climbed up inside her again, but she held it back long enough to scrawl her signature on the page. Then, standing up, she bolted from the room to the bathroom where she retched out her heart and all her secret sins.

No one even cared that she had left the room, for the papers had all been signed.

It was no more than an hour later, as Rena lay in a fetal ball on her bed, that Giselle came into her room. "Tough day, huh?" she asked in a voice that bordered on kindness.

Rena didn't reply.

"You don't have to worry, Rena," Giselle said, sitting on the bed beside her. "No one knows but me."

Rena sat up slowly. "What are you talking about?"

"You and Joe Holifield, of course. I'm not stupid."

"Then why haven't you told them?"

Giselle smiled. "There's no need. Not as long as you do what I want."

"And what is that?"

Giselle stood up and prowled across the room, picked up John's Rolodex, set it down. "Tomorrow I'm going to hire my own lawyer," she said. "One who has no stake in our family."

"For what?"

Giselle turned back to Rena. "To draw up new papers, in which you sell your share of Dobias Enterprises to me."

"No, Giselle. I can't do that."

"You have no choice," Giselle said calmly. "If you don't I'll tell Dad everything. And John, too."

Rena balled her hand into a fist and pressed it against her mouth, shutting her eyes tight against the ugly reality that faced her. "It's really to your advantage, Rena. You hate business, and you aren't very good at it. This would leave all the decisions to me. You'd have nothing to worry about. In return, I'd take care of you financially for the rest of your life. And it would be our little secret. We wouldn't even tell John."

"What about when Dad gets it all back?"

Giselle shrugged. "When that happens, our agreement would be null and void. So you'd really lose nothing, after all."

Rena wiped her eyes, took a cleansing breath, and regarded her sister again. "Why would you do it this way?" she asked finally. "Why didn't you just tell him to begin with? He would have cut me out, and it would have all been yours, anyway."

Giselle couldn't tell her that she'd considered doing it that way, but then she would have been forced to fight

John for Rena's share of the money. It was easier this way, easier to let him go on thinking he had her share in the palm of his hand. That way, she'd still have the benefit of his experience in the company. And it made her affair with him infinitely more exciting. It put her in control. It gave her an edge.

Now, she met her sister's eyes and said, "I did it this way to protect you, Rena. So that your marriage won't be jeopardized. I think you deserve another chance. So . . . are you in agreement?"

Rena sucked in a ragged breath. "I'll sign whatever you want."

"You won't be sorry," Giselle whispered.

Rena watched as Giselle started back to the door. "But will Dad?"

Giselle turned around. "What do you mean?"

"Do you really have any intention of giving it all back to him?"

"Let's just say that I'll do exactly what he would do in the same situation."

Giselle left the room, and Rena stared at the closed door, hating Giselle, hating Joe Holifield, hating Adam Franklin.

But more than any of those, she hated herself, even though she knew Giselle's betrayal would be far greater than her own.

chapter
32

EARLY THE NEXT MORNING, COREY FOUND A NOTE on her door from Adam, pleading with her to talk to him. At the same moment, in Brookline, Dobias found the morning paper on his step where the security guards had left it.

At 10 o'clock, a delivery boy brought Corey three dozen red and white roses from Adam. At roughly the same time, Dobias's secretary delivered the airline ticket to Barbados.

At noon, one of Adam's people knocked on Corey's door to tell her that he needed to see her and had sent a car to pick her up if she would come. She refused. At the same time, in Brookline, a black stretch limousine pulled through the reporters at the gates of the Dobias estate.

At two o'clock, climbing the walls with want of news on her father or sister since the paper had come out, Corey ventured out of her apartment and was immediately detained by a swarm of reporters who had discovered where she lived. At the same time, Dobias was detained by federal and state agents working in conjunction to bring about his arrest.

By four, Corey, defeated by the silence peppered with radio news reports of her father's arrest, went down to Dee-dee's to watch updates on television. At the same time, Dobias was being locked in a cell and denied bail on the grounds that he had the means and the motive to leave the country, and had been caught trying.

By dusk on the fifteenth of May, Corey reeled from the barrage of accusations that, according to the *Bulletin*'s evening edition, had come in from other enemies of her father since they'd read the article that morning. At the same time, defeated by the overwhelming evidence and speed with which everything had come about, and hoping to allay any probes that might thwart the sale of his company to his daughters or freeze his assets, Dobias bucked the advice of his attorneys and made the decision to plead guilty to all the charges waged against him.

At nine, Corey tried to call Rena, then Giselle, and then Emily. None of them would come to the phone.

It wasn't until that moment that Corey realized the world she had left behind would never be there for her again. It had been sucked into a raging vacuum, and it was gone.

At the same time, across town in a jail cell among thieves and drug addicts, Dobias came to the same realization.

After all the allegations had been tallied and the formal charges drawn up, Dobias was convicted of conspiracy to defraud the Internal Revenue Service, tax evasion, bribery, and a handful of other crimes.

The good news was that, because of his confessions, Dobias's sentence was reduced to one year in the Danbury Federal Correctional Institute, a minimum security prison camp in Danbury, Connecticut. He was also assessed fifty million dollars in fines, which Giselle had no choice but to pay, despite the transfer of ownership.

Of his three daughters, only Corey came to say good-bye before he was taken to prison.

Dobias ignored her as if she wasn't there, and except for the guards escorting him, left Boston completely and utterly alone.

chapter

33

THE LACK OF PRIVACY WAS THE WORST PART, even worse than the kitchen labor where he blistered his hands washing dishes for hours on end and scrubbed the floors until he could see his aged face in the shine, all for eleven cents an hour. The dormitory where he slept at night was crowded and loud and too bright, and he found little refuge in the cubicle he shared with an old black man named Thomas Spencer, who had been convicted of forgery and fraud and was serving out a two-year term. At first, Thomas had intimidated him beyond belief, for he came across as a tough-as-nails convict who'd just as soon spit at him as look at him. He soon found out, however, that the man's crimes were even more minor than his own.

Thomas was near sixty, Dobias guessed; his hair was peppered with gray and he wore wire-rimmed glasses with a bent arm and a crack in the lens. He also wore a leer that spoke of death and murder, a look that shook Dobias to his core.

"Don't give me no shit, and we won't have no trouble," the man told him the moment Dobias was assigned the bunk next to his. "I know who you are, and it don't mean a fuckin' thing to me."

"Oh yeah? How do *you* know who I am?"

"I read a lot," he said, brandishing the book he had in his hand. "My son brings me a bundle of newspapers a couple times a week. I've read all about you and your family. A lot of the inmates here know who you are, and it won't get you nowhere here. Most of them was even hotter shit than you."

He decided not to honor the remark with a reaction, for there was no way to gauge how volatile the man could be. Sitting down on the empty bunk, he glanced toward the dusty books stacked on the floor of the cell, piled four feet high against the wall.

"What are those books for?"

The man dropped his big legs and raised up from his position on the bed. "For reading, man. You got a problem with that?"

Dobias scanned the books. *Einstein*, Dante's *Inferno*, *The Brothers Karamozov*, the Bible. "*You're* reading *these*?"

"Yeah, I read 'em. Just because I'm in prison don't mean I don't have a mind. I'm smart as you are, asshole. That's how I wound up here and not Angola. I knew my rights, and I fought for 'em."

Dobias took a step backward but didn't lose eye contact with the man who could have snapped his neck with his bare hands. "I wasn't implying that you were stupid. I just didn't expect to find books like these in my room."

"It's *my* room, asshole. I'm just lettin' you stay here. But you cross me, and you won't ever leave. Got that?"

Dobias didn't honor the threat with an answer, but as if he had, the man lay back down on his cot and picked his book back up. "Now, shut the hell up," he said. "I'm reading."

The other inmates, "white-collar criminals" as the press loved to call them, seemed to accept their plight with a rare humility that Dobias found disheartening. Some even laughed about the books they were writing, which were filled with remorse and psychological justifications for the crimes they had committed, the books that would make them millionaires all over again. His shame, if he admitted to any at all, was not in having committed the crimes, but in having to serve time for them. He shouldn't have pled guilty, he told himself a million times. He should have fought it, risking a loss, then set about appealing the verdicts, tying the matter up in court until the day he died or everyone forgot about it. But he had panicked.

He wasn't like the other inmates here, he told himself. The others were crooks, liars, thieves, hiding behind tanned faces and perfectly groomed teeth. He was not.

But the greatest difference between Dobias and the others, the difference that became more vivid than he wanted to admit on Mondays, Fridays, and alternate weekend days, was that they had visitors, and he did not.

He had made out his own visitors' list the week they had checked him in. On it, he had listed Rena, Giselle, Emily, John, Robert Gloster, and a handful of others. Corey's name was conspicuously absent.

Criminal checks had been run on all of them, and each had been approved. But still no one came.

During his first six lonely weeks in jail, his thoughts continually sank back, back, back to the memory of his wife and the happiest years of his life. Shara became his solace, his refuge, his sanctuary. The more he took shelter in her, the more sanctified she became.

He didn't remember much about the bad times, when she'd burst into tears over nothing, cried for an hour, then pretended that nothing had happened. He blocked out the nights when she slept in another room or was away from home altogether, out of town shopping with a friend or skiing in Vermont.

What he remembered, instead, was the serenity of her

smiles during the last three years of her life. The secret, longing looks into space, the way her skin had taken on new, younger tones as she'd worked harder to look her best, the leanness of her shape, as if she wore the body of a woman half her age. He had never found her more attractive.

Or less accessible.

But he would not remember that. She had grown up, he'd told himself, and if that meant growing away from him a little, he supposed that was the price he'd had to pay. He saw her spending his money joyfully for the first time in his life, finally making him feel as if the wealth he had achieved had brought her happiness, after all.

He had never forgotten the sparkle in her eyes the morning she had come home from an overnight trip to New York, wearing that emerald and diamond necklace she had bought for herself. Though it hadn't been like her, he had been so pleased with the pleasure on her face when she wore it, the way her fingers fondled it with gentleness and disbelief as it draped her throat, the way she held it in her hand when she took it off and brought the emeralds to her lips as if it were the most precious jewel she possessed.

He had considered her new, inner joy his own achievement. At last she was enjoying what his hard work, his years of neglect, had meant. At last she could appreciate all that he had done.

That warm, secret smile when she thought he wasn't looking, that beauty that radiated from within, that glow of life and love in her skin before she got ill, all wrapped him in a cocoon of memory and made his incarceration easier to bear. He would be all right as long as she was with him, he told himself. Now he had time to savor what he'd never had the time to consider before.

*   *   *

Shara's presence haunted Corey, as well, for the next three weeks as she tried to reconcile her feelings for her father. She reached Rena once, just long enough to learn that she had taken Corey's advice and kept her indiscretion from her father and husband. But her own self-abhorrence had turned her to more drinking than she'd ever done before, and she had sunk into a reclusive depression that kept her from taking more calls from Corey. Corey tried to reach Giselle, hoping that the family crisis would at least serve to bond the sisters closer together. But Giselle was buried in work, she was told, and couldn't be disturbed.

The only person she did manage to contact was Emily, and got the cold, firsthand account of the events that had transpired before her father's arrest. She also felt the loneliness emanating from her niece, for Giselle was rarely home now, and when she was, she was far too distracted to pay Emily more than passing notice.

"Aunt Rena isn't helping," Emily told her. "She just stays in her room all the time. Doesn't even go into work. Mother has to run everything all alone."

It was three weeks into Dobias's prison term when Corey realized her father's downfall had changed her status: No longer was she the one on the bottom; now her father was. And in her mind, his humble state redeemed him in some ways.

She called the prison to inquire about visitation rights and learned that her father did not want to see her.

Instead of letting the reality of his rejection crush her, Corey wrote him daily, begging him to put her on his list.

Finally, after two months, when he realized that none of his approved visitors—with the exception of Robert Gloster—had bothered to come even once, Corey heard from Danbury officials that her father had put her on his list and that a criminal check was being done on her.

Two weeks later, she was granted approval to visit him.

Not knowing what she expected, or what she hoped to gain, Corey made a visit to the prison camp one Friday morning, posing for her picture ID, then making her way into the visitors' room with the other families of inmates. Nervously, she waited for her father.

When he came, her heart stopped at the age defining his face and burdening his shoulders. The pallor of his skin concerned her, and his hair appeared to have turned a whiter shade of gray than it had been before he was sent away. The long, neglectful stubble of a gray beard adorned his face.

Tears came into her eyes.

Dobias, on the other hand, took one look at her and scowled.

"Hi, Daddy. Thank you for letting me come." Smiling slightly, Corey reached for his hand. He recoiled.

The anger in his eyes flashed brighter than she had ever seen it, and he leaned forward as if to make his point clear. "If you came here to rub my nose in it, Corey, you'll be disappointed. This isn't going to break me. And you can tell Adam Franklin that for me, too."

"Daddy, that's not fair! I—"

His dry, dejected laugh cut into her retort. "Nothing's fair, girl," he said. "Not a damn thing in this world."

Before she could utter another word, he scraped back his chair and went through the heavy door that led to his cell.

"What have you got? Shit for brains?" Thomas asked later when he had come back to their cell from visiting with his son. "You been here ten weeks and ain't had one visitor, 'cept for that lawyer with the sour look on his face, and the first one that comes you practically spit in her face. What's the matter with you?"

"I don't need visitors," Dobias said. "Least of all, her."

"Then why'd you put her on your list and let her drive three hours to get here?"

"So she'd stop nagging me with those damned letters. And so she could see just what her betrayal with Adam Franklin cost me."

"You don't even know fo' sure she's the one did that. She the one you threw out? The one you had arrested?"

The man remembered every sordid detail he read, and Dobias gave him a searing look that warned him to let the subject die. But Thomas wasn't good at backing off. "Looks to me like you oughta be forgivin' *her*, seein' how she's forgivin' you. Ain't like you got a ton o' other people lined up to see how you're doin'. Matter-of-fact, from what I can tell, you don't have a friend in the world right about now. 'Cept maybe me, which oughta show just how low you've sunk."

That night, after lights out, when most of the prisoners rested from their day of laborious, menial chores designed to humiliate and possibly break them, Dobias stared into the darkness and, against his will, recalled the tears in Corey's eyes when she had first seen him that day.

For the most fleeting of moments, it occurred to him that he might have been wrong about her wanting to rub his nose in it. But the idea that she had come for any selfless reason was too difficult for him to grasp, for anger and impulse had driven him too long.

She was seeing Adam Franklin, had probably helped him hammer the last nail in Dobias's coffin. What more did she want? To witness the suffering? To share in the pleasure of his humility?

But there had been no pleasure in her eyes today.

Despite how he wanted—needed—to believe there had been, he knew it wasn't so. Corey didn't have that kind of hatred in her.

His eyes filled with tears, and a sob tore from his throat, but he muffled it with his fist so that Thomas wouldn't hear. But the tears came harder, and before he was done, his pillow was soaked with tears that hadn't been shed in years. But Dobias was not even sure what he wept for.

Corey held herself together for the three-hour-long drive back to Boston in the car she had rented, and told herself she shouldn't have expected more. She knew how her father felt about her. What she didn't understand was why. The car wasn't due back until first thing in the morning, so mechanically, she drove to her building, found a space out front, and sat.

It occurred to her to get out, to go in, but somehow she felt paralyzed, unable to move. Professionally, the past three weeks had gone better than she had ever dreamed. She had talked the owners of four of the buildings she wanted into selling, then had gotten a commitment from the New Jersey bank Adam had told her about. She had gone to two other banks and found that with her father out of the way her ideas for the renovations and her eventual restructuring of the Combat Zone were taken seriously. Before those two banks actually agreed to finance her project, she went to two other bankers, claiming that the first two had already committed.

The fact that she was bluffing bothered her only marginally. Her father had taught her to play things by ear, to say what needed to be said to close a deal. Success was a self-fulfilled prophecy, and he who left things to chance wound up with very little.

In the last week, she got three of the five banks to commit to loaning her the money she needed not only to buy the property, but to completely renovate the first building as well. The deals would be closed next week.

But the exhilaration she should have felt at her new upward spiral wasn't there, for she couldn't shake the distress and defeat, and yes, even the grief, out of her mind.

Tears came to her eyes, and she slumped over her wheel, trying not to succumb. But her shoulders began to shake, and the tears began to flow.

Her father had rejected her again. And for the life of her, she didn't know what it would take to ever mend things between them, for his rejection was not based on anything logical. It was illogical, and yet it existed just the same.

She didn't know how long she had sat there, but after a while, she heard a tapping on her window and looked up. Adam stood at the window, and before she could gesture for him to go away, he opened the door.

"What's wrong?"

She shook her head and wiped her swollen eyes. "I don't want to talk about it. I don't want to talk to *you*."

He took her hand and made her get out. "You can tell me here, Corey, or you can tell me upstairs. Come on. You're upset, and I'm here. Take advantage of it."

She sucked in a sob and closed and locked the door, and not having the energy to fight him, let him lead her up to her apartment.

The moment the door was closed, he forced her to look up at him. "What is it? Tell me what's wrong."

"My father," she said, her face turning red beneath the sheen of tears. "I went to see him. I thought since he'd consented to my coming, that he actually wanted to see me. But he still hates me. He still won't talk to me."

"That bastard." Adam pulled her into his arms, but she swiveled away again.

"He told me to tell you that this won't break him," she said. "He thinks I helped you get your story. I felt like a traitor, just for knowing you. Like I'm consorting with the enemy or something."

"He wanted you to feel that way," he said. "But what I did to him had nothing to do with you. You know that."

She crossed her arms and breathed in another sob. "And Rena's at the house, locked in her room, refusing to talk to anyone. Just sitting there—"

Her voice broke off, and she clutched at the roots of her hair. "It's so stupid. Dad's in prison, and he looked so old and so small. I've never thought of him as being small, but today . . . and Rena's cutting herself off from everyone when what she really needs is to talk . . . to trust again. Emily's all alone and confused. As much as I want to cut myself off from them and not feel their pain, I can't. They're my family, no matter how many times they reject me."

"But when it's all said and done," Adam told her, "it isn't your family that's there when everything is gone. It's yourself, Corey. You still have that. And in your case, that's a hell of a lot. No one can take that from you."

She didn't know if it was fatigue or distress or the simple need to touch a human being who wasn't rejecting her that guided her, but this time when Adam reached for her, she didn't recoil. His arms felt like the first glimpse of security she'd had in weeks. Like the first ray of hope. And it had been a very long time since she'd felt that.

"When I wanted you, you kept pulling away," she whispered. "And now that I don't want you, you won't leave me alone."

"That's just how my perverted mind works," he whispered against her hair. "It wasn't until you refused to let me see you that I realized how much I wanted to."

"I really hate you for what you did, you know that?" she whispered weakly.

"I know that," he said. "I hate myself for making you hate me."

When he kissed her, she felt the sparks of emotion igniting inside her, and for a moment she was able to forget her grief and anger and worry and fear. For now, she needed to believe in something good, something sweet, something without a price tag or a consequence. Adam offered her that something. And for now, she supposed that was all she needed from him.

Dobias needed to believe in something, too. He needed to know that while he sat in prison, his daughters guarded and protected what he'd spent a lifetime building. But like everything else in his life, that belief was shattered when his close friend and trusted attorney, Robert Gloster, paid a visit to him one Monday afternoon.

The man looked tired and shaken, and Dobias knew instantly that he had not come with good news. "I wanted to tell you right away," he said. "Giselle fired me this morning."

"She *what*?" He leaned across the table, studying Gloster's eyes. "She can't fire you. You've been with me for thirty years. Without you, I'd be—"

"She fired me," he repeated wearily. "She said my ideas were outdated and I was getting in her way." He took off his glasses and rubbed his face and brought his blood-shot eyes up to Dobias. "Nik, you should have let me look over that agreement you signed to sell her and Rena the company. You should have waited until I could approve it."

"But John drew it up. He's my attorney, too. I thought if I could trust anybody—"

"That's just it, old boy," Gloster cut in. "You can't trust anybody. Not your son-in-law, not your daughters . . ."

Dobias leaned back in his chair and stared at his friend. "So what are you saying? That I've been had?"

"I'm saying that you signed everything over to them lock, stock, and barrel. That agreement had no stipulation for what will happen to you after you get out of here. If they wanted to, they could throw you out into the street without a penny. And judging by the way they've been handling everything else, I wouldn't put it past them."

"That's not true," Dobias said, stiffening as reality dawned. "I insisted on a clause that said I could buy back everything. I specifically told him—"

"Well, he didn't put it in," Gloster said. "He took advantage of your panic. He knew you were in too much of a hurry, and that I wouldn't be there to read it. I'm telling you, Nik, you gave it all away. Unless your daughters give it back out of the kindness of their hearts, you're a man without a penny to his name."

Dobias raked a hand through his hair and suddenly found the air in the room to be too thick to breathe. He tried to think, tried to reason it out, tried to gauge what Giselle and John and Rena could be thinking. "They'll give it back," he said, even as a cold sweat broke out over his skin. "They wouldn't turn on me that way. Even if they could, they wouldn't."

"Wouldn't they?" Gloster shook his head slowly. "Nik, have they come to visit you here once? Have they shown any kind of familial concern for you? Have they asked you if you need anything, written you, phoned you? Even once?"

Dobias realized the significance of what Gloster was pointing out, but he didn't want to see it. "They've been busy. Corey came once, but—"

"Corey?" Gloster asked softly. "Corey, who has gotten

nothing from you, came here to see you? And the ones who have your fortune in their pockets haven't bothered? Doesn't that tell you *anything*, old boy?"

As if the news had punctured the energy right out of him, he deflated visibly, dropping his head into his hands. "I can't believe this."

"I can't believe it, either," Gloster said. "But it's true. And as your friend, I felt I had to warn you."

Dobias looked up at the man who had been with him almost from the beginning. His sounding board, his confidante, his right hand. He couldn't believe Giselle could treat Robert so badly, but why not? She'd had no trouble stabbing her own father with the blade of her newfound power.

   . . . she's never learned the art of cunning, and her judgment in business is sometimes so bad that it's a wonder she's come as far as she has . . .

His own words rolled through his mind like a slow-winding tape, and he realized that Giselle had proved nim wrong. She had enough cunning to fool him. Her judgment was going to make her one of the richest women in the country. He supposed he should be proud. He had taught her well.

But he'd never counted on being her stepping-stone to success. Somehow, he'd always thought he was invincible.

That was an assumption he knew he would never make again.

chapter
34

COREY HAD KNOWN MICHAEL STANTON SINCE her freshman year of college, when he had been in graduate school studying architecture. Since then, the short, unassuming man with so much talent had worked on the design teams of some of the best architects in the country. Corey thought it was time to give him a project of his own.

She had met with him weeks earlier, gone over designs for her buildings, and put him to work on models of the ones they had both agreed upon.

Her eyes danced with excitement as she watched her block unfold in the model he set up on the conference room table, in front of the president of Prudential Life and some of their top officers.

"Eventually, we hope to completely transform this section of Boston and redesign it so that each building complements the other. As you can see, Mr. Stanton and I have been very careful to maintain a blending of the traditional and modern to enhance the surroundings instead of detract from them."

The men walked around the table, examining the model with quiet enthusiasm and restrained interest.

"As we discussed, the revenue from the office buildings will more than cover our interest payments, in addition to paying for themselves over just a few years," she went on. "As you can imagine, the value of the buildings will quadruple as the Combat Zone shrinks."

She answered the questions that the officers had,

then reiterated that they were the last hold-out in the package she needed to get the project underway. Three other banks had all agreed to lend her the money if Prudential Life agreed. Without the proper financing, the whole deal would fall through, and Boston's Combat Zone was destined to remain just that.

Two hours later, she shook hands with the president, setting the closing date for the same day as all of the other closings. It wasn't until she was back in Mike's car and two blocks from the Prudential Building that she let out a squeal that she was sure could be heard as far away as Vermont.

"I've got to hand it to you, lady," Mike said, laughing. "You know what you're doing."

She leaned her head back on his leather seat and closed her eyes. "What can I say? I have more of my father in me than I realized."

"Not too much, I hope."

Her smile faded slightly, but she rallied. "I'm going to make you a star among architects, Mike. You'll see. This project is going to make both of us famous."

She saw the Franklin Tower looming up ahead and grabbed Mike's arm. "Tell you what. I don't want to go home. Drop me off here."

"Going to tell Adam?"

She smiled. "I have to tell *somebody*, don't I?"

She pressed a kiss on his cheek, then let out another squeal. "After the closing, we're going to celebrate. Tell your wife to buy a new pair of dancing shoes. On me."

He laughed again. She got out of the car and waved him away, and hurried up to tell Adam her news.

On the morning of the closing, Adam woke her up in his bed with a rose and a *Wall Street Journal*. The rose seemed infinitely more romantic until she saw the page-

3 article about her project, and the fact that they were closing the deal that day.

"You're famous," he said. "And to think that the *Journal* scooped me on it."

She grinned and stretched her arms above her head. "Hey, you had your chance."

They indulged themselves in lavish lovemaking until it was time for her to dress and go to the meeting that would be talked about for weeks, and as she buttoned the last of her buttons on the suit she had bought for the occasion, Adam slipped up behind her and slid his arms around her waist. "You're getting too successful to live in a one-room apartment with warped floors and no furniture."

She smiled. "I was just thinking that myself. Maybe after I've closed this deal, I'll do something about that."

He looked at her reflection in the mirror. "I have an idea."

"What?"

"You could move in here. I could get used to having you around all the time."

Corey breathed a quiet laugh and shook her head. "No way. I'm not ever getting caught in that trap again."

He let her go. "What trap?"

"Depending on someone. Intruding on their space. Living under their roof and their rules. Let's just say that between my father and Eric, I've been completely broken of that."

"It wouldn't be the same," Adam said. "We'd be equals. Two professional people involved in our own separate projects, sharing an apartment."

Corey laughed. "Oh, it sounds nice and neat, Adam, but I'm not interested in sharing an apartment with you or anybody else."

"Then what do you want? Marriage?"

Her face fell with his sarcastic emphasis on the word, and she shook her head. "You still don't know me very well, do you, Adam? And you honestly want us to live together?"

He set his hands on his hips and stared down at her, and she could see that he still did not understand.

"I want my own place," she said. "I want a nice big apartment of my own, one that I can decorate the way I want, one that's just mine, without anyone to answer to or clear things with. Until I've had that, how can I even consider anything else?"

He leaned back on his dresser and watched her slide the brush through her hair. "So when do you get started?" he asked. "As I see it, the sooner you get started, the sooner we can cut our living expenses in half. They say it's cheaper for two to live than one."

"Since when did you care about expenses?"

He grinned. "Since I had to justify why I want you to move in with me."

"You're sweet." She kissed his chin, then turned back to the mirror, pulled her hair back, and clamped a barrette at her nape. "But after today, I don't plan to ever be poor again. From now on, I'm going up. And you know what?"

"What?"

"This time, I'm going to *appreciate* being rich. Every minute of it."

By the time Giselle read the *Wall Street Journal* that morning and saw the article about Corey, it was too late to act. Furious, she picked up the phone and dialed Eric Gray's number.

"You moron!" she said the moment he answered.

He recognized her voice immediately. "What? What's going on?"

"You told me that she wasn't working on anything! You said that she told you that."

"She did! She said she didn't know what she was going to do!"

"Well, she obviously doesn't trust you, which makes you of absolutely no use to me."

"Giselle! You swore you'd use my prints in the casino. I did my part—"

"Casino?" she shouted. "There isn't going to be a casino. They don't give licenses to convicts or their daughters. I'm unloading it on the Burns Hotel Group."

"You're what?"

"You heard me."

"But what am I supposed to do? I've got fifteen—"

"Take them to Corey," Giselle suggested. "Maybe she'll hang them in that dump she just bought. If not, the Salvation Army might take them off your hands. I hear they make pickups!"

That afternoon, after all the papers were signed and all the money deposited, Corey hired Dee-dee to work as her assistant at sixty thousand dollars a year. "I'll work you like a dog," she warned, "and you'll probably drag in half exhausted every night."

"So what?" Dee-dee said. "I did that as a waitress and didn't make nearly as much."

Together, they went apartment hunting, and when they found Dee-dee's, Corey paid the start-up costs as a perk for coming to work for her. "Enjoy it," she said, "because it's the last extravagance I'm going to afford for a while. Except for my apartment, I'm going to put every penny I have into the renovation."

She found her own place, a plush two-bedroom townhouse on Bowdoin Street, big enough to double as her offices until she finished this first project. She started

moving in that day. Since all she owned were a few suit-
cases of clothes and the chair that Adam had given her,
she was all settled before the sun set that afternoon.

Unwilling to leave her new home just yet, she hired a
catered dinner to be delivered that evening, and served
Adam on her small patio. He grumbled a little that she
didn't have any furniture as they made love on the carpet.

The next morning, he had a huge brass bed delivered,
with a note that it was yet another house-warming gift.
She surmised that he intended to spend a lot of time in
her new home, which suited her just fine.

In the weeks that followed, as busy as she was, she
found herself missing him terribly on the nights when
he couldn't stay. On the nights that he did, she rejoiced.

As they grew closer, she began to entertain his suggestion of pooling their resources, sharing their home,
spending their lives together. The more she considered
the idea, the more appeal it had for her.

For she was in control of her life and her heart, and
she couldn't imagine what could go wrong this time.

chapter
35

JOHN STUDIED THE OFFER FROM THE BURNS
Hotel Group to buy the casino and rubbed his fatigued
eyes. "That's a third of what it's worth, Giselle. We'll lose
a fortune. We can do better than this."

Giselle had taken to pacing her office lately. It calmed
her somehow. It wasn't easy to hit a moving target, and
although John was content to rest on his imaginary
millions, she knew the day of reckoning would soon
come. For now, she enjoyed his false sense of security
and that smug smile on his face as he walked through
the kingdom over which she ruled. It made it all more
worthwhile.

"I want out, John," she said. "Our investors are starting to get crazy, and it's costing us a fortune every day
that we hold onto it. The Burns Group keeps harping
on the fact that Dad admitted to building it under code.
It'll cost them millions to upgrade it. If we could just cut
our losses and get out from under those investors, then
we could get on with things."

"Things like what?" John asked. "This is all that was
in the works, except for your little competition with
Rena."

"Don't underestimate me, John. I have several other
things in the works. Besides, we have hotels and office
buildings and apartment buildings everywhere we turn,
and as boring as maintaining them may be, somebody
has to take care of them. Besides, I can think as big as
my father. I can move mountains just like he did."

"What mountain did you have in mind?"

She smiled. "I was thinking of building a new hotel in Boston. An ultra luxurious one. One where kings and queens line up for a suite. One where the president will want to spend weekends."

"Terrific," John said dryly. "Just what Boston needs."

She sat down on her desk. The split in her dress opened over her long thighs, but she seemed not to notice. "I also have a deal in the works to buy a little furniture manufacturer in Stamford, Connecticut. That'll save us tons on mark-ups in the future. And the deal on the carpet company will be closing next week. That way, our major purchases for our properties will be minimal."

"And Nik thought you didn't learn anything from him."

"I learned everything from him," she said. "He could learn a few lessons from me."

"Like what?"

"Like how to break the rules without breaking the laws. Like staying out of prison. By the way, about that little property on Tremont Street."

John leaned back and shook his head. "Stupid purchase, Giselle. What the hell are you going to do with it?"

"Oh, I don't know," she said. "It's right across the street from the property Corey just bought. Maybe I'll paint it fluorescent pink and put a team of diseased strippers in there. And some vendors on the sidewalk out front pedaling sadomasochist paraphernalia. Oh, I know! We could put a window in the face of the building, upstairs, and have a naked woman swinging in and out."

John began to laugh, and she grinned and twirled her pencil through a strand of her hair. "But I'll wait until the building's almost finished, when she's trying to lease the offices. That should put a kink in her business."

"Or it'll give her kinky business." He stood up and slipped between her thighs, and slid his hands around to her hips. "I like the way you think."

She regarded the smile that she found so evil, and so exhilarating. "Tell the truth, John. It's not the way I think that keeps you coming back to me."

"No," he said. His breath came heavier as her hand slipped between them, released his fly. "You're right about that. And it's not my mind that keeps bringing you back, either."

"Did you lock the door when you came in?" she whispered.

"I'll do it in a minute," he said. "No one would dare come in. If they do, we'll just tell them that we're trying out new designs for the facade of the Tremont Street property."

The house was too quiet, and too big, and Rena felt lost in it for the first time in her life. As stilted and tense as things had often been when her father was home, at least there had been activity and someone around to talk to. Now John and Giselle were always at the office, and she was always tucked away in her room with soap operas blaring on the television, a couple of pills, and a bottle that could make her forget how moronic and weak she was.

"Aunt Rena?"

She turned around at the staircase and saw Emily inside the study, sitting behind Dobias's desk, looking surprised that anyone other than the servants would be downstairs. It was only then that Rena considered that Emily was even lonelier than herself.

"Hi, Emmy," she said, straightening her hair and stepping into the doorway. "What are you doing?"

"Nothing." The papers scattered out on Dobias's desk

told otherwise, but Rena didn't push it. "What about you?"

Rena shrugged. "Just wandering around. Trying to figure out how our lives wound up like this."

The philosophical statement was more than Emily expected, and her little brow wrinkled.

"Aren't you supposed to be in school?"

Emily looked back down at the papers on the desk. "I couldn't go. I—I'm sick."

"You don't look sick."

"I am, though. I can study at home."

Rena, who took small pride in the fact that she'd become a master at recognizing deception—though she'd gleaned that particular expertise too late to help herself—didn't miss the way that Emily avoided her eyes. Almost thankful for the distraction from her own problems, she sat down across the desk from Emily. "Emmy, it's September. You've only been back in school for two weeks. What's wrong? Do you miss Dad? Is that it?"

Emily breathed a laugh that sounded a bit too cynical for a child who hadn't even turned twelve. "I miss everyone. What else is new?"

Rena studied her for a moment and saw the tears beginning to well in her eyes. "Emmy, tell me what's bothering you."

Emily's bottom lip began to quiver, and suddenly she wasn't a cynical girl-woman anymore, but a child who couldn't bear the burden that had been thrust upon her. As if she couldn't stand for Rena to see her cry, she dropped her face into her hands. "It's school. I used to be popular. People liked me. Some of them even looked up to me. And now—"

Rena waited for her to go on, but she couldn't seem to get the words out.

"Now what, Emmy?"

Emily dropped her hand and looked up at Rena, tears and all. "Now everybody knows about Grandfather being in jail, and that's all they talk about. They make fun of me, Aunt Rena, and I didn't do anything."

"Oh, Emmy. I'm so sorry. No one's even thought—I mean, it never occurred to us that you might have trouble with all this, too."

"I'm not surprised," she said quietly.

The simple words cut through to Rena's heart, for she knew that Emily had come to expect even less from her family than Rena had expected as a child. But Rena had been the lucky one, she realized for the first time in years. She'd had her mother, a mother who had adored her, a mother who could look into her eyes and know when something was wrong.

"Do you want me to go talk to your teacher? Make her understand what you're going through?"

Emily shook her head. "It wouldn't do any good."

Rena reached across the desk and took her hand. "I'll tell you what. Why don't we go out this afternoon? We can have lunch somewhere and do some shopping. It'll get our minds off our troubles."

Emily's dark eyes brightened just a bit. "Really? You're not too . . . tired?"

Aware that it was no secret that she'd been drinking far too much lately and hiding out in her room, Rena decided it was time she forced herself to put her ugly part in her father's downfall behind her, and try to move on with her life. Emily needed someone, and she was the only one around.

Late that night, the hours without a drink had caught up with Rena, making her jittery and uneasy. She had vowed to keep her head clear for Emily this afternoon.

When she'd made it that long, she decided to stay sober a little longer for her husband. She wanted him to see that she was trying to re-enter the world of the living. She wanted him to hold her, love her, and reinforce the small encouragement she'd gotten when she'd helped Emily today.

But John never came up to bed.

Finally, deciding to make the most of her sobriety and take her concern for her niece a step further, Rena belted her silk robe and went down the hall to knock on Giselle's door.

"Who is it?" her sister called in a muffled voice from within.

"Rena."

A moment passed before Giselle opened the door. "What is it?" The brusque greeting was no more than Rena expected. They hadn't talked—really talked—since the night Giselle had blackmailed her.

"No whining, Rena," Giselle said in a low voice. "The papers are all signed. There's no turning back now."

"It's not about you and me. It's about Emily."

"Emily?"

Taking advantage of her surprise, Rena pushed past her into her room and saw that the bed was rumpled and unmade, a circumstance that usually meant the ass of one of the housekeeping staff. Giselle stood stiffly near the door, and knowing that she would hate it, Rena ambled toward the bed.

"Did I wake you?"

"No, I was reading," Giselle said.

Rena didn't mention the fact that there wasn't a book in sight.

"What about Emily, Rena? What's wrong?"

Rena sat down on the edge of the bed and looked up at her sister. Even at this hour, all tousled and ready for bed, Giselle was beautiful. She wondered if she even knew what a gift that was.

"Did you know she stayed home from school today?"

"Yes," Giselle said. "She's had a stomach virus or something. Why?"

"Right, Giselle. And she was puking her guts out right on the lace curtains you hung in Dad's study. Do you care?"

Giselle stiffened. "No one told me that. The staff said—"

"The staff said," Rena mocked. "Do you hear yourself, Giselle? Your daughter's going through a crisis, and you expect the staff to keep you updated?"

"Who else could I entrust her with, Rena? You?"

The arrow pierced her right where Giselle had aimed it, and Rena looked down at the satin sheet and traced a fingernail across a seam. She told herself that it was no time to crumble. She was here for Emily.

Looking up, she met her sister's eyes. "Here's a news flash, Giselle. There was no stomach virus. Emily's having trouble in school."

"Trouble? She's brilliant. How could she have trouble?"

"The kids are giving her a hard time about Dad."

"Oh, God." Giselle's defensive expression collapsed instantly. "I didn't even think about that. But of course they would. Kids are cruel like that, and all their families are probably ecstatic about what's happened. If we were Otises or Saltonstalls or Gardners, it would be forgivable. We could tuck our skeletons in the closet and no one would care. But since they still consider us the family of 'that Greek upstart,' everything we do is open to criticism. Now Dad's proved what they've all thought about him for years. And we're the ones who have to pay."

"It isn't Dad's fault that he doesn't have English barons for ancestors, Giselle, any more than it's our fault."

"Our fault? Rena, the Caine family was one of the oldest families in Boston."

"Right. But they don't acknowledge us, do they? And it isn't our fault. Now what's happened is something that Emily needs to learn to deal with. It isn't going to go away."

Giselle settled her intense eyes on the carpet for a moment, and in one of those split-second decisions that Rena always found amazing, solved the problem. "Maybe she needs a new school."

"A new school? Giselle, any of the private schools you'd consider would have children who've heard what happened. It might not be any better someplace else. We have to help her cope. Teach her to get along—"

"And she can use you for her role model?"

Rena stared at her, her eyes dull. "Either one of us could screw that kid up royally, Giselle. It's probably a toss-up who could do the most damage."

She saw that her own arrow hit its mark, wounding Giselle just where she'd hoped it would.

"I think I can handle my own dau
ghter   without   any
more interference from you, Rena. Tomorrow I'll go talk to the headmaster at her school, and if they can't promise me some changes, she's out. It's as simple as that."

"Maybe for you." Rena looked down at the elegant apricot comforter on the bed and tried hard to keep her voice from shaking with her anger. "But it isn't that simple for her. She's lonely and depressed."

"It's called puberty."

"That's just like you, Giselle. In case you haven't noticed, she's a little young for puberty. Maybe she needs a little extra attention."

"Are you saying I've been neglecting my daughter?"

"I'm saying that Emily needs—"

"I know what she needs." Giselle got up and went to her vanity table, sat down, and began to brush out her hair in rough, frustrated strokes. "I'll take care of it. Go back to your room, Rena, and plunge back into your self-pity. Everyone likes you better drunk, anyway. Especially your husband."

"What do you know about what my husband likes?"

Giselle smiled as she continued to brush her hair, and Rena's hands began to tremble as she got up and went to the vanity. "I asked you a question."

She snatched the brush out of Giselle's hand and slammed it down on the table. A bottle of hand lotion fell over, spilling some of its contents on a man's gold cuff link.

"Dammit, Rena!" Giselle jerked the bottle up and began blotting her table with a tissue.

Rena picked up the other cuff link, the one that had escaped her assault. She looked down at the initial K on it.

Giselle stood up. "I'm going to talk to Emily right now, Rena. Mission accomplished. Now get out of my room."

Rena tore her eyes from the cuff link. "What are you doing with John's cuff links?"

Giselle grabbed the other one up and dumped it into Rena's hand. "He left them in my office, Rena. He rolled up his sleeves, for God's sake. Get a hold of yourself."

Rena clutched the cuff links in her fist as Giselle opened the door and ushered her out into the hallway, and started up the hall to Emily's room.

Rena stood paralyzed for a moment, trying to still her racing heart, trying to think rationally. Giselle's explanation made sense. She had brought them home to give them back.

But the bed had been rumpled and unmade, and Giselle reeked of perfume. . . .

Still holding the cuff links, she ran downstairs and searched every room, from the study to the staff bathroom. When he was nowhere to be found, though his car sat conspicuously in the driveway, she went back to her room, praying as she did that John would be lying in bed there, waiting for her. But their suite was empty.

Feeling sick, she went to the bathroom cabinet, pulled out a just-refilled bottle of Valium, poured three pills into her hand, and washed them down. Then she poured herself a drink.

It couldn't be, she told herself as she waited for numbness to wash over her. Not her husband and her sister. Not right under her nose. There were many tragic things in her life, but that was not one of them. It was her weariness, her paranoia, her depression, that had worked on her imagination. She was losing her grip on reality. Even that was preferable to the shadow of truth that lurked behind Giselle's bedroom door.

She fell asleep in her robe and her slippers on top of her undisturbed bedspread. It was only then that she stopped waiting for John.

Giselle found Emily lying awake in her room, staring at the ceiling as if it had some answers for her that no one else could provide.

"Sweetheart, why aren't you asleep?"

Emily shrugged. "I don't know."

Giselle sat down on the bed next to her and pulled Emily's head onto her lap as she had when her daughter was much younger. As she did, she realized it had been too long since she'd babied the girl. She was so independent, so capable, it was hard to remember Emily still had childhood needs. Gently, she began to stroke her daughter's forehead. "Rena told me what's happening at school. Honey, why didn't you come to me?"

"You're so busy. I didn't want to bother you. And it's not that big a deal. They're just a bunch of snobs."

"They don't have a right to be," Giselle said. "Even with all that happened, we still have more money than most of them will ever dream of."

"I don't think they care about our money, Mother."

"Well, they will one day. Tell me what they've said to you."

"Just . . . stuff. That Grandfather is a jailbird. That he's a crook. And Monday Will Endicott said that Grandfather was a homosexual, because everyone who goes to prison is."

"That little shit!" Giselle bit out. "Who's his father? Is it Morris or Avery?"

"I don't know."

"Well, I'm going to find out, and when I do, I think I'll give Mr. Endicott a call tomorrow. I'm not going to tolerate this, Emily, and neither are you."

Emily sat up and gazed at her mother. "Is it true about Grandfather?"

"Absolutely not! Don't you even think about that! He's not locked up with hard-core criminals, Emmy. It's a minimum security prison . . ."

"Why haven't we visited him then? Are you ashamed of him?"

Giselle hesitated, trying to find an explanation that would appease Emily. "No, of course I'm not ashamed. I've just been busy, and it's so far away. A three-hour drive one way, and—and Dad said he didn't want us to come. He's proud, and he doesn't want us to see him that way."

"What way?"

"You know. In jail. He doesn't want us to see him in jail."

"Then why did they do all those checks on us? Why did they say we could come if he didn't want us to?"

"I don't know, Emily."

"But doesn't he miss us? Isn't he lonely? He hasn't answered any of my letters. You did mail them for me, didn't you?"

"Of course," Giselle lied. "I'm sure he misses us very much. Why don't you get out the camcorder tomorrow, and tape yourself sending him a message. He'll like that."

"Do they have VCRs in prison?"

Giselle breathed a defeated sigh. "I hadn't thought of that. No, they probably don't."

Emily sprang up in bed. "Maybe we could donate one!"

"No, I don't think so. Tell you what. Just write him another nice long letter, telling him how much you miss him and all that. I'll mail it for you."

Emily wilted, and Giselle could see that the idea didn't appease her. "Look, if he changes his mind and decides that he wants visitors, I'll take you. We just have to be patient, okay?"

"Okay."

Giselle tucked the blankets around her daughter. "Now go to sleep. Tomorrow I'll take you to school and have a word with the administration. We're going to get this worked out. Believe me."

"Do you really think you can fix it?"

"I can fix anything," Giselle said. She dropped a kiss on Emily's cheek and slid her arms beneath her for a tight hug. "I love you. You know that, don't you?"

"Yes," Emily whispered. "I love you, too."

"Good night."

"Night, Mother."

Giselle closed the door behind her and stepped back into the hallway, cursing the spoiled little brats at that school. Setting her jaw in a grim, determined line, she went back to her room.

John was back in her bed. "Ready to finish what we started?" he asked with a sheepish grin.

Giselle closed her door behind her. "Did you hear what your wife told me? About Emily?"

"Come on, Giselle. You know Rena. She overreacts. Everything's a big deal to her."

"Emily's feelings are a big deal. And I find it ironic that it's your wife who's concerned, and not you!"

"Give me a break." He sat up in bed, letting the sheet fall around his bare waist. "This is the first I've heard of it. I think you should do something. Put her in a different school or something."

"I plan to if I don't get the answers I need tomorrow morning."

She slipped her robe off, revealing the long, transparent negligee beneath it. "She saw your cuff links, you know."

"Yeah, I heard that. You covered very well. I even believed you for a minute." He pulled her onto the bed next to him and jerked his knee between her thighs. "She bought it, Giselle."

"And what if she hadn't? What would you have done?"

"Made up another ridiculous story that only she would be naive enough to believe," he said. "Don't worry. I've got my wife under control."

chapter
36

"CHILDREN WILL BE CHILDREN, MISS DOBIAS."

The headmaster of Emily's school, a withered replica of Winston Churchill, tapped his coat pocket and withdrew a pack of breath mints. Popping one into his mouth, he shook his head dolefully. "All I can suggest is that you begin helping your daughter adjust to the negativism. It is inevitable, you know, considering your father's prison sentence."

"My daughter doesn't *have* to adjust, Mr. Smythe. *You* do. That's why I pay so much to send her here."

The man snickered, sending Giselle's blood pressure up two notches. "I can adjust just fine, my dear, but I have no control over the gossip among our students and their families. What's happened to your father is . . . unfortunate . . . and I'm sorry that your daughter has had to suffer for it. But really, there isn't anything I can do."

Giselle stood up and leaned over his desk, skewering him with her eyes. "Then my only choice is to pull my daughter out of this school, and her exorbitant tuition and my family's ample donations right along with her. Guess you won't be building that new computer wing like you planned, Mr. Smythe."

The man wasn't intimidated, a fact that pushed Giselle's smoldering temper into the danger zone. "If you feel the need to pull your daughter out, Miss Dobias, I would certainly understand. Some of the other parents have expressed . . . concern . . . over having your child in this school, anyway. Perhaps it would be best for everyone—"

"Go to hell, Mr. Smythe. And take your student body with you."

Bursting out of his office, she found Emily sulking in the chair where she'd been waiting. Jerking her up, she started for the door.

"Mother, what is it?"

"We're leaving. Say good-bye, Emily. This is the last time you'll ever see this hellhole."

Emily looked over her shoulder as her mother dragged her out of the building, and saw that nothing had been altered. No one chased after them begging forgiveness. No one pleaded for her to stay. She saw Mr. Smythe waddle out of his office, stop at the secretary's desk, and offer her a grin as he glanced in their direction.

He was glad to be rid of her.

They were tucked inside their limousine before Emily dared to speak again. "Mother, what are you going to do with me now?"

"I'm going to find you a decent school. I should have done this a long time ago." She leaned forward and instructed the driver to take them to a competing school across town, then snapped open her compact and reassured herself that her flawless face was still flawless.

Nothing more was said during the long drive, and when her mother went into the headmaster's office, Emily sat quietly in the outer office, listening to Giselle ranting inside. They didn't want her there, either. She was rich enough, but not good enough.

Emily stood up when her mother bolted out of the office.

"I have enough money to buy this school!" Giselle cried.

The man eyed Emily uncomfortably. "Miss Dobias, please—"

"Come on, Emily." Giselle snatched her wrist up and began pulling her out. "The truth is," she said in the doorway, "she's too good for you! This child's IQ is 152. She can do a hell of a lot better!"

But it didn't appear to Emily that Giselle believed her own words when they reached the limousine that waited for them. "I can't believe that!" she cried. "They turned you down because of my father!"

The car pulled out of the long winding drive of the campus, and Emily swallowed the emotion welling in her throat and tried to still the trembling in her lips. She saw tears in her mother's eyes, a rare sight for the superwoman who admitted to so few weaknesses. She felt guilty. Her mother had more important things to think about than where Emily would go to school. Clearing her throat, she set her hand on her mother's.

"Mother, I could go away to school. Lots of girls do at my age. That way, you wouldn't have to worry about me."

A tear dropped onto Giselle's cheek. "There are other schools in Boston, Emmy. I'm not sending you away. I—I just can't do that."

"But you went away to school, didn't you, Mother? How old were you when you went?"

Giselle's gaze drifted out the window in memory, and after a moment, she whispered, "I was only nine."

"And it was good for you," Emily said. "I mean, wasn't it?"

Giselle dug into her handbag for a handkerchief and blotted her tears. "No, it wasn't," she said. "I missed my mother terribly. But, of course, my father insisted. Things were never the same for me again."

"What about Aunt Rena and Aunt Corey? Did they go?"

"No." She shook her head and made a great effort

to swallow. Reaching into her purse, she withdrew her compact again and rechecked her makeup. "My mother put her foot down when it was Rena's turn. She thought Rena was too sensitive, too fragile, to be sent away. And I don't remember the subject ever even coming up with Corey."

Emily watched her mother's face as Giselle stared vacantly at her own image in the mirror. For the first time in her memory, she saw naked emotion, raw pain, in her mother's eyes.

After a moment, Giselle snapped the compact shut and took a deep breath. "It probably would be good for you in a lot of ways to go away to school, Emmy, but I can't send you. I just can't do it. Call me selfish—heaven knows, I've been called worse. But I need you at home, with me. I'm not ready to let you go."

She opened the window that separated them from the driver, and told him the name of a third private school. The driver headed in that direction.

Emily wrapped her fingers through Giselle's and held her hand tightly for the rest of the drive.

Emily made a concentrated effort to fit into her new school, in order to lighten the burden on her mother, but nothing was different there than it had been at her other one. The children were all privy to the gory details of her grandfather's arrest, and their cruelties reached an all-time high since they had no past relationship with her to soften the blows.

But she didn't complain. At least, not to anyone who could do anything to change things. But one evening, when her mother was down in the study with John discussing business, and Rena was asleep in her room, Emily got Corey's new number from the operator and called her.

Corey answered on the second ring.

"Aunt Corey?"

"Emily!" She could hear the genuine surprise in Corey's voice, and it reminded her of home, the home she remembered when Rena still came out in the daytime and Corey sang through the halls, and her grandfather schemed and planned and grumbled. It seemed like a very long time ago.

The business was beginning to swallow Giselle, absorbing every moment of her time and energy, and she hadn't had much time with her daughter since she'd enrolled her in her new school. She had set aside tonight to have dinner with Emily out beside the pool. Then they would ride horses for a while together before it grew dark. She had penciled it in on her calendar so that she could justify it. Spontaneous, emotional needs weren't acceptable unless you made an appointment to feel them.

She opened Emily's door without knocking, as she often did, and heard her daughter talking on the telephone. It had been a long time since she'd seen Emily embroiled in a gab session with a friend. It gave her a spark of hope.

Deciding not to cut the conversation short, she backed out of the room.

"Yesterday one of them brought a picture of Grandfather to school," she was saying in a low, melancholy voice. "It was in *People* magazine, and it was of him in his prison clothes, sitting in his cell."

Giselle froze and listened from the hallway.

"I ignored them," Emily said after a moment. "But I hate all of them."

Giselle raised her hand to her worried brow and changed her mind about leaving Emily alone. Her daughter needed her. Quietly, she went through the door and started across the room.

"I miss you, too, Aunt Corey." Giselle stopped and stared at her daughter's back. "This house is so empty all the time. I'm always by myself. I don't have any friends anymore. I wish I could come visit you for a few days. Can't I, please?"

As she spoke, Emily pivoted slowly. She jumped when she saw her mother, standing in the center of her room with her arms crossed.

"Uh, I have to go. Bye." She slammed the phone back in its cradle and cast her guilty eyes to the floor. "I thought you were downstairs."

"You were talking to Corey."

Emily gave her a sick look. "I thought it was all right now that Grandfather isn't here."

"Is that why you were sneaking around?"

"I wasn't sneaking! I just—"

"What did she say?" Giselle's question shot into her defense.

"She invited me to come visit her," Emily said, her eyes lifting with the slightest hope. "Can I go, Mother? Just for a weekend?"

Giselle schooled her expression to hide her chagrin at the question. There was no way in hell that she would allow her daughter within ten feet of Corey, but she chose not to tell her that. "Emily, Corey's very busy. She was just being polite."

"No, Mother. She really wants me to come. I can tell."

Giselle ambled across the room and picked up a little porcelain clown on a table beside Emily's bed. "Emily, Corey has a life of her own now. I don't really approve of the way she lives. People coming and going. Men in and out. The people she associates with—they're low-lifes, and I don't want you exposed to them."

Emily gave Giselle an incredulous look. "How do you know how she lives? You haven't even spoken to her in months."

"I know my sister."

"Well, I know her, too."

Giselle turned back to the girl, saw the indignation on her face, and knew she'd chosen the wrong tactic. "Besides," she said, making her diversion up as she went along. "You won't have time for her. You have your party to think of."

Emily's frown was suspicious. "What party?"

"Your birthday party. You'll be twelve next month, and I was thinking that we should have a big blow-out party."

"But I don't have any friends."

"Then this will be a great way to make some," Giselle said. "We'll get a live band and invite the whole school. By the time it's over, you'll be the most popular girl there."

The ember of interest in Emily's eyes ignited into a smile. "Really?"

"Really. My daughter doesn't turn twelve every day. Besides, maybe it's time for the Dobiases to get back on the social track. Show them that we're neither down nor out."

"And people will really like me again?" Emily asked carefully.

"I guarantee it." And as she spoke, Giselle had no doubt in her mind that pouring money into Emily's social life would solve all of her problems.

By the end of the week, Giselle had booked an act called Easy Street, an up-and-coming young group from Boston complete with heartthrob good looks, soda pop music, and choreography to die for. And, oh, yes, their band would come with them.

"When I was a teenager," she told Emily, "the groups played their own instruments."

Emily, who seemed a hundred percent more ebullient since the plans had begun, laughed. "And they just stood there on the stage strumming their guitars and screaming into the microphones."

Giselle shook her head. "Not exactly. Sometimes, if their concert was really hot, they'd smash their guitars onto the stage and set fire to the set."

They giggled together, feeling closer than they ever had, and for once in Giselle's life she felt as if she'd won the unequivocal approval of someone she loved.

The plans went smoothly for the next two weeks, until it was time to send out invitations. That was when the powder keg that Giselle hadn't even anticipated released its first small explosion.

"I want to invite my father," Emily said.

"I'm afraid that's impossible."

"Why? He's my father. I'm his daughter. I'm turning twelve, and he's never come to even one of my parties before. Why can't I invite him?"

"Because I haven't been in touch with him in years, Emily. I have no interest in calling him, much less entertaining him in my home."

"It's my home, too," Emily said. "I'll call him."

Giselle struggled for a way of diverting her daughter, but the stubborn glint in Emily's eye told her it was futile.

"I'll do a lot for you, Emmy. I'll give you a huge party, I'll pay ungodly amounts for your gifts and your entertainment, but I will not allow you to invite that man here!"

Emily had run up to her room in a fit of rage. Late that night, when Giselle was sequestered in the study, Emily found Samuel Hart's address in the telephone book and scrawled out an invitation to him. He would come; she was certain of it. He couldn't deny his only daughter this one request, not after all these years.

As for her mother, well, Emily decided to handle her potential wrath the Dobias way: She would cross that bridge when she came to it.

Giselle allowed Emily to invite Corey as a concession for dropping the subject of her father. Corey imagined that her sister's greatest hope for the party was that she wouldn't show up. But she enjoyed dashing Giselle's hopes by arriving two hours before the party began, on the grounds of her home for the first time since her father had banished her.

There were subtle differences in the house, she noticed as she strolled through it, struggling to feel nothing as nostalgia swept over her. Her father's study had been rearranged to Giselle's taste, and the artwork he had bought for specific placement on its walls had been replaced with abstracts from Giselle's own collection.

Other rooms had been altered, as well, with new furniture pieces and different wallpaper, as though Giselle had chosen to put her own stamp on the house now that her father wasn't around to stop her. It all gave Corey a strange, portentous feeling.

Giselle pretended to be too busy to acknowledge Corey, so she slipped up to Rena's rooms to speak to her sister, from whom she had heard nothing in months. She found Rena lying in bed feigning a headache, with a half-empty glass of Scotch on the table next to her.

"Rena, you've got to get up and come to the party," she said.

Rena shook her head. "No, I don't. I'm staying up here."

Corey took her hand and tried to pull her into a sitting position. Her eyes were glazed, and her hair, wildly tangled, looked as though it hadn't seen a brush in days. On the big-screen television in the corner, a rerun of *Andy Griffith* blared incessantly as Barney Fife waved an empty gun at an amused prisoner.

"Come on, Rena. Think of Emily. She needs us now. She's getting a lot of crap from the kids at school, she's upset about Dad, Giselle's working all the time—she needs us to be here for her tonight."

"I know what she's been going through," Rena slurred, jerking her hand from Corey's and rolling to her feet. "I'm the one who's here all day, remember? I'm the one who brought the whole shitty mess with her school to Giselle's attention in the first place. Not that the bitch appreciated it."

"Then you should know. Come on, Rena. Come down with me."

Rena shook her head vehemently and plopped into the chair at her French provincial vanity table, and stared with lackluster eyes at her reflection in the mirror. "What if no one comes?" she asked miserably, as if she would be the one who was shattered. "Giselle told me that half the people she invited didn't even respond. She isn't sure if they're coming or not. The ones who RSVP'd had such creative excuses. I don't think I can stand it if I have to go down there and watch that little girl's heart get broken. At least somebody in this family ought to be happy."

"Really? That many didn't respond? That's odd."

"Not for the granddaughter of a convict," Rena said on a dry, miserable laugh. "Who happened to have been betrayed by his very own daughter."

Corey went to Rena and, grabbing a brush from her table, began trying to work the tangles from her hair. "You didn't betray him. You were a victim. When are you going to realize that?"

Rena brought her drink to her lips and regarded Corey in the mirror. "I guess the day I can turn back time and show Joe Holifield what he can do with his obsession. The day I can turn the tables and ruin his life instead of letting him ruin mine. That's the day I can put it all behind me. But that isn't likely to happen, is it, Corey?"

"No, Rena. It isn't."

Rena looked at Corey over her shoulder, and her eyes welled with tears. "You're really pretty, you know that?" she asked softly. "Is that what independence does for you?"

Corey smiled. "You should try it."

"Me?" Rena threw back the rest of the contents of her glass and laughed again. "No, not me. I'm not like you."

"So you've said before," Corey pointed out. "But no one expects you to be like me. And no one's comparing you to Giselle. You can be yourself."

"Oh?" She stood up and swung out of Corey's reach. "And what is that? A sniveling drunk who falls prey to every leech who comes along? An idiot who can't tell the truth from a honey-coated lie? My husband's sleeping around, you know. I know he is."

She filled her glass again, spilling some on her hand, and licked the excess off of her fingers. "It's true. And probably with someone in this very house. I've already fired every housekeeper we have under the age of thirty. I figure he likes them young, though I couldn't really know for sure, since he never really liked me . . . young *or* old."

"Rena, why would you say that? What's happened?"

"Oh, just his not coming to bed sometimes until three or four in the morning, or popping in right before dawn for a shower and pretending that he's been in bed beside me all night, like I'm the one who's crazy. And all the time, his car is parked right outside. No matter where

I look in the house, in all the obvious places, he isn't there."

Corey's face paled, but she didn't know what to say. She had known of John's philandering for years—everyone had, including Rena, she guessed—but she wouldn't have expected him to be so unfeeling as to do it right under Rena's nose. "Have you asked him about it?"

Rena burst into wet, sloppy tears and wiped her nose with the back of her wrist. "Of course. He always says he was downstairs working, only I looked for him there, Corey! And then he changes the subject, like my hysteria is boring him, and I always shut up and just accept it. Just like I accept everything."

Corey sighed and pulled Rena into her arms. Rena cried stains onto her dress, but Corey didn't notice.

After a moment, the crying subsided a little, but Rena didn't separate herself from Corey. "I miss Mama."

"I know you do. So do I."

"She would have known what to do," Rena went on. "She always did."

"Maybe," Corey whispered. "But I don't know, Rena. This is a tough one. You probably wouldn't like what I think you should do."

"What's that?" Rena pulled away from her and looked her directly in the face, hanging on every word of the solution she so desperately needed.

"I think that if what you say about him is true, you should leave him."

"Leave him?" Rena asked, as if the thought was inconceivable. "It's my home. If I left, I'd have nothing!"

"You have your share of the business, Rena. You could make it without him."

"I have nothing," Rena repeated. "Giselle has it all now. I signed it all over to her so she wouldn't expose me about Joe Holifield."

"You what?"

Rena wilted from the severity of Corey's reaction. "I told you, Corey. I'm so stupid!"

Corey sank into the chair Rena had just abandoned and stared at her sister. "You signed everything over to her? Everything?"

"Nobody knows," Rena said. "You can't say anything, Corey. John still thinks it's half mine. It's probably the only thing keeping him here. If Giselle finds out I told you, she can throw me out. She agreed to support me, but I don't know what she'd do if I crossed her."

"That bitch," Corey said through her teeth. "That conniving bitch." Red-faced, she got up and grabbed Rena's shoulders. "Rena, you won't get any arguments from me about that being a major screw-up, but it doesn't mean you're shackled and at the mercy of a philandering husband and a conniving sister for the rest of your life. It's all the more reason to put that drink down, pull yourself together, and fight back."

Rena shook her head. "I can't, Corey."

"Yes, you can! You can come live with me, and work in my company. I'm on the cusp of some exciting things, Rena. You could be a part of it. I could use your talent and experience."

Rena's eyes dulled to a dismal gray. "I can't, Corey."

Corey heaved in a deep sigh, despite the heaviness in her lungs. "You don't have to decide now, Rena. Right now, we've got to get downstairs. The guests will be arriving in less than an hour, and I'm not going without you. If I do, I'm liable to tell Giselle exactly what I think of her robbing you blind. It could get real ugly, Rena."

Rena moaned. "I look like a nightmare. I'm not in any shape to be seen in public."

Corey went into her dressing room and riffled through her dresses. "Here, you can wear this," she said, coming back to the door with a dress in her hand. "And I'll do your hair, like I used to when we were kids, remember? Besides, there're going to be some sparks down there before too long. Emily's going to need our support."

"Sparks? What kind of sparks?"

"Emily told me she's invited Samuel Hart to the party, even though Giselle told her she couldn't. She seems to think he's going to come. I have to tell you, I think if no one showed up but him, she would have the party of her life. She needs for him to acknowledge her. It's really kind of sad."

"He won't come."

"Why not?"

"Well, why should he start now?" Rena asked, emptying her glass. "He's never come before. I've invited him to her party personally every year of her life. He's shown nothing but absolute indifference."

"But this year she invited him personally. Really, how could he refuse her that one little thing?"

Rena let out a shaky breath and rubbed her bloodshot eyes. "I didn't realize how bad this is going to be. If that bastard hurts that little girl by not showing up, by God, he's going to have me to answer to. I may have a backbone of jelly when it comes to the way men treat me, but I will not sit by and watch one of them hurt my niece."

"Now you're talking." Corey smiled and pulled Rena back to the vanity table. "Now come on. We have to hurry."

The music started blaring at exactly seven-thirty, even though only a handful of people had shown up. Emily didn't go into the ballroom, but lingered instead in the foyer, as if waiting for the barrage of guests to appear.

But no one else came.

Giselle became testier with the staff as the night wore on, and Corey and Rena tried to devise ways to make

Emily join the few guests who had come. But the girl wouldn't leave the foyer.

Finally, when it was almost eight-thirty, Giselle—visibly upset by the poor turnout—put her arm around her daughter and tried to force her into the party. "Sweetheart, you're neglecting the ones who did come."

Emily tearfully turned on her mother. "I'm not going in there," she said. "They're whispering about me, and Monday they'll go back to school and tell everyone how awful this was. I'm staying right here."

"But sweetheart, it serves no purpose."

"Yes, it does," she said. "There's one more person who I know will come. He knows how important it is to me. I wrote him a personal note with his invitation."

"Who is that?"

"My father," Emily said defiantly.

Giselle's face went pale. "Honey, your father isn't coming."

"Yes, he is. I know he is. He's just late. He's a very busy man."

"Honey . . ." Giselle glanced at John, who stood in the foyer with them, and he looked at the marble floor. "I didn't tell you before because I didn't want to spoil the party for you, but Samuel did respond to his invitation. He sent his regrets, but he had to be out of town tonight."

The hot tears in Emily's eyes made Giselle's heart fall to her stomach, and she wished she'd come up with something better, something more believable, something easier to swallow. But the truth was that he'd had his secretary send back a note that said simply, "Mr. Hart will be unable to attend."

It hadn't surprised her, of course. He had no reason to come, never would, and she didn't even hold it against him. It was herself she hated more than him when Emmy started up the stairs.

"Emily, where are you going?"

"To my room."

"But the party! The band! Emily, I paid thousands and thousands—!"

But Emily was out of sight before she'd even finished the sentence.

The few guests who had come were allowed to stay until the band finished its first set, in hopes that Emily would hear the festivities and decide to join them, after all. Such were fickle adolescent minds, Giselle said. Emily would be all right.

But Corey knew better. She knew what it was like to be absolutely and irrationally rejected by her father. She knew how crushing it felt not to understand why.

So after a while, she went up to Emily's room and found her niece weak with sobs and lying in tears on her bed, her silk and lace organdy dress wadded in a puddle on the floor.

Corey sat down beside her and stroked her hair, peeling strands back from where they had pasted themselves onto her face. "Are you going to be all right?"

Emily didn't answer.

Corey just sat with her for several moments, rubbing her back and stroking her hair, until finally Emily looked up at her. "Can I go home with you, Aunt Corey? Please?"

"Of course, if your mother says it's okay. But, Emmy, I don't think she will."

"She will. I'll talk her into it. Please."

Emily threw her arms around Corey's neck and clung to her in desperation. "I'd love for you to come home with me," Corey whispered. "But just for the weekend. You have school next week, and—"

"No," Emily cut in. "I'm never going back there again. Never."

"Emily . . ."

"Really, Aunt Corey. I'm not. I'll run away before I'll go back and let those people make fun of me. I won't do it."

There was a shift in the doorway, and they both looked up to see Giselle standing there. She gave Corey a searing look, but those eyes softened as she approached the bed. "Emily, I don't blame you," she said. "I wouldn't want you to go back there."

Emily wiped her eyes. "Really, Mother? You won't make me?"

"No. I've been thinking about getting you a private tutor. That way you could study at home."

"A private tutor?" It was Corey who spoke out with surprise. "Really, Giselle. Isn't that a little extreme?"

"No, it isn't," Emily piped in. "It sounds good, Mother. I'd like that."

"But Giselle . . ." Corey stood up and faced her sister squarely. "She needs to work through this. She needs to learn to get along with people."

"There are plenty of people in her life," Giselle said. "She doesn't need a bunch of yapping little adolescents making her life miserable. Besides, she's way too advanced for the school she's in. She can move along a lot faster if she has her own tutor."

Emily's spirits seemed to lift at the news, but the pale, tired, and desperately disappointed cast to her face still made her look very small and vulnerable. "Mother, could we put it off for a few days? Getting the tutor, I mean? I want to go home with Aunt Corey. She said I could if it was all right with you."

Giselle's gaze locked with Corey's for the first time that evening. Corey saw the loathing there and wondered what she had ever done to deserve it. "No, I don't think that's a good idea."

Emily burst into tears again. "Please, Mother. It's my birthday. Nothing else has gone right. I want to go with Aunt Corey."

"But I need you here. I need you to—"

"To what?" Emily asked. "To wander around the house all alone while you're at work? To keep remembering how my father hates me?"

Giselle set her lips and gave Corey one more murderous look. Corey didn't respond.

"*Please*, Mother."

"All right." Giselle's grudging acquiescence was expelled on a quivering breath.

Emily leaped off the bed and threw her arms around her. Giselle hugged her lightly, her distress at the decision making it impossible for her to accept her daughter's glee with any degree of warmth. "Run down and get one of the staff to pack you a suitcase."

Emily hesitated. "Are all the guests gone?"

Giselle sighed. "Yes. The last one left some time ago. The band is breaking down their equipment, but you don't have to go in there."

Emily seemed relieved and bounced out in her jeans, barefoot, down the hall.

Giselle leaned against the wall and crossed her arms, locking her gaze on Corey. Corey lifted her chin and waited.

"I want you to know that I think using my daughter to get to me is the dirtiest trick you've ever pulled."

"You're the expert on dirty tricks, Giselle. Not me. It wasn't my idea to take Emily home. It was hers."

"I want her back tomorrow."

"She expects to stay a few days."

"Tomorrow," Giselle repeated.

Corey looked down at the floor, considering her sister's ultimatum, then brought her gaze back up to hers.

"What is it you're afraid of, Giselle? That she'll find out how real people live? That she'll see that there is life after the Dobias fortune? That she'll like me better than you?"

"I told you to have her back tomorrow," Giselle repeated. "And I meant it. If you don't, I'll have you arrested for kidnapping."

Corey smiled and crossed her arms. "I'm sure Emily would find that gesture real amusing. As amusing as the press found it when Dad had me arrested. She might not think too much of a mother who would do that."

"Don't you worry about my relationship with my daughter."

"I won't, Giselle. But you'd better. Because that little girl is a time bomb just waiting to explode." She pushed past her sister and started up the corridor. "We'll be leaving as soon as Emily's packed," she said. "And while I'm waiting, I'm going to get some of my own things."

"Nothing in this house is yours!"

Corey shot her a drop-dead look. "Chill out, Giselle. Your insecurities are getting out of control."

She made her way to her old bedroom, and Giselle made no move to stop her.

chapter

37

THE FIRST TWO DAYS THAT EMILY STAYED WITH Corey, Corey took her to the construction site, forcing her to don jeans and a hard hat and to stay close as they walked through the debris. Corey included her in "decisions" about the blueprints and the decor of the building, allowed her to look through swatches of carpet and drapery for her opinions on colors, and introduced her to business acquaintances and workers as if she were another adult just brought into the company.

Before her eyes, Emily seemed to blossom. She gave Corey ideas about how to decorate her apartment, and without even a second thought, Corey took her advice and ordered the items she would need. The second night they dined with Adam, and despite Emily's reluctance to like him at first, he had won her over by the end of the evening.

That night, as she said good night to Emily, the girl looked up at her with her wide brown eyes and asked, "Do you think Grandfather's all right?"

"I think he'll be fine," Corey whispered.

Emily studied Corey's shadow on the wall, frowning. "Adam is the one who got him in trouble, isn't he?"

Corey thought of lying, evading, or explaining it away, but she knew that Emily was too bright for that. "Yes. He's the one who exposed him."

"But you like him anyway?"

"At first I was very angry at him. For that and . . . some other things he did. But I finally realized that Dad did this to himself. He was going to get caught sooner or later. And by the time all this happened, I really liked Adam." She swallowed, looked down at her hands, then moved her eyes back to Emily. "I've lost a lot of people in my life, especially in the last few months, Emmy. Adam was someone who didn't turn his back on me when I needed him, like a lot of other people did. I decided that life is too short to hold grudges."

"Do you love him?"

Corey's face flushed, and she hoped Emily couldn't see the answer in her expression. "I don't know, Emmy. Maybe I do."

"What about Eric?"

"Eric." Corey smiled a weak, sad smile. "Eric is one of those people who didn't stand by me when I was in trouble. That's hard to forget, you know?"

"Yeah." Emily sank her head into the pillow, her brown hair splaying around her face like a dark halo. "I guess you'll never forgive Grandfather."

"I think I could, maybe, if he'd accept it," she whispered. "But he's not interested in forgiveness."

"How do you know?"

"I know," Corey said, "because I went to visit him in prison not too long ago. He wouldn't even talk to me."

Emily sat up suddenly. "Really? You went there and saw him?"

"Yes, of course. Why?"

"Because Mother told me that we couldn't visit. She said that he wouldn't want us to see him that way."

Corey felt that old familiar rage rising inside her again. "Emily, if anybody needs visitors, it's someone in prison. I think Dad would love to see you."

"Then will you take me there? Tomorrow? Please, Aunt Corey? Mother might not let me stay any longer than that. I had to beg to stay this long."

Corey wilted a little, for she knew that taking Emily to Connecticut without Giselle's permission would be overstepping her bounds. And yet, her father had every right to a visit from his granddaughter. If he wouldn't accept her own support, maybe he would take Emily's. She smiled even as she made the decision.

"All right," she said. "I'll take you. Get some sleep. We have to get up early tomorrow."

Dobias didn't wait for visitors anymore. On visiting days, when other inmates showered and groomed for their loved ones, he went about his work as if it were any other day. His beard had grown long, and he decided he liked it that way. There was no one who cared what he looked like, after all. His hair, too, had grown too long and scraggly, until a few days earlier when Thomas had insisted on cutting it.

"Don't worry," he said, twirling the scissors he'd gotten from the guard in his fingers. "I'm not dangerous with these things, or they'da put me in maximum security."

"Just watch where you cut," Dobias warned him. He glanced at the man's reflection in the bathroom mirror and felt him make the first snip. "Why *did* they put you in here?"

"With you rich bastards?" Thomas asked without bitterness. "You know, most of you dudes in this place did crimes a whole hell of a lot worse than I did. Still, I guess I'm damn lucky I'm not married to some three-hundred-pound murderer in Angola." He stopped trimming and waved the scissors toward Dobias's reflection. "Wanna know why the judge put me here? It's because he's a black judge, and he liked me. And he happens to think that these minimum security lock-ups are a crock of shit, that you people should be mixed in with the real hard-core scum for a while. I ain't hard-core scum, but the way some o' you look at me, I reckon I'm the next best thing. Bein' with me's what's s'posed to make you think twice before you rip somebody off again."

"I didn't rip anybody off," Dobias returned. "I didn't do anything that hurt anybody. I'm a businessman. And I didn't get as successful as I am teaching Sunday school."

Thomas snipped a little too close to the skin on the back of his neck, and Dobias winced.

"Nice to know the American work ethic still exists, ain't it?"

Irritated, Dobias looked over his shoulder. "Why do you talk like that, anyway? You read classics until your eyes are bloodshot, you know everything that's going on in the world from Wall Street to the Middle East, and still you talk like some grammar-school dropout."

"I *am* a grammar-school dropout," Thomas said. "But that don't mean I'm stupid. Maybe I talk like this to aggravate you. Maybe I do it 'cause I like it. Hell, I don't have to prove nothing to nobody. If I want to mix my metaphors and dangle my participles, ain't nobody gonna tell me I can't."

Dobias watched the flakes of his gray hair falling to his shoulders, and he dusted them off roughly as if Thomas had put them there deliberately. "What do you do out there in the world, Thomas? Besides forgery, I mean."

Thomas leered at him, unamused. "I'm a carpenter. A damn good one. Problem is, ain't much money to be made. Only reason I started forging checks is that I had a sick grandbaby needed surgery. Didn't have no insurance. A man got to pay the bills somehow."

"A sick grandbaby." Dobias uttered the words quietly, wondering why he was so surprised that the big, gruff-talking man would have a family, bills, and a host of problems. "Did the baby get the surgery?"

For a long moment, Thomas seemed intent on the haircut, but finally he answered. "No. She died before anything could be done. Heart trouble. Probably never really had a chance."

"And you wound up in prison, anyway."

"*C'est la vie*," the man mumbled. "That's Russian for 'that shit happens.' "

Dobias grinned over his shoulder, fully aware that Thomas knew the term was French and exactly what it meant. He probably spoke the language fluently. It wouldn't have surprised Dobias a bit.

Now, on visiting day, he knew better than to wait for his name to be called or hope that anyone would come. He hadn't even had a letter from Giselle or Rena in the three months since he'd been here. The fact left an uneasy feeling in the pit of his stomach, a feeling that Gloster had been right, that something was going on that he couldn't control. A feeling that his fortune was slipping out of his grasp as time went on, but that there was not a damn thing he could do to save it.

He plunged his hands into the soapy, steamy water and began scrubbing the hardened food off of the plates, and tried to think back over his talks with Giselle before he'd come to prison. She had been awfully anxious for him to sign things over to her. Though her argument had been sound, he couldn't help wondering now if her deliberate absence, her lack of respect revealed in her indifference to his plight, was any indication of how deeply her claws were sinking into his company.

And what of Rena? She was the one who would have followed him to the ends of the earth and sworn he hung the moon on his own little hook. She was the one who'd always stood by him. And yet he'd heard not a word from her. Not one word.

He rinsed the plates and stacked them in the rack where they dried, and reached for another stack. The robotic labor was almost comforting, unlike the pressure-cooker work he engaged in at home. This was mindless, mechanical, and it was becoming something that he didn't hate quite so much. It was better than the back-breaking job of scrubbing the kitchen and bath-room floors, and more sanitary than washing out toilets.

One of the guards appeared at the door to the kitch-en and, amid the clutter of other inmates doing their jobs, called his name. His hands still dripping, he turned around.

"Dobias, you have a visitor."

He picked up the towel, his heart jolting at the pros-pect. "A visitor? Who?"

"Your granddaughter," he said. "She's waiting in the rec room."

"Emily?" He dried his hands quickly and started out of the kitchen, his expression a mixture of surprise and bewilderment. As he stepped into the noisy room, full of visiting families, he quickly scanned the room. He saw Corey first, sitting alone in the corner of the room, her coat folded over her lap. She didn't recognize him, for her eyes strayed behind him to the doorway, then met the gaze of someone across the room.

He followed that gaze, and saw Emily, sitting with her hands folded at one of the empty tables, looking nervous and ready to burst into tears.

"Emily." He walked toward her, and she looked up at him, reluctant at first to believe it was he.

"Grandfather?" A smile skittered across her face. "You grew a beard."

He smiled and pulled her into a tight hug. "And you grew another foot."

"No, I still have two." She smiled, and his heart melted.

Instead of taking the seat across from her, he pulled a chair around the table to sit right next to her.

"Jeans, Grandfather? I never thought I'd see you in jeans."

He laughed, but that laughter quickly faded. "Bet you never thought you'd see me in prison, either."

She shook her head. "No."

A moment of silence followed, and she glanced awkwardly toward Corey. Dobias looked, too, and saw her soft, poignant expression as she smiled at him. He looked away.

"Corey brought me," Emily whispered. "Mother's been really busy, running the company and everything. I'm sure she would come if she could . . ."

The words died, and Dobias nodded silently. He thought of grilling her about the way her mother had stolen the company from him, about her intentions, about her plans. But something told him that Emily knew nothing of the deception, and it would serve no purpose for her to know. After a while he asked, "So why is Corey sitting over there?"

"She thought you wouldn't want to see her. I told her you would, that things had changed. They have changed, haven't they?"

He looked down at his wrinkled hands, still red and chafed from the steaming water. "So your mother's working. What about Rena?"

Emily recognized the deliberate evasion, and her shoulders wilted as she threw Corey a defeated glance. "Fine. Well, not really. She's been drinking a lot, keeping to herself. I guess she's depressed over everything that's happened."

"What about you?" he asked. "What do you think of all this?"

It was Emily's turn to look at her hands. "Oh, Grandfather," she said on a sigh. "It's been awful. Mother took me out of school because, well, I wasn't getting along well with the other kids."

Dobias's face hardened. "Because of me?"

She couldn't answer. "I don't know why. They're just all snobs. They think they're better than everybody. And then I started a new school and had a birthday party—"

"Your birthday," he cut in. "I'd forgotten."

"It's okay," she said with a shrug. "What could you have done? Uncle John said you were sending me a license plate, but you don't really make those here, do you, Grandfather?"

Dobias didn't find John's comment amusing. "He said that?"

"He was just kidding. But anyway, hardly anyone came to the party. I think I kind of know how you felt at your party now. To get all excited and dressed up, and nothing goes right." She looked down at the table, noted the stain on the grain of the wood, and rubbed at it with her finger. "*He* didn't even come."

"He?"

"My dad. I invited him, but he didn't come."

"Your dad." Dobias frowned, and Emily saw new lines pleating his face, lines that hadn't been there before. "You want to know why your dad didn't come, Emmy? It's because he's an asshole. Repeat after me. Asshole."

Emily smiled.

"Go ahead, say it."

"Grandfather!"

"Come on," he said, raising his fingers to direct her pronunciation. "Ass-hole. You can do it."

"Asshole." Emily giggled. "You've changed, Grandfather. You would have never let me say that before."

"I'm more grounded in reality now," Dobias said, smiling for the first time since he could remember. "When your mother asks you what I said to you, you tell her that we worked on strengthening your vocabulary. Particularly those words that apply to those no-good *assholes* who think only of themselves and don't give a damn what they do to anyone else."

Emily's smile faded, and she took her grandfather's hand, squeezed it. "I miss you, Grandfather. Is it terrible here?"

"It's not as bad as it could be," he said. "No one ever died from loneliness or boredom."

"I guess we have more in common now than we ever had before," she pointed out softly. "I'm lonely and bored a lot, too. I guess it'll get worse. Mother's getting me a private tutor."

"A private tutor?" He straightened in his chair. "Why? Before she resorts to that, she should at least consider some of the boarding schools. She went to one of the finest in the country."

"But she won't send me. She said she hated it, and that she would never do that to a child of her own."

"Hated it?" His forehead pleated again. "She flourished there. She graduated at the top of her class, and she had friends from the finest families—"

"She hated it, Grandfather. She said that she never understood why Rena and Corey didn't have to go. She wanted to be home with the rest of the family."

Denying her words, he began to shake his head. "If she hated it, she would have said something. All those years, she never said a word."

"Maybe you just weren't listening," Emily whispered.

Later that day, when his work was finished and many of the inmates had congregated in the rec room to watch reruns of *M*A*S*H**, Dobias lay on his bed thinking back over what Emily had said. Had Giselle really hated board-ing school?

He tried to recall the day they had left her there, only nine years old, and how Shara had broken down in the car before they'd even pulled off of the grounds. "I can't do it, Nik. Don't make me leave my little girl. She needs me."

"She needs a good education. We're doing what's best for her."

Shara ground her teeth, and tears seared her eyes. "Dammit, Nik. When do I get to decide what's best for my children? Look at her standing up there. She doesn't want us to leave her. We're abandoning her."

"She'll get over it by the time we pull away," he said. "She's a tough kid. She'll be fine."

Shara had cried all the way home that day, and when he came to their room that night and tried to comfort her, she had shaken him away. "I don't know if I can ever forgive you for this, Nik," she said.

But she had gotten over it. After a year or so, when Giselle appeared to have adjusted well and her achieve-ments in school had been meteoric, Shara stopped harp-ing on it. But by the time it was Rena's turn to go away, she had adamantly refused. "If you make me send anoth-er of my children away, so help me God I'll leave you."

Something about the finality in her voice had shaken him, so he'd let her have her way. Then, when Corey came along, well, he never even suggested it. The truth was, *he* couldn't bear to let her go.

But now Corey and he weren't even speaking. He thought of her sitting alone in that corner today, still so small and pretty, still wearing that soft smile that always melted his heart completely. The daughter he had thrown out. The one he had tried to destroy. She was the only one who seemed to care about him now, and still he couldn't make himself put the past behind him and move on. Once the lines were drawn, it was too hard to cross over them. She had fallen in with Adam Franklin. She had betrayed him, and that betrayal had cost him everything. He couldn't forget that even when his heart tried.

"Instead o' mopin' 'round here like some kinda hangdog, you oughta do somethin'," Thomas told him a week later. "You oughta try carpentry or somethin'. You could go crazy just sittin' there."

Dobias shook his head. "I'm not the carpenter type. I hire carpenters."

"Yeah, well, from the looks o' things, you might need a trade when you get outa here."

Dobias sat up and dropped his feet to the floor. "What are you talking about?"

"Your daughter," Thomas said, nodding toward the article he'd just read in USA Today. "She's a steamroller, all right. Once she gets her claws deep enough in your company, she'd be a fool to give it back. And she don't strike me as no fool."

Dobias lay back down and issued a sigh.

"I'm just sayin' it's mighty odd that she ain't come to see you."

"She's busy."

"Yeah. Busy wallowin' in your money."

Dobias closed his eyes. "Just shut up and get off my back. I'm trying to sleep."

"I'm just tryin' to make you face reality, bro."

"I'm not your bro."

"Yeah, well. As much as you hate to admit it, we're more alike than we are different."

Dobias raised up on an elbow and shot his cell mate a dismayed look. "How's that?"

"We're both old," he said, shaking out his paper. "We're

both stupid enough to wind up in a prison camp. We're both smart enough to know we're stupid, though we can't put our fingers on whether we're stupid for gettin' caught or for doin' what got us here."

"I don't know about any of that," Dobias said, lying back down, "but I guess the reasons we did anything illegal were the same."

"Shit," Thomas said. "I did it to feed my family."

"So did I."

The old black man's laughter rang out over the building. "Yeah, man, but your family eats a hell of a lot more than mine."

"That's why my crimes are so much bigger," Dobias said with a smile.

"Hallelujah, praise the Lord," Thomas said. "The man admitted he done somethin' wrong. I think we're makin' progress here."

"Progress toward what?"

"Toward your rehabilitation. We might make an honest man outa you yet, bro."

Dobias turned over, putting his back to his bunk mate. "I told you, I'm not your bro."

But this time he said it with a smile.

chapter
38

ERIC GRAY STEPPED INTO THE EXCLUSIVE RES-
taurant he'd been summoned to, and standing at the entrance next to the Victorian Christmas tree that smelled
like mothballs, he scanned the diners. He had deliberately not dressed up. He never liked to meet expectations,
for when he tried to, he fell short, anyway. This way,
there would be no question about his intention to fit in.

The hostess approached him and eyed the brown
tweed blazer with the black open-neck shirt, and the
faded jeans that had seen one too many washings. "May
I help you?"

"I'm meeting Jacob Stewart," he said, lowering his lids
and waiting defiantly for her to tell him he couldn't go in,
that he wasn't dressed suitably. That would be a hell of a
note for the old banker who placed image above anything
else in his life. He wondered if it would embarrass Jacob
Stewart if he was forced to leave his own turf and eat at
a place with piped-in rock music rather than the orches-
trated Christmas carols. But then, it would probably suit
him better. That way he wouldn't have to explain to any
acquaintances who passed their table just what his relationship was to Eric. He had never been good at explaining that.

"Yes . . . well." She stepped over to the coatroom and
came back with a tie folded in her hand. "Would you
mind wearing this? I believe it'll match all right."

Offering her a wry smile, he took the tie and stared
down at it. "Do I have to? Ties are only for weddings

and funerals. I don't plan on dying, and nobody in their right mind would marry me."

She gave him an apologetic, if amused, look. "It's policy. I'm sorry."

He grinned and pulled up his collar, and slid the tie around his neck. "Well, I'll forgive you if you'll help me tie it."

He saw the pink flush across her cheeks and congratulated himself for still having the ability to put it there.

The hostess, a restaurant copy of Vanna White, tied his tie, cocking her head to one side and studying him the way a lover might. "There you go," she said. "You're all set. I'll lead you to your table now."

He held back, casting a grudging look toward his table. "You know, I'm about to have a meeting with someone I don't like very much, and I anticipate swapping insults for the next hour or so. I'd really like it if, when I finish with this, you might have a drink with me. Sort of pick up my wilting spirits?"

"I'd like that. I'll be due for a break in about an hour." She started leading him back toward his table. "So, are you meeting with your boss?"

"I don't have a boss. There isn't anybody I answer to."

"Then what kind of person could make you sit with him for an hour if you can't stand him?"

Eric's grin faded, and he offered a careless shrug. "The worst kind," he said. "My father."

He reached the table, and with cool eyes, regarded the older man to whom he bore a striking resemblance, for all the good it did him. Jacob Stewart's hair was white now, and his skin was more withered and drawn than it had been years ago, when Eric had first discovered that the well-to-do banker had given stud service to his mother. He'd had no more tolerance for the man then than he had now.

The meal went pretty much as he expected, with sarcastic barbs passing across the table like saltshakers—mostly from him, he had to admit. It was thirty minutes before he wearied of the tension, and finally he leaned forward, propping his elbows on the table—something that he knew would drive his father crazy—and looked Jacob Stewart in the eye. "So, Pop," he said, using the name that had always made the man cringe. "When are you going to get around to the point? What was so important that you actually took the time to call me?"

Jacob Stewart set down his fork and leaned back in his chair, and surveyed his son for a long moment. "It's recently come to my attention that you've been spending a lot of time with a certain young lady. Corey Dobias."

Eric crossed his hands in front of his grin. "Just where do you get your information?"

"From various sources," he said. "One even told me you were engaged to marry her."

Eric sat back and cocked his head, and decided not to tell him that the engagement was off. It was too amusing the way he brought up ancient history as though it was current news. His sources were really on the ball. "Yeah. So?"

"Is it true?"

Eric crossed his arms again and glanced toward the hostess weaving her way through the tables. She winked at him as she passed. Wearily, he brought his gaze back to his father. "What's the matter, Pop? Is it so difficult to believe that your no-account son could hook a billionaire's heiress?"

His father shifted in his chair. "Well, frankly, I did wonder where you would have the opportunity to meet someone like that. I mean, there you are, stuck up in that room you call an apartment and barely making a living."

"Get to the point."

The banker cleared his throat. "Well, I . . . that is . . . I simply thought that if it's true that you're going to marry her, then perhaps it's time I met her. After all, if she's going to be my daughter-in-law—"

Eric laughed out loud, indifferent to the diners who turned and glanced at him. "So what are you going to do when I marry her? Suddenly admit to the world that you're my father, so you can claim your daughter-in-law?"

The comment ruffled the man, and he took off his glasses and cast his steely eyes on his son. "I admitted that you were my son long ago. It's you who could never accept it, so don't give me that poor-little-illegitimate-me crap. It's time we made peace, Eric. It's time you started acting like a man."

"A man with a billionaire's daughter for a wife?" He shook his head and let his eyes scan the room idly, and finally he settled them back on his father. "You need to get new sources, Pop. Hasn't anyone told you that Corey's father is in jail? That she doesn't even have access to his money, and might never again?"

"She has her own money. I understand she's embarking on some challenging projects in Boston. Some projects that stand to make her a lot of money. As a banker, that interests me a great deal."

A slow, deprecating smile sliced across Eric's face, and he flopped back in his chair and nodded with disbelief. "Oh, I get it. I see now. You want me to talk Corey into putting her money in your bank."

"I thought it might somehow benefit us both."

"What's in it for me?"

The man looked flustered, something Eric had witnessed only rarely in his father. "My gratitude, of course."

"Ah, yes. Gratitude. Just the thing I've always wanted from you."

The sarcasm in his voice shook his father, and he shoved his glasses back on. "Eric, if I had a clue what you really did want from me, just once we might have a conversation that didn't end in a yelling match."

"Forget it, Pop," Eric said. "I don't want anything from you. Nothing. As for what you want from me—" He leaned forward, holding his father's eyes, and decided to drop the bomb to dash his greedy hopes once and for all. "I'm not going to marry Corey Dobias."

"But you said—"

"No, you said. And your stupid-ass sources said. Corey and I were engaged, but not anymore. We called it off."

"Called it off?" His father's face reddened, and for a moment he looked as if he might come across the table and grab his son's throat. "Do you mean to tell me that you had a billionaire's heiress in the palm of your hand and you blew it?"

"I didn't blow it," he bit out. "I'm not marriage material, and I wasn't looking forward to being tied down for the rest of my life. My only role model for a family was a two-bit maid who slept with her boss, remember?"

"You idiot!" he hissed out. "You threw away the chance of a lifetime, and you're blaming me?"

"It's not my chance of a lifetime you care about, but yours!"

"You're not even worth the time it takes to choke down lunch," his father said, scraping back his chair and motioning for the waitress to bring the check.

Eric's face took on a dull, hard expression as he stared across the table at his father. "Just go to hell," he said.

He got up before his father could, forgetting the girl who'd promised to meet him and cheer him up. It would take considerably more than a martini and a roll in the hay.

He walked at a brisk pace for several blocks, as if the

sheer exercise could dash away the fury growing like disease in the back of his head. He should have taken some satisfaction in ruining the man's hopes, he told himself. But there was none. Because the old man was right. He was an idiot. He *had* blown it with Corey.

A drunken Santa Claus blocked the corner, waving a toneless bell and a bucketful of change. "Got a dollar to donate, pal?"

Eric shot him the finger.

"Merry-friggin'-Christmas to you, too, prick," Santa said.

Pushing past him, Eric cursed the season and the three million men dressed in red suits and the cheap decorations trashing the town and the maddening, inescapable music blaring everywhere he turned. He hated it all, for he had nothing to celebrate.

He never had.

Without making the conscious decision, he found himself walking down Tremont Street, coming upon Corey's building that had Boston buzzing. The facade was almost finished, and inside he could see the activity that all centered from her commands, as if she'd been doing this all her life. Some people were born with everything, he thought. People born with it could never lose it. It was part of their genetic makeup, like the structure of their bones and the strength of their teeth. Others could fake it or imitate the lucky ones, but in people like Corey, it was unmistakable.

He just wished he'd realized it sooner.

He stepped to the open doorway of the thirteen-story building, saw the massive stretch of concrete on which teams of men worked. The new staircase was in place, he noted, and pipes were being fitted for a waterfall which would be the lobby's centerpiece.

Then he saw her, dressed in a short white jacket and a

skirt that made her little rump look even cuter, stepping over boards and cords in high heels, wearing a bright yellow hard hat as if she'd chosen it to accent her outfit. She was impervious to the looks she got from the workers around her, the ones who wouldn't have dared make them to her face. But he saw them.

He was the worst kind of fool, he told himself. The worst kind. The kind that was too stupid even to know it until it slapped him in the face.

"Did you hear from Mr. Chesterfield about the chandelier yet?" she was asking her assistant—that Dee-dee person he had seen at her apartment, as she trotted along behind her.

Dee-dee checked her clipboard and nodded. "He said he'll have it ready in three weeks. He made an appointment for Thursday, though. Needs to talk to you about the weight of the crystals."

"Great." Corey shifted her thoughts to the small waterfall being built on the lower level of the lobby, and saw the contractor she had hired supervising the placement of some crucial piping. "Sam, are we still on schedule?"

"A little ahead, actually," the tall, leather-skinned man told her over his shoulder. "But don't get excited. Something'll pop up to slow us down."

Shifting focus again, she went to the mezzanine and found a crew working on the staircase. It's marble was a soft shade of pink swirled with white, which would provide a cool, luxurious look once the carpet and wallcoverings were in place.

She had good taste, he thought.

Satisfied that all was as it should be, she started toward the door with Dee-dee on her heels, and saw Eric standing there watching her. The intensity that had previously animated her face disappeared. "Eric."

He stepped inside. "Just stopped by to see how it's going."

Corey slowed her step and met him across the floor. Her shoes were covered with dust, but she didn't seem to notice. "It's going fine. I wish I had time to talk, but you know how it is—not enough hours in the day."

"Tell me about it," he commiserated, only he didn't know what it was like, because these days he couldn't manage to get a job shooting weddings. "Can I walk you somewhere?"

She shrugged and stepped past him into the winter sunshine. "I have my car."

She could have asked him if he wanted a lift, but she didn't, and he didn't lower himself to suggest it. "New car, huh? Things sure have turned around."

"Yeah." She opened the door and tossed her hard hat on the seat, then straightened and smoothed back her hair. "So what are you working on these days, Eric?"

He chose not to tell her how bad things had gotten. "You know. This and that. Listen, Corey, I know you're busy, but I'd really like the chance to talk to you about exhibiting some of my prints in your lobby. Most of them you handpicked yourself for the casino—"

She held out a hand to stop him. "I was going to call you," she said. "I might be able to use a few. Here—" She dug a piece of paper out of her pocket and jotted a name on it.

"This is the name of my interior designer. I'll tell her to expect to hear from you."

Eric took the phone number and frowned down at it. "I thought you'd be involved."

"Oh, I will. It's just . . . I have to trust the people I have working for me. Otherwise, we'd never get finished on time. The opening's in six weeks, you know. God, I hope we make it. You will be there, won't you?"

"Yeah, I guess."

"Good. I'll make sure you get your official invitation when Dee-dee sends them." She started around the car.

"I have to go now. I have to be somewhere."

"Important appointment?"

"Well, kind of. I'm going to see my father."

Something in his heart stabbed at him, and he refrained from uttering that she'd picked a hell of a time to make up with Dobias—after it was too late to do him any good. "So you two are speaking again?"

"Not exactly." She got into her car, slipped the key into the ignition, and opened the passenger window on his side. It was his cue to bend over and talk to her through it, but he didn't. Instead, he made her lean across the seat to him.

"Not exactly?"

"That is, he doesn't speak to me. But I go anyway."

The comment intrigued him just enough to make him forget his stubbornness and lean over, propping his elbows on the window. "Why?"

When she looked at him, there was a gloss of innocence in her eyes, the same innocence he'd seen in her long ago on that mountain. But he'd been too much of a bastard to remember it until now. "I don't know why," she whispered.

She shifted into drive and he stepped back from the curb as the window slowly rose. He stood still for a moment, watching her drive away.

He looked down at his watch, tapped it to make sure it was working, and started back the way he had come. Wadding the note in his hand, he stuffed it into his pocket. He could have married her, he told himself, but now he was relegated to a referral on a piece of paper.

He laughed out loud as he walked, a dry, self-deprecating laugh that brought a fine mist to his eyes, then ended in a scowl.

He had brought it on himself. The knowledge of that made it all even harder to bear.

chapter

39

COREY TRIED NOT TO LOOK SO FRAGILE AS SHE
sat in the visitors' room of the prison camp waiting for
her father to be brought in. He would snub her again,
she knew, but she hoped he wouldn't do it as blatantly
as he had on her first visit. He had seemed gentler on
the visit with Emily, but that was two and a half months
ago.

She had thought about coming every day since then,
but something had always stopped her. This morning,
however, she had gotten out of bed, glanced at her calendar of things she had to accomplish that day, crossed
off the last four, and decided that today would be the day
that she would visit her father.

She saw him step into the doorway, looking more hag-
gard and even older than he had before. He had grown a
full beard, and though his hair was still short, it waved
about his head, an unruly mess of neglect. He still stood
with the regal posture of a king, but when he walked,
she saw the age in his stride. He scanned the room for
the face of someone he knew, and when he came to hers,
he paused.

For a moment, she thought he would turn and walk
back through that door, and she knew she couldn't take
it if he did. Finally, putting a long-suffering expression
on his face, he ambled her way.

He took the chair across the table from her, but instead of greeting her, his eyes strayed indifferently to
those at the next table, an old black man with his wife

and daughter. The man gave him an amused look, and Dobias turned away.

"Hi, Daddy. You look good. How are you?"

He looked down at his hands, and she saw new blisters there, and callouses where there hadn't been any before. "You can tell your sisters that they haven't done me in yet. I'm still here, and I'm still alive. It'll take more than prison or ungrateful daughters to do me in."

Corey's lips trembled. She wet them and held them tight for a moment. "They still haven't been here to see you?"

He looked at Corey directly then, for the first time since he'd come in. "Don't you know? They've taken my company over completely. Sold off the casino and half of the other things I've worked my life for, and Gloster tells me they don't plan to give any of it back."

"But I thought your agreement was that you could get it back when—"

"It was a lie!" he said. "Your brother-in-law took the clause out before I signed it. He tricked me, so he could get his greedy hands on my money."

"Are you sure?"

"I've never been more sure of anything in my life. I've raised three daughters, and every last one of them has turned on me. Oh, you begin to see things pretty clearly when you're in here."

"I haven't turned on you, Daddy. You know I haven't. I would have been here every week, but I didn't think you'd speak to me. The way you've treated me—"

"The way *I've* treated *you*?" He shook his head, rubbed his beard, and turned away.

Corey blinked back the tears in her eyes and tried to steady her thoughts. She wouldn't let him shake her. She had expected this, and she was prepared for it. "Daddy, I don't want to talk about this. I wanted to tell you about the building I'm renovating on Tremont Street. It's opening in six weeks. Dad, you'd be proud of me. It's beautiful, and all the critics are saying wonderful things about it. Last week, the *Bulletin* did a front-page article about it—"

"The *Bulletin*?" He laughed out loud, a dry, grating sound, and shook his head. "That's supposed to be something you're proud of? That your boyfriend would publish an article about you? Why not, girl? He's been publishing articles about me for years. Don't you know it's his life's work to keep the Dobiases in the limelight?"

"He didn't even know about the article until it came out, Daddy. The *Globe* printed a piece about it two weeks ago."

Dobias slapped his hand on the table. "And you aren't even sleeping with anybody there? Amazing."

Corey lifted her purse from the chair next to her and set it in her lap, ready to leave. She thought better of it and forced herself to go on. "The point is that I'm using everything you've ever taught me, Daddy. I've already leased out every floor, which means I'll have an immediate, consistent income from the building. And I've managed to buy three other surrounding properties. I'm actually cleaning up the Combat Zone, Daddy, and I stand to make a fortune. You were a good teacher. The best."

"So good, that I have nothing left," he said bitterly. "So good, that my own daughter has finagled a way to take every last dollar I have."

"But I'm not the daughter who did that, Dad. Curse Giselle if you have to, and turn your back on her. But I haven't done anything to hurt you intentionally. I'm the one who never cared about your money. All I've ever done is love you."

Traitorous tears dropped to her cheek, and she smeared them away. Dobias settled his cold eyes on the table.

"I came for another reason," she said after a moment, trying to steady her undulating voice. "I found out that you're eligible for a furlough at Christmas. I wanted to invite you to spend it with me."

"What are you going to do? Call Adam Franklin's paparazzi to meet me at the door? Give him an update for his scandal sheet? No, thank you. I'd rather not have a Christmas this year."

Her lips trembled, and she looked down at her hands. "I guess I'm not surprised."

She pulled her chair back and got to her feet. "I'll go now," she said as her tears scurried down her face. "But I'll be back. You're a stubborn, bitter old man, but you're still my father. And I haven't given up on you, yet."

Dobias watched her leave, then sat motionless in his chair until someone forced him to go back to work in the kitchen. Burying himself in the menial labor he had grown used to, he put her tears out of his mind.

But that night, as he lay in his bunk staring up at the ceiling, he couldn't get past the feeling that he was smothering in a box without air, a box through which he was unable to reach out, even if he wanted to.

. . . *a bitter, stubborn, old man* . . .

Well, he supposed that was exactly what he was. Bitter, though he had a right to be, and stubborn, for otherwise he would break. But he was not going to break.

"Thinkin' 'bout the way you made that pretty gal cry today?"

He looked at Thomas, who sat on a stool playing solitaire on a TV tray.

"She look anything like your wife?"

Dobias stared back at the ceiling and recalled his wife's auburn hair, her dark, turbulent eyes, and her restless smile. "Why?"

"Well, does she or don't she?"

"She does. A lot, okay? What do you care?"

"Then you had yourself one hell of a little woman. Probably had to beat the men off with a stick, huh?"

Dobias sat up and leered at the black man across his cell. "My wife never looked at another man the whole time we were married, and I was faithful to her, too. So if you're implying—"

"Hey, I don't imply nothin'. I'm just sayin' that a lady like that has plenty o' chances to fool around. Any man'd be a fool not to notice when she walks by."

"People always noticed when Shara walked by," he said, lying back down, his eyes glossing over with memory. "I was the luckiest man alive, and everyone knew it. I was a nobody. A Greek kid from a poor family. She gave me class and credibility. And I gave her everything money could buy."

Thomas considered his cards for a moment, turned up the last one that won him the game against himself, and stacked the deck again. "I don't know," he said skeptically. "Some women, they don't need everythin' money can buy. Like that daughter o' yours. Don't seem like she cares so much 'bout money."

Dobias didn't answer, for there was no way he could ever explain his feelings to Thomas. He couldn't understand them himself.

chapter
40

THE FEBRUARY OPENING OF THE CAINE PLAZA ON
Tremont Street was one of the main Boston social events
of the month, and Corey shone with regal glory—the
fallen princess who'd triumphed on her own—as she
greeted celebrities and tycoons and old friends from
even older families in the great marble foyer. Outside,
snow fluttered over the limousines being spirited away
by uniformed valets. It was the coldest night of the year,
a blessing, since the frigid wind kept the Combat Zone
hookers from lingering on the street and forced the
dealers and pimps to stay inside as streams of guests
were dropped off at her door.

The lobby that had previously seemed so big now
seemed to shrink as more and more guests filled it.
But none was overlooked, for Corey spoke to each one,
even those she detested.

Theodore Winthrop, president of the bank that had
kicked her while she was down, gave her an apprehen-
sive look as she approached him with a smile on her
face. "Mr. Winthrop," she said, extending her hand and
allowing him to kiss it. "When I sent you an invitation,
I never dreamed you'd come. But I'm so glad you did."

He cleared his throat uncomfortably and dropped her
hand back to her side. "I was surprised to be invited,
Miss Dobias. After the last time we spoke . . ."

"How could I resist?" she asked. "It must have been
quite a blow to lose my family's casino account. The
bank must have lost millions on that deal."

"Yes . . . well." He cleared his throat again. "My board has instructed me to tell you that if you ever need help from our bank, we'd be more than happy—"

"I see you took my advice and bought yourself some balls, Winthrop. Too bad they aren't going to help you now." She frowned and brought a hand to her forehead. "Let's see. There must be a lesson here. What could it be?"

Then she walked off, leaving the man red-faced and flustered, and floated across the room to another guest.

It had taken Adam two hours to get one dance with Corey, but when he finally held her close and moved her in step to the small orchestra's rendition of "Sweet Caroline," he wished he could whisk her up to one of the vacant floors and stamp his unequivocal possession on every inch of her body.

She smiled at the pensive gleam in his eyes as he gazed at her. "What is it, Adam?"

"You're something, Corey, you know that?"

"And what is that something?"

"Exciting. Beautiful. Dangerous."

"That's three somethings. But if you have any more, I'm listening."

"I think I could really fall for you, Corey Dobias." He pulled her closer and buried his face in her hair.

A poignant look of gratitude flashed across her eyes as she brought her head back to look at him. "That doesn't scare you to death?"

He pulled her closer. "Hell, yes, it scares me to death. But not for the reasons you think."

"Then why, Adam?" she asked. "Why was it so important to you not to fall for me?"

He looked off into the distance, unable to meet the honest question in her eyes. "That doesn't matter, Corey. What matters now is that I have, and it's too late to do anything to stop it."

"Really? But you just said you *could* fall for me. Not that you had."

His smile faded as he settled his eyes on hers. "I lied."

She stared up at him, stricken, and if it hadn't been the kind of thing that made headlines, he would have cleared the room and taken her right there.

But they were not alone, and someone tapped his shoulder.

Looking behind him, he saw Eric Gray, dressed in a tux, clean shaven, and looking like anything but the loser Adam knew him to be.

"I'd like to cut in," he said.

Adam started to mumble "get lost," but he knew too many eyes were on the hostess. His own cameras had been trained on her all evening, for he'd instructed the society and business editors of the *Bulletin* to leave no holds barred in covering Corey's moment. Now he knew he'd have to act like the gentleman they expected him to be, and step back, allowing Eric to sweep Corey out of his arms, shattering the most important moment that had yet passed between them.

Adam looked daggers at Eric as he stepped back. Corey didn't take her gaze off Adam as Eric pulled her into his arms.

"Lover boy didn't like that much, did he? Now he sees how it feels."

"How what feels?" She glanced at Eric and halfheartedly noted that he had shaven and trimmed his hair, and for once looked like someone who'd conformed. She wondered if that was what he'd always been under the contempt and bitterness. Someone who really wanted to be what he so openly scorned.

"To have you snatched away from him."

"Nobody snatched me away from you, Eric. I ran away."

He didn't answer but looked off into the crowd, not missing a beat of the music. "You did a good job with this place, Corey," he said after a moment. "But where the prints are hung, I doubt anyone will even notice them."

"There wasn't wall space," she said on a sigh. "There are plants and stone and mirrors everywhere. We put them in the best places we could."

"What about the new building you're doing? I could do some special shoots just for it. Even handle some of the advertising shots."

Her eyes strayed over his shoulder, and she saw Rena and Emily walking in. Quickly, she pulled away from him. "My sister's here. I have to go."

Chagrined, he wove through the other dancers to the side of the room, and his gaze collided with Adam's. If looks could kill, he thought, they'd both be bloody and lifeless. And Corey would still be flitting around without a care in the world.

Corey took Rena's hand and pulled her through the crowd to where Adam stood with the mayor of Boston and his wife. It was clear that Rena had put away a lot of booze before her arrival. Her eyes had the bloodshot glaze of someone who hadn't been sober in weeks. Still, she put on her best smile and asked the mayor about his new grandchild and their son who had joined the marines. While they talked, Corey watched her polish off two glasses of champagne, then reach for another when a tray passed.

As soon as she was able, Corey pulled Rena aside. "Rena, you're drinking too much. Slow down. There's plenty to go around."

Rena finished the glass in her hand and set it on a marble sill. "He wouldn't come with me, you know. They couldn't wait to get me out of the house."

"Who? John?" Rena had started on about John when Corey had called to invite her to the opening, and Corey had seen how far her sister's spirit had deteriorated since she'd seen her last.

"He's sleeping with someone else," she said. "Right under my nose. You don't think she'd really do that to me, do you? Her own sister?"

Corey tried to grasp what Rena was saying, but found it was impossible. Taking her sister's hand, she pulled her up the staircase to the mezzanine and turned on the light in her office. It was quiet in there, and she closed the door, locking out the party. "Now who are you talking about? Giselle?"

Tears burst to Rena's eyes, and her lips quivered. "You don't think she'd take John from me, too, do you? I've given her everything else I have, Corey. Would she do that to me?"

"Of course not! Rena, you're letting your imagination run away with you. You've got to pull yourself together. You're drinking too much, and you're losing all sense of perspective."

"Then explain the cuff links!" she cried. "She did, and I bought it, until he left his belt there, too. I saw it lying over her chair when I went into her room this morning. And he didn't make it to our room with it."

A cold chill washed over Corey, and she gaped at Rena. "Well, it could be anything. Maybe she found it and picked it up. Meant to give it to him later. You can't jump to a conclusion like that, Rena."

"Then what conclusion can I jump to?" She looked at Corey, waiting for her to give her the answer that would clear up the whole ugly mess. But Corey had no answers.

"I—I don't know. But I'm sure it's not what you think. Giselle's a beautiful woman. She can have just about any man in Boston. Why would she have to take yours?"

"For the same reason that she bought that building out from under you and stole my half of Dad's company. She despises both of us, Corey. Whatever we have, she wants."

"No, I don't believe that. She's a lot of things, but she would never sleep with her sister's husband." Corey's voice fell to a softer, weaker note, as she added, "I'm sure of it."

"Really?" Rena took a deep breath and wiped the tears from beneath her eyes. Her nose was shiny and red, and her makeup ran beneath her eyes.

"Really. Now I want you to stay up here for a little while until you feel better, and then freshen up your makeup and come back down. A lot of people have been asking about you tonight."

"Emily," Rena said. "What about Emily?"

"I'll take care of Emily." She started out the door, then turned back. "Why did Giselle let her come, anyway? She was so furious after I took her to see Dad, I didn't think she'd let her within a mile of me."

Rena's face took on that dull expression again, and she uttered a heartless laugh. "I told you. She wanted to be alone with my husband. She said they were working."

"Then that's what they were doing," Corey said, but as she closed the door and left Rena alone, she knew better than to believe her own assurances. Giselle was up to something, and Corey didn't like it. But she doubted there was anything more she could do about it. For now, all she could provide was a shoulder for Rena to cry on, and the reassurances to help her make it through one more day.

Eric was waiting for Corey at the bottom of the stairs, charming a blush onto Emily's young cheeks. She saw

Adam engaged in conversation with one of Massachusetts's senators, and he smiled at her.

"Where's Aunt Rena?" Emily asked when she reached the floor.

"Upstairs. She doesn't feel well."

"Tell me about it," Emily said. "She was really quiet all the way over."

"She'll be all right." She hooked her arm through Emily's and smiled coolly at Eric. "What were you two talking about?"

Eric gave her a conspiratorial wink and Emily blushed again. "I was just telling her how much she's changed in the last year. She's turning into a beautiful young woman, with those dangerous Dobias eyes."

"She happens to be twelve, Eric," Corey said, drawing Emily away from him.

"What do you think?" he shot back. "That I'll elope with her or something?"

"As much as she's worth, I wouldn't be surprised," she muttered.

They were halfway across the floor toward Adam when Emily rounded on her. "Aunt Corey! What did you mean?"

"I mean that Eric Gray has one thing on his mind, and that's money. If you've got it, he loves you. But if you lose it . . ."

"Is that what happened with you? When you lost your money, he didn't want you?"

Corey looked down at her niece and realized that a child her age didn't have to know all the ugly realities of life. "No. What happened, Emily, is that I found out he was a jerk."

"But he's so cute! And he was really nice to me."

Corey looked down at her niece, contemplating the loneliness of a child who had only a tutor to break up her days, a child who knew only the ways of adults and their deceptions, rather than those of children her own age. A surge of sorrow flushed through her, and she pulled Emily into a hug.

"Can we finish that dance now?"

Corey looked up into Adam's eyes, and she smiled. "Yes. I don't think Eric will cut in again."

'"Terrific. Now if we could only take care of the other two hundred men in the room who might."

It was an hour later before Rena pulled herself together enough to come down, and when she did, Corey slipped away from Adam and the cluster of people surrounding them, and started toward the staircase. She met Rena halfway up and escorted her the rest of the way down.

Over the other heads, she scanned the room for Emily, whom she'd kept an eye on while Rena was upstairs. Their young niece had a charm all her own and was faring well with the roomful of adults. She found her on the dance floor with a sixty-five-year-old stockbroker. But she wasn't dancing.

Corey followed the girl's surprised gaze to the door and saw her ex-brother-in-law, Samuel Hart, enter the crowd with one of Corey's bankers, Marilyn Warner, on his arm.

"Oh, God," Rena moaned. "Why did you invite *him* here, Corey?"

"I didn't!" Corey whispered. "I invited Marilyn. I didn't know they were seeing each other."

She glanced back toward Emily, saw that she had left the stockbroker without a backward glance, and was heading toward Samuel with a look of hopeful anticipation on her fragile face.

"Oh, no. She's going toward him."

"It's okay," Corey said. "He'll be nice to her. Samuel

really wasn't such a bad guy when he was married to Giselle. I can't imagine him deliberately snubbing her if she confronts him like this."

Just the same, they both started toward them and came up behind Emily as she stepped into the couple's way. Samuel looked down at her without recognition.

"Hi," she said, and her voice was almost inaudible.

"Hello."

Emily's face paled. "You don't recognize me. I'm Emily."

He frowned for a moment, then glanced awkwardly at his date. "Oh, yes. Giselle's girl."

A look of disbelief and bewilderment passed over the girl's eyes, and after a second of gaping at him, she turned and fled through the crowd toward the door.

Corey caught her just as she dashed out into the night.

"Emily, wait! You can't just run out there alone. It's dangerous!"

"I want to go home," she cried. Tears welled in her eyes, and she held them wide to keep them from shattering. Snowflakes drifted down and gathered on the red ruffles edging her bodice. "Where's Aunt Rena? I have to go."

Rena was behind Corey, and she grabbed Emily's arm. "I'm here, sweetheart. We'll go now if you want."

"Grandfather was right," the girl bit out in a broken voice. "He *is* an asshole."

Corey didn't argue with that, for she couldn't come up with a better word for him herself. "Honey, I'm so sorry. He didn't mean it. He's just—"

"Just what?" Emily screamed. "Just forgetful? Slipped his mind that he has a daughter? I'm nothing but Giselle's girl to him!"

"Honey—"

"I'll see you later, Aunt Corey," Emily said, waving her off. "I just want to get home."

Corey stood motionless as her sister and her niece stepped to the curb and waited for their limousine to retrieve them.

Rena forgot her own worries, for Emily's were much more serious at the moment. The girl's tears made her feel helpless all the way home, and she held her and let her cry, wishing all the while that, if she had no power to repair anything in her own life, she could at least do something for Emily.

She saw her to her room when they were home, sat with her for a while until her crying subsided. Finally, telling her she would find Giselle and send her to Emily, she left her alone.

But neither John nor Giselle could be found anywhere in the house, though both cars were home. She avoided Giselle's room until last, praying she would find them both engaged in work, but she feared she would, instead, find them engaged in something she wasn't strong enough to face.

Finally, knowing she had no choice, she went to Giselle's bedroom door and knocked. It was a moment before Giselle answered. "Who is it?"

"Rena." The word came out shaky, and she held her breath, listening for the sound of tracks being covered, cuff links being gathered, shoes and clothes and belts being hidden away. She heard none of it, but she couldn't revive her sinking heart.

After a few moments, Giselle opened the door, still tying the belt around her silk kimono. "You're home early."

"And you turned in awfully early."

"I was tired."

Rena swallowed the huge obstruction in her throat. "Where's my husband?"

Giselle lifted her chin and looked Rena directly in the

eye. "Don't you know? I thought he was with you."

"You know damn well I left him here working with you."

"But he isn't with me now, is he?" Giselle stepped aside and waved a hand back into her room. "If you'd like to come in and search the place, you're welcome to."

When Rena looked as if she might, Giselle shook her head sardonically. "You know, you're losing it, Rena. You're more of a basket case than I've ever seen you."

Rena set her teeth. "I didn't come here to search your room or talk about my shortcomings," she said. "I came here to tell you that your daughter is in her room crying her heart out, because she saw her father at Corey's party tonight and he acted as if he didn't even know who she was."

"Samuel?" Giselle's face transformed suddenly, and Rena saw the genuine alarm there. "You didn't tell me he was going to be there. I would never have let her go!"

"Corey didn't invite him. He showed up as someone's date. The point is, he was there and Emily was crushed."

Giselle left her room and started off toward Emily's, without a second look back.

Rena lingered at Giselle's open door for a moment, thought of going in and taking her up on that offer to search the room. She stepped inside, glanced around, and saw nothing of John's. A subtle scent in the air was reminiscent of his cologne, but she told herself she was imagining it. She looked toward the bathroom. The door was closed, but that wasn't unusual. Deciding that she didn't want to know badly enough to look beyond it, she slowly backed out of the room and closed the door.

She went to her room and sat on her bed, staring at the door and waiting. Not ten minutes passed before John came through it, fully dressed, though his shirt was unbuttoned.

"What are you doing home?" he asked. "I didn't expect you so early."

"Where were you?" The question was a direct one that left no room for evasion.

"Out by the pool. Why?"

"I looked for you. I thought you were working."

"Giselle was tired," he said. "So she turned in early. Did you look for me out there?"

She had to admit that she hadn't, but she wasn't naive enough to think he was telling the truth. People didn't sit "out by the pool" in weather this cold.

She waited for him to undress, stoke the fire in the fireplace, and slip into bed beside her, and wished, from the center of herself, that he would hold her, tell her he'd missed her tonight, and make slow, languorous love to her. But he had only sleep on his mind.

He's already satisfied, she told herself. Someone else has already given him what he didn't want from me.

She had few doubts who that someone was.

Her own sister.

Still, the slightest doubt kept her from confronting him, or from ranting down the hall toward Giselle, demanding a confession. She had been wrong before, and Giselle was right about her being a basket case. She was insecure. So insecure that she couldn't even trust her own instincts anymore.

She didn't take a pill that night, for the first time in weeks, for she wanted to sober up and clear her mind. Her life had gotten away from her. She had been a victim for too long. Now, before her eyes, little Emily was becoming one, too.

The injustices of it all—her own betrayal by Joe Holifield, her father's conviction, Giselle's blackmail, her husband's infidelities, and now Emily's broken heart—raged through her mind, keeping her awake all night.

They crescendoed in her head like a tornado lifting off the ground, stirring her blood into a heated, vicious need to act.

Finally, as dawn broke through the curtains of her window, she sat up and decided that today was a new day, and she was going to make the best of it. If she couldn't do anything to change her own state, she would do something to help Emily. She would pay a visit to Samuel Hart and tell him how cruel and sadistic his indifference to that child was. She would tell him how crushed Emily had been last night. Maybe she would convince him to throw the child some morsel of affection that might last her a few more years. Just until she was old enough to stop believing in fairy tales and fathers and love.

For Emily was a Dobias, after all. And those revelations would come soon enough.

chapter
41

SAMUEL HART, A MAN FROM OLD BOSTON MONEY even more abundant than what the Dobiases boasted, had a house on Beacon Hill, and his visitors were screened by the English butler who answered the door and refused to let her in. "Tell him it's his ex-sister-in-law. I have to speak to him immediately. It's very important."

She waited on the doorstep as the butler went to find him, and finally, he came back to the door. "I'm sorry. Mr. Hart is very busy this morning. If you'd like to make an appointment for a later time—"

"Tell him that I'm not leaving until he sees me. All I want is five minutes. That's it."

The butler reluctantly closed the door and left her on the step again. After a moment, he returned. "He said he'll see you for five minutes, but he's going out—"

"Thank you." Rena pushed into the house and saw Samuel waiting in the parlor, wearing a pair of slacks and a silk smoking jacket.

He came to his feet when she walked in, his face a little puzzled. "Rena. What can I do for you?"

"I want to talk to you about what you did to Emily last night."

He frowned. "What I did to her? I didn't do anything to her. I hardly even spoke to her."

"That's precisely what I'm referring to."

He sat back down and leaned back in his chair, but Rena kept standing.

"We realized long ago that you weren't going to be the doting father, but you don't have to be so cruel to her. You've never once in her entire life sent her a card for her birthday. She sends you a Christmas card every year and you never even acknowledge it. Do you know that her birthday was ruined this year because she was positive you were coming, and you didn't? Then last night, when you called her Giselle's girl, like you had no claim to her at all—"

"Wait a minute!" His face had reddened by degrees the more she shot out to him, and finally he came to his feet. "Wait just a fucking minute! You should be thanking me for keeping quiet all these years. I divorced your sister, remember? I don't have to pretend for Emily or anybody."

"You divorced your wife, not your daughter. She's your flesh and blood. How can you just ignore her that way?"

"You're not listening!" he shouted. "She's not my flesh and blood. She's not anything to me, except a reminder of how my wife cheated on me! I'm not that child's father, Rena!"

"What?" For the first time since she'd stepped into his house, Rena found herself speechless. "Not her father? But you were married to Giselle . . ."

"That didn't mean anything to her," he cut in. "Why do you think I left her the way I did? Why do you think she gave me a divorce without question? Do you think Giselle does anything nice? She gave me what I wanted so I wouldn't tell the world that I hadn't even been sleeping with her the month she conceived. There's no way that child could have been mine."

"Then whose?" Rena cried. "If you're not her father, then who is?"

Samuel stared at her for a long moment, and his face took on a hard expression full of bitterness and cynicism. "Why don't you ask your husband?"

As if the breath had been knocked out of her, Rena stumbled back, gaping at him. The truth cut into her, chiseling despair and horror into her face, slashing fresh wounds across her heart. Unable to hear another word, she fled out of his parlor.

She broke into a trot before she reached the front door, then ran the rest of the way through the fresh blanket of snow to her car.

The drive home took too long. Long enough for thoughts of what Samuel's words had meant to hit home in her heart. Not John. Not her own husband. Not all these years.

She pulled to the front door of the Dobias mansion and stumbled in. She felt herself trembling as she dashed through the house looking for them, and prayed that she would hold herself together just long enough to get to the truth.

Then she prayed she was strong enough to endure it.

She found them together in the dining room, sitting side-by-side over Sunday brunch. She stood before them, her hair fraying from its coil and sticking to her damp face, her makeup smeared, and her eyes full of dread and purpose.

"Rena?" John stood up, but Giselle kept sitting, waiting for the bomb she sensed was about to drop.

"I just came from Samuel's house," she said, her voice breathless, but amazingly steady. "I asked him why he was so cruel to Emily, and he told me it was because she isn't really his daughter."

Giselle rose slowly from her seat.

Rena smiled, a twisted, painful, distorted smile. "When I asked him who was, do you know what he said to me?"

John was pale as he looked at her, quietly waiting. "What did he say, Rena?"

"He said to ask you, John." She laughed, but tears rolled down her pale cheeks as she did. "Isn't that funny? He said to ask you."

Neither Giselle nor John laughed, and they did not look at each other or Rena as she stood there, waiting for them to answer. Their very silence confirmed what Rena knew in her heart, and finally, her laughter died. Along with the rest of her soul.

"You've been sleeping together all these years, haven't you? Since we were first married."

Neither of them answered.

"You fathered my sister's child, John?" she asked pitifully, as if pleading for an answer that would set the whole thing right, clear the matter up to everyone's satisfaction.

He stepped toward her, reached out to her. "I didn't want to hurt you—"

She slapped his hands away. "Hurt me? Hurt me? My sister!"

She turned to Giselle. "How could you do something like this? How can you look yourself in the mirror, knowing that you've done this to me? To Emily?"

The question hardened Giselle's expression, and she compressed her lips and thrust out her chin, and started toward Rena. "If you weren't such a hopeless drunk, he never would have turned to me," she cried. "If you didn't wash down half a dozen pills every night and sleep like a corpse in his bed, then maybe you could have held his interest."

"Then it's my fault?" Rena cried, folding her arms across her stomach. "It's my fault that my husband cheats on me with my own sister? It's my fault that you have no morals, no values, no conscience? Either of you?"

John reached out to her again, and she recoiled.

"You were with her last night, weren't you? And all those other nights? For how many years now? Thirteen? Have you been sleeping with my sister for thirteen years, John? Screwing her and then coming to me?"

"No," he said. "Not all of that time."

"Oh, right," she said. "The rest of the time you were screwing secretaries and wives of your friends. But I knew about them. It was my sister that I never guessed! My own sister!"

Before either of them could utter another word in self-defense, Rena turned and fled from the room.

It was then that she saw Emily hunkered halfway up the steps, her face ashen as she stared at her.

Unable to undo any of the damage that she knew had already been done, and blaming herself for all of it, she whispered, "I'm sorry, Emmy," then pushed past her and locked herself in her room.

She turned on the television as loud as she could, hoping to blot out the sound of Emily crying in the hall, of John knocking on the door and ordering her to let him in, of Giselle cursing.

Trembling, she poured herself a drink, then shook three Valiums out of her bottle and threw them into her mouth. Clutching the bottle as if it were a lifeline, she curled up on her bed and tried to sleep. But sleep would not come.

She lay like that, crying until she was sick, for an hour or more. A barrage of commercials blared out from the television, and women with perfect bodies and perfect smiles and perfect lives danced across the screen, mocking her, laughing at her, torturing her.

She took another pill and refilled her glass. Then, emptying it, she drank directly from the bottle, waiting for the numbness to overcome her. But it never came.

Finally, as her body relaxed around her turbulent, wounded, miserable heart, she looked at the television and saw the model smiling directly at her.

"You don't need a new life," the model said. "You just need a new shampoo."

The irony of that statement made her laugh, slowly at first, then harder and harder, until she couldn't catch her breath and her eyes filled with tears and the bottle of pills in her hand was shaking.

The laughter turned into sobs, and finally, unable to endure another moment of her pain, she opened the bottle, poured the contents of a hundred odd pills into her hand, threw them into her mouth, and washed them down with the last of the whiskey in the bottle she held.

At last, at long last, the numbness washed over her, wiping out her pain and her humiliation and her self-loathing. With kind and gentle heaviness, the pills brought her down, down, down into an oblivion of nothingness. A darkness of unfeeling. A paradise of emptiness.

By the time John forced the door open and found her on the bed, Rena was already dead.

chapter

42

THE DAY NIK DOBIAS GOT NEWS OF HIS DAUGH-
ter's death, the sky opened up with fitful vengeance,
raining torrents over all New England, hardening the
snow to ice. The temperature dropped to fourteen degrees. He was released on a seven-day furlough for Rena's
funeral, and as he walked outside the confines of the
camp, feeling the icy rain beat down on his head and the
unseasonable lightning bolts sending jagged messages of
warning across the sky, he was overwrought with the
tragedy his life had become.

He had been in the kitchen when they told him, scrubbing scum out of the oven with a bucket and a Brillo pad.
At first they'd only told him that his daughter was dead.
His first reaction was, which daughter? Which daughter
had died?

It had seemed of paramount importance to know
which one, and now, looking back, he didn't know
why. Shouldn't a father grieve equally for each of his
daughters? Wouldn't one death invoke just as much pain
as any other?

Still, his heart had burst with anxiety as he'd followed
the guard back to the superintendent's office, where he
was told that it was Rena.

Rena. The quiet one. The gentle one. The one it was
easiest to ignore, for she demanded so little.

He had suddenly felt older than age itself, and he
didn't remember anything about his packing a bag or
being given his furlough. All he knew was that now he

was sitting in a dirty cab with torn vinyl seats, on his way back to Brookline to bury his daughter. There were reports of suicide, the superintendent told him. She'd been found yesterday in her room with an empty pill bottle in her hand. Giselle hadn't bothered to notify him until today.

He felt himself shaking as the cab took him farther and farther from the prison camp, and closer and closer to where his dead daughter lay. Tears squeezed into his eyes, tears of remorse, tears of anger, tears of helplessness. What could have been so bad that it would break her so thoroughly? Why hadn't she come to him?

The image of his wife holding their middle child in her arms flashed to his mind, and his heart swelled, then deflated. You left her to me to protect, didn't you, Shara? Only I didn't. I didn't protect her, he thought.

He felt his wife's grief, as it would have been had she lived to see it, and that grief made his own intensify. Rena was gone. It was only now, in hindsight, that he could honestly admit that he hadn't always been kind to her, hadn't always been generous with his love, hadn't always been there when she needed him. He had tried to make her tough, only some people were never meant to be that way.

The guards at the gate were somber as they let the cab in, but no one greeted him when he reached the front drive. He got out and realized he had no money, for his meager pay at the camp went into a commissary fund to buy him an occasional soda or snack. He had forgotten to request the cash for the trip before he left.

Asking the driver to wait until he could get someone to pay the fare, he made his way through the freezing rain to the front door of his home, punched out the security code on the panel beside the door, and waited for the lock to give. But it didn't open. The code had been changed.

A sense of defeat greater than any he'd ever known bled over him, and he rang the bell and waited for someone to come.

At last, the door opened, and he stood face-to-face with the new housekeeper he did not recognize.

"Yes?"

Without uttering a word, he pushed roughly past her. "Where's my daughter?"

"I'm sorry . . . I don't—"

"I'm Nik Dobias," he said more forcefully. "What have they done with Rena?"

"Oh, I'm sorry, Mr. Dobias. In the parlor. The coffin's open . . . for the family to view."

Dobias felt as if the life had been sucked from his bones as he walked through the dark, quiet house into the room where his daughter's lifeless body lay.

The moment he saw her, lying so peacefully as if she slept in a halcyon dream from which she would soon awake, he fell to his knees and dropped his forehead on the satin side of the coffin. Sobs racked his body, tearing great chunks from his soul, making him wish with all his heart it could be he lying there in her place.

"Grandfather?"

He lifted his head and saw Emily behind him, her eyes red and raw and swollen. He opened his arms and his granddaughter ran into them, clinging to him with all the strength her little body had left.

"It's terrible, isn't it?" she cried, burying her face against his neck, her fresh tears wetting his shirt. "She was so upset . . . she didn't even want to live . . . it's so terrible what they did to her!"

A tired frown altered Dobias's face, and he pulled back and looked into her bloodshot eyes. "What who did to her? Emily, what happened?"

"My mother and John," she said bitterly. "They don't know it, but I heard everything. I hate them, Grandfather. I hate them."

Before he could get more from the child, he heard the doorbell. He wiped his face, and a moment later Corey and Adam Franklin appeared in the doorway.

Corey's eyes filled with tears as she beheld her father kneeling on the floor, holding Emily in front of Rena's coffin. "Daddy?" The word choked out on a sob.

He rose to his feet, but before he could respond, Giselle stepped into the room behind them.

"Dad," she whispered, surprised. Giselle's face was paler than he'd seen it in a very long time, and her hair, rather than the carefully coiffed styles she usually wore, was limp and pulled back in a severe bun at her nape. "I didn't know you were here yet."

Emily slipped out of Dobias's arms, and wiping her face, started from the room. "Honey, where are you going?" Giselle asked softly.

"To my room," she said. She dashed out before anyone could stop her.

Giselle stared toward the door where her daughter had disappeared, then turned her strained face back to the others in the room. She nodded toward Adam. "Are you sure he isn't wearing a hidden camera? The tabloids love pictures of corpses."

The callous choice of words sickened Corey. "Adam's with me, Giselle, so back off."

She turned back to her father but saw that he leaned over the coffin now. Slowly, she stepped toward it. When she reached it, she wilted, and Adam caught her in his arms to steady her.

"I want to know how this happened." Dobias's demand was frighteningly quiet.

"I don't know why she did it, Dad," Giselle said. "As

a matter of fact, I don't think she did. They're saying it was suicide, but I think it was an accident. An overdose. She was always taking those pills . . . drinking too much . . ."

"Shut up, Giselle." Corey's words slashed across the room, cutting her sister off.

Dobias turned around, looked from his youngest daughter to his oldest. "Somebody had better tell me what in God's name happened before I rip it out of you one word at a time."

"It was suicide, all right," Corey cried. "She came to me the other night and told me she thought you were sleeping with John, Giselle. I told her you would never do that, that you were her sister. But I was wrong, wasn't I?"

Dobias took a step forward, his eyes searing into his firstborn. "Is that true, Giselle?" When she didn't answer, his voice thundered out again. "*Is it?*"

Corey didn't give Giselle a chance to answer. "It's true, Dad," she bit out. "Emily heard it all."

Shock rounded Giselle's eyes. "What did you say?"

"That's right, Giselle. She called me last night. She was so distraught she could hardly talk. She told me she heard you admit that Samuel Hart is not her father. She heard you say that John fathered her, and that your affair has been off and on for years!"

"Oh, my God!" Dobias wavered where he was standing, and feeling for the chair nearest him, he dropped into it. He looked up at Giselle, standing so straight and so still. "What's gotten into you, girl? What have you become?"

Giselle shook her head slowly from side to side. "I never meant to hurt anybody. None of it was planned. I tried to protect Rena from the truth all these years. I tried to protect Emily."

"Well, she knows the truth now!" Corey cried. "What is

she supposed to do with it? What does a twelve-year-old girl do with a surprise like that? The same thing Rena did? God, Giselle! When do *you* start taking responsibility for all you've done?"

Corey crumpled with the last words and turned back to her dead sister. The sight was too much for her, and she felt dizzy. Adam closed his arms around her again, and she laid her face on his chest and allowed herself to melt into his strength.

The sight of that support after Corey's condemnation made something inside Giselle snap. "You're so smug, aren't you, Corey?" she sneered. "Everything's so simple to you, isn't it? Standing there with Adam Franklin, the man who sent our father to prison, and acting like you're the only pure one in the room."

"Leave her alone, Giselle," Adam warned. "You can't hurt her."

"Oh no?" A slow, ominous smile came to Giselle's lips. "I wouldn't count on that. Because I know some things about you that would knock little perfect Corey right off her feet."

Corey looked up at Adam and saw the uncertainty in his eyes. "What are you talking about?"

Giselle straightened as the feeling of power seeped like a drug through her bloodstream. "It's no wonder Adam wants you, Corey. He was our mother's lover for years."

Dobias shot to his feet, a guttural sound of disbelief gasping from his throat. Corey pulled out of Adam's embrace and reached for a chair to steady herself. She looked up at him, waiting for his denial. His face had drained of all color.

"How dare you?" Dobias shouted, but his outburst was directed at Giselle, not Adam. "How dare you slander your mother's good name?"

"Because it's true!" Giselle cried. "And you would have

realized it, too, if you hadn't always been at work, trying to figure out new ways to make a buck!"

He raised his hand to strike her, but Giselle backed away. "Ask him, Daddy! Just ask him! I saw them together more than once myself. The last time was that New Year's Eve party we had here. He came, remember? And then Mother disappeared, and I went looking for her. I found them outside, behind the pool house."

Dobias's hand lowered slowly as the words sank in, and Giselle spun to Adam. "You remember that party, Adam. It was the night my mother ended it with you. She said she couldn't leave Dad. I saw her crying, and she kissed you for the last time. She didn't tell you that she was dying, that that was why she wouldn't leave him and marry you. But later, when she was gone, I knew that was why!"

The pain on Adam's face was as vivid as the memories Giselle had dragged up, but it was not as great as the anguish twisting Dobias's expression.

Corey still watched Adam with a look of horror, waiting for him to react in self-defense, to set it all straight and expose Giselle for the liar that she was. But he didn't utter a word.

"I never told anybody," Giselle went on, turning back to her father. "I didn't want to believe that Mother could betray you, Daddy. And then she died, and there was no reason—"

"No!" Dobias's raging denial thundered through the house as he bolted across the room and grabbed Adam's collar. "I'll kill you, you bastard!" Adam braced himself as he crashed back against the wall, but he couldn't escape Dobias's fist swinging at him with the force and hatred of a twenty-year-old street fighter.

"Stop it! Daddy, no!" Corey threw herself between them just in time to catch her father's second deadly swing.

It knocked her down, and she scrambled to her feet, smearing blood across her face.

The shock of what had happened stopped him, rendering his rage impotent. Struggling to catch his breath, he gave Adam one last lethal look. Corey stayed where she was, blocking another attack, and finally, Dobias backed away.

Before anyone could stop him, he left the parlor with the weary, aged gait of a man who had lived too long. The cab still idled in the drive, waiting to be paid, and without looking back, Dobias climbed inside it and rode away.

Corey waited a moment in the crackling silence left in his wake, staring at Adam's bloody nose as her own lip began to swell.

"Are you all right?" he asked.

"No," she said, feeling a rise of nausea that she couldn't quell. "I'm not all right."

She turned back to her sister and saw, ironically, that Giselle had begun to cry. When she finally summoned enough courage, she looked at him again. "It isn't true, is it, Adam? Tell me it isn't true."

He looked at the floor, unable to meet her eyes, and suddenly she knew without a doubt that it was. Her face twisted in despair, and she covered her bloody mouth with her hand. "You slept with my mother, Adam?"

"Corey, it wasn't what you think. It wasn't some dirty little affair. I was in love with her . . ."

"God." Her voice cracked, and she stood still for a moment, letting the hateful words sink in.

"Corey, you have to understand. She wasn't happy, and when we met—"

"Just tell me one thing," Corey cut in on a tremulous breath. "Did she love you?"

His own lips trembled as he struggled with the words.

"There was the age difference, and you girls—"

"I asked you if my mother was in love with you!"

He raked a shaky hand through his hair as he looked at her fully. "Not enough to leave your father."

His teeth came together, and he wiped his bloody nose on the sleeve of his shirt. "The bastard was just too greedy to realize what he already had. He still hasn't learned."

A deep sob racked her body as she doubled over and turned away.

"I love you, Corey," Adam said. "And that has nothing to do with the way I felt about Shara. It was because of her that I helped you when you were in trouble. But it turned into more. You've got to believe me."

"Get out," Corey said in a flat voice that reflected all the weariness she'd felt over the last year, all the pain she'd endured, and all that she had yet to suffer. "I don't ever want to see you again."

He lingered there a moment. "Corey, please. Listen to me."

"I said get out!"

Helpless, defeated, he turned and slowly left the room.

For a moment after he was gone, the three sisters were alone in the room where they had spent so much of their childhoods, where they'd all learned the high cost of love, where they'd all forged their own ways of playing "the game." Only now, as one lay dead, and the other two faced each other like bitter enemies, Corey realized that everything made a cruel kind of sense. Everything except the hatred and the vengeance and the death.

"Are you happy, Giselle?" she asked, her voice hollow in the quiet room. "You've finally managed to destroy two of the people who cared most in the world for you. Who's going to be next?"

Giselle made no move to answer her. Instead, her eyes

fell to Rena's body, and more tears slithered down her face.

Knowing there was nothing more to say, Corey pushed past her and left the mansion, hoping from the depth of her heart that she would never set eyes on it again.

The funeral ceremony at Rena's burial plot near her mother's grave was something of a cruel joke. Giselle stood stiff, assuming the posture of the Dobias matriarch, listening with dry eyes to the priest's mumblings about death being a door through which we all must pass. Emily stood several feet away from her, her face still wet with tears as she stared at the flowers she had brought to lay on Rena's grave. John stood across the casket from Giselle, avoiding her eyes and looking, instead, at the closed casket as it was lowered into the grave. Corey stood back from the family, unwilling to join Giselle in her mourning, for they did not share the same grief or the same guilt or the same blame. Nothing about them seemed to resemble a family anymore. Except for Emily, she wanted no part of them.

Her dull, raw eyes scanned the crowd that had turned out for the burial, and with a wry acceptance, admitted that most of them were probably tabloid reporters hoping for a flare-up in the family that they could write about in their next issue. The rest, acquaintances Rena had known over the years, had come out of respect, she knew, but she wondered how many of them waited breathlessly for a morsel of gossip about the suicide and the sordid events leading to it, to share with those who hadn't come.

Toward the back of the crowd, she saw Eric, unshaven and shaggy once again. Farther back stood Adam, dressed in black and looking at her with sad, remorseful eyes that didn't come close to satisfying the misery in her heart. Quickly, she turned away.

Then she saw her father, hanging on the outskirts of the crowd like someone who had no business coming forward. He was still dressed in the jeans and khaki shirt that he'd worn from prison, his hair uncombed and his beard was ragged. She wondered where he had slept last night, if he had eaten, if he had gotten over the pain that had driven him from his own home. She waited for the priest to utter the last words of the prayer. When at last he did, the crowd broke up and hampered her view of her father. Ignoring the condolences of those she passed, she threaded through the crowd, searching for him.

But he was gone, and she didn't see him again for the rest of the day.

Later that afternoon, when she had made her way back to her apartment and sat in the darkness of it staring at the wall and contemplating the deflation of the world she had known and the loss of everyone she had ever loved in her life, a knock sounded at the door.

At first she sat motionless, unable to answer, but finally, the knock came more urgently. "Aunt Corey?" the feeble voice called through the door.

Quickly, Corey got up and pulled open the door. Emily stood before her with a suitcase in her hand. "Emmy!"

"I'm running away from home," the girl said. "I want to stay with you." She burst into tears as she uttered the words, and added, "If you won't let me, I'll find someplace else. But I can't go back home, Aunt Corey. I just can't."

Corey pulled the child into the townhouse and took the suitcase out of her hand. "Of course you can stay here, Emmy. As long as you want."

Emily threw her arms around Corey's neck, and Corey held her for a long time before either of them spoke. "I hate her," she whispered finally, in a voice so soft and resigned that Corey didn't doubt her words. "And I hate him. It's because of them that Aunt Rena's dead. And nobody knows where Grandfather is . . . I hate them, Aunt Corey. I hate them."

Corey held Emily, crying with her, until the night filled the house and Emily fell asleep. Then, leaving her lying on the couch, Corey picked up the phone.

The housekeeper at the Dobias estate answered. "This is Corey Dobias," she said in a metallic voice. "I need to speak to my sister."

"I'm sorry, Miss Dobias. I'm afraid she isn't taking any calls."

"Has she noticed that her daughter is not in the house?" Corey asked through her teeth. "Or has it even occurred to her to look?"

The housekeeper put her on hold, and a few moments later, Giselle snatched up the phone. "Corey, where's Emily?"

Corey's voice wobbled as she answered. "Your daughter ran away from home. She showed up at my door with a suitcase."

"I'll send a car for her. It'll be there in fifteen minutes."

"Don't." Corey stood up and took the cordless phone upstairs into her bedroom to keep from disturbing the sleeping child. "I'm keeping her here until she calms down. She doesn't think a lot of her mother right now, and she says if I make her go back, she'll just run away again."

"Corey, you've put ideas into her head!"

"Ideas?" Corey laughed, but there was no joy in the sound. "Giselle, nobody has to put ideas into her head. She's stood by and watched you destroy everyone who's ever meant anything to her. What did you think she'd do? Just forget everything that's happened?"

"I want my daughter!" Giselle cried.

"Well, she doesn't want you. I thought you should know where she is." She swallowed, then took a deep breath. "One other thing. I saw Dad at the funeral. Has he come home?"

"No," Giselle said. "I haven't seen him. Corey, about Emily—"

"I'll call you tomorrow and let you know how she's doing." Corey punched the button that cut off the line, and sat down on her bed.

She stared at the phone and thought of her father's pain after years of believing in his wife. Pain much like hers at discovering that her mother had carried dark secrets, that she wasn't as pure and clean as they all had believed. Then her thoughts drifted to Adam, as they had a thousand times that day. But she had to get him out of her mind, because whatever precarious bond they had built between them had been destroyed, too. She could never love a man who had slept with her mother.

She had no more tears to cry, so instead she wilted back onto the bed and stared at the ceiling. She had to stop picturing Adam and her mother. She had to cling to the picture of the woman who had loved and nurtured her, the woman who had protected her, the woman who had been so close to perfect. She had to think of her father and help him to remember those parts of her mother, as well. She had to figure out where he could be. She had to find him before he did something drastic.

Wearily, she pulled herself back off the bed and dialed Dee-dee's number.

"Dee-dee, it's me. Corey."

"Corey, are you okay? You didn't look so good at the funeral today . . ."

"I'm fine. Listen, I wondered if you could come over for a little while and stay with my niece."

"Your niece? Well, sure, but . . ."

"I'll tell you about it when you come," she said. "Just . . . please hurry."

Dee-dee was there in ten minutes, and quickly explaining to her that her father was missing and that she had to find him, she left her with the sleeping girl and rushed out into the night.

Giselle's eyes were tinder-dry as she descended the steps to the dining room where John sat alone over a meal that no one would eat.

Clutching the file she'd dug out of her personal safe, she went in. "Emily's gone."

He didn't look up from the spot his eyes had settled on. "Gone where?"

"To Corey's. She refuses to come home."

"Can you blame her?" He moved his bloodshot gaze to hers. "I don't much like the idea of sleeping in the same house where I found my wife's corpse, either."

"Then leave."

An amused, lifeless laugh broke from his throat. "Oh, no, Giselle. I'm not going anywhere. This house is half mine now."

For the first time since they'd found Rena's body, Giselle smiled. "No, John. You're wrong about that." She tossed the file onto the table in front of him. "Rena and I had these papers drawn up months ago."

Frowning, he opened the file and picked up the document.

"Let me save you the trouble of muddling through it all, John," she offered. "It says that Rena signed her half over to me."

His alarmed eyes snapped up to hers. "It won't work, Giselle. Nobody's going to believe that. Even you aren't so stupid that—"

"Then read it," she offered. "It's airtight. I made sure of it."

He flipped through the pages, scanning the contents and the key clauses. His breath grew shallow as he read, and his face turned an unsettling shade of red.

"No," he said as the truth became clear to him. "She wouldn't do this. She would never sign everything over. It would mean—"

"That you don't get a dime," Giselle provided.

"The hell I don't!" John bolted out of his chair, knocking it over. "It's half mine, Giselle! Without me, you wouldn't have any of it!"

Giselle gave him a pitiful look and clicked her tongue. "Poor John. I'd think you were used to being a loser by now."

He grabbed her shoulders and threw her against an antique china cabinet in the corner, cracking the glass. "You bitch, you set me up!"

"Damn right, I did!" she shouted, unafraid. "You fathered my child and never did anything about it! You thought staying with my sister would be safer financially, since you couldn't manipulate me the way you could her."

She shoved him away from her and reeled across the room, putting a safe distance between them. "Then when you thought it could all be mine, you came back to me again, straddling the fence between the two of us, just in case. But all that planning didn't do you any good, did it, John?"

A fine sweat broke out over his lip, and he shook his head wildly as he started toward her. "That's not true, Giselle. I've always wanted you. I love you!"

Giselle's palm slammed across his face with the force of her rage, and he stumbled back. "Don't you ever say that to me again! You don't love anybody but yourself!"

His breath was labored, and he rubbed his face where her handprint was beginning to show. "That's why we got along so well, Giselle. We both look out for number one."

"There's only room for *one* number one in my house."

She started from the room, but he grabbed her arm and swung her around.

"You need me, Giselle. You can't do it alone. Together, we could make twenty times what the old man made. We could own this town!"

"Face it, John. The competition's over, and I won. While you were using your cock, I was using my brains."

"You can't do this!" His desperate voice shook the house as she started up the staircase. "I'm Emily's father! I have a right to—"

"You don't have any rights," Giselle cut in. "And if you ever try to manipulate her feelings to get at my bankbook, or hers either, for that matter, you'll hate the day you ever met me."

"I do already."

Giselle resumed her climb up the staircase. "I'll have a guard here to escort you out of the house in fifteen minutes," she said. "Make sure you're ready. And John, don't try a last minute dash for the silver. I'll make sure they search you before you're out the door."

As she reached the upper floor, she heard glass crashing on the tile floor. But she didn't turn back, because it didn't matter. He couldn't hurt her.

She was in control now.

Four hours after she had left her apartment, Corey gave up looking for her father and drove back into the parking space in front of her townhouse. Hail plundered down on the roof, and the sky cracked with deadly bolts of lightning. She sat in the car for a long time, staring dully into space and racking her brain for some place she had forgotten to look. She had tried every one of his favorite haunts, the restaurants and bars, the stores, even the few people he could have claimed as friends.

Finally, she had driven to Robert Gloster's house, whom she had phoned earlier, but he still hadn't heard from him, either. So she had begun checking as many of the hotels as she could, from the most expensive ones to the ones that rented out by the hour. No one had seen him.

Now, sitting alone in her car, she prayed that wherever he was, he would be safe tonight. Safe from any more pain. Safe from any more memories. Safe from himself.

But even as she prayed, she knew the hollow feeling of inevitability. The worst had not yet happened. There was still a bomb ticking. Only time would tell where it would explode, and when.

chapter
43

THE SKY SPLIT WITH A SEARING BOLT OF lightning, and Dobias, soaked and freezing, ducked into the doorway of a garment factory and huddled there for a moment. His feet were tired and aching, and his stomach growled out its discontent. Since the funeral, he'd been walking. Just walking.

The night was different in Boston than it was in the day. At night, during a storm, the buildings cast ominous shadows on the street, darkening the alleys where people like him roamed without direction. But he was not afraid. He had nothing else to lose.

The thought of going home never crossed his mind. He could not even consider it. The house was no longer his. Giselle had stolen it. Even if he swallowed his pride, what was left of it, and slept under her roof, he'd have to deal with the ghosts of Rena and Shara, ghosts with secrets that he'd never had the sense to guess when they were alive. No, the joy of his loving family and his home and his accomplishments were overshadowed, now, by the ugliness of what he'd learned yesterday.

He had hit Corey. He dropped his head into his icy hand and reproached himself one more time. He had meant to hit Adam, to kill him, to take him apart limb by limb, but Corey had come between them. He hadn't meant to hurt her.

But he had hurt her in more ways than that, he reminded himself. The one daughter he could count on. The one who loved him not because of his money or his power, but in spite of it. The one who had the integrity and dignity that he himself had never managed to achieve. He had thrown her away, because she had hurt his pride.

God, what a fool he was. He looked up into the heavens, thick with threatening clouds and fierce fissures of lightning, and wondered how he had accomplished so much in some areas of his life and failed so miserably in others?

The rain and hail slanted inward, catching him in the doorway, soaking him even more, but he didn't make the effort to move.

Shara . . . Her name played over and over in his mind, like a song that he couldn't bear to hear. She had betrayed him. She had loved another man. And if not for the cancer that stole her from him, she would have left him, anyway.

Hot tears escaped his eyes and mingled with the tears on his face, and his body shook with all the misery of an old man who'd lost everything, including his memories. It was all a farce. A huge joke. His life was his own illusion.

Aimlessly, he left the doorway and started down the sidewalk. A bolt of lightning shot out behind him, and he stopped, looked up at the sky, and dared it to strike him dead.

But only the freezing rain beat down on him.

He smelled smoke from just inside the next alley, and idly he followed it. Looking through the small drive between stores, he saw a fire blazing in a garbage drum, and a few ragged vagrants huddled around it, beneath an overhang of one of the buildings. Slowly, he started toward it.

The men idling there, smelling of whiskey and dirt and

smoke from the fire, looked as spent and disillusioned as he.

"You got any cigarettes?" one of them asked as he approached.

Dobias looked down at the man hunched in the light of the fire. His front teeth had rotted out, and his beard was long and crawling with lice. Filthy fingers peeked from the tips of his gloves as he reached up toward Dobias.

"No. No cigarettes."

The other man handed Dobias a bottle that was half-filled with Jim Beam. "Have a drink. It'll help warm you."

Dobias took the bottle gratefully and sat down on a crate next to the one who'd offered it to him. Slowly, he drank. Wincing at the bitterness, he handed the bottle back to the man.

"You need a box?" the derelict asked. "I got a extra box over there."

Dobias looked toward the boxes he pointed to, saw the Lazy Boy logo on the side, and surmised that it must have contained a recliner before it had been emptied. With his sleeve, he wiped the drizzle running from his forehead into his eyes. "What do I need with a box?"

"It's gonna get mighty cold here tonight," the man said. "Wet, too. Box'll help a little. Keep the wind out, at least."

A sense of profound devastation eased over him as he realized they were offering him the box to sleep in. Nik Dobias, the man *Forbes* had applauded in more issues than one, the man who had been known as a real-estate genius, the man who had invented the art of dealmaking that Trump had been arrogant enough to write about, had nothing more than a box to protect himself from the elements.

The crazy thing was that he didn't care. He had no wish to find comfort or peace or rest for his head. Hatred and anger poisoned his heart, but it was self-directed. He had achieved more than any man he'd known, and still he had nothing. Just as he had accused Corey so long ago, he had never learned to climb the mountains that mattered.

The man handed him the bottle again, and he drank from it, feeling the warmth seep into his shivering bones. His saturated clothes plastered themselves to him as the temperature dropped lower.

He wondered if these men, sitting here like rodents in a dark Boston alley in the middle of the night, wet and cold and hungry, had started out the way he had. Had they been billionaires, too? Had they been blind with greed and selfishness? Had their wives betrayed them? Had they buried their children?

For the first time, he realized that, whatever had brought them here, he was no better than they. Tonight they were each just as empty, just as broken, just as impoverished as the other. Tonight they were all fallen kings, stumbling blindly through the hell they had created for themselves.

"You should get out of those clothes," the toothless man told him. "There's some newspapers stacked in that garbage bin over there. They'll keep you warm in the box."

Lacking the energy to move quickly, Dobias got to his feet, and started toward the bin. He needed to lie down, he thought. He needed to try to stop shivering. He opened the bin, and a rat scurried down into the garbage, out of sight.

He grabbed a stack of newspapers, hugged them close to him, and claimed one of the boxes tucked out of reach of the rain. He stepped inside it, peeled off his shirt and his wet pants, kicked off his sloshy shoes. Hugging his trembling arms around himself, he lay down and spread the newspapers over him.

The raging storm outside the box and the freezing cold within it kept sleep from coming, so he lay there for hours, until his body no longer had the energy to shiver, until the memories and recriminations fell to nothingness in his mind, until finally the rain stopped and the light of morning dawned bright and cruel over the alleyway where he lay. The water puddling around them froze to ice, and the fire died out.

His clothes hadn't dried, but he put them back on nonetheless, ignoring the frosty sting of them against his skin. He crawled out of his box and struggled to rekindle the fire. But the last sparks had died away.

Acceptance washed over him like a rising fever, and he fell back into his box and lay down in his damp clothes. Finally, sleep fell over him, a deep, drugged sleep from which he didn't care ever to wake up.

Eric Gray awoke cold and cramped from sleeping in his car and took a moment to orient himself. He straightened behind his steering wheel, rubbed his eyes, and cursed that he had fallen asleep when he'd been onto the story of his life. This picture, taken at the right moment, could make him big bucks. He just hoped he hadn't blown it.

Morning shone with icy brightness, and sunlight danced from the icicles hanging overhead. He must be crazy to have stayed out all night in weather like this. But no crazier than Dobias.

He had seen him at the funeral yesterday, looking like a man whose marbles weren't all there, still wearing the clothes he'd probably worn from prison, lingering on the outskirts of the crowd like a wandering bum who'd just happened to come upon a funeral. Eric had recognized him only when he saw Corey staring at him, and he had been so curious about the man's new, humble, almost

crazed look, that when Dobias had left the crowd, Eric
followed him.

He had taken a cab downtown, then was let out on a
street in the garment district. Eric had followed him,
sometimes on foot, but mostly from his car, as Dobias
wandered aimlessly through the rain, then wound up
in an alleyway.

He wasn't crazy enough to go in there himself, for
one never knew what kind of men loitered among trash
bins and garbage drum fires in twenty-degree weather.
He had not seen Dobias come back out of the dead-end
alley, and he had waited for hours before he'd fallen
asleep.

Now, as the first lights of morning glistened off the
icicles hanging from the electrical lines, he got out of
his car and decided to take a chance that Dobias was
still there.

It was during these deep, deadly cold snaps that the
ugliness of human suffering was more pronounced,
and it was just such shots that his photographer's
eye thrived on. He saw the garbage drum that smelled
of smoke, the bin nearby, and two or three big boxes.

He knew that people slept in them, for alleys often
swarmed with such people—the homeless—and they
were a source of great fascination to magazines. Eric
decided that if he couldn't find Dobias, he could at
least photograph some of the bums and take a shot
at selling the story to *Life* or *National Geographic* if it
had a sensitive enough angle. Something with emotion
that could grab hold of the old heartstrings and make
the toughest SOB cry like a baby.

Something that could make him a lot of money.

He looked in the first box, saw that it was abandoned,
and cursed himself again. Dobias wasn't here; he'd lost
him. And why not, after all? What would make him

think that a billionaire would spend the night in a cardboard box in an alleyway on one of the coldest nights of the year?

He saw another box, and a pair of bare feet peeking from under the damp cardboard. Deciding to give it a try, he stepped forward, bringing the camera up, and snapped the picture of the Lazy Boy box. He stepped to the other side. The box flap was half open, and inside he could see a man huddled up in a fetal position, out cold in clothes that looked to be wet and partially frozen. Clothes that looked like they'd come from a prison camp. Clothes a lot like those Dobias had worn yesterday.

With no regard for the sleeping man, he quietly tore back the flap of the wet box and saw the man's bearded face. His heart leaped as he recognized the fallen tycoon, and he knew that he had hit paydirt.

Quickly focusing his camera, he snapped one shot after another, from every angle, until he ran out of film.

Dobias never even woke up.

He unloaded the film as he ran back to his car, mentally calculating the amount of money he could demand for the shots, and deciding who would be his first prospect.

He would take the finished prints to Adam Franklin. As much as he detested the man, he knew that the *Investigator* would offer the most for pictures like these. After all, Franklin had put Dobias away the first time.

Feeling as if he had found his gold at the end of the rainbow, Eric drove back to Cambridge to develop the film.

Eric Gray was the last person Adam Franklin expected to see that day as he sat in his office, nursing a strong drink and smoking a cigarette, staring into space but seeing only Corey's face as she'd told him to get out.

He had known it would happen sooner or later, that Corey would discover his affair with her mother, that she would despise him for it. It had just come sooner than he expected.

Now Eric Gray stood before him with a Cheshire-cat grin, as if he had some secret that they could share and delight in. He had probably heard about his falling out with Corey, probably wanted to twist the knife a little. But Adam had little patience for him today. "What do you want?" he asked, not bothering to get up from his desk. "I'm sure my secretary told you I'm busy."

"Not too busy for this, Adam, old boy." Eric plopped into a chair and threw his ankle over his knee. "I have something that I think you'll be real interested in."

"I doubt it."

Eric's smile didn't falter as he dropped his foot and leaned forward, and tossed the manila envelope he'd been holding onto Adam's desk. "I'm giving you first shot at these," he said, "but I have to warn you, the price is high. As you can see, this is a one-in-a-million shot."

Adam took the envelope and opened it. He stared down at the photo of the pitiful, withered old man sleeping in a wet cardboard box and scowled. "A picture of a bum sleeping on the street? Not interested, Eric. I have my own photographers."

Eric's eyes only grew more electrified. "Look at it, Adam. It's not just any bum. Don't you recognize him?"

He frowned and looked closer, trying to place the pale, wrinkled face relaxed in sleep. It came to him all at once, and he turned his gaze back to Eric. "Dobias?"

"The same," Eric said, sitting back and crossing his arms. "He slept in that box last night."

"In this weather? Why?"

"Got me, although I have a theory that the man has

finally snapped. I saw him at Rena's funeral yesterday, and he didn't look like he was all there. I followed him, and it paid off."

Adam flipped to the next print, and the next, and saw that each one showed a clear picture of the tycoon sleeping in a Lazy Boy box, in a filthy Boston alley. He drew in a deep breath and regarded Eric again.

"What do you want for these?"

"Ten thousand dollars."

Adam shook his head. "You won't get it. I'll give you two. And I want an exclusive for the *Investigator*."

Eric laughed. "An exclusive? You've got to be kidding! The other papers would pay an arm and a leg for pictures like these."

"What would it take?" Adam asked. "If I paid ten, could I get the exclusive?"

Eric hadn't expected him to be so blatantly anxious, so he hesitated for a moment, rubbing his mouth. "Fifteen for an exclusive," he said. "Not a penny less. I could sell these over and over and make a killing."

Adam studied the photos again. "If I paid fifteen, I'd want the negatives, too."

"The negatives?" Eric asked. "Why?"

Adam met his eyes. "Because I don't trust you. If I pay that much for these shots, I expect to be the only one who has them."

Eric stared at him for a long moment, and finally his grin broke again. "All right," he said. "Fifteen thousand, and you can have the negatives."

Eric watched him as he wrote out the check, and Adam knew he was so anxious to cash it that he was ready to piss in his pants. Eric handed over the negatives and all the prints, then reached for the check.

Adam held it back. "One more thing," he said. "Where were these taken?"

Eric told him, and Adam jotted it down and gave him the check. Then, just before Eric left the office, Adam stopped him again. "When did you take them? Was it long ago?"

"A couple of hours," Eric said. "Why?"

Adam shrugged. "Just wondered."

He watched Eric leave his office, watched him get on the elevator, then turned back to the photos on his desk. Slipping them carefully back into their envelope, he unlocked his top drawer and slipped it inside. Then, grabbing his coat, he stepped out of his office.

"Where are you going?" his secretary called as he headed for the elevator.

"Out," he said. "I'll be back in a little while."

"But you have a meeting in half an hour!"

"Cancel it," he said.

Ignoring her protests, he stepped onto the open elevator and headed down to the parking garage for his car. As he pulled out into the traffic, he wondered if Dobias would be where Eric had left him.

As if he'd been put there as a prop on the set of some class-B movie, Dobias still lay in that wet, torn cardboard box when Adam found him. Immediately, he stooped and tried to wake him, but Dobias didn't stir.

He felt his forehead, found that it burned with fever, and his pulse seemed weak and erratic. Around his mouth, his skin was a pale shade of blue, and Dobias's breathing seemed too labored and rapid for a man who only slept.

Quickly, he lifted Dobias into his arms and carried him to his car.

He was still unconscious when they reached the closest hospital, Massachusetts General. Adam lifted him again and carried him in, praying that it wasn't too late.

Corey attacked the telephone the moment it rang, her eyes clashing with Emily's in intense hope. "Hello?"

"Corey, it's me. Adam."

Corey slammed the phone back in its cradle.

"Who was it?" Emily asked, hugging her knees as she sat in the recliner Adam had given Corey.

"Wrong number."

The phone rang again, and this time she let it ring twice, three times.

"Aren't you going to answer it? What if it's someone who has word on Grandfather?"

"It isn't. It's Adam."

Emily stared down at the phone as it continued to ring, and finally, she reached for it. "Aunt Corey, if you don't answer it, I will."

Corey let out a heavy sigh and jerked up the phone. "Adam, leave me alone."

"It's not about us!" Adam shouted. "I have your father."

Corey sprang out of her chair. "What do you mean you 'have' him?"

"At Massachusetts General," he said. "I found him this morning. He'd been out all night in wet clothes, and he's got pneumonia. I got him here as fast as I could."

"Oh, God. Is he going to be all right?"

"I don't know," he said. "You'd better get here as soon as you can."

Corey threw down the phone and turned back to Emily, who had already gotten both their coats and was pulling hers on.

"Is it Grandfather?"

"He's in the hospital," Corey said, heading for the door. "Come on, we've got to hurry."

They reached the hospital in record time and saw Adam standing in the waiting room, pacing as if his own flesh and blood lay struggling in the room behind him. He looked at her with deep compassion and hesitation, and she lifted her chin and cast her tired, raw eyes on him.

"I suppose you expect me to thank you for bringing him here?" she asked in a shaky voice. "Well, you can forget it. If it weren't for you and your ugly secrets, my father wouldn't be in this condition."

He nodded toward the intensive care unit. "He's in there. They said he's been asking for you."

"For me?" Her face softened and her eyes filled with tears. "Are you sure?"

"Positive," he said. "He's been calling your name since he got here."

When she had been briefed on the seriousness of his condition, they let her in, reminding her that he drifted in and out of consciousness. Quietly, she stepped into the room alone and caught her breath at the tubes and machines hooked up to the small body that seemed to wither away before her eyes.

She went to his bed and took the hand not hooked up to an IV. "Daddy? Daddy, can you hear me?"

For a moment he didn't answer, but his fingers seemed to close more tightly around hers. "Daddy, please wake up. Just long enough to let me know you're all right." She touched his forehead, felt the fever burning there, and stroked back his stiff, tangled hair. "I was so worried about you, Daddy."

She looked over him to the machine that monitored his pulse, saw the sporadic lines moving across the page, and her own heart jolted. She squeezed his hand tighter and brought it to her face. "Oh, Daddy, please don't leave me now. I'm not ready to say good-bye again."

Slowly, his eyes opened, and his hand trembled around hers.

She caught her breath on a sob. "Daddy?" She smiled at him, stroked his forehead again. "Can I get you anything? Anything at all?"

He pulled his hand back, tried to prop himself on his elbow, tried to sit up. Corey forced him back down. "No, you have to lie still, Daddy. You have pneumonia. You have to rest until you're well."

He collapsed back on the bed, as though the effort to move had been too much for him. His breath came in short, unsatisfying gasps, and he began to cough.

She checked the tube beneath his nose, saw that it was still attached, and glanced over her shoulder toward the door, wondering if she should call someone. "Just a minute, Daddy. I'll get the doctor."

"No." The word came out in a hoarse, breathless whisper, and he took her hand again.

His eyes were more alert, more alive, than she'd expected, and she looked at him fully, struggling to blink back her tears. She heard the monitor beep in warning, and knew that she was upsetting him.

"Daddy, I'll go. Please, calm down."

A tear fell from his eye to roll down his temple, and he pulled her closer, closer, until her ear was next to his mouth. "What, Daddy? What is it?"

The words he uttered came out with the greatest effort but went straight to the wounded places in her heart. Only two words.

"Forgive me," was all he said.

And then, as if sleep had drawn him under, he closed his eyes and relaxed his hold on her hand.

She stared at him for a second, letting the sweet, soothing words sink into her heart to heal her, not yet aware that they were the last he would ever speak.

Then an alarm sounded and the doors burst open and a team of doctors and nurses shoved her away and began attempts to revive the old man who had no further wish to live.

She stood back, watching in horror, as her father's body was shocked and pumped and drugged, but still he lay limp on the hospital bed.

After a while, the doctors, damp with perspiration and weary from the effort of a lost battle, gave up the fight.

"No," she whispered, looking frantically from one to the other. "No, you can't stop. He's not dead. He's *not*. You have to try harder."

With quiet words meant to help her, they ushered her out of the room. Emily was just outside the door, crumpling in her own sobs, for she had seen the whole thing through the window.

They held each other for a short eternity, neither knowing how to comfort the other. For they both knew that the scars they wore would last them the rest of their lives, and that their wounds might never heal again.

chapter

44

GISELLE WAS IN HER ROOM, SITTING ALONE IN the dark, when Corey called her with the news. She didn't remember if she had said anything at all before she'd hung up the phone.

Feeling nothing but numbness, Giselle got up and began to dress. At first, she picked a white suit and had the skirt on before she decided it wasn't appropriate. Then she took it off, leaving it in a heap on the floor, and found a black silk dress that she hadn't worn in a year. It, too, seemed wrong, so she shed it, as well, and walked through her closet again.

At last, she chose an ivory sweater and a brown skirt, the most nondescript outfit she had, then agonized for a moment over the shoes. What did one wear to the hospital on the day of her father's death?

She found a pair of brown pumps and went to her vanity table, sat down, and began to apply her makeup. She looked too old this morning, she thought. Her eyes were tired, and fine lines showed around them, despite the collagen treatments she'd had not two weeks ago. But the makeup helped, so she meticulously applied it, taking great pains to look her best.

When she was perfect, right down to the color of her lips, she sat for a moment, staring into the mirror. She told herself to get up, to go downstairs, to get in the car.

But she couldn't move.

It was then that the tears had come, great, deep, destructive tears that she hadn't been prepared for. She doubled over as the sobs shook her, and tried to muffle the groans tearing out of her throat.

She must have wept for more than half an hour before she managed to pull herself together. By then, her make-up was washed away, and her eyes were smeared in long, wet streaks of black. After summoning only enough energy to wash her face, with none left for more makeup, she got her purse and started out of the room, no longer caring how she looked.

There was work to be done today, she told herself. The worst work she had ever faced. And she had to admit that her father was right. She wasn't ruthless nor cunning enough for this. The toughness she had nurtured and cultivated in herself wouldn't serve her today. Nothing she had ever done had prepared her for the task of burying her father. She didn't know if she was strong enough to face it, or her part in bringing it about.

Wearily, she called for the driver to bring the car around.

Corey and Emily stayed at the hospital until Giselle arrived, and when she reached for Emily, the girl recoiled.

Holding her porcelain expression blank, Giselle sat down on the vinyl sofa next to her. "Emily, he's my father. I'm as upset as you. Don't shut me out when I need you the most."

Emily wiped her tears across her face and shook her head. "*You* need," she muttered. "It's always what you need, isn't it, Mother? What about what Grandfather needed? What about what Aunt Rena needed? Did you ever once think of that?"

Giselle's hand trembled as she pinched the bridge of her nose and squeezed her eyes shut. "Emily, what happened to Dad was not my fault. You can't blame me for this."

"Yes, I can," Emily said. "And I'll never forgive you for any of it."

Giselle opened her eyes and looked at Corey, who sat limp in a chair across from them, staring with vacant eyes into nothingness. "Corey, tell her . . . You know this isn't my fault."

Corey moved her empty gaze to Giselle. "She wants to stay with me, Giselle. I told her she could stay as long as she wants."

"No!" Giselle came to her feet, assuming the CEO posture that had always gotten her her way in the boardroom. "That's out of the question. Emily is *my* daughter and she belongs with me. I won't allow her to stay away another night."

Emily stood up, facing her mother like an equal in age and maturity, and Corey grieved over the years of childhood the girl had lost in just a few short months. "I know you have the legal power to make me come home, Mother," she said quietly. "And you could make me stay. But only for a while. For a year, maybe. Possibly two. But then one day you'll push me as far as you pushed Aunt Rena and Grandfather. Is that what you want? To destroy me just like you destroyed them?"

"Emily, I would never hurt you. Never. You're the most important person in my life!"

"You already have hurt me, Mother! Don't you understand?"

Corey stood up and pulled Emily into her arms, and held her as the girl began to weep again.

Giselle's eyes were wild with fear as she shook her head violently. "Corey, don't do this to me. Tell her . . . tell her how much I love her. You know I love her more than myself. You know it!"

"Then let her go," Corey whispered. "If you really care for her, let her go."

"I can't!" The words came out in a high-pitched moan, and Giselle covered her mouth with her hand and touched Emily's shoulder, trying to pull her out of Corey's arms. "She's mine, Corey. You can't take her from me! You're not her mother. You don't know anything about being a mother!"

"And you do?" Corey asked. She settled her dark eyes on Giselle. "I know that she needs time to heal. That she needs to forget some of the horrors. That she needs time to be a kid. I can give her what she needs."

"So can I," Giselle said. "Anything she needs. I'll put her in therapy. I'll—I'll take time off work, and we can spend more time together. We'll travel . . ."

Emily looked up at her mother, her face red and wet and distorted. "I want to live with Aunt Corey," she said again.

Giselle collapsed on the couch, covering her face with both hands, and wept like a child who'd been abandoned in a fierce, cruel world. Finally, trying to control her voice, she looked up at her daughter.

"Go home with Corey today," she said. "Just for now. I'll—I'll call later this afternoon. We'll talk."

Emily started toward the elevator without a word, and Corey lingered behind and looked down at Giselle. "I'll take care of the funeral arrangements."

"That won't be necessary," Giselle said. "I can—"

"I said I would do it," Corey bit out. "You robbed him blind, you destroyed his daughter, and then you crushed the only thing he had left, the memories of his wife. I'll be the one to bury him, Giselle."

Sick with grief over the loss of her daughter even more than the death of her father, Giselle went back home to the elegant mansion she had stolen from her father, to the money she'd manipulated from her sisters, to the servants and the corporation and the possessions—

everything she had ever wanted in her life.

And she realized she had nothing.

When she called Corey's that afternoon and Emily again refused to speak to her, she had curled up in bed alone and wept for hours. The next day, she was still in bed, still alone, still unable to function, when time for the funeral arrived.

Too sick and broken and defeated, and too consumed with guilt and self-recrimination to pull herself together and attend, she went down to the study in her robe and phoned Robert Gloster. Forgetting that she had fired him months before, she asked him to draw up the papers making Corey Emily's legal guardian. She would sign them the moment they were ready.

Since Robert considered that the contract was for a good cause, he agreed without argument.

Once the phone call was made, Giselle sat at her father's chair behind her father's desk and stared into the dim nothingness. It was her kingdom, she thought, ironically. A kingdom of great wealth, but nothing of any value. She had won everything she'd fought for—it was all hers.

But for the first time in her life, Giselle knew what it was to lose.

Corey knew that her father's greatest wish, for most of his life, had been to be admired and accepted by Boston society. Ironically, his funeral was a quiet, barren affair with only a handful of mourners. That was the greatest tragedy of all, she decided. That of all his crowning achievements, none was remembered on the day of his burial.

Adam attended the funeral, but she kept her distance from him, still unable to overcome the myriad feelings haunting her like a scene from the past replayed—her lover, making love to her mother. During the entire morbid ritual, she avoided even looking at him.

Giselle was noticeably absent, which proved to be a relief to Emily, whose own fragile spirit seemed close to breaking. It wasn't until Gloster told them of Giselle's decision that the slightest hint of relief came to the child's face.

Corey was the last to leave her father's grave after he'd been lowered into the ground, but there were no more tears left to cry. Instead, she stood there, staring at the place where they had yet to put a headstone, and wondering what it should say.

Beloved husband? No, that would mock the fate that had done him in.

Beloved father? The thought brought new tears to her eyes, and she shook her head slowly. That, too, would be something of a mockery. She didn't want her father mocked. She couldn't bear it.

A hand touched her shoulder, and she turned and saw Adam. "Are you all right?" he whispered.

She nodded.

"Corey, I'm sorry. I'm so . . . so sorry."

She squinted into the icy wind, her eyes mercilessly dry, her hair flapping into her face. Her father had asked her forgiveness, but she never got the chance to tell him she had forgiven him long ago.

Somehow, though, she felt he knew.

Now Adam was asking, but the grief was too great. With her father, she buried a lifetime of memories that had become nothing more than distortions and deceptions. Nothing was the way it had once appeared.

With dull, tired eyes, she looked up at him. "It's not the transgression, Adam," she whispered. "It's the heartache."

"Time will heal that."

"Will it?" The question, in itself, was a denial, and she turned away and saw Emily waiting for her beside the limousine. Time didn't have power enough to heal her own bruised spirit, she told herself, but perhaps it would be enough to salvage Emily's before it was bent too badly to be redeemed.

"Emily needs me." Without looking back at him, she started walking toward her niece, leaving Adam behind her. There was really nothing more she could say.

Motionless, Adam watched her as she got into the car with Emily and drove away. He tried not to dwell on the feeling of desolation that had stricken him the moment Corey turned her back on him. Instead, he turned to the grave, to the mound of fresh earth covering the elaborate coffin that very few had seen.

He had hated the man, as much as any man had ever hated. He had watched him neglect his wife, and then he had lost Shara to him. When she died, he had grieved for years, blaming Dobias for the misery in his own soul. And then he had stood and watched him drive his own daughter to her knees, stripping her of everything he had spent a lifetime lavishing upon her.

Yes, he had hated him. But even so, he had to ask himself if any man deserved to end it all as a pauper in a cardboard box in the freezing rain.

He had kept it all to himself till now—where he'd found Dobias, the condition he'd been in. The public would love it, he knew. The gory details of the depths to which the tycoon had sunk. They would devour the images of the Lazy Boy box, the prison clothes, the alleyway. It would sell a hell of a lot of papers.

Leaving the grave, he went back to his car and drove home, the events of the last few days, the last few months, the last few years, playing like newsreels through his mind. When he got home, he went up to his office, unlocked the desk drawer where he'd kept the photographs and negatives.

Fifteen thousand dollars. An exclusive. It had been money well spent.

He swiveled in his chair toward the computer on his desk, turned it on, and began to type. The story would go on page 1 of tomorrow's edition, he decided. And the by-line would be his.

He had already lost Corey, and she wasn't coming back. And as his fingers hammered out the words he couldn't wait to get down, he realized that he had nothing else to lose.

Corey slept late the next morning, for she hadn't been able to fall asleep until almost dawn. Emily woke her gently, handing her the *Bulletin* that had just been delivered.

"Aunt Corey?" she whispered. "It's about Grandfather. The front page."

Corey sprang up in bed and grabbed the paper out of Emily's hand. The headline read, The Death of a King. And beneath it was Adam's name.

Combing her fingers through her hair, she began to read the article.

Adam was in his penthouse stoking the raging fire in his hearth when Eric showed up demanding to see him, now that the morning edition of the *Bulletin* had been delivered to all its subscribers. Adam wasn't surprised. He'd been expecting him.

"What the hell's going on?" Eric demanded when he let him in. "I gave you those pictures in good faith. I thought you were going to use them."

Adam smiled and looked down at the front page lying on the coffee table. The picture he'd used of Dobias was one that was a couple of years old, a portrait he'd had on file of the man in his prime, smiling with the arrogance of a monarch who had no idea how far it was possible to fall. "I didn't say I was going to use them."

"Then why the hell did you buy them? If you didn't want them for the *Investigator,* I could have sold them to a dozen different tabloids. The *National Enquirer* would have killed for them!"

"Exactly," Adam said. "Which made them worth every penny to me."

Eric was silent for a moment, but when he spoke again, his voice quivered. "You think anybody who knew him is going to believe that garbage you wrote in that article?"

"That garbage was all true," Adam said. "Every last word of it."

Eric picked up the paper and sneered at the article. "You talked for a full page about all his achievements, but there wasn't a single mention of his conviction or his imprisonment or the fucking way I found him lying in a box! *That's* news, Adam! Not this shit!"

Adam sat down and crossed an ankle over his knee. "What do you want, Eric? The pictures back? I don't remember you balking when you took my check. I'd even bet you've already cashed it."

Eric pulled out his wallet and the thick stack of bills inside it. Dropping the money on the table in front of Adam, he said, "Here. Take it all back. Just give me the pictures. I can sell them to another tabloid for twice what you paid."

Adam laughed. "You think I'm stupid, don't you? Why do you think I was willing to pay fifteen thousand dollars for them? To keep them from being printed, that's why."

"What are you trying to do, Adam? Score brownie points with Corey?"

Adam's smile faded. "Corey doesn't even know about those pictures. I didn't tell her the way I found him, or that it was you who led me to him. I figured I'd let the man die with a little dignity. Even Nik Dobias deserves that much."

"What about what I deserve? I didn't sit out in my car on a rainy twenty-degree night watching some back street alley for my health. I want those pictures back!"

"What *you* deserve?" The question made Adam laugh. "You left the man lying there freezing to death, because you were so all-fired anxious to develop your film!" Adam got up and went to his fireplace, stirred the fire a little more, then reached up to the mantel and got the envelope he had set there earlier. "You want to know what you deserve, Eric? This is what you deserve."

Eric started toward him as he shook the prints out, but before he could reach him, he had dropped all of the photographs into the fire. Flames embraced them, encompassed them, devoured them.

"You bastard!" Eric lunged for the envelope that still held the negatives, but before he could reach them, Adam tossed it into the flames, as well.

He grabbed Adam's shirt and flung him away from the fire, but it was too late. There was nothing left.

Adam picked up the stack of money, more money than Eric had ever seen at one time in his life, and slapped it into the photographer's hand as he continued to stare into the fire. Then, he forced him to the door.

"Get out of my house," he said. "And don't ever let me see your sleazy face again."

"I'll get you for this, Franklin," Eric cried. "You won't get away with this!"

Adam slammed the door in his face, and Eric stood staring at it, his rabid anger fading into impotent bitterness. Finally, he looked down at the cash in his hands, counted the bills, and stuffed them back into his pocket as he stepped onto the elevator.

chapter

45

THE COLD LIFTED TWO WEEKS LATER, AND THE
temperatures shot into the fifties, as Corey stood
on the balcony of Adam's penthouse, her hair blowing
in the breeze. She looked out over the Boston skyline,
at the buildings her father had owned. Because Giselle
had taken the corporation from him, it all belonged to
her now.

But that was all right, for Corey didn't want his fortune any more now than she had when he'd ordered her
to compete for it with her sisters. Of all the lessons her
father learned before he died, she was quite certain that
was one of them.

The article in the *Bulletin* on the day after Dobias's
death had confused her, and she'd spent the last two
weeks deciding just how to react to it. Adam had made
her father look like a financial genius, someone who
had started with nothing and ended up with everything,
someone who was loved and would be sorely missed. She
had finally admitted he deserved her thanks for that.

He stepped out onto the balcony with the Perrier he
had gone to get her and gazed quietly at her. Closing
her eyes, she drank.

She felt him touch her neck, push away her hair, and
drape something around her throat. Opening her eyes,
she looked down and saw the emerald and diamond
necklace he had bought from her a year ago. Her hand
came up to touch it.

"You kept it," she whispered. "For her, or for me?"

There was no room for dishonesty between them, so he told the truth. "For both of you."

Corey breathed a sigh and dropped her face. Adam touched her chin with the tips of his fingers and made her meet his eyes again.

"It's not Shara Dobias who's made me ache for the last year," he whispered.

Corey turned away from him and stepped back toward the rail. Her hands trembled as she felt for the clasp of the necklace, opened it, and slipped it off. Turning it over in her fingers, she gazed down at it. "You gave this to her, didn't you? That was why you wanted it."

For a moment he didn't answer, but finally, he whispered, "Yes."

She looked up at him, and he saw no bitterness in her eyes, only a deep, weary sadness. She took his hand, dropped the necklace in his palm, and closed his fingers over it. "I want you to keep it," she said. "I don't want that memory of her, or of you."

She struggled with the emotion obstructing her throat, but her gaze remained locked with his. He touched her face, grazed his thumb across her cheek. "I just had to thank you," she said. "Things could have turned out so . . . so much uglier than they did. You were kind to my father at the end, when he was all alone. And then . . . the article—"

"What are you going to do?" he cut in, unable to accept gratitude from her when he wanted so much more.

She sucked in a deep breath, and a slight smile lifted her lips. "I have the income from my office building, and since my father died they've released the trust fund my mother left me. Besides, a lot of Giselle's people have jumped ship and come to work for me. My projects are in good hands. I can afford to take some time off. I'm taking Emily to France for a while. Maybe I can undo

some of the damage the past year has done to her. She
needs a rest, and so do I."

"You're running away," he said. "From me, from Giselle, from everything."

Her expression was accepting, serene. "Maybe," she
said. "But it's what I have to do."

Adam blinked back the mist in his own eyes and
looked off over the skyline, then turned back to her.
He frowned and threaded his fingers through her hair,
slid his hand down to her neck. Her skin was so soft, so
sweet, he couldn't bear the thought of never touching it
again.

"Run if you have to," he said quietly. "But one day
you're going to look up, and I'll be standing there."

A sad but forgiving smile played across her lips, and
unshed tears glistened in her eyes. "One day I might look
up, and want you to be."

Then, pressing a kiss on his cheek, she left him on
the balcony and walked out of his life . . .

In search of her own.

TERRI HERRINGTON graduated *magna cum laude* from Northeast Louisiana University. She is the award-winning author of more than twenty books and has written novelizations for television. She currently lives in Clinton, Mississippi, with her husband and children.

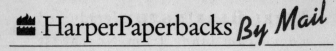